A MOST PRIVATE BANK

Also by **Andreas F. Clenow**

Following the Trend
Stocks on the Move
Trading Evolved

A MOST PRIVATE BANK

A Novel by

Andreas F. Clenow

Equilateral Publishing
A Division of
Equilateral Capital Management GmbH
Zurich, Switzerland

All rights reserved under International and Pan-American Copyright Conventions. Published by Equilateral Publishing, a division of Equilateral Capital Management GmbH, Zurich, Switzerland. To request permissions, contact the publisher via the author's website at www.clenow.com.

Cover artwork and design by Alejandro Colucci.

Copyright © 2022 by Andreas F. Clenow.

All rights reserved.

Hardcover: 978-3-9525566-1-0
Paperback: 978-3-9525566-0-3
E-Book: 978-3-9525566-2-7

The story which you are about to read is a work of fiction. At the same time, it is very much true. The author of this book has lived and breathed this world, navigated the dangers, and survived the shark infested waters described herein.

This is a world that may seem absurd to outsiders, a world to which few are ever admitted, and fewer still manage to thrive in. A world with rules of its own.

Any resemblance of characters in this book to real life persons may be coincidental. Or it may not. Which parts of this book are true to life and which are not, is a matter that the author will take to his grave.

"In this world, you either become a shark, or you become lunch."
  – Jim Dixon

A MOST
PRIVATE BANK

Monday

The Client

"Ms. Rosenbaum is in the meeting room," she said. "Been waiting half an hour."

The coat was building a puddle on the carpet. The shoes had been polished an hour ago, whatever good that had done. Ten years in Switzerland and I was still unprepared for the November weather.

"Twenty minutes early. She can marinate a few more."

I uttered a curse under my breath. With the soaked trench coat secured on its hanger, I had once more forgotten how the local hats seemed to be designed as rain barrels. Not quite a fedora, not quite not a fedora. You didn't stand out if you wore one in Europe, not in this part of Europe. Now it had left an unmistakable wet patch on the chest of my jacket and the white shirt under it, and there wasn't time to do a thing about it.

"She got coffee?" I asked, looking at the watch on my wrist. My favorite watch. The only one that actually mattered.

"Three cups. Should be bouncing off the walls. You need one, Jim?" she asked.

"No. No thanks, Sandra," I said. She had been here early. Then again, she was always here early. Dependable, much like the timepiece on my wrist. She had been with me since I crossed the pond all those years ago. Not sure how I would have made it without her.

"What's she like?" I asked.

"Oh, right up your alley," she said. "Try not to give the store away, will you?"

"No promises. Say, be a good girl and interrupt us in ten."

"Behave in there!"

"No promises."

I heard the keys hammering away. She was already ignoring me, whether actually busy or pretending to be. Outside the meeting room, I stopped to straighten my tie, only to find none. I hadn't worn one since I got here. Old habits.

A double knock on the door and I swung it open. There she was. That was the first time I laid my eyes on her. If I had been warned, if I had been told what would come of this, what this week would bring. If I could have understood just what this very meeting would set in motion and the consequences of it, I still wouldn't have done anything differently. She simply took my breath away.

I had stopped dead in my tracks and I was staring and she saw it. Couldn't have been more than twenty-five. If that. Sitting there, in that sky-blue Thierry Mugler outfit, her knees together and gracefully tilted to the left. The deep-cut blazer jacket immaculately form fitted and flowing effortlessly down over the matching skirt, separated only by a matte silver-tone waist chain.

The shade of blue perfectly matched her eyes just as the manicured fingernails were in the exact same blood-red shade as her lipstick. She rose to her feet slowly and with the grace of a gazelle, brushed back that long straight dark hair behind her shoulder and extended that hand toward me. She was tall and slender and with the kind of smile men would kill for and if she spoke I hadn't registered it.

I forced my brain back on, reminding myself of who she was and why I took this meeting.

"Ms. Rosenbaum. My apologies for having kept you waiting. Jim Dixon," I said in my best German, shaking her hand, unable to take my eyes off hers.

"Make it Chris," she replied in an unmistakably American

A Most Private Bank

English, holding on to my hand for just a second longer than customs dictate.

"Your father never told me his daughter grew up in the States," I said. She sat down first and I followed.

"My father was not one to volunteer information."

I could only agree. I had considered the old man a close personal friend for decades. I was as close to him as anyone, and I didn't know more than I had to. Not about his family, not even about his business dealings. I knew enough to do what he hired me to do.

"Quite. I'm sorry for your loss," I said.

She paused for a moment and looked at the desk. It gave me enough time to glance at that shiny little thing on her wrist. Chopard Imperiale, case in rose gold set with diamonds around the bezel on a brown crocodile band.

"Bank Niederhauser is against the ropes. I want to build a controlling stake," she said.

Whatever I might have had expected when I agreed to this courtesy meeting, those words were not part of it. Bank Niederhauser was one of hundreds of small private banks scattered around the country and it had been in the news for the past weeks and not in a good way.

Most people misunderstand the term *private bank*, assuming it refers to the private nature of the services they provide to wealthy individuals. What it really refers to is that a private bank, a real private bank, is privately owned by a family or small group of individuals who are privately and unlimitedly responsible for the bank's finances.

Traditional private banks have been family owned and operated for centuries, providing bespoke services to the elite of the world. Private banks are based on trust, stability, and discretion. They will safeguard your money and your secrets. Until recently, when globalization started putting pressure on business models based on facilitating tax evasion.

"Banks aren't interesting businesses. Not anymore. Certainly not private banks. Besides, I'm retired."

Christina Rosenbaum flashed that warm, white smile at me, her eyes not moving from mine for an instant. Her voice bearing the confidence of someone who never had to contemplate the idea of actually working for money, even less having a request refused.

"It's a good bank underneath and once they get out from under these current little issues, I'm sure they'll do just fine. Besides, Jim, you're not retired. You just retreated into your little family office."

I thought I had managed to keep a neutral face and hide how her words cut. She knew very well why I didn't have clients anymore. I could see it in her eyes. I kept my lips together, looking at her, considering how to best get rid of her. The ultra-rich were rarely good observers. The skill of being able to read someone's emotions or show empathy had never been of much use to them. But few things passed her unnoticed.

"Oh, you know what I mean. After how things went back home, you got your fresh start here. What are you managing these days? Ten? Twenty million? I'm sure you're comfortable, but you don't strike me as a man looking for comfort."

She was pushing it and she knew it. Worse. She was enjoying it.

"Why take this to me?" I asked her.

"Father always said that Jim's the man who gets it done. The dealmaker."

"He tell you I'm a sucker for female flattery?"

"He told me you deliver. And I hear you have a long-standing

A Most Private Bank

relation with Niederhauser, that you have his ear."

"I see. What are you looking for from me?"

"Due diligence. Look into the finances and valuation. Set up a holding company to acquire a controlling stake. Assist in raising short-term financing. And ensure buy-in from the Niederhauser family."

I sighed and leaned back in my chair. When I was asked to meet Benjamin Rosenbaum's youngest, I had assumed she wanted a private shopping session at Louis Vuitton or VIP tickets to the opera.

"Sounds messy," I said. "It's privately held and opaque. Ownership is probably spread out in the family. You're unlikely to get hold of enough shares to matter. My advice is that you drop this entire idea."

"This is important to me, Jim. My first big deal, if you will. I want this bank and I want it before the end of the year. Your assistance would be invaluable, Jim. Shall we say a five percent fiduciary fee, based on a target hundred-million-dollar valuation?"

It didn't make sense. None of this made any sense. But here she was, seemingly real and seemingly reasonably sane, making me a ridiculous offer.

I opened my mouth to speak. "That is—"

A firm knock on the door interrupted whatever I had planned to say and a wavy blond head poked inside.

"So sorry to interrupt, Jim," Sandra said. "But I have Mr. Ghaly on the line. Regarding the Mirimar Holdings deal. Rather urgent, I'm afraid."

I looked at the scratched-up old watch on my wrist. Dependable. Like clockwork.

"Ms. Rosenbaum. Chris," I corrected myself as I stood up,

extending my hand. "I'm afraid I'm going to have to cut this somewhat short."

She too took to her feet, shaking my hand. "Say you'll look into it. Please?"

My intention was to forget about this. To move on to some more realistic project, away from the insanity of the Rich and Dysfunctional, away from the world I knew far too well. But her eyes were relentless and her smile provided them with overbearing fire support.

"I'll make some inquiries. Out of respect for your father. That's all I promise," I said, cursing my own weakness.

"That's all I can ask for," she said. "For now. I'm staying at the Baur au Lac. Your girl has my number."

She had a triumphant smile on her face when she fetched her coat. In the corner of my eye I notice Sandra rolling her eyes at how Chris picked up her little green leather Chanel purse from the floor, bending by the hip. The outsoles of the black stilettos were in the signature dark red of Christian Louboutin, the same dark red as her lips and nails, and I watched as Christina Rosenbaum and her heels clicked their way out of my office and out the front door.

"Your girl?" Sandra asked. "That's me, I suppose. You can close your mouth now, Jim, she's left already."

I shook my head and couldn't help a chuckle. "Barking mad, that one. Cute, but barking mad. Wants me to buy a bank for her. Wants me to front it. A hundred mil…"

"She any good for it?"

"Damned if I know. Her father sure was. Far as I know, he's got to have at least five kids. God knows how many ex-wives. Offered me a five percent fee on a hundred-mil deal and she wants it done by Christmas. We'd clear five mil in a month and a half."

"Yeah. *We*," Sandra filled in. "You trust her?"

"'Bout as far as I can throw her. None of that made any sense. Hell, if she had offered me a couple of hundred I might have written it off as a vanity project for a silly rich girl. And the flirting? No, something's not right. Not that it matters though.

"These people never have enough. They're all the same. The people I made wealthy over the years. This girl, even if she only got a small part of Benjamin Rosenbaum's loot, she's set for life. She's got enough to settle down and enjoy. Learn the piano, travel the world, go scuba diving. But no, they always need more. And they always go risking what they have for just a few more bucks that they'll never spend anyhow."

"You also have enough to settle down and get out of the game, you know," Sandra said.

The interruption made me lose my train of thought and my rant got cut short.

"You gonna take the deal?" she asked, changing tack.

"Wasn't planning on it. Good payout, sure, but only if it gets done. I'd probably spend a month hitting brick walls with nothing to show for it. Not like she offered me money up front, is it. Might take another meeting. To find out more."

"You do know she's half your age, right?" she asked, collecting the empty coffee cup on the table.

"Uh-huh. I'll be on my best behavior."

"Uh-huh," she repeated on her way to the kitchen.

Raphael Bosch

The old floorboards under the carpet creaked, as they always did. A prestigious office location wasn't a shiny new glass tower, not here, not in this part of the world. This was a place where heritage mattered, down to the very walls around you. A place like this was protected by a hundred different building codes and even if I wanted to make the floor flat and replace the creaky old boards, I couldn't swing a permit for it.

Spend enough time in Europe and you can't miss it. How most cities are a mix of modern and 1960s concrete. How there's not much older, just the odd anachronistic church. This was the exception, this was the place that hadn't been leveled by B-17s back in the day. The Swiss took pride in their ancient architecture and this particular building was smack in the middle of Zurich's Old Town.

My office was small and so was my payroll. No sense in building up overhead cost, not in this business. Just a Yank, a Kraut and a native. A reception area, a meeting room and a trading room. Four identical office desks with identical dual screens and identical leather chairs. Three of the desks empty, not just of people riding them but of papers or other signs of life. The fourth desk manned by my native, by the only Swiss.

The size of a family office isn't measured in head counts. It's measured in how much money you're managing. A family office, a real family office, manages the wealth of a single family. For older family offices, those that have been around for centuries, there could be hundreds of family members. Some family offices have billion-dollar real estate portfolios, manage fleets of cars and planes, and pay an allowance to all members to make sure that none of the descendants of the founder ever has to work again.

A Most Private Bank

By their very nature, family offices are secretive. Most manage hundreds of millions of dollars. How much mine manages is none of your business.

Raphael Bosch hadn't seen me yet or at least not acknowledged me. His eyes stared intensely at the monitors, typing with his right hand, left hand on the mouse, earphone in one ear. Thirty-four years old, ex-JP Morgan trader, prone to wearing one size too small slim-fit shirts to show off the excessive time spent in gyms.

Dumping Rosenbaum on him had no downside. The chance of this turning into anything real was far too low to get my attention, and I wasn't about to spend the rest of the year running errands for anyone's spoiled daughter. Had I thought for a moment there really was five million to be had, I'd be all over it. But the real world doesn't work like that.

It wasn't just the obvious fact that the golden days of private banking were long over. The business model of hiding foreign money, black or gray, shielding it from taxation and authorities, was a dying industry. No, this particular bank was without a doubt in the worst possible situation. A pariah in the business.

They had gone and opened a branch office in New York. That's just all kinds of stupid. The traditional business of private banking is based on taking advantage of certain legal discrepancies across jurisdictions.

More precisely, the fact that it is not illegal in Switzerland for a bank to assist foreigners in hiding their money from their government. As long as you stay in the land of Alps, cows, and cheese, you could simply refer to banking secrecy and decline to share any information with anyone. Unless of course you go and open a foreign branch and get caught soliciting tax avoidance schemes on foreign soil.

Bank Niederhauser had done the unthinkable. In a furious fit of hubris, they had opened an office in Soho and started actively courting American clients. It hadn't taken the feds long to build a case and raid the place. That was the beginning of the end, or so it seemed at the time.

Why anyone in their right mind would be interested in a radioactive firm like that was beyond me. And here came some girl barely out of school telling me that she's sure they'll recover from their little problems.

Better to get Raphael to check it out. I knew he'd be all over it, after he was done pretending not to be interested. People in the financial industry are greedy and greedy people are predictable. All I'd need to do is to give him a potential upside, a tiny fraction of potential profits, and he'd spend all his free time pursuing it. It wouldn't even cut into his regular duties around here. It was his time to waste and if he against all odds turned this into profit, most of it would come to me anyhow.

The back left corner of the trading room was glassed in, a private office. My private office. A desk, a phone, a couple of black leather visitor chairs, a small couch, nothing fancy. Nothing but the floor-standing safe box by the window.

"Morning, Raph. How d'we look?"

"One sec." He lifted a finger off the keyboard without taking his eyes off the screen. Then a few more button presses, a brief pause and a double tap. "…And we're done. Locked in the trade."

He pulled the earpiece out and picked up a pen off the table and spun it around his fingers, a parlor trick anyone who spent time on a trading floor has deep in muscle memory.

"Hey Jim. Vola's moving up, looking solid on the dispersion trade. Swissie ticking down, Mirimar acquisition unchanged. My book lost a couple of points this morning, nothing to get your knickers in a twist over. Who's the babe?"

"Got a minute? Need a word," I said and proceeded toward

A Most Private Bank

my personal glass corner castle. Raphael followed and sat down in one of the chairs in front of my desk.

"Have a seat," I said before seeing that he was way ahead of me.

I turned and opened the safe box next to me, taking out a glass-top mahogany case, setting it down on the desk. Three rows of gray pillows, four wristwatches around a pillow on each row, only one lone pillow without a watch. I snapped open the steel bracelet of what I had been wearing all weekend, my favorite among my collection.

"Can't you at least polish that scratched piece of junk?" he said. He knew the answer, he just liked pushing me.

"One day when you're all grown up and can afford a 1962 tropical Rolex Submariner, you can polish it as much as you like," I said. Many would make the same observation as he did. The watch looked like it had taken a few spins in a washing machine. "My father bought it for two hundred and fifty bucks, brand new. Was a high-price watch back then. Now it's worth six figures. What's your shiny fifty worth anyhow? Ten? Twenty K?"

He was proud of his watch and there was no easier way to take him down a peg than to criticize it. Blancpain Fifty Fathoms in stainless steel, a classic diving watch with a bezel reminiscent of a life buoy, supposedly favored by the Navy SEALs. Named after its ability to withstand water pressure of fifty atmospheres - five hundred meters - this particular one was the flyback chronograph version on a textile strap. A respectable choice, but I wouldn't let him hear me say it.

"Niederhauser. You familiar with them?"

He shrugged and leaned back in the chair, his fingers interlocked behind his head. That pen had followed him in and was sticking up like an antenna from his head. My father's old Submariner took its place around the empty pillow, and I picked a steel Daytona to wear for the day. A classic sports Rolex chronograph.

"Yeah. Well, somewhat anyhow. Been around since seventeen hundred and whatever. Supposedly preferred bankers of Joséphine Bonaparte back in the day. Old-school, no-risk private banking and such. No risk on the part of the bank, that is. Stability, generational wealth protection and all of that. Probably ridiculously profitable back in the day. Back when any money was fair game, back before you had to start asking where it came from. Centuries of *omertà* was a great pitch."

None of this was new to me. Everyone knew of this bank. Small as it was, it had heritage, history, and until recently credibility.

"Sure, until they got themselves on the American radar. Bank's been on the way down since they caught those Muppet bankers playing James Bond over there, pitching buckaroo tax schemes to anyone with a few hundred thousand and the time to listen."

"Too bad they only snagged a few juniors," Raphael said. "Serves them right. Been downhill for the bank since then, but this week things are really getting juicy."

"In what sense?" I asked.

"You really didn't read the paper this morning, did you? The leak. Someone on the inside is shopping client data. A few high-profile guys in trouble. Could be a one-off, could be an ongoing leak. No good for the bank. Kills trust."

This I hadn't known and he quickly filled me in on the morning's events. Someone at the bank had stolen information, stolen records on clients, and sold it to the German government. A bunch of corporate executives over there will have lengthy court cases and painful fines to look forward to. Some might face jail time. Tax evasion may be a joke in Switzerland, but to the

A Most Private Bank

northern neighbors it's certainly no laughing matter.

"You think it's the US bankers? Stealing the data before getting fired?"

"What else would it be? These guys are outsiders. Americans. No offense, Jim. But they're not Swiss. Lacking the banking culture, you know. Probably shat themselves when they got pinched, and now they're trying to remember any secret they ever overhead, spilling it all."

I nodded in agreement even though I didn't buy that for a second. That just wasn't how these banks were run. Information that mattered, client information, was on a need-to-know basis and the New York branch office simply didn't need to know about German clients.

No, this was something else. This was someone at their head office in Zurich who had broken ranks. Someone had violated the most sacred vows of Swiss banking, someone had ratted out their clients.

"Perhaps," I replied. "You think the bank can come back from this?"

"Unlikely. Not to its former glory, no way. It's been on the way down for some time, even before this mess. You wanna tell me what this is all about?"

"You don't see them returning to profitability any time soon?" I asked.

He rubbed his face with his palm from his forehead down to his chin, exhaling slowly and loudly.

"Please tell me we're not buying a bank, Jim."

I grinned, seeing him make that face, give me that look that I usually got when I was up to something.

"Who, me? Nah, I'm not that vain. Not yet anyhow. Bank Dixon, how's that? No, don't worry. Just need you to look into it for a potential client. Probably a waste of time. But has to get done."

"What d'you need?"

"Benjamin Rosenbaum's daughter's in town. One of 'em, anyhow. She wants a stake. For God knows what reason. Doesn't matter. She's way out of her depth. Most likely, she'll lose interest and move on."

"Poor little rich girl wants her own private bank?" Raphael suggested.

"Something like that."

"Explains the legs I saw in the lobby before." Raphael grinned.

"Listen, Raph, I need you to run with this one. Just gotta find out if there's anything to it. Check it out, you don't like it, we kill it. No biggie."

Raphael sighed and brushed nonexistent dust off his sleeve.

"Look, cute as she seemed, I've got better things to do. You can't put me on this nonsense this late in the year, Jim. It's crunch time. Final inning. My focus is on closing the Mirimar deal and hitting a fresh high on the trading book. Can't babysit Little Miss Spoiled on some vanity adventure."

"Worried about your bonus, Raph?"

"Damn right, I am! I'm well on track for half a mil, and you know it." Raphael crossed his arms and leaned back in the chair. "No way. I'm not wasting time on this. I should be out there hustling."

"Need you to deal with this," I said, leaning back, crossing arms in a mirror movement.

"Tough."

The usual ritual. He wanted the project, he wanted it badly.

A Most Private Bank

He smelled money and he had seen the girl and he wanted both. This was nothing but a negotiation. The room was quiet for a few seconds, the two of us staring at each other.

"Potential on this project is a mil," I lied. "Your end would come to ten percent of that."

Raphael drew in air slowly for a long, deep breath, eyes locked with mine.

"Twenty. Mirimar stays in my book."

"Fifteen. You keep Mirimar. Don't get greedy, Raph. You'll hit your five hundred once Mirimar comes through. Best case, you'll do another hundred and fifty on this deal. Worst case, you waste a bit of time."

I had poached Raphael from JPM four years ago. Natural trader, great instincts, but easy to read. As much as he argued against it, he wanted in, anyone could have seen it. Even if he hadn't picked up the scent of money, he wanted an excuse to get to the girl.

He leaned forward in his chair, pretending to think it over, his thumb tapping my table.

"Fine. I'll trade the US late sessions. And deal with this in the mornings. Fine. Deal."

"Good. You can stop pretending to be pissed now. Can we move on?"

He sat back up with a victorious smirk on his face, leaning back with a relaxed posture. He thought he had won this negotiation, and I had no plans on correcting that misconception.

"What's the game plan, skipper?"

"Groundwork first. Due diligence on the bank and the client. Find out what you can about the bank's finances, see if there's any actual potential. If you still think there's something to it, set up a meet with the client. Christina Rosenbaum. Sandra's got her details. See if she's good for the cash and if she's for real. These people change interests like regular folks change underwear. I'm leaning toward dismissing the entire thing quickly. If your conclusion is the same, we drop it and move on. If you find something of interest, pitch me, and let's see."

"Right. Fair enough."

"Keep it on the q.t., will you? Under the radar just in case. Word gets out the bank's in play, all hell breaks loose."

Raphael Bosch stood up from his chair. "No sweat, Jim. Not my first rodeo."

Approached

The Dolder Golf Club is located on the slopes of Zürichberg, one of the two hills surrounding the city on either side, and adjacent to the hotel with the same name. The Dolder Grand, known to be one of the most expensive hotels on the European continent, has an exterior design befitting a Disney castle. Dating back to the late nineteenth century, the hotel is adorned with towers and spires all overlooking not only the city but a large part of Lake Zurich with surrounding snow-covered Alps.

The rain had subdued somewhat by the afternoon but the thick fog that replaced it had not helped my game. It had been one of the worst rounds of the year and on my home course to boot. Hadn't been easy keeping my composure when I lost three strokes in the bunker on the sixth.

When I had finally sunk that last putt I couldn't take it anymore. The bad game I could deal with but not the rest. I pocketed the ball, looking out over the misty landscape. On a clear day you could see the whole city from here. The lake, the marina, and the white rocky Alps all around. This day, you could see your own hand.

"Wanna tell me why you're jerking me around?" I asked.

"Why'd you say that?"

"You'd beat me on a good day. And today was not a good day."

He leaned down to pick up a ball. He spun it in his hand silently a moment before replying.

"Got time for a drink, Jim? Need a chat."

"Thought you might," I replied.

He was short, a full head shorter than me, overweight enough to give a round physical appearance. Steven Hill wore horn-rimmed glasses and had a short, well-trimmed beard that had turned gray along with his hair with age. He was a good decade older than I and spoke with a slow, Southern drawl, giving away his Georgian origins.

We walked in silence back to the clubhouse by the first hole, at the top of the slope, up the stairs from the course, up to the back entrance and stepped inside.

The club room was nearly empty on account of the season and the weather and the two armchairs near the fireplace were free. Best spots on a cold and rainy day. As soon as we sat down, a young man in a white shirt and black pants came up from behind the bar to take our orders.

"Bourbon… Make it Knob Creek. Two, neat. Thanks," Hill said in English to the waiter before turning his attention back to me.

"How's business, Jim? Must be nice working for yourself these days. You miss the days of having clients?"

"Considering a change of career, Steve?"

"Just friendly curiosity, Jim. You strictly a family office these days? No external clients anymore?"

I turned my face to the fireplace, watching the glowing ember. The log on the bottom had just burned through, snapping and sending a cloud of sparkles up the chimney.

"Five years."

"What's that?" Steve asked, caught off guard.

"Five years we've played. Never threw a game, and never asked about my business."

Steve grinned through that beard.

"Suppose you want me to get to the point."

"Suppose I do."

"Fair enough," the fat, bearded man started. "I hear you got an interest in Niederhauser," he continued.

I had been watching the fire. I didn't like where this was going, I didn't like it one bit. I felt my eyes narrow as I turned to look at him. He too was watching the fire and he too didn't like this conversation one bit.

Until a few hours ago I couldn't have cared less about that bank. Even after that morning meeting, I didn't care all that much. There was really no reason for him to ask such a thing, no reason for him to think that I had an interest, no reason to care if I had one or not. Yet here he was, risking our friendship, asking about things that were none of his business.

"State Department's dabbling in banking now, are they?" I asked, intent on giving him no information of any kind.

"We'd like to understand your interest," the gray-haired little man said after a brief silence.

"We?"

The young waiter's return with two glasses of Kentucky bourbon interrupted the exchange. "*Zum Wohl, meine Herren,*" he said, setting down the glasses on the small, round table between the two armchairs.

We both paused for the waiter to step back behind the bar. Each man lifted his glass close to his nose, taking in the aroma of the bourbon before having a small sip. For a moment, the faint breathing of the fireplace was the only sound heard.

The silence had grown uncomfortable by the time Hill cleared his throat. "Inquiries made on your behalf had some people concerned, Jim. We would like to understand your involvement."

"I always wanted my own bank and, this seems like a good

time to go into private banking," I said with a blank face, maintaining eye contact.

Hill let out a soft chuckle. "Come now. There's no need for that. I'm sure you have a perfectly good reason. I'm assuming you're acting on someone else's behalf."

I took a sip of bourbon, intent on not giving him an inch. No expression to read, no indication of any kind.

Hill continued, "I made it clear to them that we've known each other a long time and that I have full trust in you, of course. You are not a target of any sort of... investigation at this point."

"Swell. Thanks."

"This really doesn't have to be difficult, Jim. Niederhauser has been on our radar for some time. Given recent events, both back home and around here, we'd like to see things neatly wrapped up without any unexpected... interference. We have no problem with you making a buck. But we'd like to know who you're fronting for and what their interest is.

"In fact, we're quite comfortable with you taking on this bank. That is, more so than if it would be some local who actually bought into all of that Swiss secrecy nonsense. No, one of our own is a better prospect. We'd like you to keep your eyes and ears open for us, Jim."

I felt my chest heave. I felt the blood vessels in my forehead pound, my face getting redder, my temper rising. I wasn't sure what made me more upset. That he somehow knew that we were looking into the bank, just hours after I gave Raph that task, or that he actually seemed to take me for some amateur who would just hand him information.

"I'm sure you can see the sensitivity of the subject," he continued. "The ongoing case against them can very well turn into a larger situation and have lasting bilateral consequences. With the political connections of Mr. Niederhauser... Well, you can see

A Most Private Bank

how we would like to ensure that there are no unwelcome surprises coming up. And who better to give us a real time insight than one of our own. An American patriot and veteran."

I turned my face back to the fire, another big sip to keep my mouth from saying something I might regret. The patriot card, that's the best he could think of? I nearly lost my temper, nearly raised my voice. This was the second meeting this day that didn't make any sense, and as upset as I was, curiosity was starting to grow stronger. A small private bank in financial and legal difficulties shouldn't be this interesting to anyone.

The Daytona told me it was 1:32 p.m. Not even five hours since I gave Raph that task. Five hours. Whatever this was about, it was a priority for the US government and that's not something I want to be anywhere near.

"Sounds like you're working your way to a proposal. Suppose we cut the foreplay and get to it, Steve."

The bearded man instinctively checked his own wrist. A quartz Seiko was quite a contrast to what most members of the Dolder Golf Club would normally wear.

"Certainly. Nice to deal with professionals. Quite frankly, we need eyes and ears on the ground. We have a specific interest, but it appears we are not the only party. We need to stay ahead of the opposition and you appear to be in a unique position to assist."

"You expect me to run errands in exchange for some kind words about my patriotism and my service to my country, do you?"

"As I said, it is nice to deal with professionals. Whoever your client is, they are likely paying well for your services. Otherwise you wouldn't have gone back into the game. We are prepared to stand by and let your deal go through, not acting until after you are paid."

"My end is my end. I can get that without your benevolent

assistance."

"There is also the matter of your culpability. Of how your government may see your involvement in a matter such as this. Given your previous legal history. We may be able to expunge that SEC ruling against you. You could operate in the financial industry back home again, Jim. But on the other hand… if you would work against us here… we would be unable to protect you from any potential fallout."

"That a threat, Hill?"

"Merely the facts on the ground, as they stand. I'm sure it won't come to that. Now, what can you tell me about those who approached you?"

My blood was boiling. Until this day, I had seen him as a casual acquaintance, some diplomatic bureaucrat of little importance. Not someone who could get this kind of information this fast. My history, my pressure points. He wasn't supposed to know that I was barred from the financial industry back in the States. This was too much, and I had to get out of there before things turned nasty.

I set my half-full glass of bourbon down on the table and stood up slowly, "I can tell you that it's lunchtime and my wife's making pork chops."

Hill rose to his feet as well, extending his hand. "That's fine. That's not the most important part at the moment. Tell me when you can. My card has my direct number."

I took the card and left without a word. Once past the gates I stopped and looked at it. *Steven J. Hill Jr., United States Consulate, Zurich*. No title.

For a moment I held the card over the dustbin by the gates. It went into my coat pocket instead and I headed to the parking lot. The rain had started again.

A Fool and her Money

Navigating the city in a car was far more manageable outside of rush hour. That's not to say it was a relaxing drive. European cities aren't designed for cars, not like American cities. Single lanes, traffic lights every few yards, one-way streets, and suicidal cyclists everywhere. Having a decent car only made city driving more frustrating. The BMW growled each time the lights finally turned green only to whimper at the inevitable next red light.

The city of Zurich, just like most of this Alpine nation, had been carped-bombed with speed traps. A tiny touch too much with the right foot and you'd be greeted by a bright and brief flash. Smile for the camera. You just lost fifty bucks. Don't even think about rushing past that yellow. A split second too late, and you're down two-fifty.

An office in the Old Town has its advantages, but parking is not one of them. This neighborhood was around long before Columbus got lost on his way to India. Narrow cobblestone paths, centuries-old colorful stone buildings with ornate crests and historical paintings on the facade. A fairy-tale landscape. With no underground parking.

The spot I found wasn't too far away, and I dropped a few coins in the meter. Not sure why I bothered. I'd probably get a fine anyhow. The restaurants were nearly empty by now, about to shut for the afternoon. The daily routine of the business lunch crowd vying for tables with the tourists was already played out. In this part of the city, restaurants opened for lunch and dinner only, closing all afternoon.

Lunch was the last thing on my mind. If I was hungry I didn't notice it. Passing the slow-moving tourists and the suited bankers,

I headed straight for the door. There was a discrete sign towards the cobblestone path, one you wouldn't see unless you were looking for it.

Elevator out of service again. Three flights of stairs were quickly scaled. The sign on the outer door of the office was more prominent than the one by the street. A rectangular steel plate with the engraved words Dixon Capital. I rushed past it.

She was right there in the lobby, behind her desk, as she always was.

"Bit chilly for golf, isn't it? Ms. Rosenbaum stopped by again, left a message for you and —-"

My hand up, I didn't even look at her. Not now. I headed straight down to the trading room, my coat and hat still on. I had held back my temper at the golf club, I had held it back all the way to the office and now I was looking for someone to take it out on.

"Who'd you speak to?" I said. I was out of breath from rushing up those stairs, and it bothered me.

He was sitting where he usually sat, in the same manner as always. Predictability is an underrated quality in employees. He pulled the earphone out and, looked up at me.

"About what?" Raphael asked.

"Niederhauser. Who did you speak to and how?" I demanded, hearing my own voice raised more than I had intended.

The young trader wasn't used to being spoken to like that, nor did he like it very much. He pushed his chair back a bit, leaned back and crossed his arms.

"There's a problem?"

"Could be," I said, taking it down a notch or two. "Just had a conversation I didn't like one bit."

He was quiet a moment, relaxing his posture somewhat. My lowered voice was as much of an apology as he could ever expect from me.

"Your office?" he asked.

"My office," I replied.

He got up and walked ahead of me into my private glass cubicle. The two glass walls making up my corner office might have been somewhat anachronistic in the otherwise old-style office decor, but they were practical. He slumped down in the chair in front of my desk.

"Talk to me," he said.

I took my seat and collected my breath for a moment.

"I need to know who you approached on Niederhauser."

Raphael just shrugged back.

"I made a few calls. Few guys I know at the bank, just to chitchat and feel out their views of the bank. Hell, they probably thought I was shopping for a job."

"Just guys at the bank?"

"Well, I met the chick too, " Raphael added, smirking with closed lips.

"You mean the client. Ms. Rosenbaum."

"Yeah, that chick. We had a chat."

"Anything stand out?"

"I can think of two things off the top of my head."

"Save it, Raph. Bad time for that stuff," I snapped.

"Fine," Raphael said, pulling his left foot up over his right knee. "One call did stand out. Most of them were a waste of time, but one got kinda weird."

"Why's that?"

"You met Dick, right? Von Baerenfells. Bit of a pompous prick. In my squash club."

I nodded. Zurich is a small town, and I had come across Dick von Baerenfells a couple of times. He was the typical old-school Swiss banker, been in the game for at least four decades. Back then, the way to get into Swiss banking was to start as a teenage intern, spending a decade doing the most menial tasks. Back before anyone cared about university degrees and certifications, back when all you needed was a high school diploma and blind loyalty.

There were lots of people like him in Swiss finance, people with no education, with no real knowledge of finance or the world. People who made seven figures or more, simply for having been at the right place and time, having gotten the right internship as a teenager.

"Can't say I know him. Know the face. You called his mobile or office line?"

"Office line. He's still head of their Balanced Mandates team. I just felt him out a bit. He loves to play the big shot. I figured, if he knows something, he'd love to tell me how well-informed he is. I chitchatted a bit first. Asked what he's planning to do, now that the bank looks like it might shutter."

"And?" I asked.

"That's the weird part. He didn't exactly seem worried. Said he had been working plan B for the past few years. Got all secretive on me, trying to impress me with this big secret that he can't tell me. He said that he had a hot tip. That we should check out this local hedge fund, Global Possibilities or whatever, something generic. Figured it's just some bucket shop he's got a kickback on."

"You said anything about the bank being in play? Anything to indicate we may have an interest?"

A Most Private Bank

"Not particularly. Asked if he thinks the bank will go belly-up or if someone's gonna bid for it."

"That light him up?"

"Like a Polish church. Said he already planned to talk to you about that. Something about hidden reserves and unique opportunity, and all of that. He actually started whispering about how it's all a secret. As if the whispering would somehow make the compliance guys not hear… Dumb sap." Raphael shook his head in disbelief.

Private banks, like any other banks, had been recording all phone calls by routine for decades. With plenty of orders and deals done over the phone, all was recorded. These days, with compliance rules up to the ears, calls were also monitored in search of all kinds of ethics breaches. Which is the reason why truly secret conversations were done in person or over private cell phones.

"I could almost hear him winking over the phone," he continued. "He said someone will call you. That there's this incredible opportunity."

"What's your take on it, Raph?"

"I think he's full of it. Probably making a few bucks on the side on referrals and thinks we're an easy mark."

I thought about what was said. For a few seconds I sat with my elbows on the desk, my face leaning against my fist. I took a deep breath and nodded to him. On a normal day I would agree with him. It made sense. That's how Zurich finance works. It all spins on kickbacks.

When someone gives you a friendly suggestion to invest in some fund, to open an account with some bank, or to do business with someone, that's usually not just a friendly suggestion. He'll get a cut of the revenue, and you can make a pretty good living just making these friendly suggestions.

No, on a normal day I wouldn't care about another banker recommending another fund manager. Doesn't mean a thing. But this hadn't been a normal day so far - far from it. My instincts told me to just walk away from anything even remotely connected to Bank Niederhauser, but there was no way my curiosity would allow that.

"Right. What about Ms. Rosenbaum?" I asked. "Assessment?"

"Seems serious about bagging the bank. God knows why. I sure didn't get a straight answer on that point, but as you like to say, a fool and her money—-"

"Are lucky enough to get together in the first place," I finished the saying for him.

"Gotta tell you, though, I'm not convinced. I mean, some broad barely old enough to date shows up and wants to make a huge deal, just like that. This kind, these spoiled brats, they get some harebrained plan and in a few days they're onto something else. Next week she might decide to buy a beach resort in the Maldives instead."

"You wanna drop it? Your call, buddy."

It was his time to pause and think and he mimicked the same position I had seconds ago, elbow on the table, head on the fist. He didn't believe in this thing. I could see it. He didn't want to give up on the profit potential either. I saw that too.

"Lemme do another pass. See if I can figure something. Give me two days, three tops. If it doesn't look solid by then, we'll kill it."

"Works for me, Raph. Do some initial due diligence. It's probably a waste of time, but I don't want to be caught off guard here. Start with the usual. Balance sheet, income statement, cash flow reports, if you can get hold of them. Not exactly a public company. Approach them correct, say that you represent me and we are looking into taking a stake. They're in deep and should jump all over it. Let me know if they give you a hard time about getting the info. Don't expect surprises, just do it anyway. As far as anyone is concerned, the interest is mine and mine alone. After the scandal, customers are jumping ship. Expect their finances to be a disaster."

"Shouldn't take too long. It's a dog with fleas. A distressed firm in a deteriorating industry. Even a healthy private bank, in this environment—"

"I know, I know," I interrupted. "But we're not risking firm assets on this one."

"That's for sure. I almost feel like talking her out of it. But then I remember that I've got 150 reasons not to. Got any idea what this is all about, Jim?"

I studied him for a moment. Raphael Bosch was a clever guy - some may even call him a sneaky bastard. Par for the course in this industry.

I didn't tell him about what happened at the golf course. Didn't want him to understand the potential importance, didn't want him to see any larger picture. If he had, he would have wanted more money. Greed makes people predictable.

"Can't be sure. Probably nothing. But might be something there. Something off the books."

"Like what, safe-deposit boxes filled with bearer bonds?" Raphael suggested.

"I wish! Probably nothing. Hell if I know. Might be something, might be nothing."

"I always wanted to rob a bank," Raphael said, rubbing his palms together.

"Bank robbers are amateurs, Raph. Professionals start banks," I said, rising to my feet, signaling the end of the meeting.

Sandra Joseph

The conversation with Raphael hadn't been particularly enlightening. He knew as well as I did that this was a dead parrot - he was just too blinded by a bonus check and a pretty girl to give up right away. Whatever my old golf partner was up to, I had no interest in playing along. Nothing good could possibly come from it.

I should have put an end to it. Should have just walked away. It would still have been possible. There wasn't much at stake, not yet. Perhaps if I had ended it there, if I had told Chris that I wasn't interested, told Sandra not to accept her calls, if I had told Raph to drop the idea, perhaps then, everyone would still be alive. Perhaps.

Remembering that I had interrupted Sandra earlier, I walked back out to the reception. She was busy typing away and didn't look my way.

"You were saying?" I asked, using that tone of voice that was the closest to an actual apology that I ever gave her. She stopped typing and pushed the keyboard to the side, reaching for her notes. She accepted my apology - I could see it in her eyes.

"Ms. Rosenbaum came by again."

"Met with Raph?"

"That too. They went out for lunch. Two hours. Came back a bit tipsy. At least him."

"No big surprise. That it?"

"Well, she came to me after. Wanted to have a chat. Bit odd. She waited for Raph to go back to his desk."

I wiped nonexistent sweat off my forehead and walked

around behind her desk and pulled up a chair. She had something to say, and better if the trader in the next room didn't hear it. Sandra was good with people, good with reading them.

"Fishing for information?"

Sandra shook her head. "Not at all. You know I'm always on my guard. No, at first she just wanted to chat. About nonsense. The city, the language, the weather... Tourist stuff."

"Right," I said. "Bet that didn't impress you at all."

"She got to the point in the end. Had an odd way to it, but she finally did. Asked me to get you to come meet her for a drink tonight."

"What for?" I asked. "Raph's got this. And frankly, I'm not terribly interested in this project."

"She asked for you. Made sure he was out of earshot."

"She gave a reason?"

"Didn't ask."

"So she prefers older men?" I said with a big grin. She rolled her eyes at me and was about to speak.

"Sorry, just kidding, Sandra. She said when?" I added before she could scold me.

"The Baur au Lac at six."

I reached for a yellow sticky note and a pen on her desk and made a note. I didn't like this, how Chris tried to play me. I had been in this business far too long to be played that easily. Her little feelings had been hurt when I put Raph on it and now she was trying to go over his head. Hoping that I would just drop everything and jump at the chance for a drink with a pretty girl. I'd go, all right, but just to set her straight. Enough's enough.

"Yeah, I'll be there. What's your take on her? As a woman."

"My womanly intuition? Is that still a thing?" Sandra said.

"Well, I like her. I'd say she seemed worried. Tough cookie, putting-up-a-brave-front, kinda gal. Probably has her reasons."

"You think she's trustworthy?"

Sandra paused and thought about it. I hadn't just asked to make conversation, I actually cared about her view. More often than not, Sandra read people correctly even when I missed something.

"I think she's good people. If she's not giving you the whole story, she probably has a reason. Hear her out, will you? She seems like an honest person to me. Be nice to her, Jim."

I thought about that for a moment, trying to parse what she said and figure out what to do with it.

"That all?" I asked.

"That's not even the half of it. I had a very odd call just now. Two of them, actually. Thought it was a prank at first."

"Oh?" I leaned closer in my chair. "First that creepy banker called, Dick von Baerenfells. Not sure if he was drunk or high. Or just being a slimeball. He was kind of whispering. Weirdly cryptic. Said that I'd get a call in five minutes and that I should take it seriously. Then he said not to tell anyone but you. And just like that, he hung up the phone."

"And did you? Get a call?"

"Sure did. Damn near on the second five minutes later. I checked. Didn't know if Baerenfells was calling in a bomb threat or what. 'Take it seriously'. The hell does that mean?"

"What was the second call?"

"Just some sales call. The kind that I would normally not even mention to you. Some punter looking for investments in some hedge fund." She lifted the notebook in her hand up to read something. "Global Opportunities Fund. Local guy, Swiss, sounded young. Markus Bühler. Nervous fellow. Not very used to pitching over the phone. He said that your mutual friend would like you to stop by their offices down on Talstrasse. Mutual friend… that's what he said. Supposed to be Baerenfells?"

More childish games. Just what I needed. Things were already looking dicey and here's some bargain-bin hedge fund kid joining the fray. This was another fine chance to call it a day, to drop the entire matter. Of course, I passed it up. Curiosity can be a dangerous thing.

"Thanks, I'll deal with it," I said.

"This Baerenfells guy is with Bank Niederhauser, isn't he? This related to Ms. Rosenbaum?"

I set her pen back on her table and pocketed the yellow note I had been scribbling on. She's sharp. Cleverer than Raphael, that's for sure. In a fair world, she'd be making ten times what he's paid, instead of the other way around.

"I'm not too big on coincidences. Last week, no one in their right mind would touch this bank. Now everyone and his grandmother is interested."

That piqued her interest more than I had intended, and she leaned in closer to me. "Really? Who else?"

I hadn't planned on telling her about Hill, but I trusted her and didn't mind her knowing. She had no economic interest anyhow.

"Keep this between us for now. I don't want Raph getting greedy on this one. Hell, I'm not even sure what we're dealing with yet," I half whispered. "I was approached by Steve Hill at the golf club. Wants to know why I'm looking at Niederhauser."

Sandra's eyes sparkled and she couldn't contain an excited smile, "He's CIA, isn't he? Was stationed in Caracas before he came over here. That's what I heard."

"Honestly, I don't know. Never cared until today. I heard the rumors but never figured he's smart enough for that."

"He dated a friend of mine for a while. Likes to talk about being a big-shot spy. Not sure what's true or not, but he likes to impress girls with these stories."

"I'm not sure what he is. I had him pegged for some low-level bureaucrat. Most of these so called intelligence guys aren't exactly James Bond, you know. He somehow knew we're looking into Niederhauser but apart from that seems clueless. Didn't even know who the client is."

"You tell him?"

"I told him what he's entitled to. Squat. Until I know what the play is, nobody gets anything."

"You have any idea what this is all about, Jim?" Sandra asked, lowering her voice.

Sure, I had some ideas. I had plenty of ideas. It's not like I lacked the imagination to make some educated guesses. None of them turned out to be correct, of course. The one thing I was sure of, though, was that this wasn't about some cute little heiress buying her own private bank in a sudden and furious fit of vanity.

No, whatever this was about, it was bigger than that. I saw that already and that made me curious. No, curious isn't the right word. Greedy. I really didn't care all that much what this was all about, not at this point. What I did care about was the profit potential. It had been far too many coincidences for one day and all pointed to one thing. There was something going on here, something that I might be able to find a way to profit from.

I looked at Sandra. She deserved an answer, a real answer. But I wasn't about to give her one.

"No idea. Probably nothing interesting," I told her.

Global Opportunities

The man opening the door was clearly old enough to shave - the goatee was proof of that. He was slim and short, wearing spectacles with rectangular black plastic frames, extending his hand.

"Markus Bühler. Come on inside, Mr. Dixon. Great that you could make it so quickly."

"Jim." I stepped past the diminutive man in the jeans and checked shirt and into his office.

The room was small and barely fit the IKEA office desk and the two cheap chairs. Couple of computer monitors on the desk, surrounded by a jungle of paper, notebooks, pens, markers, and leftover food. Next to the keyboard a half-eaten Subway sandwich in its open wrapper. A whiteboard leaning against the wall covered in illegible handwriting, perhaps a list of stocks. The room smelled as if the windows hadn't been opened in quite some time.

"Let's talk in here," the eager young man said. He was motioning to the second room. Identical to the first in size but with kitchen sink in the corner and a meeting table with six chairs around it, all bearing the unmistakable IKEA hallmark. On the wall a six-feet-wide artwork, painted on a metal canvas. The motif a dark and stormy sea, waves crashing against a barren shore.

"Ah, yes, one of our investors owns a local gallery," the young man explained seeing his visitor stop for a moment to look at the painting. "We had it custom made by an up-and-coming artist attached to his gallery. Cost us twenty grand."

"We?" I asked, pulling out one of the plastic chairs, brushing some dust off it before taking a seat.

Bühler glanced out the window and pulled out a chair opposite the one I had chosen.

"Well, I did, that is. We, as in my company did. Got a good deal too. These things sell for far more at the gallery. Great deal, really."

"Uh-huh. Why am I here, Markus?"

"Right, right, let's get to it," the young man said as he shuffled around some papers in front of him and turned a laptop to the side so that we could both see the screen. "So my fund was launched two years ago. It's a Caribbean setup, with the Global Opportunities Fund domiciled in the Cayman Islands."

He kept on talking and I did my best not to let my thoughts wander. He was excited about all of this, excited in that way that rookies in the industry tend to be. Before you grow cold, hard, and cynical. He was explaining how clever their company structure was, as if this was something new. As if this was something interesting.

Work in finance long enough and you learn to hate regulation. It's expensive to be regulated and it means following rules. This little fund had bypassed regulations by having a fund company in the Caymans, a fund management company in the British Virgin Islands, and an advisory company in Zurich. Three countries, all pretending that they didn't need to regulate you, that this would be the responsibility of one of the other countries.

My thoughts were drifting off. This was just another bucket shop, another little pretend hedge fund. Regular folks hear the term hedge fund and they think of Gordon Gekko, of billionaires in New York. Truth is, a hedge fund can be anything. It can be a twenty-year-old in a shabby office playing around with a few million bucks of other people's money. This town was full of these little shops, most of them doing nothing but dream and lose money.

He was droning on and my attention was on the skies outside the window. The dark clouds were moving, but in which direction? I had been politely pretending to listen for long enough.

"What's your AUM?" I said, interrupting whatever he was talking about. I looked at the Daytona and I made sure he saw me looking. He had lost his train of thought and was struggling to recover.

"Your assets under management. How much money do you have in the fund right now?" I said, getting impatient.

"Eh… well, at the moment the assets under management is at about forty-one million, but—"

"Redemptions? Subscriptions? Any money in or out?"

"Well… no, just the initial seed money," he said. He knew where this was heading by now.

"So you spent two years and lost nine million. Eighteen percent down in the first two years?" I asked.

The previously enthusiastic young man hesitated. He shuffled around some papers on the desk again, until he found one with the month-by-month results for the Global Opportunities Fund. He turned the paper the other way, so that I could see the monthly numbers and the various charts and figures on the fact sheet.

"We… we had some initial teething problems… but this is to be expected from time to time. It's been a difficult couple of years for our kind of strategies, but we're well on track and expect a strong bounce back. In fact, this is probably a good time to invest, given the drawback. Many sophisticated investors prefer to buy a fund like ours after a losing streak to get a better entry price and to be part of the recovery."

"You got a rich uncle, Markus?"

"What? No, not that I know of," he replied.

"You just stumbled upon fifty mil to manage, all by your lonesome?"

He got suspicious, hesitating.

"Who's your mysterious benefactor?" I asked.

"I'm not allowed to talk about that. Bank secrecy, you know."

"You're hardly a bank."

"Call it Swiss discretion, then. I'm sorry, I can't."

I sighed and looked at the Daytona again. I had never understood why this model got so popular. Impossible to get ahold of, at least in steel. Lacking the simple beauty of the Submariner, the hard lines and clear definition, and with a tachymeter that can't stand a polish or two. This particular one was an earlier model, with the Zenith movement, trading at three times its list price on the secondary market. Nobody cared about this model until it got scarce. The more they can't have it, the more they want it.

Bühler had something on his wrist too. I hadn't seen it before - his shirt had covered it. A steel Longines Master on a brown alligator strap. A classic chronometer, white face with three sub dials. Month, weekday, day, and moon phase indicators, along with the chronograph, made an unbeatable complications-to-price ratio. Not a big-league watch by any means, but certainly one of the most respectable choices in the budget range, sub $5,000. It made me wonder if I had judged the kid too quickly.

"Look, Markus," I started off. "You seem like a nice enough fellow. But you're a junior without market experience, running a dodgy offshore vehicle for some secret investor, and your stellar strategy finds itself in an eighteen percent hole after the first two years. Again. Why am I here?"

He actually smiled. Here I had half expected him to run off

A Most Private Bank

crying. He took a moment to collect himself and pushed the papers aside.

"It was suggested to me that I try to pitch the original fund to you. Before explaining our shift in focus," he said.

"What's the shift?" I asked.

"We're mounting a raid on Bank Niederhauser," he said.

I watched him closely as he said it. Sizing up the person in front of me.

"Why would you want to buy a distressed private bank?"

"We have on good information that… that the book value may not accurately reflect the actual value of the company."

"How's that?" I asked.

"There may be something of great value… in the vault."

"What's in the vault belongs to customers. Not the bank," I said.

"Yes, of course… Unless it's legally deemed to be abandoned and is without known owner. You know, like if it had been abandoned for half a century or more. Rumor is that there are thousands of safe-deposit boxes all over town that hasn't been touched for ages. Back in the day, ownership wasn't even registered. Whoever had the key owned it."

"And if no one's been around to access the box in fifty years, the bank can legally drill it open and pocket what's inside?"

He nodded slowly. I wasn't sure if he was trying to convince me with this explanation, or himself.

"So what exactly is in these boxes?"

"I can't tell you much. But I hear there's gold. Lots of gold."

"You hear?"

"That's what I hear," he said.

"Is this when we get to why I'm here?"

"It was suggested to me that you might be interested in assisting. On the financing side," he said.

I had heard enough. If the project looked questionable this morning, it was setting off Geiger counters by now. Anyone could figure out what he was hinting at, what kind of safe-deposit boxes might be abandoned for that long and why. It didn't sound like anything I wanted to be near, for a whole range of reasons.

Besides, if there really was something big here, something secret and valuable, someone like this guy would be the last to find out. The interesting secrets, the ones you can actually make some money on, tend to trickle down slowly. Money can be made when you're close to the source, when you're one of the first to know. If a tiny little failed fund like this knows, it would be in the newspaper soon and by then it's all over. If there ever was anything of interest in the first place.

No, he seemed like a decent guy but decent guys don't get far in this line of work.

"Thank you for your time, Markus," I said, extending my hand. "Tell your silent partner that I'm not in the habit of investing in secretive ventures or risking money on hearsay. Good meeting you. Best of luck."

Dick von Baerenfells

A waste of time, no more, no less. I hadn't expected anything else. The walk back to the office was a mere ten minutes. If the problem with old European cities like this was the frustration of driving, the advantage was the ease of walking. Nothing was really too far to just leg it.

Coming up the stairs I saw Sandra through the glass entrance door. She was on the phone, and she had seen me too. She lifted a finger to her temple and spun it around in a circle.

"Hold one moment, please. He just walked in the door," she said and muted the phone. "Jim, I've got that banker on the line again. Baerenfells."

The timepiece on my wrist showed 4:35. Most of the day already gone with just a crappy golf game to show for it, and my patience was wearing thin. I nodded to Sandra and held my hand out for the phone. I was going to make this short - no need to transfer the call to my desk.

"Yeah, Jim speaking."

Pressing the receiver to the ear wasn't enough. I had to cover my other ear with my palm.

"What... Speak up..."

She nodded knowingly. The man on the other side of the line was drunk. Loud music in the background. At half past four on a Monday.

"Fine... Where?" I had him repeat the address twice and I still wasn't sure. Never heard of the street, must be a small one. Close to Stauffacher he said, a major inner-city tram junction.

"Right... Uh-huh... Yeah, just came from there... Look, just tell me what… Fine… I'll be there in fifteen," I said and set the receiver down.

"Tried to warn you," Sandra said.

"Getting ridiculous," I said. "I'll go put an end to this nonsense."

I had barely got in and I wasn't in the mood for another hike and another pointless meeting. My coat still on, I grabbed the hat and went out anyway.

The sun had managed to break through and the fog was lifting. I kept a brisk pace toward the Stauffacher junction. A small side street he had said. Couldn't make out the exact street names but I might recognize them when I saw the signs.

I crossed the bridge by the casino, the most unassuming casino in the world. Outside it looked like an office building, and I couldn't care less what the inside might look like. There were all kinds of tiny roads and alleys around Stauffacher. The first sign I saw said St. Jakobstrasse. Sounded familiar. A bit of luck for the first time this day.

Following St. Jakobstrasse a hundred yards down, there was Müllerstrasse. That must have been what he said. St. Jakob and Müller. A quiet little street, barely any cars around. Small round tables on the sidewalk, two chairs for each. It was far too early for any bar to be crowded. Just a few people. The windows of the bar were tinted, impossible to see what was inside.

The door was just at the corner. I headed straight for it and stepped inside. What I saw stopped me in my tracks.

I looked around slowly, from left to right. Something surreal came over me, something I had not expected. The lights inside were dim, and despite the sun breaking through the cloud cover outside, the room was dark. It took a moment for my eyes to adjust.

At the bar sat three girls, all facing me, all smiling at me. Slavic features, Eastern Europeans. Early twenties. The first wearing a short black leather skirt with a matching top. The second in red hot pants, a top that barely covered its silicon-infused contents.

The third girl stood and approached me. Slowly. Making a show of it. One high-heel black boot in front of the other. My mouth half-open, I stood frozen until I felt her hand on my hip, her smile right in front of my face.

"I... I'm sorry, I'm clearly in the wrong place," I said and turned. "My mistake."

A soft giggle came from the bar when I stepped out, my surprise mistaken for shyness. If this had been someone's idea of a joke, I wasn't amused. This was a type of place I hadn't seen before, hadn't even been aware of. A brothel, disguised as a regular bar. There were no laws requiring such a disguise, not in Europe. When I turned to leave, I wasn't completely sure, but that's what I assumed the place to be.

Once outside I looked around to make sure I was in the right place. A brief, loud whistle cut through the quiet air, and I spun around. A familiar face occupied one of the chairs outside the bar. Someone I had met in the past, quite some time ago.

A man in his late fifties, silver hair, double-breasted gray pinstripe suit with a purple tie and matching pocket square. A phone pressed to his right ear, he was waving the left in my direction. The sun reflected in the shiny piece of kit on his wrist.

It wasn't surprising to see the forty-four-millimeter Audemars Piguet. My impression of him so far fit well with that choice. The original Royal Oak was designed by the legendary Gérald Genta and played no small part in rescuing the Swiss watch industry during the quartz crisis. With the hexagon shape, reminiscent of an antique diving suit helmet and the integrated wide bracelet, it was one of the most recognizable watches in the world. Which was the point for most buyers.

The standard model is larger than most watches, but this was the extra-large Offshore variant, and it was objectively huge. Even the regular version, even in steel was meant to be seen. And this particular one was in yellow gold both for the case and the bracelet. Black face with three golden circles for the chronograph, everything about a watch like this was meant to scream money.

He was having a conversation in slurred French on the phone. The hand graced with the enormous watch had picked up a cigar from the ashtray, and next to him sat a girl. Not European, not like the ones inside. She had a milk-chocolate complexion, long black hair, dark sparkling eyes and a friendly smile. I grabbed a chair from the next table, pulled it over and sat down opposite them.

"Jim. How do you do?" I said and offered the girl my hand.

"And I'm the Queen of Sheba," the girl said as if that was the most common thing in the world to be saying.

"But of course you are," was the best reply I could come up with.

"*Pardon*... Sorry, just a moment," the drunk banker said to me and continued what sounded like a heated discussion in French. By the time I had turned my head to nod to him and turned it back, the queen had waved over a blond girl from a nearby table.

"You like her?" the queen asked. "My friend. She can join us."

"No," I said as firmly as I could, motioning toward the clownish banker. "No, thanks. I've got some business with Dick."

"Don't we all," she replied, making me regret my choice of words.

I was just about to get up and walk away from the mad house when one of the girls I had seen inside came out with a tray. She set down three glasses, leaving a fourth on the tray after noting that the blonde had gone back to her own table.

A Most Private Bank

I put my hand up to refuse the drink. "I'm not staying."

"What's the matter?" the waitress said, pouting her lips. "Don't like blondes? We have more inside for you."

I had had enough, and got up to leave and he quickly got off the phone.

"Jim, Jim, what's the rush?" he said with an outstretched right hand.

Regretting having shown up to this meeting, I shook the hand. "You said it was urgent. You got five minutes. Ladies, please excuse us."

I waved the girls away without looking at them. The queen took her purse and scooted over to the next table, and the waitress approached the next punter. "Come back anytime, Jim!" said the Queen of Sheba.

Dick von Baerenfells corrected the rimless glasses and took a big puff on the cigar. The label still on, still visible. *Romeo y Julieta No.3*. I waited for him to exhale the smoke.

"I hear you beat my guy up." He grinned. "Bright kid, not much of a sales guy, I'm afraid."

"You mean the poor sap you have running your secret offshore fund?" I asked.

He chuckled and puffed that big smelly cigar. "Go easy on him, he's just the front. Mr. Visible."

"So you call in trades to him during lunch hours, I suppose. Anyhow, I saw the result. Not interested."

"Yes, yes, of course. Had hardly expected it. The fund is, shall we say, more of a tax and compliance construct than anything. Not easy to manage your own money when you work for a bank, not these days."

"Right. Pesky little things like tax declarations and insider trading rules can be a nuisance, I can imagine."

"Quite," he replied without picking up on the sarcasm. "I assume you have your own fund too somewhere, Jim. But what is of importance here, why I asked to see you, is our special investment project."

"Buying your employer before they figure out that you're running an illegal investment shop on the side and robbing their vault of their stash of stolen gold?" I asked.

Dick von Baerenfells broke out in a loud laugh, turning the heads of the girls and the few punters on the other tables. After he stopped laughing, he tapped his nose with the right index finger with cigar ashes predictably falling down over his bespoke suit.

"Top secret. No one knows. No one… but me. Don't ask how I found out. This is the big one, Jim. This one can make us all rich."

"You're not already rich? I would have thought you've been clearing seven figures for a few decades. Niederhauser always rewarded lifers, I hear."

"I'm talking real money, my dear! Real money! Generational wealth."

I looked at the drunk lunatic in front of me. Hard to imagine this was supposedly a respectable Swiss banker, someone responsible for hundreds of millions of client money, someone trusted by wealthy individuals and institutions. Hard to take him seriously, sitting there in his loud outfit, getting drunk, and trying to impress working girls in the middle of the day.

"It all sounds like quite a tall tale," I said.

"This one is real. Solid information. Take my word for it."

"When it comes to big deals, I'm not in the habit of taking anyone's word," I said.

"You lost your appetite, Jim? I thought you were the guy to talk to for larger deals."

I picked up the drink that had been put in front of me, smelled

A Most Private Bank

it and, changed my mind.

"What do you know and where did you get it?" I asked.

"Oh, I can't tell you where I got it. But what we're looking at is at least two full metric tons of gold. All unclaimed. No beneficial ownership, my dear! All that gold, and it belongs to no one! Best of all, the current bank management knows nothing about it."

That required at least a second thought. Metric tons. Would explain all the hoo-ha this morning. The senior banker in front of me gave a comical appearance, the combination of being drunk in the middle of the day and the peacock outfit, cigar to crown it. The words metric tons went through my head and I did some mental arithmetic.

"And where would this supposed hundred million dollars' worth of metal have come from?" I asked. There was only one possible source, but I wanted to hear him say it anyhow.

"Back in the thirties, this was the only safe place in the world to keep your money. For all sides. Everyone knows that plenty of rich Jews stashed their gold here. But they weren't the only ones, were they? No, there were plenty of rich Krauts too. Some senior party members even. As it turns out, much to our benefit, quite a lot of people in both of those categories met an untimely demise before they could pass on the proof of ownership to anyone."

He stopped for effect and grinned triumphantly. I motioned for him to go on.

"Back in those days, banks didn't keep much information on ownership. Any sap with the key could come and claim what's in the boxes. But of course... if some unforeseen incident should happen, and you had no way of passing on the key... or telling people what the key is... well, then the boxes become orphan, don't they?"

A spectrum of reactions went through my brain along with all kinds of possible replies to such a story. They would all have to remain in my brain for now. Showing my true feelings about that little story and his glee about it wouldn't be productive, not now.

"Two tons of gold," I said, running the numbers in my head. "That'd be about twenty-six gallons. A hundred liters. Enough to fill three bathtubs. Doesn't exactly fit in a deposit box, does it?" I asked him.

"Sure, it does. The vault is enormous. Plenty of private little rooms in there. Lots of space for your gold bars, bullions and trinkets. Funny, really, if you think about it. Jews and Nazis had their little stashes just next door to each other. In the same vault!"

I looked away and exhaled slowly as he tried my patience.

"Uh-huh. You seen this gold?" I asked.

"Certainly not. No one can go in, you see. No one can open it. It's not like banks have spare keys. But we do log when someone accesses it, and if no one has been there in fifty years... it's all up for grabs."

"How do you know it's there?"

"I have very reliable sources. High-level sources."

As much as I despised people like him, I had to concede that what he was claiming wasn't impossible. Unlikely, perhaps even outlandish, but not impossible. His job was to smooch the rich and obnoxious, to gain their trust and their investments. He could have overheard something.

Still, I had no intention of going anywhere near this. If he was right, if his story turned out to be true, anyone involved could expect to be tied up in legal proceedings for decades. Besides, having my picture in the newspaper next to a headline about theft from Holocaust victims wasn't on my bucket list.

"Where do I fit in?" I asked anyhow, for some reason.

"Front the project for us. Help raise some assets for the deal and keep it quiet."

A Most Private Bank

"You're not looking for an investment from me?"

"No, no, Jim. I don't expect you to take risks of your own. Just set it up and run it for us."

"And what's my end?"

"Half a mil, Jim. That's your end. Paid off the books, if you like, to any bank anywhere. Good enough for you?"

It was time to leave, for all kinds of reasons. I stood up and shook his hand.

"I'll let you know," I said and walked away.

When I passed the girl who had kept him company earlier I tipped my hat and muttered, "Your highness…"

The Baur

The darkness set on the city early this time of the year. It was shortly before six when I got to the Baur au Lac. With the lake on one side and the canal on the other and a history going back two hundred years, this was the hotel of choice for financiers and visiting film stars. Three flags flew from the top of the main building, a Swiss white cross on red background flanked by dual Zurich cantonal blue-and-white banners.

The driveway as usual was surrounded by a selection of exotic cars. Today's lineup included a pair of black Bentleys, a silver Aston Martin Vanquish, a Blu Swaters Ferrari Portofino, a Rosso Folgore Maserati Quattroporte, and a bright pink Lamborghini Aventador. Only the Vanquish caught my eye. Not every day you see the Shooting Brake model. Not with just ninety-nine of them ever manufactured.

Twilight was setting and the fog was sweeping in from the lake. Cold enough for my coat to remain buttoned up. The garden patio was a bright oasis in the dark and foggy surroundings. White marble pillars holding up marble roofs, white canapes, white chairs and tables, all well-lit with the grass and trees all around.

A lady on the piano provided soft, soothing background music. By the bar, an elderly gentleman in a blue blazer, white shirt, crimson ascot and matching stuffed pocket square. The soft sound of subdued conversations from the guests enjoying their evening drinks.

By the bar sat a beautiful young woman. She was in a black evening dress, one knee over the other, sipping a martini. Her finger twirled her long black hair. I watched her for a moment.

Lost in thought until the concierge approached.

"Mr. Dixon, always a pleasure. Would you like a table?"

I snapped out of it and shook his hand. "Just here for a drink tonight, Fred. Say, the girl by the bar, you seen her before?"

"Been sitting there a good hour, sir. Nursing the same drink the whole time."

"Anyone spoken to her?"

"Japanese guest of the hotel got swatted away half an hour ago. Surprised me. I took her for a pro, if you beg my pardon, sir."

I looked back at her. Pretty girl, all alone by the bar. The only pretty girl around.

"See what you mean. She a guest at the hotel?"

"Oh no, sir. Not staying here. I would have known. Never seen her before tonight. Came walking in. In those heels. Unusual, sir. Not many would walk far in such shoes."

"I see. Thank you, Fred. You've been most helpful."

"Anytime, sir. Anytime. Enjoy your evening."

I resisted the habit of slipping him a twenty. That's not the European way. Hotel staff are paid well and would be offended if handed some little trinket.

She spotted me when I walked into the patio space, past the white marble pillars. With the soft spotlights aimed at the white outdoor ceiling and canvases and with the dark surrounding greens, there was a glowing, dreamy feel to the place.

She uncrossed her legs and got up from the barstool, a confident warm smile on her face, letting me come to her.

"Jim, thank you for seeing me," she said and gave me the traditional Swiss triple cheek kiss greeting. Left, right, left. A trick she had picked up quickly.

"Apologies for being late," I said, despite being right on time.

"Hope I didn't keep you waiting too long."

"Oh, not at all. I just arrived myself. Please, have a seat." She turned to wave the bartender over as she sat back down on her barstool.

"Jack Daniel's. On the rocks," I said to the bartender.

The man behind the bar turned his attention to my companion. *"Et pour vous, Madame?"*

Speaking French in high-end hotels and restaurants was somewhat of an annoying habit in this multilingual little country and she was caught off guard. A touch of blush on her cheeks as she searched for a reply. The waiter read her confusion quickly and switched language.

"*Ah, pardon, Madame.* May I offer you another drink?"

"Another martini, please," she said.

"You're not happy with the way Mr. Bosch is handling his matter?" I asked, straight to the point.

"Oh no, Raphael was most helpful," she replied.

"But?"

"I would very much appreciate your personal attention, Jim."

The drinks had arrived in front of us, and I picked mine up. It had been quite a day so far and having a sip of whiskey was the only part of this meeting I had actually looked forward to.

"Gotta tell you, Chris," I said. "I'm not overly keen on this idea. Too many moving parts, too much that can go wrong, and I frankly don't see the point in the first place."

She took her time with that martini. Perhaps she wanted a moment to think, perhaps she wanted some distance to what I had just said. When she finally broke the silence, she acted as if I hadn't said it at all.

"It seems as if the schedule may have changed slightly. We

A Most Private Bank

may need to move a little faster. I might not be the only interested party, and you would be in a better position than Raphael to get this little project wrapped up swiftly, Jim."

"We?" I said, studying what looked like a slight chink in her confident armor. "I don't recall agreeing to anything."

"Oh, we both know you want to do this, Jim. There's a deal to be made and you're the dealmaker, aren't you? At least you used to be. Don't you miss the old days? Just managing your own money can't be the same. What are you doing these days? Allocating to hedge funds and doing the odd private equity deal? Must be a little dull after swinging billion-dollar venture portfolios for people like my father."

It was my turn for some quiet time with my drink. The first words that came to mind would not have been helpful, not now. Benjamin Rosenbaum's daughter would know very well why I was not doing those things anymore and I didn't like the way she kept rubbing it in. But that didn't make her wrong.

"Not the same action, is it?" she said, pushing me some more.

I kept quiet a little longer and my drink got a little shorter. Then I set my glass down and looked into those big blue eyes of hers.

"You wanna tell me what this is really about, Chris?"

She looked away. Her face shifted hue. A small shift, and anyone not looking for it might have missed it. I had been looking for it. She lifted the Chanel purse up from the floor and set it down in her lap and started searching around inside it. I waited patiently.

Up came a hand holding a pack of Dunhill cigarettes and a Ronson lighter. I let her take her time, watching a bright flame caress the tip of the cigarette, watching her inhale and blow the smoke up toward the spotlit ceiling.

"I think the timing is perfect for a takeover. Father always said that the best time to buy is when everyone in the world thinks it's crazy. Buy when you hear the sound of the cannons, he said."

"Uh-huh," I muttered, waving away some leftover smoke from my face. "But I asked for the real reason."

She had pushed me, and I enjoyed getting back at her. She didn't want me to ask, didn't want me to dig further. So that's what I decided to do.

"I'm not delusional," she said.

I wasn't about to take the pressure off, not now. In seconds she had gone from a spoiled brat demanding a new pony to something very different. Insecurity and stress were on display. That didn't take much.

"Didn't say you were," I said.

"I... I have my reasons. I can't explain. Not yet. I know what I'm doing, Jim!"

There was something to her voice. Perhaps a sense of desperation. Perhaps fear. Perhaps I was the delusional one. I needed to take my foot off, if just for a moment. A glass of whiskey can be a godsent prop, and I used it to ease off.

"I met Dick von Baerenfells this afternoon," I said as I set the glass down.

She looked away from me, out of the patio, her eyes following the spotlight trained at a tall pine tree.

"You're not going to rummage around your purse for another cigarette, are you?"

She turned back to me. The redness in her face was all gone and it had gotten paler than when the evening started.

"What did he tell you?" she asked.

"He told me a story."

"What about?"

"A wild story about a hundred million dollars' worth of metal in the bank's lost-and-found basket," I said without taking my eyes off hers.

She reached for the purse again, searching around inside it before her hand came up with a cigarette between her fingers. She searched the purse once more and I picked up the Ronson for her. It was on the bar table, next to the ashtray and the still-smoking, half-finished previous cigarette. She put the fresh one between her lips and I lit it for her.

"And you believe that I have something to do with this story?" she finally said.

"I wasn't too sure until just now."

She puffed on the cigarette between her manicured fingers. The prior confidence in her face for a moment seemingly diminished.

"I was worried about this," she started. "I was hoping I had enough of a head start."

"Who's behind Baerenfells?" I asked.

"He's a dangerous man, Jim."

"What, Dick? He's a buffoon."

"No, no. Not him. Sasha Petrov. He's a Russian businessman."

"Businessman or gangster?"

Chris put her barely started cigarette out in the ashtray, squashing it down hard.

"In the East the lines aren't so black and white."

"And now he's looking for leprechaun gold?" I asked.

She hesitated, picked up her martini, and finished what was left in it.

"I can't tell you the whole story. Not now. Can you trust me, Jim?"

I felt her finger touch the hand I was holding my drink in and I pulled my hand back. This was a business meeting, and that's the way I intended to keep it.

"I'm not a very trusting person. This business does that to you," I said. "I asked Raphael to take the lead on this, and he's more than capable. It's in his court now. He tells me it can't be done, we walk. He wants to go ahead, I'll assist, but it's his project. His call, you deal with him. No promises, no guarantees."

I got up from the stool, and so did she. She looked shook up. She looked amazing. I saw her move closer for the triple Swiss cheek kisses, and I preempted it with an outstretched hand.

"I understand," she said, shaking it.

I left a fifty on the bar for the drinks and headed back. It had started to rain again, and I raised the collars of my coat and picked up the pace.

Evening Plans

The rain was light, and the hat provided sufficient protection. The shops around Bahnhofstrasse, Zurich's Main Street, were closed by now, but all the storefronts were lit up. The route led me past Trois Pommes, the very store that had caused such a stir not long ago when they refused to wait on Oprah Winfrey. From an American perspective it looked like racism. You would have to spend some time here to realize that it's not racism but merely the run-of-the-mill contempt for poor people you'd see from most shops of its kind. Just last summer I had been asked to leave Giorgio Armani a few yards away when I had dared to show up in cargo shorts.

The walk gave me some time to think the day over. There were alarm bells all over this thing, so many reasons to walk away. You don't want to be anywhere near something that draws the interest of the US State Department, and if the story of stolen war gold was true, it would be a disaster in the making. The five-million fee she had dangled in front of my eyes didn't make any sense and I just couldn't see a path for that to become real. Weighing the sides of it, all that was in favor was my own curiosity. That and the fact that the annoying girl was starting to grow on me. But the whole situation looked like a lemon even before she mentioned some shady Russian guy.

No, better to steer Raphael out of it.

I slowed my steps passing Beyer, one of the oldest and most respected watch stores in town. There were a few interesting items on display, and I decided to come back another day for a closer look.

The lights were on. Most other upper-floors windows were

dark at this time but those for my office were shining bright. I made it up the stairs and past the lobby.

"Hey, Raph. How's the market treating you?" I asked.

He was in the same spot where I had last seen him, still slumped back with earphones in. After a delayed reaction, he pulled the earphone out of his left ear and looked up at me.

"Huh? Oh, excellent. Nearly fifty K up the last hour. All on track."

"Good to hear."

I reached for a nearby swivel chair and pulled it up to Raphael's desk. "Listen, I just met Chris and—"

"No. There's no way you're taking it away."

"And here I thought you didn't want to babysit Little Miss Spoiled."

"You're not taking my cut, Jim."

"Look, I'm not even sure this whole thing is worth doing. If it is, I need your help anyhow and you've still got your fifteen percent."

Raphael's composure relaxed and a he gave a smiling nod.

"Fine. Tell me."

"There's a possible joker factor here. Ever heard of a Sasha Petrov?"

"Should I?" he asked.

"Never heard the name. Supposedly some Russian with money. Wants the bank too. Look into him, will you?"

Raphael made a note on a pad in front of him.

"Will do. He legit?"

"How many legit, wealthy Russians have you met?"

"Got it. I'll be careful."

"Look, I gotta tell you, I'm not overly convinced about this whole thing. I think she's full of it. Not sure why or about what, but she's lying to me."

"I lie to you all the time. You lie to me. You think I wouldn't figure out the profit potential is five times what you told me? Hell, we're in finance, Jim. Who doesn't lie?"

He had picked up the scent of money, and like a hound he was locked on target. If I told him to back off now, he'd work twice as hard on it just to prove me wrong.

"All I'm saying is that this may be just a wild ghost chase. Might not be any money in this at all. Let's go get a beer and see if we can figure this out together."

Raphael looked at his Fifty Fathoms. It was a nice piece, respectable. Avoided the mainstream and cliché, clean and stylish. Only reason I didn't have one myself was that I didn't want to validate his choice.

"You know, I'd love to… but I can't today."

"Planning on trading the late session? Seems like someone's eager to hit that bonus target, huh?"

The younger man swirled the pen in his hand. "Can't hurt… My new Porsche isn't going to pay for itself, is it."

I laughed and stood up, shaking my head. "What are you going to do with a six-hundred-horsepower convertible? You really have that much to compensate for?"

"Sex on wheels, Jim. Sex on wheels. Hey, rain check on that beer, okay?"

"Yeah, no worries. Next time."

I walked into my glass fortress, squatting down by the floor-standing safe. It clicked open after a few spins of a dial, and I reached for the wooden watch box. Raphael had followed me in and saw me place the box on my desk, opening the lid. My finger moved from left to right over the timepieces until it stopped at a classic.

The Patek Philippe Nautilus range was probably the most sought-after watch model in the world. Designed by the same Gérald Genta who was behind the Royal Oak, it was hard to grasp how the same man had made something so elegant and something so clunky. The 5711 steel Nautilus was for all intents and purposes impossible to buy new. The waiting list would be decades if you somehow managed to get on it. That's why those who for some reason had them could off-load them at three times the thirty-something-thousand list price.

Mine had the classic blue shimmering face and was bought long before collective insanity had skyrocketed the price. I picked it up and replaced it with the Daytona I had been wearing. That too was a hard-to-get piece but in a whole different league. Rolex produces two million watches a year. Patek makes fifty thousand.

Raphael was looking at the box like a starving child looks at a pizza menu. He was just about to speak when the phone rang.

"Dixon Capital, Raphael Bosch speaking," he said to whoever was on the other side of my desk phone. "Repeating. Eight a.m., code eight four six seven, confirmed."

He set the receiver down and pushed over the paper where he had noted down the code. "You got a SecurePost delivery in the morning."

"Good, thanks. I'll get you your cash once it arrives," I said.

"Don't think I've forgotten, Jim. A bet's a bet."

"Don't I know it. Hey, don't stay too late, huh."

I started off toward the door.

"Sweet Patek. Who you trying to impress?" he asked behind me.

"See you tomorrow, buddy," I replied and walked out the

door.

Tuesday

Wake-Up Call

"Turn it off!"

The pillow against my ear didn't make it stop no matter how hard I pressed it.

"Turn if off!" I repeated.

"It's not mine," she said. "Must be yours."

I ignored it. Most things go away if you pretend they don't exist. This one proved my point and quieted up. I rolled over and eased back into a dream.

It started again. The angry, unrelenting, rude interruption. I sat up and tried to locate the culprit. The noise came from the chair. From my jacket on the chair.

The room was dark and I hit my toe on the bed trying to navigate to the noisy offender. I found the phone and moved toward the window.

"Yeah, what?" I said, ready to explain a thing or two to whoever was on the line.

"Wait, what? Slow down… No… no, stay right there. Twenty minutes."

I stared at the phone a moment. My heartbeat had doubled in the last ten seconds and I stood frozen, unable to move.

"Your wife?" a sleepy voice from the bed asked.

"I've gotta go. Right now."

Snapping out of it, I flipped on the lights by the bed. My clothes were all over the floor. Hers too. I can't remember getting dressed but I must have. All I remember was snapping the Nautilus back on.

She sat up in the bed now, the blankets pulled up over her chest, brushing her long, flowing blond hair back. "Something wrong?" she asked me softly.

"Yeah," I said. "Room's paid for, just drop the key card in the reception on your way out."

"Will I see you later?" she asked.

"I don't know, Nina."

My mind racing, I headed for the elevators, put my hat on, and hit the button for the ground floor. I hit it again and again as if hitting it more and harder would make the elevator move faster. This couldn't be happening. I couldn't have been that dumb. This was my fault, all my fault.

The only person I could see in the lobby was the night manager. It was that time of the night where neither a good evening nor a good morning would feel entirely right. He nodded and gave me a safe 'Mr. Dixon'.

I didn't mind the rain, not at the moment. The wind brought the drops of cold November water to my face, and I needed that. I needed to focus, I needed to be the strong one, I needed to be a rock.

An ambulance passed me by Bahnhofstrasse. The blue lights were on but not the sirens. It was heading the same direction I was and it wasn't in any hurry. I was.

I picked up the pace, walked as fast as I could without running. Then I started to run. I ran the last two hundred yards.

The footpath outside my office was busy. At this time it was never busy. The Patek told me it was 4:16 a.m., two minutes from breaking my twenty-minute promise. Lights. Blue and red. A squad car and a police van. The ambulance. No sirens. No one in a hurry.

Blue uniforms were busy cordoning off the area outside the

A Most Private Bank

entrance of the building. Not the regular police, not the city cops. These were the state troopers, the cantonal police, and they were carrying Heckler & Koch MP5 submachine guns. The word *Polizei* in shiny reflective letters on the chests of their ballistic vests.

They saw me head straight toward them and they turned to face me. Weapons trained at the ground, fingers straight.

"Move away, please, this is a crime scene," one of the officers said in Swiss German.

My hands low, palms on display. I was out of breath - I had been running, I was unshaved and in stress. Swiss cops are well-trained and not likely to shoot me just for the hell of it, but why take a chance? I took a moment to catch my breath, to collect my thoughts.

"It's my office," I said. "I was called for. Dixon. Jim Dixon."

"Identification, please," the officer replied.

I reached for the wallet in my coat. I did it slowly, very slowly. I found my Swiss driver's license and showed it to them.

Once past the downstairs entrance, I wanted to run up the stairs. I wanted to sprint. But I knew it was a poor idea. Never sprint among nervous people carrying machine guns - if that's not a proverb it ought to be.

Behind me two men in blue and yellow. Paramedics carrying a folded-up stretcher. I tried not to think about what it was for. It took self-control to scale the stairs in an orderly fashion. Gave me time to think. Whatever good that would do.

I prepared for the worst and opened the door.

A uniform in my lobby, by Sandra's desk, looking through papers. Later. I continued past him and he didn't stop me. The trading room, chatter, talking, voices, camera flashes. There were people in my private office.

"Jim..."

My focus broken, I spun to the right and there she was. Sitting in a chair, her eyes all red, a tissue in her hand. I was lost for words.

"Jim… he's gone, Jim…" she said. She had been crying. She was still crying. Sandra didn't cry - I had never seen her cry before.

I put my arms around her, and I hugged her hard. I rocked her slowly in my arms.

"Are you okay?" I asked.

"I'm fine… I mean, not fine, but… okay."

I looked into her eyes, my arms still around her. Noise, chatter, camera flashes. Her eyes moist, red.

"Sure?" was the best I could come up with.

"They called me… Couldn't get hold of you."

"Go home, Sandra. Go rest. I've got this."

"No… No, I'll stay. I'll be all right. Perhaps I can do something… I'll be here. Go… Go deal with it. Please."

She wiped her eyes with the tissue and nodded to me as if I was the one needing comfort. She looked toward my office, toward my private office with strange men inside, she looked at them with horror.

"Stay strong," I said. "I know you can."

There was no avoiding it. I walked to my office.

He's Dead, Jim

They hadn't seen me yet, the three in my office. A uniform squatting down by my safe. It was wide open and his hands were inside it. Another uniform flipping through papers on my desk. The third was no uniform. A man in a long beige overcoat stood behind my desk facing the window toward the street.

"Get your hands out of my safe!"

I took a decisive step forward, about to slam the safe shut in his face. That's when I saw it. Something that would stay with me for as long as I live. There he was. Facedown, next to the safe, next to the officer poking around in my private things. My friend, my colleague, my employee. He was on his chest, his face toward me. Expressionless cold eyes seemingly looking into eternity.

I saw his eyes first and his eyes were what would always stay in my mind. It wasn't until I managed to take my eyes off his that I noticed the soaking-wet, crimson shirt. It had been white yesterday.

The man in the beige overcoat by the window turned.

"Ah, Mr. Dixon—"

He stopped as the two paramedics made their way into the room. I stood there motionless and watched them kneel by Raphael's body. The man in the coat continued to talk, but I didn't hear a word of it. One man lifted my friend's shoulders, the other his legs. I was aware of someone talking but I didn't hear the words. They lifted the stretcher, starting to carry him away.

I snapped out of it.

"Jesus, cover him up! There's a woman out there!"

The uniform nosing around my desk complied, pulling up the

blanket over Raphael's dead eyes.

"Mr. Dixon," the coat said. "Need a word."

I turned slowly until I faced him. I felt my teeth grinding, I could hear them grind. My mouth barely open I hissed at him.

"Get your man off my safe before I pull him off it."

"We are gathering evidence, sir. The safe was open and we have every right—"

I stepped up to the safe and snatched the papers from the uniform's hand and threw them back in and slammed the safe door shut.

"It's damn well closed now isn't it?"

The uniform looked up at his superior and the coat held out a palm as a response.

"Mr. Dixon," the coat started. "I appreciate that you are under a considerable amount of stress. I'm Inspector Schmidt, *Kriminalpolizei*. Fedpol. I do need to ask you a few questions."

I took a deep breath and tried to steady myself. He was right, and I wasn't doing much good.

"Get the goons to take their paws off my stuff and I'll answer anything you like."

"We have what we need. For now. Officers, would you give us the room, please?"

I waited for the uniforms to leave the room before I spoke. It was a well-needed pause.

"What happened here?" I asked Schmidt.

"Robbery homicide, it would appear. No forced entry. The victim was either tricked or coerced to open the front door for the perpetrators. The safe box was not forced open, and I assume that the victim was made to open it under duress.

"He was shot in the back standing near this window and shot

again while he was on the floor. I assume the victim had access to the safe combination?"

"Mr. Bosch," I said.

"Excuse me?"

"He had a name. Yes, Mr. Bosch had access to the safe. He was my head of trading."

"Of course. Mrs. Joseph has explained as much."

"Anything taken?"

"There was a watch box on the floor with a few watch pillows less than what such a box normally would house. We would appreciate an inventory from yourself, as to what might be missing."

Schmidt motioned to the wooden watch box at the far end of the desk and I reached for it and pulled it closer to us.

"Anything missing?"

"Yeah. A gold Jaeger-LeCoultre Grande Reverso and a bimetal Rolex Datejust."

"You find that odd?" the inspector asked.

"They left a steel Daytona, a Grand Complications, and a 1962 Tropical Dial Submariner."

"That strengthens our initial theory that they are amateurs. Took the shiny stuff. Junkies who saw a chance, perhaps."

I looked up at him with raised eyebrows. I hadn't expected that.

"You're dealing with the Swiss federal police, Mr. Dixon. Not the NYPD. It's not every day I see burglars leaving a few hundred thousand francs behind."

I nodded and reached for my chair. The wheels were just next to a dark wet stain on my carpet. I let go of it and sat down in a visitor's chair.

"Except that junkies aren't exactly known to be armed around here, are they?"

"True, we don't see much gun violence. We had a cruiser responding to possible gun shots earlier. The hole in your window toward the street narrowed the source down."

I looked at the window, at the small circular hole in it, at all the tiny cracks from the hole in all directions, at the almost beautiful sunshine pattern it formed in the glass.

"Can you tell me if Mr. Bosch had any personal trouble? Any enemies, large debts, or such?" Inspector Schmidt asked, after a few seconds pause.

"I thought you had this pegged as a random robbery?"

"We have to check all angles. I'm sure you understand."

"Yeah. No, I can't imagine him having enemies like this. He's a gambler, for sure, but not into any debts as far as I know. It's not like he's underpaid here."

"What was he making, if you don't mind me asking?"

"Three hundred base. On track for at least half a mil bonus this year. Probably would have hit six hundred."

The inspector whistled. "I'm in the wrong racket. Can you tell me where you were a few hours ago, Mr. Dixon?"

I had been staring at the sunshine pattern in the glass, lost in thought, answering robotically. Until now.

"You think I bumped him off to save money on the bonus?"

"As I said, we have to rule everything out. But no, I don't think so. We tried your home. Your wife said you travel a lot and that she wasn't sure where you were."

"My business is my business. If you want to make it yours, I'll lawyer up and you get squat."

The inspector sighed.

"Fine, we don't need to know at this point. But I might come back to you on that. Was Mr. Bosch working on any particular project? Any particular client relationship he was tending to?"

I looked at the floor. The size of the stain was growing. It didn't look red. It looked more like black. Perhaps it wasn't growing, perhaps I was imagining.

This was on me. I should have dealt with this personally and Raph would still be around. I had failed him but I would not fail him again. This was on my shoulders.

"We don't have clients. Not anymore. This is my family office. Managing my money."

"Of course. We have what we need at the moment, Mr. Dixon, but I will be in touch. Please make a complete inventory and let me know if anything else is missing from your office."

"Have you notified next of kin?"

"Not yet, no."

"Don't. I'll see to it," I said.

"As you like. Contact me directly if you think of anything else that might help."

Inspector Schmidt placed his business card on the table in front of me and silently left the room and my office. I don't know how long I remained motionless in that chair. Until I remembered that Sandra was still out there.

Her eyes were dry and she looked composed. Calm and collected. She had recovered quickly.

"No way some junkie got the drop on Raph," she said.

"I need you to go see his parents, Sandra. Right away."

"Me? And... they're in Basel."

"You know I can't deal with those kinds of things. Please, Sandra. Take the BMW. It's parked down the street."

I reached into my pocket for the key, handing her the rectangular piece of plastic, black with blue, purple, and red stripes.

"What are you going to do?" she asked.

"Call Guy."

Hardening the Office

The first time the buzzer rang, I ignored it. Hours spent sorting through papers, tidying up my office. A leather-bound notepad on my desk kept score of what was accounted for and what was not. All the coffee in Brazil couldn't have kept me more focused.

The buzz was longer, more impatient. I opened my mouth to shout toward the reception but closed it again. She wasn't there. She was racking up speeding tickets on her way to Basel. I hated doing that to her, but what else could be done? I sure as hell wasn't going to break it to them.

She had a button by her desk that opens the ground-floor door. I found it. Opening the door toward the stairwell I heard footsteps and waited as they grew closer. Someone better fix that elevator.

"Thanks for coming so quickly," I said.

Guy Katz was nearly a full head taller than I with a wiry frame akin to a long-distance runner. Trimmed black hair and an unshaved face. The handshake firm, strong, and reassuring. It's not every day you need the services of a private security consultant, but when you do, you want to have one on speed dial.

"You look like you've seen better days, Jim. Sorry about Raph," he said. The strong intonations of his Rs was the only indication that this was not a man of North American origin. I held on to the handshake for a moment and he let me.

"You wanna show it to me?" he asked.

I nodded for him to follow and headed over to my private office. To the scene of the crime. He went to work. I stepped back and watched a detached professional do his job.

He worked the scene. What was left of it. The blood-stained carpet, the hole in the window, the holes in floor. I didn't interrupt. He squatted down over the still-wet stain and poked the carpet with a pen.

"You saw him?"

"Yeah," I said. "Facedown, right there."

"Two slugs have been dug out from the floor. Tightly grouped. You saw where they went through?"

"Behind the heart," I said. "Powder burn on the shirt, point-blank."

"Double tap in the heart when he was on the ground? What about the first round, the one that went out the window?"

"Center mass."

Guy scoffed and went to examine the window. "Junkies, eh?"

"Never thought it was," I said.

Guy was moving around the room, one eye close, aiming a finger like a gun at the hole in the window.

"Cops are either incompetent or playing it coy. Raph was what, six-one?"

"More like six-two. Weight lifting, squash, tae kwon do. Not exactly an easy target."

"Uh-huh," Guy said, looking down the sight of his finger. "Not a pushover."

We both knew none of that really mattered, not when you're staring down a barrel. No amount of bodybuilding and martial arts helps against a loaded weapon - only an idiot would put up a fight. Even a junkie with shaky hands is likely to tag you if you try to slap the gun away.

I inhaled slowly and looked around the mess that used to be

my most sacred place, my private office, my personal glass fortress.

"Need you to secure the office, Guy. State-of-the art stuff. This never happens again."

"Figured as much. I'll have a team here in an hour. Security glass on doors and windows. Motion sensors covering every inch. Concealed CCTV. You want panic buttons as well?"

"In every room. Ballistic glass for my personal office. Turn it into a fish tank panic room. And I need a better solution for the safe."

"On it. What else?"

"Sasha Petrov. Ever heard of him?"

Guy shrugged. "Not on my radar."

"Supposed to be some Russian businessman. Not sure if he's on the level. Look into him, will you?"

"He got a hand in this mess?"

"Could be. Could be nothing. I need to know who he is. What he is. Keep it quiet."

Guy looked closer at the broken window.

"If you're worried about snipers, we could tint the window. Ballistic glass will deflect but not stop a supersonic round."

"That's a little paranoid," I said, smiling for the first time that day.

Our conversation was interrupted by the doorbell. I checked my wrist. The same steel Nautilus on from last night. Eight o'clock, sharp. Swiss reliability.

"Excuse me a moment, Guy."

I went back to the lobby and buzzed them up. A moment later someone emerged from the stairwell and stepped inside. A thirtysomething man in a trimmed beard wearing the gray-and-yellow uniform of the Swiss Post stepped inside. The only visible clue that this was not a regular mailman was the sidearm snapped to his hip and the unusual case cuffed to his left wrist.

"Morning, Mr. Dixon. Today's code, please."

He set down what he was carrying. An oversize metal briefcase with an electronic lock on top of it. More than twice the size of a regular briefcase and with the weight of reinforced steel.

I squatted down and the man turned his eyes away while I entered the code. Eight four six seven. As soon as my fingers hit the seven, the side of the case snapped open. Nearly empty inside apart from a vacuum-pressed plastic brick, about four inches thick. I took it out and closed the case.

The man in the postal uniform said, "Enjoy your day, Mr. Dixon," and took his leave.

"Must be nice to have the government's armed personnel carry cash across the border for you," Guy commented from the doorway to the trading room.

"It's convenient. I suppose I might as well pay you, then, now that I can't deny having the cash anymore," I said and reached for a paper knife on Sandra's desk.

"Cash up front works for me," Guy said. "We'll have this place locked down like Fort Knox by the afternoon. My boys are en route."

I cut open the white plastic brick, exposing eight stacks of dollar bills, each with a yellow-and-white paper ribbon tying them together. I counted up five stacks and handed them to him.

"Hope dollars works for you. Fifty K for now? Bill me for the rest."

"Works for me. I can arrange close protection. Three shifts, alternating two-man teams. Licensed to carry."

"Thanks, but that won't be necessary. Whatever this was, it

wasn't a hit. Wouldn't make any sense. No reason to think they're coming for me."

"Want a piece, just in case? Got an unregistered Glock 19 in the bag, no serial, no history," Guy said, motioning to the bag by his feet.

I looked at the bag for a moment. He had offered it to me as protection, but protection was not on my mind. Perhaps I should have been worried about my safety, but that never entered my mind, not at the time. My mind was elsewhere, consumed by anger and thoughts of retribution. Thoughts I knew did no good, thoughts I knew better than to let anyone see. It wasn't easy suppressing them, and I wouldn't trust myself with a gun, not in this state.

"Not a good idea to walk around strapped, not over here. Thanks, though. Just harden the office for now. Oh, and one more person to look into. New client. Could you run a background check on a Christina Rosenbaum?"

"Common enough name. Got anything to narrow things down?"

"Benjamin Rosenbaum's youngest."

"That'll do it. I'll have an update on Petrov and Rosenbaum by tomorrow at the latest."

Guy picked up his bag and slung it over his shoulder, heading to the exit.

"You got any idea what this was about?" he asked as he opened the door to the stairwell.

"Yeah."

"They got what they were looking for?"

"Nope."

"Glad to hear it."

The Vault

Three stacks of hundreds were in the torn plastic on the desk. I stood there holding them, watching him leave the office. He'd be back. He'd gotten the key. It'd be a long day for him. Hell, it'd be a long day for us all.

All alone in the office, all quiet once more. Sandra was probably there by now, talking to them. She wouldn't be happy about it. Wouldn't be happy about me sending her. It had to be done. Someone had to go and it sure wasn't going to be me. Better a woman's touch. Least that's the excuse I gave myself.

I have no idea how long I was standing there. Alone with my thoughts, with my anger, my guilt. All alone with my hidden rage. It was seeing my white knuckles crushing the stack of money in my fist that woke me from my trance. Rubbing my eyes I looked for water to throw in them. Didn't find any.

Sandra's desk phone was right there, and I used it. Hammering in the numbers as if I was punishing the phone for some transgression. She answered before it could ring twice.

"It's me. We need to talk... Not over the phone... The Pavillon at twelve, lunch... See you there."

She sounded concerned. Who wouldn't? Here I am, calling her early in the morning probably sounding like I was just in a car crash. Get it together, Jim.

Hanging up the phone, I saw my hand shaking. I turned it over, looking at the palm of my hand, trying to get it to stop shaking. Closing it into a fist, I headed into the bathroom.

Hitting the soap dispenser, rubbing my hands together, putting them under the hot water, burning my hands, more soap on my hands, rubbing them again under the scolding water.

I stopped and looked at my own reflection. Deep in my own eyes I found what I was looking for. It was there all along. I just needed to remind myself.

Resolve.

Quarter past eight in the morning. People to see and things to get done. Never let them see you bleed.

I threw cold water in my face, washed it off, and checked my hands. Steady as an aircraft carrier. Let's get to work.

Coat, hat, out the door.

A light drizzle still, the wind had eased off. Heavy clouds laid thick over the city. Coat buttoned up all the way, collar folded up, covering my neck.

This part of the city was a dizzying labyrinth of winding alleys surrounded by centuries-old buildings. The boutiques that occupied the ground floor of these buildings were just opening for the day. Jewelers and bespoke fashion interlaced with cafes, restaurants, and the occasional hotel.

Scores of tourists wandering the cobblestone maze, photographing the architecture and landmarks. Keeping a brisk pace, I rounded yet another baroque stone building. A small kiosk by the corner, a newspaper stand outside under a rain cover. A familiar name in the headlines, a familiar face on a photo.

I picked up a copy of the NZZ, the *Neue Zürcher Zeitung*, paid for it, and found a dry spot to read. The latest installment in what the paper called the "Niederhauser scandal". The article was illustrated with a photo of a man at a podium. A shareholder's meeting. I should know - I was in the audience when it was taken.

"Automobile chairman Victor Schreiber among implicated tax evaders," the caption said. Flipping to page three, I read the article. More leaks from Bank Niederhauser, a drip feed to the press. Someone's bragging. A well-placed source quoted about dozens of high-profile prosecutions in Vienna. My old friend and former client one of those caught in the net.

Speculations on the bank, if it could survive, editorial outrage, pundits providing unsolicited opinions. I didn't need to read the rest. No need to bring the paper. I put it back where I found it and went on my way.

Not much farther. I pushed my way past a group of slow-moving tourists, past Hotel Storchen, slowing my steps approaching a solid oak door facing the square. Windows on both sides of the door fitted with metal bars, rebarred into the stone walls.

An unassuming sign outside read *Bank Niederhauser & Cie*. I hit the button, turned my face to the well-hidden camera and waited for the door to click open.

On the other side of that door, a space large enough for three, perhaps four, persons. The glass walls all around had a slight greenish shimmer, reminding me of the work being done to my own office. Behind the glass in front of me, a pair of elevators and a carpeted marble staircase. A man on the other side of that glass in a black suit and tie, a white folded pocket square, and a build like a bricklayer. If the bad suit didn't out him, the white wire from his shirt to his ear did.

To my left a receptionist, she too behind a glass barrier. Turning to her, I showed her the two items I had just fished out of my pocket before I spoke.

"Jim Dixon, here to visit the vault."

My Swiss driver's license held facing her in one hand and a brass mortice key in the other, about two and a half inches long with the bow-shaped crest of the Niederhauser family.

She squinted at my identification for a second.

"Certainly, Mr. Dixon."

She motioned in the direction of the glass doors and the gorilla opened them for me. He held it hand out, pointing to the elevators.

"This way—"

"Not my first time," I interrupted him. The elevator opened and I entered it. No buttons inside, no floor numbers, no labels. Only a card reader for those in possession of one. I was not.

The doors closed and I felt it move. Two floors underground in a slow-moving elevator gave me time to look at my own reflection in the mirror. I was back. Calm, collected, no signs of distress.

A distinctly modern security door greeted me down there. I tried it and it was unlocked, remote controlled from the lobby. No staff down here, no cameras, no prying eyes. What happens in a private bank vault stays in a private bank vault.

Thousands of boxes in each room, five rooms that I knew of. Who knows what those other doors led to. They had never been opened while I was around. Most boxes the size of half a briefcase, some a full briefcase, a few the size of two or even three. The back room had larger boxes and always made me associate to a morgue with those pull-out drawers of bodies you saw on television.

My own box was in room three. This place looked like it had barely changed since Napoleon's days. Barring a few modern security measures, the entire building and all inside it had barely changed.

I found the box that belonged to me. Inserting the key, twisting, pulling out the box from the wall. It was heavy and I needed both hands to carry it to the table. I opened it and looked at the contents.

Starting with the documents, I lined up the contents on the

table. Share certificates, a property deed, personal documents, my old NYU diploma. Then the heavy stuff. A gold bar is nearly impossible to pick up with one hand. At four hundred ounces, it's not the weight but the shape that makes them hard to lift.

I took them out one by one and placed both of them next to each other on the table. My rainy-day insurance.

For a moment I remained there, deep in thought, looking at my stash, thinking about the morning's events. Then I put the bars back in the box. I pocketed the blue passport and returned the rest of the documents. The box went back into its slot, and I locked it in, taking my key and returning out the door.

Nicholas Niederhauser

The elevator door had just opened on the ground floor, and I was about to continue down my list of errands for the day. What I hadn't expected was for someone to be waiting for me.

The man standing by the elevators had a three-piece pinstripe suit of considerably higher quality than the off-the-rack outfit favored by the security staff. A younger banker but not a junior. Not someone I had met before.

"Mr. Dixon. Mr. Niederhauser would like to invite you to his office, should you have time, sir."

Private bankers had an annoying habit of being overly polite to clients, at least when the clients were within earshot.

"He does, does he?"

"May I take you to him, sir?"

I looked at the time, sighed and nodded, and he entered the elevator with me, swiping a key card. There was no conversation while the elevator gently slid three floors up. When the doors opened, we were facing the antechamber of the bank's chief executive.

Much like the vault, this area of the bank probably looked exactly the same when the Napoleons stopped by. That's the impression it was designed to give anyhow. An antique desk was manned by a horse-faced middle-aged lady who could have been an extra on *Downton Abbey*. She wore a smile that was both sleepy and exceedingly polite at the same time and greeted me in the local dialect.

"Herr Dixon, thank you for taking the time. Go right ahead, he's expecting you."

The man in the three-piece quietly slipped away and I knocked on the door before opening it.

The room I entered would not have looked out of place in Versailles. Tapestry art covered the walls, bronze sculptures and wooden panel decorations with carved motifs. The desk at the center held no computers or other signs of modernity. Merely feather fountain pens and leather-bound notepads.

In the far corner of the room, a four-foot green floor-standing safe with rounded corners, considerably larger than mine, the paint sporadically chipped and torn with time. The bronze plaque at the front, between the polished wheel handle and the numeric combination knob, read *Franz Jäger, Berlin, 1944*.

The man who rose from behind the desk was in his mid-sixties, slim as a shovel, his hair long and silver and wavy, parted at the middle with thick, round horn-rim glasses. The suit was pinstripe of the same color as the banker from the elevator, even if a trained eye could identify the immaculate Savile Row tailoring. He corrected his spectacles with his left hand, and I caught the glimmer of a beautiful A. Lange & Söhne. A small watch at just thirty-eight millimeters but one that stood out in its elegance. White face with two off-center sub dials and a retrograde seventy-two-hour power reserve indicator, moon phase in the main sub dial, a large date display in the northeast, less than ten millimeters thick, and all of this in a discrete platinum case on a black crocodile strap.

"Jim, great to see you! Been a while! Bloody shame what happened this morning. Bloody shame. Bet you could use a whiskey. Single malt, on the rocks?"

I shook his hand and sat down in front of his nearly empty desk. This particular office always reminded me more of a museum than a place of business.

"Thanks, Nick. Seems like you guys have your fair share of

trouble as well these days," I said and toward Nicholas Niederhauser who was standing by the vintage drinks trolley near the window. The silver-haired man lifted the square peg of a whiskey decanter and poured two glasses.

"Quite, old boy, quite," the old man replied. "The business just isn't what it used to be. Not the same respect for the rules anymore, I'm afraid."

I had a sip of the whiskey. He was right, I needed it. I had another.

"What's today's topic of conversation, Nick?"

The CEO and chairman of the private bank grinned and tapped his finger on the desk in front of him.

"Always straight to the point. Still haven't lost touch with your American side, I see. Well, I certainly shan't waste your time."

I had another sip without interrupting. Local customs dictated ten minutes of chitchat before getting to business, but I was in no mood for that.

"Right," the old banker continued. "I was of course briefed first thing this morning on the situation in your office, and I wanted to be the first to offer my condolences and my assistance."

I held my glass and I held my piece, merely nodding as a reply.

"Truth be told, I was scheduled to contact you this week for other reasons. As you bluntly but rightly point out, we've had more than our fair share of egg on face lately."

"Word on the street is that the bank may not survive the year."

The banker paused with a horrified expression on his face.

"Oh, God forbid. Heavens no, nothing that bad. Far from it.

This bank has survived wars and disasters for centuries. We're not about to fold now."

I had finished my drink and I set it down on his antique desk. The old banker looked at the glass on his wooden table, a good foot from the coaster.

"I'm not here for sympathy, and I'm not here as a valued customer. The bank is in play. Where do I fit?"

I wouldn't normally be that rude, not to a man in his position. But today I had better things to do.

"Yes, straight to the point... Always nice to work with professionals, Jim."

"Well?"

"The situation is rather delicate. There is an intensifying light shining upon us and, as you know, light is not something that we are used to. Or prepared for, for that matter."

"You have an active leaker, and with every new headline, the bank and the family name lose more of their former luster," I said.

"In so many words, yes. We do feel that there is an unhealthy confluence of the bank and the family and that perhaps some decoupling may be in order."

"You're worried that foreign law enforcement not only will run your bank into the ground but will go after the family directly."

"As a family-owned private bank, there are certain liability issues, of course."

I got up, took my glass off his desk, and stepped over to the drinks trolley. Without asking, I poured myself another.

"You looking to sell part of the bank or the whole shebang?"

"We have been advised to divest a controlling stake. Forty to sixty percent range. You need to appreciate, of course that the bank is the lifework of not just the contemporary family but of our ancestors as well. We are not simply looking to… exit."

"Tell me what you need, and I'll tell you if I can help."

"The ideal scenario would be for the divested share to be taken by a consortium of multiple investors, preferably of non-Swiss origin. If this… consortium could be de facto controlled by a trusted non-Swiss professional, so much the better."

"You want the bank to be perceived as a reformed, multinational organization. One that does not have as much connection to your family as people may think. You want me to organize a group of investors and acquire share from you and other owners."

The banker, leaning back comfortably in his chair, now had a relieved look on his face.

"I'm glad we understand each other, Jim."

I looked out the window down the narrow alley, rubbing my forehead with my hand. This was just too much. Something larger was at play here, something larger than I had expected. The old saying came to mind. Once is happenstance. Twice is coincidence. Three times is enemy action.

Yesterday I had thought it impossible to buy a stake in this bank. Now the main owner was begging me to do just that.

"If I would do that, and I'm not saying I will… I would need full access. Total transparency."

"I would expect nothing less."

"I suppose you also expect me to rip you off on the valuation."

"Certainly. But money isn't everything, as you know."

I took another look at that beautiful platinum chronometer before standing up.

"I'll let you know."

Alexander Mikhailov

The windshield of the white van outside the office was decorated with a furiously red parking ticket. Leaving a car on the cobblestones in the Old Town is practically a dare to the parking attendants. As if they needed one.

Two men carried a sheet of glass from the side of the van and into my building. By the way they held it and how they walked, it seemed unusually heavy. Bet they were more upset than I about the out-of-service elevator.

From the stairwell I heard the noise. Guy was earning his money. My office was already a construction site. The fourth-floor entrance was not only open, the entire door was taken off its hinges. A man was on a ladder in the process of fixing some device in the ceiling corner.

Sandra's desk empty still. The ungrateful mission I sent her on would take half a day at least. She wouldn't be happy about it, not one bit.

I followed the noise inside the trading room, finding Guy there directing the men with the heavy sheet of glass.

"Jim, glad you're back. Got some stuff for you."

Guy picked up two binders off the table and motioned for me to follow. We went into the meeting room, and he pulled out the same chair that Chris had sat on yesterday. I shut the door and sat down opposite and looked at the two unmarked binders that he had placed in front of me.

"Petrov. Nasty fellow," Guy said, opening one of the binders. "Real name Alexander Mikhailov. Started out as a foot soldier in a Russian syndicate. Spent as much time in prison as out of it.

Bodyguard for Gregor Lebedev before he wound up in the Moskva River with taped hands and a leaky chest. After that he went missing for a while. Presumed dead for years until he resurfaced. Gone independent, it seems."

"I see. What's he into now?"

"Poses as some sort of oligarch. Nobody buys it, nobody with brains. He's small-time. Money-laundry restaurants, garden-variety fraud and scams. Cops have him on their radar but nothing that sticks, not yet."

"Any violent stuff?"

"Capable of what happened here? Certainly."

Guy turned the binder around and pushed it over the table. I glanced over the first page. A black-and-white mug shot of a man in his lower forties in the upper left corner, just below the Interpol symbol, a sword stabbed through a curiously flattened planet Earth.

Two hours I had been gone, and here he had a full Interpol jacket on the guy. The summary profile listed convictions and ongoing investigations. Multiple stints in Russian and Ukrainian prisons. Acquitted twice for murder by a Moscow court.

The next page was an extract from the World-Check database of heighten-risk individuals and organizations. Considerably more detailed than the Interpol report, it ran for five more pages, listing links to drug smuggling, trafficking, extortion, and fraud.

Guy waited in silence while I got what I needed from the documents. The final page of the binder had recent color photos with today's date on them. The shallow depth of field indicated that they were long-lens photos. The focus was on a man in a track suit sporting a bald head, an acute lack of neck, Ray-Ban Aviator sunglasses and a distinct resemblance to the low-quality black-and-white photo from the Interpol report.

I squinted at the pictures, looking closer at the blurry background behind the white Lamborghini that the man was just entering. The uniform of the valet opening the wing door of that ridiculous sports car seemed familiar.

"That's taken outside the Dolder Grand. He staying there?" I asked, breaking a five-minute silence.

"Under the Petrov alias. Been there since Sunday."

"Got the room number?" I asked.

"Don't be a fool, Jim."

I looked up from the photos and stared into his eyes. My old friend and security consultant was a hard man, one whose stubbornness rivaled my own. I kept staring at him.

"Can't help you, not on this one, Jim."

"Not asking you to. Give me the room number."

Guy stared back with the same steadfast resolve.

"This is not a guy you confront, Jim. Pass it to the locals. Let them deal with him."

"Give me the room number, Guy."

He leaned forward, elbow on the table and the hand on his mouth. The room was quiet for a few seconds.

"Thirteen eighty-one. If I get a direct question from the cops, I'll tell them you got that from me."

"Fair enough," I said. "What about Rosenbaum?"

The pent-up tension in the room swept away with the change of topic and Guy slid the second binder over to me.

"That's a different story. Nothing surprising. Youngest of the second-generation Rosenbaums, daughter to Marie Rosenbaum, wife number three. Seven half-siblings. Went to school in Switzerland, place called Institut Le Rosey."

"Well, that explains a few things," I said. "Quarter mil per semester, summer campus in Rolle on Lake Geneva, winter campus in Gstaad. Schooling of choice for royals and billionaire brats."

"Grew up with the rich and famous," he continued. "Current residence, Benedict Canyon, Los Angeles. Secretive lot, these people. Nothing odd about that. No warning flags."

I spent a few minutes reading the sparse information in front of me. A background of educational history. Family members' names, residences and current occupations. Satellite pictures of a mansion in California.

"Give me a day or two and I can get more details," Guy said.

"I've got what I need. Thanks. Good job," I said, closing the binders. "I've gotta keep moving. Sandra should be back in a few hours. Show her how the new alarm system works, will you?"

The Pavillon

The dual-Michelin-star restaurant was inside the Baur au Lac hotel compound, facing the small canal that formed the moat around the historical inner city of Zurich. Once a defense parameter against neighboring city-states, it now held long rows of small boats moored side by side, covered in white-and-blue canvas for the season.

Despite the small size of the boats on the canal, this was a place where none but the old families of the city kept their boats. Finding a mooring anywhere within an hour's drive from the city was not a matter of money. They were passed from generation to generation and were simply not available.

The sun had temporarily broken through the dark clouds, and the reflection shimmered in blue and green as I entered the bustling restaurant. With an elongated shape, the place ended in a round pavilion toward the hotel gardens. The floor, walls and ceiling painted in blinding white with purple velvet chairs and matching flower decoration in the exact same purple shade. Most of the purple chairs held nearly interchangeable men in dark suits engaged in conversation.

I hadn't been in this place for some time and I was always impressed over how the staff remembered faces and names. The maître d' all in white with discrete purple highlights spotted me and met me by the door.

"Welcome, Mr. Dixon. Your table is ready, if you would follow me, please."

Following the man through the busy lunchtime crowd, nodding silent greetings to some of the suits, letting him take me to the far end of the restaurant. A waitress materialized out of thin air to pull my chair out, and a wine menu was soon in my hand. I had just about picked a suitable wine when I saw a familiar figure, escorted up to me.

I rose to my feet, extending my hand. "Good to see you, Chris."

She looked smaller somehow, as if carrying a heavy weight, or perhaps it was the flat shoes. Black, just like the conservative dress she wore. Full-length cashmere, form fitted with long sleeves, covering all the way up to the turtleneck. She shook my hand with hesitation and timidity. The long nails the same shade of red.

"Jim. God, I just heard. It's all over the news. Raph... I... It's my fault, Jim. I should have warned him. Should have warned you both."

"You did warn us. Raph was no pushover. A stronger warning wouldn't have helped."

"But... if I hadn't come to you..." Chris brought her half-closed fist to her mouth, biting the knuckle.

"Don't beat yourself up about it, Chris. There's no way you could have known. Hell, might not even be connected. I can't see why this Petrov would want to break into my office."

Chris opened her mouth to speak, but the waitress's approach made her close it again.

"Would you like me to order for you, Chris? They have a marvelous three-course lunch set."

"Please do," she replied so softly that I barely heard it.

"We'll start with the seasonal mushrooms... Pike perch for mains... and the assorted matured cheese for dessert. And a 2015 Gewürztraminer, please. I hope you like Alsace wine, Chris."

Chris let the waitress disappear beyond earshot before continuing.

"I have to confess something, Jim…"

I unfolded the purple napkin in front of me and placed it across my lap. Something was on her mind, that I had seen from the moment she walked in.

"Shoot."

"I haven't been entirely honest with you."

I leaned back in my chair as the waitress came back with the wine. Pulling the cork out in front of us, she poured a mouthful in my glass, spinning the bottle around to show me the label. She held it up with both hands while I slowly swirled the wine in my glass, bringing out the aroma.

I inhaled it. Then a small sip, letting it move around the palate for a moment. A tiny nod without looking up, and the waitress proceeded to fill our glasses. Chris's first then mine.

The waitress set the bottle down in a pedestal-supported ice bucket next to us and seemingly vanished as discretely as she had materialized.

"Your story didn't exactly make sense to me," I said, lifting my glass to hers.

I hadn't thought it would be possible for her to get any smaller. Her shoulders low, her face insecure, her white teeth biting on her red lower lip, her eyes on the glass in front of her. Any cuter and she would have had her own Disney show.

"You… You didn't believe me… but still agreed to help me?"

I shrugged back. "I haven't agreed to anything yet. But let's just say that the five million dollars got my attention."

Her hand trembled slightly as it picked up her glass, lifting it up to mine. Those blue eyes looked into mine as our glasses touched and I saw the sides of her lip move just a tiny bit, just enough to qualify as a smile.

A Most Private Bank

"Petrov. His real name is Mikhailov. Petrov is an alias. I hired him to help me with the bank. But it didn't work out."

"Why would you need an exiled Russian thug to help you buy a bank?"

Chris's color shifted to ladybug red, making her freckles stand out. The hint of a smile was all gone and her mouth partly open, those deer eyes looking even larger, as if looking into the headlights of an oncoming truck.

I had thrown that out there, that I knew more than she expected. I had done it to see her reaction. She was holding back, she hiding things from me, this I was already sure of. What I wasn't sure of, not yet, was why.

"The bank has something... something that belongs to me. I had to explore different ways of getting it back."

"You're just full of surprises, aren't you?"

"Jim, this is important to me. This means... more than anything."

"What happened with Mikhailov?"

"He figured out the true value... of what I'm seeking. Tried to kill me. I think. God, Jim, you have to help me. I need you."

I studied her while I had some more wine. There was a lie in there. I had spent decades in a profession where everyone lies for a living, and you don't get to where I got without being able to spot a few. But you can lie about all sorts of things and for all sorts of reasons. I wasn't sure what she was lying about but her fear sounded real enough.

"What is the true value of what you're seeking?"

Chris picked up her glass. Swirled it a moment. Drank a good part of it.

"Please, Jim. Can you trust me? I'll tell you when I can... I promise."

I observed her for a moment in silence. Perhaps I was just lost in those eyes. The waitress returned with two tiny white plates containing mushrooms, risotto, leek, and turnip, at a quantity where most adults could probably swallow it all in one go. We both went for the little starter forks.

"Haven't decided yet. I'll let you know. What about von Baerenfells? He working with Mikhailov?"

Chris stabbed a diminutive piece of mushroom and brought it to her mouth.

"I don't know. I suppose so."

"It would help if I know what you're looking for. Properly motivated, I can be a pretty resourceful guy."

She moved her left hand forward on the table, slowly, until a finger touched the hand holding my fork.

"How do I make sure you're properly motivated?" she whispered.

I returned her piercing gaze, lifting my hand up and away from hers, scooping up some risotto. Her hand remained where it was while I swallowed, more on my side than on hers.

"How much money have you got?" I asked.

She pulled her hand back, her eyes wide open in surprise.

"What? Why?"

"You heard me," I said as the waitress removed our empty starter plates. "You want my help, you come clean."

Chris bit her lip again, looking at the empty table in front of her. She looked afraid, alone, and desperate.

"You have no idea how hard it is... growing up with expectations and preconceptions. Father barely gave me anything. How did you know?"

A Most Private Bank

"You're wearing a fake Chopard and you pretend to stay at the Baur au Lac. How much money you got left?"

She looked at the fake diamond-encrusted watch on her wrist and pulled out her sleeve to cover it.

"A... a hundred and fifty. Thousand. That's all I have left. The house is rented. I have almost nothing left..." She whispered it, hushing her voice, glancing around as if confessing her most dirty secret.

"Transfer it to me. Today."

"What? That's all I have, Jim!"

"You want my help? Transfer the money."

Chris nodded slowly, looking at the white table.

"Yes... yes, I'll transfer it. I suppose I have no choice. It's all I have, Jim. Please help me do this."

"If I see the cash tomorrow morning, I'll push ahead. You want to tell me where you're staying?"

"The... the Fleming's, it's up by—"

"I know where it is," I interrupted.

"I... could show it to you. Later. If you like."

"Perhaps another time. I'll think about it."

Chris glanced at the exit when the waitress came back to serve the fish.

The restaurant may have been bustling with activity and chatter but our table was as quiet as the dead fish being consumed. Chris pushed her gold-plated watch higher up on her wrist in a renewed attempt to hide it from view. Her face lacked the cold confidence it previously beamed with. It was not until halfway through the main dish that I decided to cut through the thick silence.

"Don't think that there's no plan, Chris. I already have a large shareholder interested in selling."

Chris lifted her gaze from the near-finished perch, pink color back in her cheeks, those eyes sparkling at me again and that irresistible smile beaming at me once more.

"So you can really do it?"

"It will take hard work. And it won't be cheap. It will take more funding than you've got."

"Jim... I promise you, I swear... I don't have anything left. Not after the one-fifty."

This time I was the one to reach across the table, my hand on hers. She was surprised but she left her hand right where it was, letting me take it.

"I know. I have a plan for that too. We need to raise some money to get this done. But that's why you came to me, isn't it? That's what I do best."

"How much do you think it would take?" she asked with palpable enthusiasm in her voice.

I took my hand from hers and continued with the perch.

"It depends on what we need to get done," I said, finishing my glass of Gewürztraminer. The moment I sat the empty glass down on the white tablecloth, the waitress discreetly picked up the bottle from the ice bucket and refilled it. "I need to know what the score is. If we really need to buy the entire bank or if the goal could be achieved in other ways. And I need to know the value of what you're looking for."

Chris hesitated for a moment, finishing up the last pieces of her main dish before replying.

"Can you trust me on this, Jim? This is not just about money. I'm in danger. And so is anyone who knows."

"I can trust you to some extent. But not blindly. If I'm going

A Most Private Bank

to do this, I need more to go on."

Chris finished up her white wine and leaned forward, her hands on the table next to her plate. She lowered her voice and started talking, but as the waitress once again came up to refill her glass, she had to wait a moment.

"We need... a large enough ownership of the bank to be able to do what we want in there. In the bank. Without anyone stopping us or asking questions."

I mirrored her movement and leaned forward, lowering my voice. Part of me was telling me that I really shouldn't ask, that knowledge could be perilous, that I didn't even need to know. But another part of me was screaming of curiosity.

"So there's really something locked up in there that you're after?"

Chris bit her lip and nodded slowly. "There is. But please don't ask me what it is. If we can get it... the rest of the bank... it doesn't matter."

"What's the value?"

Chris glanced her around her before continuing her whisper, "Forty... perhaps fifty million dollars. Enough to matter. Enough to change my life. And to make me safe again."

"Who's the rightful owner?"

Now she was shaking her head, a smile spreading over her lips. "There is none. That's the beauty."

"Because they all died in the war?"

The smile was suddenly nowhere to be seen. She looked down at the empty plate in front of her. Once again the waitress provided a welcome distraction as she approached to remove the main dish plates.

"I can't tell you more. I don't want to place you in danger.

Please don't make me."

"If there's anything illegal in what you're up to, I rather not know. Your business, your risk. But I'll facilitate it. If you get what you're looking for, you pay me another two-fifty. If it doesn't work out, I still keep the one-fifty."

"I suppose I don't really have a choice."

"That's probably true. But if the value to you is anywhere near what you say, it's not a bad deal. And don't worry about this Mikhailov character. I'll sort him out."

Chris froze up and looked at me with wide-open eyes, "No! No, don't go looking for him. He's a dangerous man."

"Wouldn't be the first time I deal with his kind. I know how to handle myself. But sure, I'll be careful. You should be too, at least until I've figured this joker out. Stay in your hotel room and don't open for anyone but me."

Consequences

The sunlight I had seen on the way to the restaurant was all gone by now. I didn't mind the rain much. A bit of chilly wind and rain in my face was what I needed to shake the effect of half a bottle of fine wine. It shouldn't take more than ten minutes to walk back to the office anyhow.

It had been an interesting lunch, an informative lunch. I had some of my suspicions confirmed, some theories strengthened. More importantly, I had started to figure out who she really was, my new mysterious client.

The white van was no longer parked outside. No sign of the security team from this morning. The rain had made the cobblestones slippery and I had to slow my steps coming off the main street into my alley.

Dripping all over the steps, I made it up and to my entrance. A brand-new frosted-glass door was put there to replace the old one, with the same Dixon Capital sign on it. About to use my key to unlock it, I noticed the distinct lack of a lock on the new door. Pushing it didn't do much either but hitting the doorbell did. The door buzzed open and I saw her inside. She was back.

"It's a new system," Sandra said from behind her desk. "You need to have the thing in your pocket, just like unlocking your car. Just touch the handle and it opens. There's one on your desk, from Guy."

"Great, more junk to carry around. How did Basel go?"

"How do you think, Jim?"

I let my wet coat dry off on a hanger and let the hat rest on top of the coat stand. She was angry and she had every reason to be. "Yeah. Thank you, Sandra."

"Never make me do something like that again."

"I have a good idea what happened here. And I'm gonna do something about it," I told her.

"Don't do anything stupid, Jim."

"I won't let this stand. There will be consequences. Believe it."

She was quiet for a moment, just looking at me, looking at what was probably wild and perhaps frightening eyes. We had known each other quite some time and if anyone could see through the facade, it was her.

"How are you taking it, Jim?" she finally asked.

"I'm fine."

"No, Jim. How are you really taking it?" she asked me.

"It happened. Move on," I tried.

"I worry about you at times," she said. "Sometimes I worry that you actually believe all of that nonsense. What you like to say about ideal traders. What is it with you finance boys and this ridiculous tough-guy act?"

I pulled up a chair and sat down by her desk. Getting off my feet for a moment wasn't a bad idea at all. It had been a long day and we were barely past lunch.

"Comes with the territory." I sighed. "In this business everyone strives to be the perfect functional psychopath. Cold, rational, ruthless, without remorse. Never show weakness, never hesitate to strike at your enemy's weakness. Eat or be eaten. You know how the game is played, Sandra. Hell, it's an act. For most anyhow."

"And for you?" she asked me.

I looked away. Searching for an answer that I didn't have. A week ago, I wouldn't have hesitated, but this day I did. I was quiet. My thoughts going over this morning's events, yesterday's events. My friend's dead, open eyes. My guess of what had happened. Then my thoughts narrowed on that bag with that gun I had been offered. A nine-millimeter semiautomatic. I had used the same model in the service and knew it well. The weight, the feel, the double-action trigger, the textured grip. In my mind I was holding it, I was discharging it. In my mind, I was already at the Dolder. Finding answers any way I could. If I had taken that gun.

"Couple messages for you," she said, rescuing me from my own thoughts. "Steven Hill wants you to stop by the consulate this afternoon. Offered his condolences and all of that. Said that he'd like you to come over sooner rather than later."

"He mention what it's regarding?"

"Just that he needs a face-to-face. Didn't sound like he's calling to reschedule the tee time."

"Fine, call him back and tell him I'll be over by four. Anything else?"

Sandra flipped to the next note in her diary.

"Nina Meier at Pierce & Pierce called, wanted to know if you'd like to postpone the meeting. I guess word is out already."

"They say bad news is the only thing traveling faster than light. Especially in small towns. I'll do the meet. Never let them see you bleed."

"That didn't work out for Raph," Sandra said, nodding toward the inner office on the other side of the trading room.

"Poor choice of words. You know what I mean. The sharks are always circling. Show weakness and they'll attack. Tell Ms. Meier that I'll be there."

"Oh, Ms. Meier, is it? You serious about this one, or just another fling?"

I shrugged back. "I'll tell you when I know. I'll be out most of the afternoon. Probably won't be back before you leave."

"Oh, there's one more thing," Sandra said. "I got flashed twice." She slid the BMW key across the desk. I grimaced and picked it up.

"What's the point with a fun car when they put speed traps every few miles." I sighed and walked over to my inner office.

Pierce & Pierce

The offices of Pierce & Pierce stood in stark contrast to those of Bank Niederhauser. The American investment bank was housed in the top floors of the Prime Tower, a building that stood out in the Zurich skyline like the family jewels of a Rottweiler. In a city where most buildings were either centuries old or at least designed to blend in with the old style of construction, Prime Tower was impossible to miss. Twice as tall as any other building, the juxtaposition between the blue glass skyscraper and the low stone architecture was an eyesore.

The decision to name the building Prime Tower reflected the American design and thinking behind the monstrosity. I passed the automatic glass doors of the ground floor and proceeded through the brightly lit lobby toward the elevators. It was like being back home, back in New York. Shiny steel and glass all around, even a security barrier with turnstile gates and uniformed guards you had to check in with if you lacked your own key card. I had to wait for a rent-a-cop to make a call upstairs before I got through and into the elevator.

By the time it reached the thirty-sixth floor, my ears had popped and I had to pressure equalize to restore my hearing. Two people side by side were waiting for me when the doors opened, standing in front of the unnecessarily wide receptionist desk. A man in his early forties with a slick-back black mullet in a blue shirt with white collar and cuffs under a black suit, pants held up by red suspenders. Next to him a knockout ponytail blonde in a two-piece gray business outfit and steel spectacles.

"Jim, great to have you here. I believe you know Nina?"

I shook his hand first. Then I shook the hand of the girl I had woken up next to this morning.

"We've met."

The banker motioned toward a door, showing the way as we passed the receptionists. "I'm glad you reconsidered, Jim. I know that there's been some friction in the past and we're all eager to put that stuff behind us and do some business."

I walked side by side with Todd Preston into a glass-walled boardroom, letting Nina Meier follow us closely behind. An all-glass table in the center, twelve chairs all around. Six of them were already occupied. Five by men in unimaginative dark suits and the sixth, a woman, in an almost identical outfit as Nina. A projector was on, and the far wall was lit up by the front page of a PowerPoint presentation, sporting the crimson-and-gold Pierce & Pierce logo. The presentation headline was in oversize Times New Roman. *P&P Welcomes Jim Dixon Back*. Below the headline, the text continued in somewhat smaller letters. *Investment opportunities: Funds, Execution, and Structured Products.*

The man in the oily mullet beamed with energy, motioning to the six people by the table who rose as one to come shake my hand. I shook them, one by one, politely listening to their corporate titles and platitudes. Fund managers, analysts, quantitative finance specialists.

"Hate to do this to you, Todd," I said. "At this point, I'm not looking for investments and execution. But I do have something for you. A confidential project. Something in the mergers and acquisitions space."

The investment banker hid his reaction well, while Nina was busy catching flies. She just wouldn't stop staring at me.

"Of course. Whatever you need. Gentlemen, ladies. We need the room. Kill the projector on the way out, will you?" he said.

I took a seat at the table as the assorted collection of investment bankers gathered their papers, doing their best not to look like children who were just sent to their room without supper. Weeks of work on the documents and spreadsheets in front of them. They had probably rehearsed the meeting, the pauses, the jokes in their presentations. One by one like a row of ducks they left the room. Nina, by the door about to exit was shooting daggers with her eyes.

"Nina can stay, of course. She is my new relationship manager here after all, isn't she?"

The senior banker looked at his junior for a second, nodding to her before taking a seat opposite me. "If that's what you want, sure. I'll be overseeing your account, of course."

Nina came to the table and sat down next to her boss, taking out her notepad and a pen.

"I know you guys are eager to have my business back, and I can't blame you. I might not have the largest accounts, but I make up for it in turnover activity. Should make a nice contribution to your bonus pool," I started. There was nothing to be gained by letting Preston know just how much contempt I had for him and for the bank I was in.

"We're here for you, Jim. Whatever you need, we'll make it happen."

"Glad to hear it, Todd. If all works out well on this special project, I'd be more than happy to look at your funds and derivatives next time around," I lied.

Nina remained quiet next to her manager, making notes but no noise.

"I'm buying a Swiss private bank, and I need you guys in on the financing," I continued. "It's a straightforward deal. You provide partial debt funding against the security of the shares purchased."

The two investment bankers exchanged a quiet look. Neither

was able to hide their surprise over what was being proposed to them.

"That... certainly sounds intriguing. Not exactly what I had in mind for today, of course. We usually don't do straight-up financing deals. After all, most people get their loans from commercial banks, not investment banks."

I pulled my hand forward to expose the Patek. An equally childish as effective power move in this town. He saw it, I caught him looking at it and even he would recognize it. As if by automatic reflex, he mirrored my move, pulled out his arm and looked at his wrist. An Apple Watch on a plastic strap.

"Well, if I were most people, I wouldn't be here. With all due respect, of course. You interested?"

"We're here to help any way we can. Give me the details, and I'll see what we can do."

"Good to hear it, Todd. I need financing on forty million US and I'll get you a floating rate of LIBOR plus four. I'll match your forty with equity, giving you at least 100 percent coverage. Proceeds will be used in full to buy shares of the bank, which will act as security for the loan. I expect to have the deal wrapped up this week. Need your commitment tomorrow and money on account Thursday morning."

What I was proposing wasn't complex, but he must have thought I had lost my marbles. I had just asked for a bank loan of $40 million dollar and I had implied that I would put up the same amount myself. Not too different from buying a house, with half the money in down payment and half in a mortgage. If you can't pay your interest, the bank takes the house. But I wasn't buying a house, I was buying another bank.

The investment banker had a worried look on his face, and a red vein on his forehead became increasingly visible. "That's quite a tall order. What duration did you have in mind here?"

A Most Private Bank

"It's a quick turnaround. A month, two at the most. But it has to be done now, this week."

Nina was scribbling notes all over her notepad, flipping to a fresh page but not joining the conversation.

"If we can arrange this... and I'm not saying that we can... What can we expect from your end?"

"All goes well on this deal, I'll make P&P my primary investment bank. I'll ditch Goldman and I'll make it public."

"Which bank are you planning to buy?"

I gave it a pause for full effect. "Niederhauser."

The investment banker corrected his steel-rim glasses and let out a little chuckle. "Well, anyone else tell me they want to buy a toxic shop like that, I'd say they're off their rockers. I assume you've got some angle that others haven't spotted yet?"

I shrugged back at him. "If that was the case, I wouldn't be able to tell you. I'm sure you understand."

"Yeah, I don't need the details. What would the setup look like?"

"The usual. A fresh offshore special-purpose vehicle, limited liability company style. I'll appoint the director, with sole discretion over the SPV. Contractually obliged to use the company only for the purpose of acquiring a controlling stake of Niederhauser. You put up your forty and I'll have it matched, pound for pound. Eighty is enough to get the job done. The entire SPV acts as security for the loan. Should be no-brainer for you guys, Todd."

Todd Preston was rubbing his hand over his chin, nodding slowly.

"You know I can't approve this. Not this size. Need to run it past the M&A guys."

"Sure. Propose it up the chain," I looked at the Patek again. "I've got my next meeting in an hour. Better get going."

"If I'm going to take this to the executive directors, I need a better deal. I need LIBOR plus six."

I rose to my feet and shook his hand.

"And yet, you'll only get LIBOR plus five."

The slick mullet smiled back. Five percent above the so-called risk-free interbank rate was more than fair.

"I can work with that. I'll have a firm reply by end of play tomorrow."

Nina finished up her notes and stood up. "I'll see Jim to the door," she said to her manager and followed me out of the boardroom.

We parted from Todd Preston, proceeding past the inner rooms of the bank and out to the elevators. She held her moleskin notebook with two hands in front of her during a long and uncomfortable silence. I put my coat and hat on and waited for the inevitable elevator chime to break the silence. We stepped in and she hit the button for the ground floor. The silence remained for the eternity it took for the elevator doors to shut.

"What in the hell was that?" she said, the moment the doors had firmly closed.

Nina looked absolutely furious, her face red, veins by her temple pulsating and her eyes cutting into mine.

"What? I said I'll go back to doing business with P&P, didn't I?"

"A loan? A bank loan? That's what you ask for? The margin is razor thin, and you know it. Doesn't matter how many millions you want to borrow, it's not going to make a dent on the bonus."

"You had expected me to just move my accounts over, trading

with P&P as if nothing ever happened? Under the circumstances, I think that just being in this building is a pretty big concession."

Nina took a deep breath, calming a bit.

"You could have told me, you know. Could have prepared me. The team spent weeks making that presentation for you. Do you know what kind of crap I'll get when I go back in there?"

"Still kept you in the room, didn't I? Mr. iWatch in there was about to get rid of you, if you didn't notice."

"I suppose you did. Well, thanks... You're really going to invest forty million of your own money?"

"Don't worry, Nina. I know what I'm doing."

"And then you're going to move your accounts to us? Do all your trading through us?"

"Sure. If this project goes well. Look, I'm still pissed about what the bank did to me. I won't be an easy client, that's for sure. But I'll be a profitable client. You'll get your bonus. You might be sick of having me as a client, but you'll get paid."

Nina nodded and looked up at me.

"Thanks, Jim. This means a lot to me. Not easy getting taken seriously in this bank. Or this industry."

"Looks to me you did all right for yourself. Can't be many executive directors around your age. How many of them female? I hear you're the rising star, no matter what those guys might say behind your back."

Finally Nina smiled back.

"Will I see you tonight?"

"Perhaps. Busy day. I'll let you know, okay?"

The elevator opened on the ground floor. Nina quickly took a step back, away from me.

"Thank you, Mr. Dixon. We'll be in touch on your project."

"Ms. Meier," I said with a sardonic tone, tipping my hat before leaving the elevator.

American Soil

Contrary to most cities, the tallest buildings in Zurich are not in the most central location. In the actual center, few buildings have more than four floors. The tram ride on line four took nearly half an hour from the Prime Tower to the US consulate in the Seefeld area by Lake Zurich. Driving would have taken much longer.

The consulate was housed in an otherwise regular office building, on a small quiet side street. It was a mere stone's throw from the lake promenade where street performers vied for tourist attention and donations. From there snow-covered Alpine mountain ranges were visible in the distance around the year with the crystal-clear water shared between ducks, swans and sailboats.

I hit the buzzer at the ground floor of the anonymous-looking building. Remembering the blue passport, I fished it out of my jacket pocket and held it up to the camera, hoping that may speed things up.

The front gate opened quickly enough and I headed up the stairs toward the consulate floor. I had been there before, as most with expats who occasionally need to renew a passport. But this was the only time the door had opened from the inside when I approached it.

The young man's biceps bulged out from the short-sleeve khaki shirt. A sidearm and a baton were attached at the hip of the blue pants with the red stripes along the sides. The posture of the man was that of a vertical ironing board.

"Sir, Mr. Dixon. Welcome to American soil. Mr. Hill has requested you be escorted to the secure area. If you follow me, sir," the man said in quick succession and a decibel or two too loudly.

I followed the man but made no particular rush out of it.

"This being a consulate, I'm not sure it's actually American soil. But thank you, Lance Corporal."

The marine security guard passed through two locked doors, remotely opened as we approached, before swiping a key card through a scanner by a metal security door. He opened it and stepped inside, holding it until I passed through.

The secure area was a small part of the floor. This was an area not seen by the foreigners applying for US visas or the expats looking to renew their American driver's licenses. I counted three offices, all with closed doors, and two meeting rooms. The young marine took a few more brisk steps up to the conference room door and stopped.

"Sir, I require your cell phone and any other electronics you may have on your person."

I sighed but kicking up a fuss at this point would be counterproductive. I reached for my phone, handed it to him and watched him place it in a thick metal box outside the conference room. The man knocked twice in rapid succession and opened the door.

"Sir, James Dixon, sir," he announced and stepped aside. I entered the room, the door closed behind me and the annoying marine was gone. In front of me, two men stood to their feet and came around the table to greet me.

Steven Hill was in a white shirt and slim black tie. No jacket. "Jim, how the hell are ya? This is Mike Donahue, State Department."

I shook my golf partner's hand first before turning to the other man. The bland suit almost made the investment bankers' from

A Most Private Bank

earlier seem tasteful. Off the rack, not very well-fitting, black cotton and polyester mix, and with the kind of slim black tie that made him look like he was on his way to a *Reservoir Dogs* convention.

The three of us sat down, them on one side of the table, me on the other. The room was just large enough for a conference table with six chairs. No teleconference unit on the table, no power plugs or decoration anywhere around on the windowless walls.

The man next to Steven Hill was younger, but his posture and confidence signaled that he was the senior. I directed my attention toward him.

"I believe I was summoned. What can I do for the State Department today?"

The serious face of Mike Donahue broke into a broad white smile.

"Steve told me you're a no-nonsense kinda guy. That suits me just fine. First, let me just say that I'm sorry you got caught up in this mess. We hadn't anticipated anything like what happened in your office."

"What had you anticipated?" I shot back.

"Here's the deal, Jim. You're in a unique position to assist us on a delicate matter. I can brief you on parts of it, but I can't give you all the details. What I can commit to is not to bullshit you. I expect the same in return."

I nodded in agreement and surprised myself by actually warming to this bureaucrat.

"With you so far. I'll either volunteer information or I won't, but anything I do give you will be accurate."

"And, of course, needless to say, anything said in this room is to be treated as confidential information," the supposed State Department official continued.

"Needless to say," I agreed.

The round bearded man sat quietly and observed the conversation, outranked by the tall man next to him.

"There is something of value in this particular bank. Of enough value to be of interest to the US government," Donahue said. "Something that multiple parties are trying to extract." He stopped and looked at me, waiting for a comment.

"I have concluded the same," was my only reply.

"Do you know what the value consists of?"

"I don't. Quite frankly, I don't really care."

That was a lie. Of course I cared. Of course I wanted to know what was really going on and why my friend was in the morgue. But curiosity can be dangerous and showing it even more so.

He glanced at Hill next to him and then back at me.

"You'll have to excuse me, Jim, but I find that hard to believe."

"Which part?"

"I buy that you might not know. But if you're aware of a substantial value, why wouldn't you care?"

I shrugged and leaned forward on my elbows. He was smarter than Hill, and he wasn't boring me.

"You don't seem to be familiar with this part of the financial industry. I couldn't care less what the value is. I intend to get paid either way. Whether there is a value there or not."

Donahue nodded slowly, pausing a moment before continuing.

"You're getting paid to arrange a takeover, but you have no direct interest in how that takeover turns out. As long as it happens."

"Correct. And I'd rather not have you guys meddle with my deal."

"We have no issue with you making a buck, Jim. We're just looking for information. There's no reason why we can't all win on this one."

"What are you offering?"

"For starters, we have a pretty good idea who's responsible for the incident in your office," Donahue said, reaching for his briefcase. He snapped it open and put a manila envelope on the table between us.

"Would that be a file on an Alexander Mikhailov, aka Sasha Petrov, current resident at the Dolder Grand?" I asked.

The two men in front of me exchanged a look. Hill shrugged to his superior and shook his head.

"You met him?" Donahue asked.

"No. Just found out about him this morning. Don't ask me how. You know any other players?"

Donahue pushed the envelope to the side. "It's unlikely that he's acting on his own. He's working with or for someone but we don't know whom. We'd like to find out."

"You and me both. I have no reason to protect whoever hit my office. What's being done about Mikhailov?"

"The local authorities have him on their radar, and we're actively sharing what information we have. There's no proof, of course, and I imagine that they can't do much but keep an eye on him. Now, what can you tell me about your client? Who are you doing this takeover for?"

I shook my head back. "Can't answer that, Mike."

"You can't or you won't?"

"I won't."

Donahue's body posture and tone of voice shifted. He crossed his arms in front of him on the table, leaning in closer to me.

"Listen here. We need to know who you're dealing with."

"Ain't gonna happen."

"This can get real nasty for you if you jerk us around, Jim. You don't want the United States government as your enemy."

I leaned back in my seat, my arms crossed in front of me.

"There may have been a time when some vague threat from some agency Muppet would have sent me running off to my room crying. But this wouldn't be the first time I tell a government bureaucrat to get stuffed and unless you're planning on having the lance corporal outside the door pull a black bag over my head and ship me off to Gitmo or have me dismembered and buried in the garden, you can do just that. Get. Stuffed."

It was at this time that Steven Hill decided to break his silence. He did nothing to hide the smile under his beard as he put his hand on his colleague's shoulder.

"I don't believe it would have to come to that. In particular as we lack a garden here on the third floor and the compost bin is rather small. You're worried about your end. I get that. If you give up your client, you risk them getting a proverbial black bag over their heads, never to be seen again, am I close?"

"Mostly it's just none of your business."

"Come now, Jim," Hill tried as Donahue grinded his teeth. "I'm working with you here. We did give you information on Mikhailov, remember."

"You gave me jack. I already had that."

"Granted, but we tried. Would you be able to reveal the client at a later stage?"

"I don't see how it could be kept secret for long anyhow."

"We can work with that," Hill continued, stopping his colleague from interrupting. "Here's the thing. We have reason to suspect high-level involvement. There may be multiple parties involved, but at least one is likely to be of the heightened-risk variety."

"Meaning?" I asked, my voice now calmer but my body language equally defensive.

"Would you be able to tell us if your client is high profile? Watch-list material."

"No. My client is not high profile. Not of the kind that would hit your radar."

Hill smiled to Donahue, as if they just got a key piece of information.

"Good to hear. If you do get contacted by any such entity or individual, we'd like to know about it."

I thought about that for a moment. "I don't see an issue. In principle."

"Listen, Jim," Hill said. "Here's what we're offering. Your SEC ban from operating in the financial industry back home seems rather unfair to me. We could get that lifted. We could also apply some pressure to get you exempt from potential violations you may need to commit in relation to this situation. If you, for example would need to deal with some questionable individuals, there's no reason why that should reflect poorly on you. Perhaps we can help facilitate the process, helping you make this deal happen. What we're looking for is information. Real-time updates on the situation, information on the involved principals.

"I'm not about to enlist, Hill. Been there, done that. I won't be your agent. If I come across information and if there is no economic downside for me, I will consider passing it on. But I don't make promises."

"That's fine. For now. We expect regular updates."

"One more thing. Unless you've got some top-secret briefing

for me, don't bring me here again. I have neither the time nor the inclination to play games, and the secure room in the secure area of the consulate with the marine security guard kid outside doesn't impress me. If you gentlemen will excuse me, I've got business to attend to."

Forty Million

It was past fourthirty when I left the consulate. It was drizzling. Not quite raining, not quite not. I put the hat back on, my only cover from the cold water, crossing Dufourstrasse, heading toward the lake, away from the tram stop. It was a good fifteen minute walk back to the city center and I needed the air. Rain or no rain.

Picking a fight at the consulate was dumb. My own pride and stubbornness got in the way. The old knee-jerk reaction to getting bullied. Someone pushes you, punch them in the face. They pull a knife, you pull a gun. The laws of the jungle. You let them push you around, they'll do it again. Sometimes it makes good business sense. Sometimes it's just a childish reaction.

They had made me a reasonable offer, a good one, even. And I threw it back in their faces. They could lift my industry ban back home, end my exile. That was a prize worth fighting for, but the last thing I needed was for them to realize how much it meant to me. They don't run me - nobody runs me.

Reaching the lake, I took the promenade back to the city. Long, fast, determined strides, standing out like a hippo in a stable next to the slow-moving tourists. Rounding a crowd watching a juggler, nearly stepping in a busker's hat, bumping into a Japanese group walking backward taking photographs of themselves with the mountains. Crossing the Quaibrücke back into district 1, the heart of the city. I took my cell phone out of my pocket, looking at it for a brief moment before deciding against. Might as well have left it in that lead box. Never liked the damned thing much anyhow. I picked up the pace, heading up Bahnhofstrasse. My neighborhood.

Zigzagging the smaller side streets, stepping over puddles of water on the uneven pavement, finally into the building, pouring out the water that had built up on the hat.

Markus Bühler was taken by surprise, opening the door with a cup of coffee in his hand.

"Oh, Mr. Dixon. I hadn't expected to see you so soon."

I took it upon myself to continue straight into his tiny office.

"I need to talk to Dick. Right away. I can't call him, and I can't go there. I assume you have some way of getting him here when he's needed?"

"Um... Yes, I can get him to come here. If it's important."

"Listen, Markus. This may be the most important call you'll ever make, so why don't you just go ahead and make it. I'm gonna help myself to your coffee machine."

I walked past him and into his meeting room, up to the little red machine by the sink. A sink in a meeting room. A red shiny little thing, a box of Nespresso capsules next to it. If there was a coffee machine equivalent of an Apple Watch, this was it, and that's not a flattering comparison.

I put the prepackaged orange capsule into the machine and hit the button. In the next room, Junior was placing a call, raising his voice to talk over the loud coffee maker.

"Yeah, hi, Dick. Markus here. I need to talk... No, right away... It's important... Great, see you soon..."

He came over to me in the meeting room, coffee cup still in his hand.

"He'll be here in fifteen," he said.

"Thanks. Have a seat, Markus," I said, inviting him to sit by his own conference table.

I sat down as well. If I had to wait around in this stuffy little

A Most Private Bank

room, I might as well be comfortable.

"What's your story, Markus?"

"I'm sorry?"

"Your story. What are you doing running a dodgy offshore vehicle for a guy like Baerenfells?"

He hesitated, looked suspicious. That did him credit.

"I applied for a job with Niederhauser a few years ago, interviewed for Dick's team. As a junior analyst. In the end, they needed someone with better French skills, but Dick made me a different offer."

"To front his offshore holdings?"

"To... to be Mr. Visible, as he put it. He wanted me to start a business, to be the owner and the manager. On a, well, fiduciary basis."

I took a swig of the bland, mass-produced coffee and grimaced.

"Right. So to the outside world and authorities, you own the company. But he actually paid, for it and you've got a paper somewhere, stating that he's the actual beneficial owner and you're just a fiduciary holder. A front."

He was nodding along, confirming what I said.

"He said it's legal and common. That the fiduciary contract removes any liability for me and that I only need to show it to the authorities if asked to."

"He's correct," I said and finished the bad coffee. "That setup is highly illegal in most of the world, but in this particular country it's quite normal to front a false owner, as long as you've got that fiduciary agreement in place and as long as you receive payment for it. You happy doing this, Markus?"

He twisted uncomfortably in his plastic chair and hesitated

again, and I continued.

"My friendly advice is to keep a critical mindset, Markus. You're probably covered with the fiduciary agreement, but there's also the matter of where the money comes from, if it's taxed and clean. Offshore money rarely starts out being offshore."

He studied me carefully now, paying attention and guarding his reaction and his words. I might have been too quick to write him off after our first encounter.

"I'll keep that in mind," he said.

The sound of someone barging in without knocking interrupted us. He was out of breath, breathing like a chain-smoker after a hundred-meter dash.

"Jim! I was hoping this had to do with you. You decided you want in on the raid?"

His breath betrayed the bottle of Bordeaux he had at lunch as he got a little too close shaking my hand and grabbing my shoulder.

"I decided to mount my own raid and offer you to join in."

Dick let out a high-pitch nervous laugh.

"Once a raider, always a raider, is that it? You're gonna threaten to do this without me if I don't raise the stakes?"

Markus's eyes were darting between us both, sizing up the verbal jousters.

"Here's what's gonna happen, Dick. I'm setting up a special-purpose vehicle to take over the bank. You'll liquidate whatever you've got in this little fund and wire the full amount to the SPV."

Von Baerenfells crossed his arms in front of his gray double-breasted suit and paused a moment.

"We can get about forty all in all. That may not be enough, as I told you we'll need to raise some assets."

A Most Private Bank

"I'm running this now. I'll match your forty in debt financing, it's already lined up."

"You... you already have that lined up? Since last night?"

"Welcome to the big league, Dick. That's why I'm in charge."

"What about the vaults? How do we gain access?"

"I've got no interest in that and don't want to know. Once the deal is done, you'll be a controlling owner and can access any area of the bank you please. I assume you plan on having your fund get the shares of the worthless bank, while you take the loot for yourself. Either way, I don't want to hear a word about it - that's your end."

Von Baerenfells glanced over his shoulder at Bühler who had his mouth wide open. Good. This was new information to him.

"Well, it's good to know that there are options open. I assume you've got your own angle, Jim?"

"I want my half mil. Up front. That's your ticket for joining this expedition."

"That's ridiculous! I came to you with this, Jim. You wouldn't even know about this opportunity if it wasn't for me!"

I shrugged and got up from the table, brushing some imaginary dust off my collar.

"If you think you can get this done alone, go for it. I'll have the entire thing wrapped up by the end of the week. I can do it with or without you. If you want in, make the transfer. Half a million up front. Forty tomorrow when I've got the SPV set up. If I don't see the half mil by end of business tomorrow, I'll do this without you."

He was grinding his teeth loud enough for me to hear it - he was furious but he was also greedy. Greed makes you predictable.

"Fine," he finally said.

"Always a pleasure, Dick. I'll be in touch."

Evelyn Walker

From the Global Opportunities office, I headed on foot up Talstrasse, wondering how many other shady little pretend hedge funds were housed in the nondescript buildings I passed. How many other bankers had some twenty-year-old fall guy behind those windows, helping them steal clients from their employers, front run the bank's trades and violate a dozen financial regulations. Not that it mattered.

The wind picked up as I reached the Selnau bridge, crossing the moat. Small leisure boats lined up in the water, all the way up to the lake. Ironic. Now that there was actually wind, it was getting too cold to use those boats. In spring, that wind would be long gone.

It wasn't far to my destination. A highly trafficked street corner, complete with the Orwellian traffic light cameras, my target was housed in a gray stone building shared with residential apartments and shops. The entrance had all the charm of a funeral parlor, and the sign above it could easily be mistaken for some sort of cheap wine dive. Baur au Lac, this ain't.

When I pulled open the door to Fleming's Hotel, I found myself surprised that it wasn't locked, requiring a key card to get in, like some of the other budget places. The lobby, if it could be called that, was even manned. A lonesome young man in an off-the-peg bargain-bin suit looked up from his smartphone.

"Evening," he said, glancing up at me.

"Good evening. I'm here to see one of your guests. She's expecting me."

"Do you have the room number?"

"I don't. I'm looking for a Ms. Christina Rosenbaum. Perhaps you can call her room and let her know I'm on the way up?"

The fresh-faced kid finally pushed away his iPhone, but forgot to turn the screen off. Colors jumped all over the screen. Some sort of game. Can't blame him. Can't be fun standing around here all day.

"Rosenbaum... Rosenbaum... Sorry, there's no guest with that name."

"Are you sure? Please check again."

"I'm sure. I checked already."

I couldn't help but smile. At a high-end hotel, they would have pretended to check again, but this kid just told me straight up instead of playing that game. Good for him.

"You seen a cute American girl, well-dressed, couple of years younger than you, long black hair, short, slim, great smile?"

Now his eyes lit up. Finally he came alive.

"Oh, you're looking for Ms. Johnson? Sure, she's up in room 24. That's on the second floor. You could take the stairs."

"Thanks," I said, sliding a twenty across the desk to him. "I need a key card or something to get up to second?"

"No, no, just walk up. And no need for a tip. Have fun!"

The kid wasn't smiling, he was grinning. Jesus, he's assuming she's an escort. Well, let him think that.

"Thanks, I'm sure I will."

I left the twenty on the desk anyhow and headed up the creaky wooden stairs. There was a sign mounted on the wall. Rooms 21 to 24 to the left, 25 to 28 to the right. It wasn't a long hike to 24.

Nothing happened after the knock on the door. I repeated the motion.

A Most Private Bank

"Chris, it's Jim. You in?"

Now there was sound. Footsteps. The chain being the door removed, the bolt turning, the door opening.

"Jim! I haven't gone out or answered the door all afternoon. Even turned housekeeping away."

"Well, Ms. Johnson, I'm here now," I told her as I walked in, shutting the door behind me.

She was wearing that same black dress she had on for lunch but had ditched the shoes. Barefoot, she gave an even smaller and more timid impression.

The balcony door stood open, and I could smell the ashtray from where I was. She walked back out there and picked up the still-smoking cigarette from the ashtray, inhaling deeply and blowing the smoke out of her nostrils.

"Well, I couldn't bloody well register in my own name, could I? I knew I was in danger, but not until this morning did I know how grave the danger was. God, I can't believe the situation I put myself in."

I followed her out on the balcony. It was barely large enough for two people to stand, let alone sit. Its view was of the inner courtyard of the dull, gray block with the air-conditioning units mounted up and down the facade. A few delivery vans parked in the courtyard, pigeons doing what pigeons do best.

"I'm glad that fake passport turned out be handy, then," I said to her, watching her reaction carefully.

She put out the cigarette and pulled out a fresh one from the pack of Dunhills. I waited patiently, having seen this routine before. Then I spoke before she had a chance to.

"You chain-smoke when you're caught off guard. That's a bad habit. No need to lie about having a fake passport. As smitten as the kid downstairs must be with you, he wouldn't break the law and check you in without seeing a passport."

She lit the second cigarette but didn't take a pull on it. Instead she looked at me with those big blue eyes. Her lip was trembling and she bit the side of it.

"Jim. I have to tell you something. Please don't be mad. I... still haven't been entirely truthful with you."

"I've been told quite a few lies this week."

She swallowed and looked down at my feet. I gave her a moment. This time she didn't go for another cigarette.

"What if... what if there's more? More that I haven't told you?"

"Look, there's a deal to be closed here and money to be made. I don't need to know all the details. It's your money to lose. But it would be nice to know your real name."

When I dropped that last one on her, she gasped. She was surprised, and I enjoyed surprising her. It was a guess, but an educated guess.

"Well, that was what you were about to confess, wasn't it?" I grinned at her caught-in-the-headlights expression.

"How... did you know?" she whispered.

"There were plenty of clues. But it was the French that sealed it."

"The French?" she asked.

"Christina Rosenbaum spent five years at Institut Le Rosey. Private school for royalty and billionaire brats. It's like the Foreign Legion. They'll speak French to you until you get it. Won't care if you don't know a word when you show up."

She nodded slowly, thinking back.

"The waiter. At Baur. I should have just waved him off, shouldn't I?"

A Most Private Bank

"I assume the accent is fake too. You're British, aren't you?" That took her off guard. Good. I enjoyed knocking her off balance. This one was a long shot, a wild guess, but her reaction told me I had hit the bull's-eye.

"I had my reasons to do what I did. Please don't be angry with me, Jim," she said in a very different accent. Her face changed somehow as well. No more quivering lip, no helpless doe eyes.

England but not London. Traces of the north, perhaps Leeds or Sheffield. Educated but with a working-class background. British English gives away so much more about a person than any version of American dialect would. She didn't ask and I didn't tell her about the Dunhills.

"I'm not. You dropped a name to get in the door. And you're right, the only reason I took that meeting was out of respect for Ben Rosenbaum. But now you're in the door and you paid for my attention. If I was angry, I wouldn't have solved your financing this afternoon."

"You what? In the half a day since we had lunch? You found a hundred million quid?"

"We'll only need eighty. There's a reason you didn't just go down to the local UBS branch and ask for a loan, isn't there?"

"Thank you. Thank you for helping me, Jim. This really does mean a lot to me."

"I have a condition," I said and paused, watching her face change. She got that nervous, girly look in her eyes again. She even twirled that long black hair with a finger, biting that lip.

"What... what's your condition?" she whispered. I could hear in her voice what she feared or at least expected the condition to be. That's what she thinks of me? Or is that just what she thinks of men?

"My condition is that there will be no more lies. You got

secrets and perhaps I got secrets. That's fine. We're in a secretive business. If there's something you can't tell me, I'll accept that. But don't feed me false information."

I was trying to see if there was disappointment or relief in her eyes. I couldn't be sure. Perhaps I didn't want to be sure. But she was smiling again.

"Just that? Can I expect the same in return?"

"You got my word. Respect for secrets but no lies."

She had that mischievous smile on her face again, back in her comfort zone, back to feeling in control.

"Will you shake on it?" she said, putting that second cigarette out in the ashtray and extending her hand. I shook it, looking into her eyes, confirming this new partnership.

"Having that out of the way, what do you say we move inside? It's getting mighty cold out here on the balcony. I'd say it's time to share a drink and see what secrets we can spill."

"I'll call room service!" she said, heading for the phone on the little wooden drawing board.

I headed in the other direction, squatting down, opening the minibar cabinet. "No need, there's a bottle of red and glasses here. I'm sure there's white in the fridge too, if you prefer."

"Red is fine," she said, turning to the tiny round glass table with the two black wire chairs on either side. She sat down while I put the two glasses on the table, looked for a corkscrew, realized it was a budget wine with a screw top, twisted it open and poured. I took a seat, lifting my glass to her. "To new beginnings."

"To new beginnings!" she repeated, and we drank in silence.

I broke the silence first. "You wanna tell me your name?"

She stood up, went to the wardrobe and opened it. I heard her enter an eight-digit combination on the mini safe box. She came back, sliding a crimson passport over the table, with the ever-absurd UK coat of arms. A lion and a unicorn, seemingly humping each side of a shield stuck in a tire. But it was a real British passport, all right. I opened it without speaking. It was her picture. Twenty-two years old. Evelyn Walker.

"This the real one?" I asked.

"Of course it's real."

"What about Ms. Johnson's passport?"

"What?"

"Didn't we agree on no lies? How did you manage to check into a Swiss hotel without showing a passport?"

She had me on that one. I could see it in her smirk. She wanted that question.

"I think you're overestimating Swiss diligence. Either that, or you're underestimating what female charm can get done."

"Pimple Face down there checked you in without a passport? He could lose his job for that."

"Oh, Stefan was soo helpful." She giggled.

"He thinks you're an escort, you know."

"Oh, don't be jealous. I kinda implied that when I paid him an extra hundred to check me in. I also implied that I'm faar too expensive for him. Does that make me a bad girl?"

This mock innocent question had me in stitches. It'd been an eventful day. A stressful day. I needed that laugh.

"Okay, okay, you win that one," I said, holding my hands up, palms to her in a motion of surrender.

"Your turn! What about this financing?"

She sounded eager. Excited. Impressed, perhaps.

"I've got eighty million dollars lined up. Equity and debt.

Tomorrow you and I set up a shell company for the takeover. You'll be in control of it. I expect to have this deal wrapped up before the end of the week."

That perfectly composed, confident face of hers was now speechless. Her mouth was open as if she lost her words mid-sentence and I confess that I enjoyed causing it. She was not used to being surprised. Perhaps she was just not used to positive surprises. Hell, she'd probably been knocked around more than a bit by life.

"It's not all locked in yet, but it will be by tomorrow," I added.

"What about Mikhailov? Don't underestimate him, Jim. He's a dangerous man, I told you."

"Trust me a little, will you? I only had half a day. I'll deal with him tomorrow. He won't be a problem. Might help if you told me something more about him. Something true this time. Remember our deal."

She lifted the wine glass to her red lips and emptied half of it in one go. She bit that lip again.

"I won't forget our deal. I worked for him. No, that's not true. We worked together."

This didn't surprise me.

"Running long cons?"

My guess didn't surprise her either.

"Financial fraud, mostly. Never anything violent. Nothing big really. We took a few hundred thousand now and then from some banks. Moving between countries and continents. Been doing it for three years now." Her eyes studied mine, posing the obvious question without saying a word.

"I appreciate your honesty, Chris. Evelyn. Honesty buys you a lot of trust with me."

I gave it a pause and she gave me her full attention.

"I'm not going to be involved in any illegality, Evelyn, but as long as there's no violence and neither I nor anyone who matters to me are victimized, I don't care about your angle. If you're holding back because you've got a score lined up, that's fine by me. If I don't know, I don't have to lie if I'm asked."

"We had a falling out," she continued. "A big argument. We… had a relationship. I wanted to break it off. He didn't."

"Common enough reason for people to kick up a fuss."

"He tried to kill me, Jim. I barely got away. I'm afraid of him."

"Don't be. I'll deal with it. Trust me."

She lifted the glass again and finished what was left of the cheap Bordeaux. Her fear of this Russian looked genuine.

"Stay with me tonight?" she said, barely more than a whisper.

"Because you're worried about him finding you?"

"Because I want you to."

She was half my age. Less. Best-looking gal I've seen in years. Con artist perhaps but clearly in a bind. She kept looking at me with those big deer eyes.

I stayed with her. And you can't blame me.

Wednesday

The Shadow

At six in the morning the city was pitch black. I reached for my office key before remembering the new lock system. I expected an eventful day but at least one without anyone dying. Turns out I was wrong on one of those accounts.

It had been good to clear things out with her yesterday, to speak frankly. I had been right so far, and I was on track. On track to do what needed to be done. I still wasn't completely sure but everything pointed in the direction of my initial instincts. Nothing was forgotten and nothing was forgiven. I wasn't going to fail him again.

No one was in the office, not this early, and I headed straight to my private area. Not much trace of the work done to the place yesterday. The glass panels all had a slight greenish shimmer and there was no more hole in my window. The stain in the carpet was still there. Blood is a hard substance to clean, in particular in large volumes. The stain on the carpet was wide and reached nearly all the way to the wheels of my chair.

Out of habit, I followed my usual morning routine. Opening the safe, taking out the watch case. I removed the Nautilus from my wrist, closed the bracelet around a watch cushion, and set it back down. Looking at the few pieces left in the box after last night, choosing the appropriate one for the day's planned activities.

Selecting the right watch for the right purpose, to invoke the right reaction from the right people, is an art form few outside Switzerland would understand or appreciate.

I reached for the smallest in the set. A thirty-six-millimeter chronometer, which would for the uninitiated barely register as anything noteworthy. A platinum case easily mistaken for steel, the diminutive cream dial had a discrete moon phase at the six and a round layout of the numbers one through thirty-one in a circle around the center with tiny indicators for weekday and month at the nine and three and a platinum Patek logo on the deployant clasp of the crocodile strap. The kind of watch that doesn't stand out to anyone unable to recognize a perpetual-calendar Patek Philippe Grand Complications or who fails to appreciate an incredible masterpiece of mechanical engineering, which only a handful of master watchmakers in the world are able to construct.

Next stop, the coffee machine. A real coffee machine, not the plastic Nespresso junk I had yesterday. Nothing better to wake you up in the morning than the smell of freshly ground Arabica beans.

I hadn't checked any messages since yesterday afternoon, and there were plenty of them impatiently waiting for my attention. Most of them could keep on waiting. I went straight to the message from Pierce & Pierce. I bet those bastards had some interesting meetings after I left. Those bankers were probably swearing like sailors as soon as I stepped out.

Three voice messages in one afternoon, all overly polite, though with growing undertones of impatience. As soon as I heard them reassure me all was on track I knew there was a snag. The first two messages didn't mention an issue but the third did, indirectly.

Preston was speaking on the recording. At first reassuring for the third time that everything's golden. Then finally we got to it. They just needed sign-off from the New York headquarters. Should be just a rubber stamp, just a piece of cake handled in a jiffy, he said. Yeah.

I wasn't worried, not about that. They'd get it done. They

were far too greedy not to. They could wait.

The next message was from Bühler. He didn't even try to hide his excitement. He only left one message agreeing to my terms and committing the full value of their little fund. Nice enough kid but he was walking around blind without a cane. Like a teen skinny-dipping in shark-infested waters, giggling, throwing a Frisbee without a care in the world. In this world, you either become a shark or you become lunch.

My thoughts were interrupted by the sight of Sandra setting her purse down and taking a seat by her desk. I put my hand up and motioned to her to come over to my office. She took her own sweet time. My own fault for waving her over like that. She never took crap from anyone, least of all me, and I've always respected the hell out of her for it.

Five minutes later, after she'd made herself a coffee, she came over. I didn't give her any lip about it. Wouldn't do any good anyhow.

"Morning, Sandra. Need you to make a few calls. Gonna be a busy day, and I'll be out most of it."

She put her coffee down on my desk and opened her little notepad.

"Sure, go ahead."

"First, call Todd Preston at Pierce & Pierce and—"

"Pierce & Pierce again? You're not really going back to them, are you?"

I held the palms of my hands up to her in a disarming gesture.

"There's not enough to time to explain now. I promise I'll tell you when I can. Don't worry, Sandra. I haven't forgotten. Or forgiven."

She shook her head in disbelief and shrugged.

"As long as you're sure."

"I am. Please call Preston and remind him that he's got until the end of the day and to stand by for a wire transfer once all's done. No need to tell him anything else."

She made a note on her pad, nodding.

"Then call Markus Bühler, the kid at this Global Opportunities fund. Tell him the same thing, to stand by for wire details."

"Last one. Call Jacques at LGT in Vaduz. Tell him I'll come over before lunch today with a client. I need a clean shell company setup ready to go by lunch. Got all of that?"

She finished scribbling before looking up at me with an expression that in no uncertain terms told me that this last question was more than redundant.

It wasn't exactly sunny but at least it was dry. I left the hat in the office for the first time this week and headed in the direction of Fleming's, starting down Bahnhofstrasse where the boutiques were just opening for the day. I passed the Bucherer window and stopped for a moment. After the loss of those watches in the break-in, I contemplated filling the empty slots in the watch case.

That's when I noticed it. I squinted and looked in the reflection. That man across the street behind me just standing there. Looking at me. Gray overcoat, Swiss-style Tyrolean hat.

Perhaps I was being paranoid. Perhaps I was imagining. Perhaps I wasn't.

I looked a bit longer, moving along the wide display window. Then I turned and crossed the street, making no rush of any kind, heading up to the Beyer display window, taking my time looking at all the watches there too, but even more so at all the reflective areas around them.

Most watches were displayed on mirror cubes or polished

A Most Private Bank

steel pedestals, both making for perfectly adequate countersurveillance aids.

Sure enough, the trench coat still appeared to be looking my way. Short, stocky. Couldn't make out a face.

The mirror display cases in the window were too small to make out much detail in the reflections and the longer and closer I stared at him, the more likely that this joker would make me. I checked the time on my own wristwatch and turned up in the direction of the train station, picking up the pace, walking with a purpose, not once stopping to look back.

I was nearly all the way up to the train station when I made a sharp left, holding my palm out. Raindrops. No matter. I'd be indoors in a minute.

The Jelmoli department store was just what I needed. Six floors of brand-name shopping, everything from groceries to stationaries and electronics. I slowed my pace once inside, taking the escalator up to the second floor, making a point out of standing to the side like a tourist rather than walking up the steps.

The urge to look behind me was growing every second, like an itch that just wouldn't go away. Stepping off the elevators, walking up to the floor directory, finding what I needed. Onward, past the men's fashion into the glassware section. Low shelves, none higher than eye level and clear glass and crystal products on the shelves. I walked slowly, up and down the aisles as if I was searching for something in particular.

Stopping by the wine section I lifted a large multifaceted crystal wine glass, spinning it slowly, admiring the reflections. In the crystal I could see the outlines. Easy when you know what to look for. A diminutive gray frame with a black hat. And there it was. Keeping his distance but following me like a bad smell. I set the glass back down, looked at the price tag, nodded, and continued.

The department store had just recently opened, and in the morning of a weekday there weren't many people in. This yokel was already standing out like a clown at a funeral. She was waiting for me. Time to shake the tail.

The lingerie department was nearly empty when I strolled in. It was the perfect spot. Open-floor layout, low shelves, two exit points to other departments plus elevators and a staircase nearby. I continued my leisurely pace down the aisles, my back to the entryway that I came from. He couldn't risk loitering around there, with no place to hide and he couldn't very well follow me in to the lady's undergarment section.

I picked up a pair of tiny white panties and held them up, spinning them around for a moment. A friendly young Swiss sales assistant shuffled over and asked if she could help me find something. I told her I was looking for something special for my wife.

Ten minutes later I was a hundred and fifty bucks poorer and a nice red-and-white gift-wrapped pair of skimpy little panties richer. I hoped it was at least her size. I couldn't see any trace of the shadow. Seemed like he wasn't too keen on hanging around the unmentionables section.

I exited through the staircase, then the back entrance through the travel agency. This time my pace was brisk, speeding up, at least until I got a few hundred yards from the building. Let him explain that to his handlers. Goddamn Hill.

I shifted direction a few times on the way, making sure my cell phone was properly turned off, just in case. If this was Hill's idea of figuring out who or where my client was, who knows how far he'd take it.

I glanced into every window, checking every reflection as I made my way to her hotel. No one.

Pimple Face barely looked up from his phone game as I

walked past the reception, up the stairs. He grinned knowingly when I looked back at him from the stairwell. She opened the door on my second knock. Evelyn. Takes getting used to.

My mind had been focused like a laser all the way here, until now. Until she opened the door in that oversize white hotel robe with her long black hair all wet. The robe was tied, but she hadn't done a good job of it, with the cleavage showing all the way down to her belly button. I must have stood there like a fool, mouth all open.

"Hey you…" Her soft whisper sounded so sweet. So innocent. So…

I felt her hands on my hips and her soft lips to mine and I struggled to regain my focus. I moved my arms around her and kissed her back gently.

"Evelyn… we need to get going. Quite soon. All is lined up, but we have to keep the ball moving," I managed to whisper between kisses.

She looked into my eyes, her nose nearly touching mine. She nodded slowly, wetting those cherry lips.

"I know… I'll be ready in just a moment."

My focus was just coming back. The plan was crystallizing in in my mind again, the activities that need to happen today, the work that needed to be done. But when she turned around, let her robe drop to the floor, and walked naked to the bed where her clothes were laid out, I lost it all again. It took every inch of my willpower to remain there, by the door. Watching the most beautiful girl I had ever seen getting dressed in front of me.

It must have been obvious - it must have been so easy to read me. I could see it in her face when she came back in that blue Mugler, the same she had on two days ago when she came into my office. She saw my reaction and she liked it.

"I... I got you something. I'll explain later," I said and put the wrapped box from Jelmoli on the desk.

"You went out and got me a gift?"

"Long story... I'll tell you later. Ready?"

"Uh-huh!" She took my hand and did that thing with her lip again, biting the side of it, looking at me with those Bambi eyes. I kissed her again before we left her room.

In case this bozo was still scouting for us, I took her on a ride through the Zurich tram system, changing a few times to different lines to make sure no one was around. I didn't explain and she didn't ask. Perhaps she didn't realize the extent of the detour.

There was no way I could hide her from view for very long, but that didn't matter. It wouldn't be possible to hide much longer anyhow. At least I could make sure they didn't know where she was staying. It took half an hour for us to get back to the office but she did get a nice tour of a gray, rainy Zurich.

The Unexpected Visitor

The blood in my veins froze to ice when I opened the front door to Dixon Capital. This was the last person I had expected to see that day, and one I had never wanted to see in my office again. Not after yesterday, not after the memories that were now forever associated with his face. Inspector Schmidt of the federal Swiss *Kriminalpolizei* was leaning over the reception desk, engrossed in polite conversation with Sandra, and hadn't noticed the front door opening behind him.

I stood there for a moment, frozen in my steps. My initial instinctive fear subdued after seeing the body language indicating a casual conversation. At least there wasn't any fresh incident.

"Can I help you, Inspector?" I said loudly, perhaps too loudly.

He spun around, taken by surprise by the unnecessarily aggressive question behind him.

"Mr. Dixon. Good that you're here. I was just asking about you."

"Excuse me?"

"Ah, my mistake. I was just asking for you. English is my fourth language, after all. My apologies."

I nodded an acceptance of this unnecessary apology but decided to continue the conversation in English out of habit. Why give away home-field advantage.

"How can I be of assistance? Any new leads on the homicide?"

"There have been some developments, yes. Can we go somewhere to talk?"

I looked at my watch. I didn't mean to be a jerk, but I didn't care if I came off like one.

"I'm good here. What's the news?"

Inspector Schmidt looked around for a chair, realized there was none in the reception area, and leaned casually against the counter instead. He was in a gray coat and had a hat in his hand. I'd seen someone else wearing a similar outfit today. Someone shorter. Could be a coincidence. If you believe in those sorts of things.

"Well, Mr. Dixon, I'm afraid I will have to start off by asking a couple of questions. Could you please tell me where you spent the night?"

That question threw me. There would be no reason for the law to ask me that. I could see Chris next to me, looking at me. I didn't look back.

"No."

That reply threw him. Good. He's in my shop - he'll play by my rules or he'll get the hell out of here.

"Excuse me?"

"No, I can't. Or rather, no, I won't. My whereabouts are not your concern."

He took a little notebook out from the left inner pocket of his coat, flipping the pages around the spiral spine.

"We tried to find you in your home this morning, Mr. Dixon, but you were apparently not there. Your wife was kind enough to inform us that you hadn't been home as far as she knew. She was unaware of your whereabouts, and it sounded as if she hadn't seen you in days."

"My patience is running thin, Inspector. If you want to contact me, leave a message with my assistant and I will get back to you. I would not look kindly on you bothering my family again."

"Alexander Mikhailov. Ever heard the name?"

Smart cop. Well played. Throw a curveball when cornered.

"Why do you ask?" I shot back, not feeling terribly inclined to trust this lawman.

"Small-time Russian hoodlum. Had an outstanding Interpol arrest warrant for a few bank scams. Money laundering, fraud, bit of extortion."

"I don't deal with that particular type of clientele."

"Quite." Schmidt nodded, and I could see in this bastard's eyes that he was finally about to get to some sort of a point.

"A gun was found in his hotel room. Same caliber as what we dug out here Monday night. Still waiting for the ballistics report."

He got me on that one. I was left speechless for a moment.

"So you see that I have to ask you if you have heard this name before, Mr. Dixon," he continued.

I nodded slowly, wishing she wasn't there next to me to hear this.

"I have. I was informed about his name and possible involvement by a private security firm yesterday," I admitted, seeing a possible danger in lying outright about this point. Sooner or later they'd figure out that I was on to him. "So you got the bastard?"

"Possibly. We don't see much gun-related crime around here, and it's an unusual caliber."

"I can only hope you found the weapon still stuck in his mouth with his hand around it, and a brightly painted red wall behind."

He sighed and looked at me as if I had just said something problematic.

"Unfortunately, Mr. Mikhailov was deceased by the time we

found it," he said.

A faint four-letter word escaped my lips, and I wish I hadn't been a jerk and just accepted his suggestion to have this conversation in private. But this was no time to backtrack.

"I'm afraid I can't reveal the details of his demise at this time, but we are investigating it as a homicide. Now I will have to ask you again. Where did you spend last night, Mr. Dixon?"

The four-letter word slipped past my lips again, more at myself than at anyone in particular. I brought my hand to my mouth and rubbed it, thinking for a second.

"I see. You believe that I found out about this Rasputin fellow yesterday, figured out where he is, and iced him for what he did to Raphael. Fine, at least I understand your rather unusual line of questioning. I have a permanent room at the Hyatt. Had for some time. It's convenient for staying in the city instead of making the commute out to the house."

"Yes, we are aware of your room there. We are also informed that no one has gone on record so far to confirm you being there last night. The staff do not remember seeing you."

"I came back late. Alone. That's a shame but hardly a crime," I said.

He was making notes in his little flip pad, nodding. That's the time she decided it was a good idea to speak up.

"He was with me all night at Hotel Fleming's," she piped up for some goddamned reason.

Inspector Schmidt raised an eyebrow as he looked up from his pad.

"Is that so? And who might you be, Miss?"

She stepped up, extending her hand, putting on the East Coast accent again. I wanted to stop her, but it was far too late.

"Christina Rosenbaum. I can vouch for Mr. Dixon's whereabouts all night and I'm prepared to testify to that affect," she spoke with the confidence and certainty of someone born with more money than they could ever count.

"Well. I suppose we've cleared that detail up, then," Inspector Schmidt replied, shaking her hand. "We could have just done this right away, Mr. Dixon. I do understand the… sensitivity of the issue, and I will treat it accordingly. I had to ask, of course."

I nodded back to him, showing some gratitude for the Swiss discretion.

"Thank you, Inspector. Much appreciated."

"There may be some follow-up questions later on this week. For now, that is the extent of my visit. To inform you of developments and to settle the question of your personal whereabouts. I should be on my way."

I watched the gray-haired man put his hat back on and leave the office. Not as dumb as he lets on, that one. After the door was shut and he was well out of range and I was left with the two ladies, I spoke first.

"We're taking the car to Vaduz, Sandra. Got some business to settle there."

"I'll just be a moment, need to use the little ladies' room," said the girl who had just lied to the police.

Once she was out of earshot, Sandra looked at me with a puzzled face.

"Why didn't you just tell him that you're separated? He went to your place as a courtesy, to tell you about this. Then your wife's too proud to tell him that you're not living there anymore, and now you're playing the same game. What's the point of that? What the hell are you doing sleeping with barely grown-up clients anyhow?"

She scolded me like a mother, the way no one really dares to scold me anymore, and I found it so refreshing that I let her drone on for a while.

"I know, Sandra. You're right. There's a lot going on at the moment. Much at stake. I'll let you in on it all, but not yet. Trust me."

I could hear the door to the ladies' room open and her Louboutins clicking their way back this direction.

"Ready for a road trip?" I asked as she came around the corner.

"You bet!" she replied, keeping the American accent.

Road Trip

The roar of the twin-turbo engine firing up reverberated through the narrow alley, and I could see how the volume startled her. She did a good job pretending it didn't but she was clearly taken by surprise.

"Quite a car, huh?" she said with an abashed little smile. "I wouldn't have guessed from the outside. But that's the point... isn't it?"

I signaled and pulled out on the street, starting to navigate the minefield of stoplights with automated traffic cameras in the inner city, heading toward the A3 freeway.

"Eh... what is?" I asked, distracted by the early-afternoon traffic.

"To brag without bragging. I haven't been in Switzerland very long, but I'm not all that dumb. I bet this beast costs as much as a Lamborghini. But a Lambo would be tacky, wouldn't it?"

I nodded without taking my eyes off the road. A few more stoplights before we cleared the inner city.

"It would be like walking around with gold chains around your neck. Not the Swiss way," I said.

"Some sort of pretend modesty, then? Pretending to have a low profile while you really just try to show off to the right people?"

We had finally reached the freeway, and in a moment of childish lapse, I settled on a nonverbal reply. Slapping the stick to the left put the sports automatic gearbox in manual mode, with the paddles behind the wheel shifting up and down. Pushing the left paddle, shifting down, I brought the pedal down slowly to the resistance level and then slammed the kickdown. Predictably, the twin-turbocharged 450-horsepower engine howled like an F-35 fighter taking off from a carrier.

I should have known better. A few seconds after my childish display, there was a brief and bright white flash in front of us, followed by a four-letter exclamation from me. I hit the brakes, going down to just above the limit of seventy-five miles an hour.

"What just happened?" she asked, sensing my sudden change of mood.

"I just lost a hundred bucks or so. I'll get over it. These damned speed cameras are all over. Bill will arrive in the post in a few weeks. Takes the joy out of having a decent engine."

She decided it was a good idea to giggle at my sour face.

"So you just lost a hundred dollars trying to impress a girl with your big engine? Doesn't sound very Swiss to me!"

Slapping the stick back to auto, two thumb presses on the left side of the steering wheel, the car settled in a smooth steady cruise. I didn't reply, and she let it slide.

We came out from the cover of the trees, the freeway parallel to the lake across the hillside landscape. Her reaction to the scenery revealing itself on the left side was palpable.

This she hadn't seen before. Snow-covered rocky mountain ranges in all directions, the sun breaking through cloud cover, reflecting in the clear blue water of Lake Zurich, old Swiss villages dotted around the lake. Up ahead a causeway crossed a narrow part of the lake, leading up to a thirteenth-century castle on a hilltop overlooking a picturesque Swiss town where no building looked to be younger than a few hundred years.

The town marina held at least a hundred small leisure boats, tourist peddle boats, and a few commuter boats going up and down the lake between towns. She was breathless, stunned by this quintessential Swiss landscape. It made me remember how I had the same reaction once and how easily you get used to these views, even take them for granted.

"Pretty neat, isn't it?" I said to break the silence.

"It's the most beautiful thing I've ever seen," she said without taking her eyes off the landscape. "It's like something out of *Lord of the Rings*."

That made me chuckle. "That's because Tolkien based the books on this. He spent quite some time here, not far away from where we are now."

I had my left hand on the wheel and the right arm resting on the cream-colored leather between our seats. She put her hand on mine.

"I'd love to explore. With you."

I turned my head and leaned to her for a kiss, but she quickly pulled away.

"Hey, eyes on the wheel, Mister! That lake looks great but I'd rather not go for a swim today."

There was something about her that brought out the worst of my childish impulses. I let go of the steering wheel without taking my eyes off her.

"You don't trust my driving?" I asked as the car started turning without my guidance, perfectly following the bend in the road. "Oh, don't worry, the car is in self-drive mode."

She was staring at the road with her hand ready to grab the wheel.

"If it's all the same to you, I'd prefer you to keep your eyes on the road. And your hands on the wheel."

I kissed her cheek before turning my attention back to the road, both hands now on the wheel. We had passed the lake and entered the valley areas. In front of us, flat as far as the eye can see. On either side of us, ten-thousand-feet elevation, rocky, snow-covered mountains.

"Another half an hour or so. Ever been to Liechtenstein?"

"My local travel agency didn't offer any charter tours," she said.

"Yeah, no daily Ryan Air flights either. Of course, that may have something to do with the acute lack of airports. A country with less than forty thousand people has very little need for one. It's just a tiny patch of land between Switzerland and Austria that refused to join the modern world. It's not even a proper democracy. The prince has veto power over anything their parliament decides."

"What about the king?" Her naive question made me smile and remind myself that all of this was so new to her.

"It's not exactly Prince Harry. This is a principality. The ruler is called a prince. Blame whoever came up with that lousy English translation. The original German title makes more sense. This guy's a multibillionaire and a sovereign ruler with actual political power. He's got a pretty neat house too. You'll see."

"So kinda like the British royal family at a smaller scale?"

"Sure. If the Windsor family bought the title for bragging rights and didn't bother to visit England in a century."

She looked at me as if I said something crazy and I tried to explain myself.

"Three hundred years ago some rich Austrians who had run out of stuff to buy figured that having their own country would be good fun. So they bought the title. Seems more like a joke in retrospect - they didn't even bother to visit the place in over a hundred years."

"They ruled the country and didn't even visit?" she asked.

"Can you blame them? Just less than a hundred years ago, it was nothing but a patch of empty land with a few sheep farmers with funny accents. When they finally bothered to show up to their country, they realized that they needed a flag and a national anthem. So they just swiped the British national anthem and Haiti's flag. No kidding, they just added new words to "God Save the Queen" and a bland two-color flag. Caused a bit of embarrassment in the thirty-six Olympics, so they added a little doda on the flag to make it look different."

"That was a long time ago. I guess things are different now?" she asked.

"Oh yeah. Even women can vote now. Since nineteen eighty-four. But the prince can still override any law as he pleases, dissolve parliament on a whim, and he pretty much owns the country anyhow. Nice part of the whole slacker way of running a nation is that they use Swiss francs rather than wasting time with their own currency, and there are no borders checks and no military."

"This is in Europe? In Western Europe?" she asked, as if I was making this stuff up. "How big is this place anyhow?"

"Blink and you miss it. Less than forty thousand people, five miles across. Bank secrecy is pretty much the only business around. The prince throws a party every year, a little garden party at his place. The entire country is invited, and they show up too."

She was staring at me as if trying to figure out if I was making this whole thing up as I went along or not. I let her keep guessing and drove on, smiling the whole way.

Half an hour later we turned off the freeway, approaching the river crossing.

"The bridge is the border. Just a hidden camera recording the license plate, nothing else. You're now officially in the principality of Liechtenstein. That's Vaduz, the capital up ahead. Keep looking up and to the right."

"The capital is a tiny little village. What am I looking for?"

I drove on, slowing as we headed into the town, waiting for her to see it.

"Oh, wow, look at that castle!"

She spotted it. The town of Vaduz was located at the foot of a steep mountain, and a mile or so up, watching ominously over it, was a twelfth-century castle. Something out of a Disney flick, the castle looked as if time had stood still for hundreds of years.

"Yeah, that's his crib. The prince. Would make Blofeld jealous."

"Nice job… if you can get it," she agreed, staring at the cliffside keep right above the center of the tiny European capital.

The nondescript four-floor white building had a discrete blue logo on the side, diamond shaped with a yellow crown and three large white letters. *LGT*. I pulled up behind the building and parked outside.

"One of the perks with this demi-nation is that you can actually find a parking space," I told her as we left the car. "This is my main bank."

She looked up at the dark blue diamond sign. "Never heard of it."

"It's got a good owner," I said and pointed up to the castle on the mountainside. "Don't go mistaking this bank for a little family business like Niederhauser. These guys are thoroughbred professionals. You don't want to underestimate them."

"I'll keep that in mind." She reached for my hand as we walked to the entrance but I moved mine away.

"Not here. There are eyes on everything in this town. No need to give them any more than required."

A Most Private Bank

She looked around the quaint village, quiet with homey little houses on either side of a main street.

"What do you mean?" she whispered.

I grinned as we stepped up to the entrance. I paused to explain before pressing the buzzer.

"It's likely that at least three different security services already photographed us. Don't worry, nothing to care about. They're just nosy, hoping to catch some of their own citizens visiting their stash of hidden money."

A Princely Bank

The interior of the LGT lobby bore no resemblance to the kind of banks that most people see. Apart from the receptionist behind a glass window to the left of the entrance, the lobby was more akin to a modern art gallery. White walls with original artwork, floor-standing marble sculptures, and brown leather sofas.

We were expected, and there was no need to make use of the sofas. A man in his sixties with salt-and-pepper hair, horn-rimmed glasses, and a three-piece charcoal pinstripe suite stood on the ready and approached us as soon as we entered.

"*Guten Tag, Herr Dixon*," he said in German, offering a firm handshake.

"No need for the formalities. Great to see you, Jacques," I replied in English for her benefit. "Thank you for taking the meeting on such short notice. May I introduce Ms.—"

"Christina Rosenbaum. Chris," she said.

"A pleasure, Ms. Rosenbaum. My name is Jacques Dumas, and I oversee the trust business of the bank. Mr. Dixon, Jim, has indicated that time is at a premium, so I propose we get started. If you would follow me, please."

He spoke English with just a hint of a French accent, though clearly and distinctly with the air of education and confidence.

Dumas whisked us into a meeting room on the ground floor with a door facing the art gallery that served as their lobby and waiting area. The glass table was diamond shaped with four chairs at the straight sides. A projector in the ceiling, a whiteboard covering an entire wall, and a conference phone in the middle of the table.

A Most Private Bank

He pulled a chair out for her, and she played the part, sitting down and letting him push the chair in for her.

I pulled my own chair out and sat down, as did he. His finger on the conference unit, he said, "Mrs. Schnieder, could we please get an espresso for Mr. Dixon and…" He looked at her with raised eyebrows, posing a silent question.

"Just a coffee, please," she replied.

"An American coffee for Ms. Rosenbaum and another espresso for myself. Thank you," he took the finger off the phone.

"I understand you need a legal entity for an acquisition project and that you need it up and running by this morning, Jim."

He went straight to the point, rather than spending fifteen minutes talking about the weather, as local protocol dictates. Good man. But I pressed my lips together and shook my head.

"Not me, Jacques. Not my show, not today. I'm here strictly in an advisory capacity. She's your customer."

Without batting an eye, he turned to her.

"My apologies, Ms. Rosenbaum. Can I assume that you would prefer a pre-setup structure with no prior activities?"

She glanced at me, and I nodded slightly.

"Would you prefer onshore or offshore? Are you looking at any particular jurisdictions?" the banker continued. She had a pretty good poker face, but his face-reading skills were well-honed. "Well, why don't we get the inventory for you to have a look at."

The door opened behind him, and a young assistant entered holding a tray. She approached soundlessly and set down a large coffee mug in front of Evelyn, a small espresso in front of me, and another for Dumas.

"Thank you, Mrs. Schnieder," he said. "Would you be so kind

as to fetch the current company inventory?"

"Certainly, Mr. Dumas," she replied in a formal tone, following the local protocol of mutual formal address in front of third parties.

She didn't take more than a minute before returning with a set of binders, placing them on the glass table before making a discrete exit.

The binders all had labels with jurisdictions on them. Panama, Val Verde, Marshall Islands, Cayman Islands, British Virgin Islands, Jersey, Guernsey, Liechtenstein. She looked to me for guidance, and I pushed the binder labeled Marshall Islands a little closer to her. She got the point.

"A wise choice. As a United States-associated nation, there are some clear benefits, in particular for an American person. Apart from the company maintenance fee, there would be no tax implication as far as the Marshall Islands are concerned, and at present no automatic information exchange. We presently have over three hundred Marshall setups, all fresh setups with no prior economic activities. Assuming you'd prefer a limited-liability company, the list starts on page four."

She flipped the binder open to that page, and I watched her eyes in amusement, thinking back to the first time I picked a company out of a binder like this, watching her first exposure to this world. Her face stern and professional, not giving away the confusion that I knew she felt as she saw the endless list of company names.

She was nodding to herself, going through the list, and I let her continue a moment.

"Find any name you like?" I asked, trying to help her out, hinting to her that the names were the only differences.

"This one. Orphelia Holdings Corp. That's the one we need," she said confidently.

A Most Private Bank

Dumas took the binder that she pushed over to him, made a mark with a fountain pen next to the name, and closed it.

"It's yours. The shareholders' capital is fifty thousand US, no other assets, liabilities, or transactions. You buy the company at par, and we charge a yearly fee of one percent for custody, administration, and fiduciary directorship."

"When can everything be up and running?" she asked.

He looked at his wrist. A sublime Glasshütte Original, the blue-face PanoMatic Reserve model, two-off center sub dials, one for the seconds, a power reserve indicator on the right, and a date display. A beautifully understated timepiece and incredible German engineering. "We should have all papers in order in, say, fifteen minutes?"

"That'd be great," she said, this time unable to hide the impressed smile.

"Will you serve on the board, Jim?" he asked me.

"This is her show. She's your client, not me." I exchanged a look with my longtime friend and banker, making sure he got the point. He did. I wanted no liability of any kind.

"Very well. In that case, all we need is your passport, proof of residence, and a statement as to source of funds, Ms. Rosenbaum. If you have the paperwork in order, I can make the copies right away."

She opened up the little green Chanel purse and rummaged around. I never could tell a genuine Chanel from a fake, and staring at it didn't help. She found what she was looking for.

"This should be what you need, Mr. Dumas. My passport and a copy of my electricity bill in California."

I remained quiet when I saw it. A blue American passport. A bill from Southern California Edison. We hadn't talked about this. Even if I wanted to stop her, it was too late now.

"Source of funds is inheritance from my late father, Benjamin Rosenbaum," she added, sealing the deal. Dumas looked at me, and I gave him a blank stare back.

"Very well, I will be right back."

He took her papers, stood up, and left the room, closing the door behind him. I leaned over the table close to her.

"I thought you didn't have a fake passport," I said so softly it was barely a whisper.

"All I said was that I didn't use one to check in."

I grimaced but decided to let it go for now. This was neither the time nor the place.

Dumas came back soon after, handing her papers back to her along with a fresh binder with paperwork.

"Please sign all the places that are marked, Ms. Rosenbaum."

She opened the binder. Red adhesive stickers poked out the side of the stack of papers, and she flipped the pages one by one, signing on the dotted lines without hesitation. I felt my pulse racing as paper after paper got signed with the name Christina Rosenbaum. There are laws you can bend, and there are laws you can't. She was far over the line, and every signature was another serious crime.

"That's all I need. You are now the proud owner and director of Orphelia Holdings Corp with headquarters in Majuro, Marshall Islands, and a PO box here with us. You have sole ownership and executive power, Ms. Rosenbaum. All the documentation is in this binder, along with the details of the company's bank accounts with us here at LGT. In other words, you're all set."

She rose to her feet, extending her hand, shaking his.

"Mr. Dumas. Thank you for an impressive demonstration in banking efficiency. I'm sure we'll do business again."

I gave Dumas an appreciative nod as he escorted us to the exit.

Roadblocks

The rain was relentless on the way back. The windshield wipers moved at full speed, slapping bucketloads of water off the glass, making for a visibility of a few hundred yards at the most. The traffic was moving slowly but at least it was moving. The incredible views of the Alpine landscape were nowhere to be seen. The first half hour of the drive, the heavy rainfall demanded all my attention, and we drove in silence.

I don't know why I was so upset. It was my own fault. I knew she had spent years working financial fraud - I should have figured out that this wasn't as new to her as I had thought. It wasn't the first time that I had been taken in by her naive and innocent appearance. She had the forged documents all ready, and she had used them before I could do anything about it. She had broken some pretty important laws in front of my eyes, potentially making me an accessory to a crime.

I couldn't be sure at the time. Had she done that out of habit, or was she playing me? I had my own plan, my own secrets. Perhaps she did too. Why hadn't she just used her real name, her real passport? There was no need to break the law, not for this. Perhaps she had thought that a good family name would help. I wanted to trust her, I really did. Even more, I wanted to remain in the belief that I was the smartest one in the room and a few steps ahead of everyone else.

My plan was still intact, and what I wanted was still within grasp. There was nothing to do but to stay the course.

"Using the Rosenbaum name was unnecessary," I started. "But the damage is done, and there's nothing to do about it now. Chris Rosenbaum is now the name on the papers, and you better stay in character. From now on, you'll be Chris until all of this is over."

She sounded surprised, insecure. As if I had just scolded her. Conflicting emotions and thoughts ran through my head.

"I thought it would make things smoother, to stay with that name," she said in her original accent. Northern England. "Perhaps we can change it," she added to my disbelief.

I continued driving in silence, weighing her explanation, considering the possible options. Naivete. Ignorance. Recklessness. Stupidity. I hadn't expected either from her. No, she had her reasons, and pushing her about it now wouldn't help.

"Done is done. It's a complicating factor. We'll figure it out. Now that you started down that path, you better continue. You'll be Chris full-time now. I'll call you only that. Better stay in character. If any of the players figure out you're not Chris, the entire deal falls apart and you better get the hell out of Dodge before they lock you up."

I glanced over at her. She looked shook up. Her face all scrunched up, looking down at her feet.

"On the positive side, you make a pretty convincing Chris Rosenbaum. Stick with her until we wrap this up. You probably need to vanish after that. But something tells me you're used to vanishing."

She looked back at me with a smile back on her lips.

"We could vanish together."

"One thing at a time, Evelyn. Chris. One thing at a time."

I smiled back at her for a brief second before returning my attention to the road. Self-driving mode is unreliable in these weather conditions.

"What's next? You gonna tell me the plan yet?" she asked, back to the American accent. I couldn't help but feel impressed over how easily she did that.

"Three boxes to be checked. We've got financing lined up. Eighty mil. Now we need to get papers signed, money wired, negotiate a deal, and have sales contracts for the bank shares drawn up."

"I like it! What are the boxes?"

"Half the financing comes from an amateur wannabe hedge fund. They're putting up forty mil, based on the absurd belief that there's an enormous amount of unclaimed gold in the vaults. I assume that they've been misinformed. Whatever you're looking for, it's not two tons of stolen World War Two-era gold, is it?"

She hesitated a moment, but then shook her head without speaking.

"Good. Thought so. They also seem to be under the illusion that I'm putting up forty million of my own money to match theirs. Something I have never promised them."

"With you so far. You'd do well in my line of work!"

I'm sure that was meant as a compliment. That's the way I decided to read it anyhow.

"Next we're seeing a cowboy investment bank so horny for my business that they're putting up forty million in debt financing for the takeover. Coincidentally, they also seem to be under the impression that I'm personally matching that investment. Yet all I told them is that I will ensure that their capital is matched."

She laughed. This was her game, and I enjoyed showing off. She's not the only one who can play the confidence game.

"We'd make a great team, you and me!"

I smiled and nodded. "Yeah, if you don't go to jail first. The difference here is that you broke the law and I didn't."

"What's the third box to tick?"

A Most Private Bank

"Getting the Niederhauser family to sell a controlling stake of the bank for eighty million or less. I've already been approached by the head of the clan. Should be a piece of cake."

At that point, I was just showing off. I was bragging, and I liked it.

"I knew I came to the right person. Father always told me to go to Jim Dixon if you need to get deals done," she said, deliberately overdoing the posh Manhattanite accent.

I shot her a grin back. Her act was good. Well-rehearsed. She could have been on *Geraldo* with that.

"Any idea why someone would follow me around Zurich this morning?"

She paused, her smile suddenly nowhere to be seen, her eyes on the watery barrage on the windshield.

"Is that why we jumped back and forth on the trams this morning? How did they look?" she answered my question with a question again.

"Only saw one guy. Doesn't mean there weren't any more. Short, stocky, coat, hat. I didn't stop to make conversation. Didn't make eye contact. Sound familiar?"

She hesitated.

"I don't know. I can't explain. Not now. Can you trust me?"

"You didn't lie about it. Our deal is still intact. There a problem? Danger?"

"Not to you. At least I don't think so. To me, perhaps. Don't let them find me, Jim."

I felt a pulsating vein popping out over my forehead. This was not the kind of complication I needed right now. This was supposed to be a simple deal. In and out. Quick and dirty.

"We're talking legal danger or physical danger?"

Instinct told me that I didn't want to know. Curiosity got the better of me.

"Could be either. Or both."

"Better move you, then. Somewhere more secure. I've got a room at the Hyatt. I'd need to make some arrangements... but I'll put you up there for now. If you don't mind staying with me."

"James Dixon, are you asking me to move in with you?"

She giggled again. She was enjoying this. The danger, the chase.

"I'll get you checked out of that roach motel you're staying at and get your stuff. Don't go back there. I need you for some meetings. After that I'll take you to my hotel."

"Why do you have a hotel room?"

"In case I need to hide small-time British grifters from mysterious men in gray overcoats."

Her mouth snapped shut and she sat there quietly as we headed into the inner city. Whether it was my refusal to answer or because I called her a grifter, this was the longest silence between us all day. Either way, it suited me just fine.

I parked by the street, in one of the white squares with a maximum parking time of thirty minutes. There would be a ticket on the car by the time we get back. Impossible to avoid parking tickets in this town. She still hadn't spoken to me after my remark in the car.

"Bring the folder. We're gonna need those documents."

She held the folder with the papers in her hand, as she had done the entire ride back, nodding but not replying.

"Oh, fine. I'm sorry. I was just kidding, Chris. I didn't mean to call you a small-time grifter. In fact, you're not only a great grifter, you're a cute one too."

A Most Private Bank

Now I saw a smile. She turned her head to look at the building we were heading toward, trying to hide her face, but I could tell she was smiling. I walked up next to her, brushing my finger over her hand. She took my hand in hers.

"I'll tell you my story one day. How I got into this line of work... why I do it. I haven't had an easy life, Jim. Not one with many choices."

I held her hand. I held it firmly, looking down into her eyes.

"I don't judge you, Chris. You think my line of work is so honest? Finance is an industry of thieves, con men, and sociopaths. At least those are the ones that do well in this business. I see people lie, cheat and steal every day. Most of them end up getting seven- or eight-figure bonuses for it. Most private bankers in this town make a living helping rich people dodge taxes or assisting corrupt businessmen, politicians, and criminals clean their dirty money. For all the anti-money-laundering laws, know-your-customer protocols, and automatic-information-exchange schemes, finance is still a dirty business.

"There's over two trillion dollars managed by Swiss asset managers. Anyone who thinks those assets are here because the Swiss are outstanding money managers is far too naive to work in this industry. Hell, I don't judge you for lying or stealing for a living. The only difference between your lies and the lies I hear on a regular Wednesday is that your kind are more likely to gain the attention of law enforcement. I don't care what your endgame is. The risk and the upside are both yours. I'll stick to the reasonably legal part of it, and I expect payment for it. That's a financial risk assessment, not a moral one."

I stopped talking and she stopped hiding the smile on her face. We stood there by the entrance to the beige office building with her smile turning into a smirk.

"Perhaps when all of this is settled, you can teach me how to play the game your way. We'd make a pretty good team, you know," she told me.

I opened the door and let her in first, following closely behind.

"One thing at a time, princess. Let's get this caper wrapped up first. All goes well, the bank is under our control by tomorrow. Something important I need to ask though. Before we go up there. Baerenfells was under the distinct impression that there's old war gold in the vaults. Someone gave him that impression. Have you had any dealing with him at all? Would he know your name? Any of your names? Would he recognize you for any reason? I need to know before we get in the room."

She shook her head without hesitation.

"No. He wouldn't know me in any way. Not the name or the face."

I accepted her reply and knocked hard on the nearly unmarked door, the fifth in a nondescript hallway of similar doors. Only a computer-printed white paper taped to the door informed of what company hid behind the it. Global Opportunities Fund Advisory.

A minute later a key turned in the lock from the inside and the door opened. Bühler hadn't shaved since my last visit, and the room smelled of feet and leftover food. He was surprised to see me, more so to see a pretty girl. It would be a fair guess that no female had visited these offices before.

"We need to talk," I said as I barged in past the surprised young man in the flannel shirt and jeans. "Everything is arranged, and we're all set. We've got a company set up for the takeover, and I need you to make the transfer today. The contracts are all drawn up, ready to be signed. Oh, and this is your new business partner in this venture - she'll be heading up the special-purpose vehicle for us."

I motioned to her without saying any names and she got the

hint. She gave him a firm handshake and a big white smile.

"Chris Rosenbaum. Great to meet you."

"Eh… Bühler. Markus Bühler," he said meekly. He was as smitten with her as I'd imagine most straight men would be, and it amused me. "Jim, I tried to get hold of you. I tried to tell you."

I continued into the little meeting room. "Crack a window, will you. We've got female company. Tell me what?"

He got my point about the window and tended to that first, opening one wide toward the street. An ambulance was heading past. He returned to the conference table and sat down opposite me and her, waiting for the noise to subdue.

"The… circumstances have changed. We're no longer in a position to, well, to complete the project on schedule, and perhaps it might make sense to slow things down and reevaluate the… situation."

I stared him down until he looked at the conference table.

"That word salad better not mean that you're backing out, Bühler. We've got a deal, and you will honor it."

There was a drop of sweat on his forehead slowly making its way down the side of his face. He was scrambling for words, struggling to find any that made sense.

"I… I've been told to, to postpone. Until we can figure the situation out. We'll have to wait."

"The hell we will. It's ready now. Next week it may be gone. You got the money? Transfer it!"

The kid looked like he just took an open-handed slap across the face. He was scared. Scared of something.

"I'm sorry. I can't do anything."

"Then get me someone who can. Call Baerenfells. Get him here right now," I said, raising my voice, feeling that vein on the right side of my forehead pulsating again.

"He told me not to call him today. Under any circumstances. He just told me to postpone. For now."

I took a deep breath. Then a few more. This path wouldn't lead anywhere.

"Fine. You got the forty million in liquidity as we discussed?"

He nodded eagerly, relieved that the confrontation deescalated.

"We do. But as I said—"

"Yeah, got that part. So the cash is there, and if Baerenfells gives the go-ahead, you can make the transfer. Correct?"

He seemed to think about it for a moment. His lips pressed together, he nodded slowly.

"I suppose so. Yes."

At those words, I stood to my feet. She caught on quickly and did the same.

"Seems like I'm in the wrong office. Keep the fund liquid, Bühler, this deal will still happen, and it will be the stuff of legends. Stand by, don't leave the phones."

I left the office without shaking his hand. She was better mannered.

Ambush

We walked out to the car, finding an angry red plastic-encased paper on the windshield. I tore it off and put it the door compartment, next to the other unpaid parking tickets accumulated the past week.

"No point in arguing with someone who can't make decisions. He probably doesn't even know what changed."

"What are we gonna do? We need this. If we don't get the equity part, that investment bank won't give the loan, right?"

My face had returned to its normal color after nearly losing my temper up there.

"You think I give up that easily? I'll get it done. I need to go talk to some people. Better I do it alone. You think you can handle my car?"

"Does it corner like it's on rails?" she asked back.

"Funny. Get her back in one piece, will ya?"

I reached for the key in my pocket and threw it over to her, watching her catch it easily with one hand. She looked at the BMW display key, at the tiny color LCD screen on it, twisting and turning the somewhat unusual, oversize-looking key.

"The only thing you need to worry about is that round button on top with the BMW logo. That locks the car. You won't need anything else. It unlocks when you touch the handle, as long as you've got the key close by. Drive straight to the Hyatt. Set the GPS. Zurich traffic is a mess. Park in the underground garage and take the elevator up. Go to the lobby, say that you're with me, and they'll give you a key card. I'll call ahead. Stay in the room and don't open for anyone. I've got my own card - I'll knock first and then open."

She went to try the unlocking mechanism, touching the driver-side door handle, the display key in her purse, smiling back at me when the doors unlocked, mirrors folded out.

"Fun toy. Where will you go while I play the damsel in the tower?"

"I've got a surprise visit to make. Gotta find out what the hell happened and kick this deal back in gear. I might be paranoid, but turn your cell phone off, just in case. If I need to get hold of you, I'll call the room."

"Can't I come with you? I hate sitting around waiting."

"The longer you're out in the open, the higher risk of having whoever followed me this morning find you. Better that you keep a low profile until I can sort out this holdup."

When she opened the car door the instrument panel display turned on, showing a sleek BMW M Sport logo before fading over to something that looked almost like a regular mechanical dashboard.

"Don't be long. I can only stand so much of hotel CNN."

I was just about to reply, but the roar of the car starting up drowned out all other sound. I was bracing for the worst, expecting her to needlessly rev up or even lose control and reverse into the car behind. Instead I was left smiling, shaking my head at how she handled the car effortlessly, reversing and pulling out into traffic. That wasn't the first time she'd handled a powerful car. Of course, she never claimed it was.

I cursed my own stupidity. My hat was still in the car and the rain had just started again. Folding up the collar of my coat, I started off with long strides in the direction of Bank Niederhauser.

Just a couple of minutes later, I crossed Bahnhofstrasse again, and the main street of the city was full of shopping tourists.

A Most Private Bank

Keeping my head straight forward, I glanced around for a suitable window before picking the Prada boutique.

It had nice big polished windows and mirrors behind the purses on display. It seemed unlikely that my shadow would let himself be rumbled by the same trick twice, but it couldn't hurt to stop a moment.

I couldn't believe my eyes. There he was. Just across the street. The same stupid trench coat. Perfectly camouflaged. If he was hiding in the 1940s. Standing out like a cockroach in a Caesar salad. Shorter but wider than most people around, dressed the same, standing still in the rain. Amateur. But he still picked up my trail in a matter of minutes. Unless he was just standing around Bahnhofstrasse all day. Goddamn Hill.

Taking my phone out of my coat pocket, I started off eastward. I aimed for the old cathedrals by the river, the ones overcrowded by tourists from the four corners of the world. Searching my pockets, I finally found the card, turned my phone back on, dialed the number, and held it to my ear, walking at a brisk pace.

"Hill, get your goddamned goon off my back!" I nearly yelled when he picked up. He sounded surprised. I yelled at him again. I told him in no uncertain terms that he was full of it and if I spotted a tail again they get nothing. Still he insisted on being as ignorant as he was innocent.

"Someone's tailing me, and he's not very subtle about it. Talk to that bureaucrat boss of yours. If I see this guy again, I won't be a happy camper!"

I hung up on him hoping he was just a good liar. The square outside the cathedral was full of Asians with umbrellas in one hand and oversize cameras in the other. Making my way through the crowd I kept low, staying out of sight, zigzagging the crowded area while switching off my cell phone. I shouldn't have turned it back on in the first place. A sharp turn, a change in direction. If they were well-funded professionals they'd have electronic surveillance and this little runaround would be a waste of time.

I doubled back, blending in with a group of French tourists following a lady holding up a little yellow flag, exiting the same direction that I came into the square.

This time of day the Old Town is full of slow-moving tourists. I walked with swift, long strides, making it near impossible for anyone to follow me without standing out, moving in a straight line toward the bank. At the end of a long stretch of a cobblestone pedestrian street, I turned to look behind me. No one. Satisfied I pushed the bell to the bank and the same security guard as yesterday opened the door for me.

"Jim Dixon. I've got an appointment with Mr. von Baerenfells," I lied.

The receptionist knew my face already. It was her job to know the faces of customers and potential customers. She was on her feet in no time, leading me to a conference room.

"Certainly, Mr. Dixon. If you care to follow me, please. Would you like a coffee?"

"Double espresso, thank you," I replied, handing her my coat and taking a seat in the conference room. She left the room and I stood up again, walked to the window, and watched the sea of colorful tourist umbrellas moving around below me like some sort of animated modern art exhibition. No trench coat, not that I could see.

A knock on the door and the lady from the reception returned with my espresso, setting it down on the table. I nodded a polite thanks to her before she left the room. After that, silence. Ten minutes passed, and then another five. The next time the door opened, there was no knock.

"What the hell do you think you're doing here?" the agitated banker said after he made sure the door was closed. If it's possible to whisper and shout at the same time, that's what he was doing. "You can't come here! I work here! They can't know that I do business with you!"

I watched his red face, his big white panicked eyes and enjoyed taking his sense of home-court safety away from him.

"But we're not doing business, are we? That's why I'm here. I just came from your other office."

He gave a somewhat comical impression as he tried to hush me, looking around as if checking if anyone could hear us. Meeting rooms in private banks are by their very nature soundproof and regularly swept for recording devices. I could confess to being the second shooter on the grassy knoll in here and no one would be the wiser.

"Bühler says something changed but he can't tell me what. Would you care to enlighten me, Dick?"

I pulled out the chair and sat down, making it clear to him that I wasn't planning on leaving anytime soon. He reluctantly got the point and pulled out the chair next to mine. Not across, but next to me, leaning a little too close, his breath giving away the seafood contents of his lunch.

"There... there are big things going on, Jim," he whispered. "My... my contact passed away. Unexpectedly."

It made me laugh, and my laugh shocked him.

"Lemme guess. Big Russian guy short a neck who seems to have had some accident at the Dolder?"

This man should never play poker. The surprise of my question wouldn't have been any clearer if it was tattooed to his forehead.

"You know Petrov?" he whispered.

"Know of him," I said without explaining anything. "So that's where you got your info. What does it matter if he's moved on to the happy hunting grounds?"

"Well, the thing is, that... He knows, or rather knew I suppose, which exact safe-deposit boxes contain the... the valuable items."

It made sense to me now. I should have seen this coming. If my head was a vending machine, the stuck quarter finally shook loose and fell down the slot. That's the connection. That's the play.

"Why don't you just drill them all open? All that lack a documented owner?"

He hesitated, just as I had expected him to, struggling to come up with a plausible reply. He looked out the window, clearing his throat, sitting up straight, trying to look important. As if this was one of his regular pitch meetings, conning high-net-worth people into buying underperforming mutual funds.

He opened his mouth and started with whatever lie his coked-out brain just came up with.

"First you have to appreciate that—"

"I'm not the guy you bullshit, Dick. Give it to me straight and I might be able to help. Tell me a tall tale and I walk."

His jaw remained clenched as he considered his options. He didn't seem to like them much. The silence grew longer and for him no doubt uncomfortable.

"It might be... that some of these safe-deposit boxes... actually do have a registered beneficial owner," he finally whispered, once more leaning too close for comfort.

It took a substantial amount of self-control not to laugh. This respectable banker, a lifer who had been in this very bank for over four decades, working his way up from the bottom, who was probably clearing seven figures a year without having as much as a community college degree, is now planning an actual bank heist.

A Most Private Bank

What he was talking about was far outside the garden-variety unethical behavior of banks and bankers. This was bank robbery, plain and simple.

"You plan to drill open a few boxes, get a truck or two for transport, and get the hell out of Dodge. South America or Asia, I'd guess. Don't tell me, I don't want to know. In fact, I know all I need to. Don't tell me anything else. Here's the deal."

I forced a smile and contemplated the supposed big-shot banker. For some reason the sight reminded me that I had been too busy to eat lunch today.

"You'll wire me the half mil today. That's my fee. I want no stake in whatever you're after. Your upside, your risk. I'll get the missing information for you, and I'll get it today. You're in a hole and you need this deal. From where I'm sitting, you look pretty desperate. I'm the only shot you've got at this."

He drew his lip back in a snarl. His contempt for me was obvious but so was his predicament. I hadn't been entirely sure until just now.

"Fine," he said. "You'll have your half million within the hour. But if you don't find that information, and if we don't close this deal within a month, I want that money back."

"If we don't pull it off, you can have half back," I said as I stood up. I didn't wait for a reply, nor did I bother with any polite parting phrases.

Werner Adler

I left the meeting room and went down the stairs and past the guard and past the receptionist without as much as looking up at anyone. I had far too much on my mind, too many thoughts knocking around like so many billiard balls after a strong break. It made sense on some level. I wasn't as far ahead of the game as I thought. At least I knew what shape a piece I was looking for.

I folded up the collar on my coat, walking out in the drizzle, heading off the small windy tourist alleys and out of the Old Town. I walked at a slower pace turning up on Bahnhofstrasse. A tram rang out its angry buzzing noise at a tourist couple walking out in front of it, making them jump back in fright. I kept away from roaming packs of Asian tourists, away from the crowded tram stops, making myself as visible as I could. He must be somewhere nearby. Trying to reacquire his target. This time I wanted him to find me.

I stopped to look into the Audemars Piguet display window, squinting at the new forty-one-millimeter Offshore, wasting time. Getting eager I turned and scanned the streets. No coat in sight. Starting off slowly in the direction of my office, planning on stopping by a few more display windows along the way, I spotted someone. But not whom I was looking for.

For a world financial center, Zurich is a very small town. It's hard to take a walk in the city center without running into familiar faces. She hadn't spotted me yet, not until I was almost all the way up to her. Sandra was just walking out of a Starbucks with a white paper cup in her hand, heading in the direction of the office when I caught up with her.

"Something wrong with the coffee machine?" I asked her.

"Jesus, don't sneak up on me like that, Jim!" she snarled.

"Say, you wouldn't happen to have seen a short Bogart knockoff with an acute neck deficiency hanging around the neighborhood, have you?"

She brushed my question off with a look. That familiar look she gives me when I'm misbehaving and should be taking things more seriously.

"I tried to reach you on your mobile. Did you forget to charge it or something?"

"Yeah, something like that," I said, not feeling like explaining how my paranoia got the better of me. "Busy day. You know how it is."

"Sure, I bet barely legal socialites can wear out the best of them. Listen, you had an odd phone message before. That's why I tried to reach you."

We walked together up the side street to the office. I looked behind me but didn't see any shadow.

"My definition of odd has been somewhat revised in the past couple of days."

"He didn't leave a name. Well, not a real one anyhow. When I insisted on a name, he called himself Mister C."

"Well, what did he want?"

"He said that you have a mutual problem that he wishes to discuss. He suggested that you join him this afternoon for a chat. He sounded... scary. Eastern accent. Used polite words but it still felt like a threatening phone call, you know what I mean? Left a number for you. Jim, we should call the police. This could be one of the guys who killed Raph! Gave me the creeps, the way he spoke to me."

We came up outside the office and I came to a halt. I couldn't go up yet. I had just spotted something.

"Stakes are too high at the moment. I've got to see this through. Don't worry, I know what I'm doing. Listen, you go ahead. I'll be up in a moment."

She looked scared and she doesn't scare all that easily. I hated to have to leave her like that. She continued up to the office while I turned in the direction of the corner cafe.

I didn't walk in a straight line, didn't want to spook him. I headed in an arc as if my route was through the nearby alley, only turning at the last moment into the coffee shop where he sat waiting for me. Once inside I went straight for his table. He had the perfect spot for observing who enters or leaves my office across the street.

He looked startled when I approached, and I didn't give him any time to react. I pulled out the chair opposite his.

"Suppose we both stop sneaking around and have a chat," I said as soon and sat down.

His face was pale and round, his eyes tired with bags under them, his nose wide and flat - his hair now freed from the hat was sparse and dark with gray streaks. I hadn't noticed the mustache earlier. Thick and bushy, all gray with little curls by the ends. Best guess would be early sixties.

Seeing his face made me doubt my assumption about him. The heavily accented reply removed all doubts.

"Suppose we would, Mr. Dixon," he agreed as his surprised expression turned into a smile. "Suppose we would."

"You want to tell me who you work for and why you're following me?"

The portly Swiss man set down the white ristretto cup and reached for the left side of his jacket. I leaned closer to him over the table, my own hand at the ready, showing him that it was at the ready.

A Most Private Bank

"You'll have to excuse me if I'm a little paranoid, but you may want to be real careful in what you do next, Mister." I spoke slowly, perhaps in an overly hostile manner, to compensate for my somewhat empty threat. If there would have been a gun in that jacket, there'd be little I could do about it. He seemed surprised, taken aback from my change in demeanor. His hand froze where it was.

"My good sir. I merely intend to reach for my wallet so that I can offer you a business card and explain myself. May I proceed?"

Bloody overly polite Swiss. I remained at the ready, nodding to him. "Nice and slow now."

His eyes remained locked on mine and his hands moved slowly. The left hand opened his jacket, showing a lack of concealed weapons while the right hand fished up the wallet from the inner chest pocket. He laid the black leather wallet down carefully on the table between us and set his hands down visibly on the white tablecloth. He was not nervous. Not concerned in the least. This was nothing new to him.

"Go ahead, Mr. Dixon." He nodded toward the wallet, inviting me to examine it. Somewhat calmer I picked it up and opened it. "Side pocket," he suggested. A few credit cards. Plenty of cash. The Swiss driver's license was the first thing I took out, laying it down on the table in front of me. Werner Adler.

The side pocket had his business cards and I laid one out next to the driver's license on the tablecloth. *Adler & Frey Privatdetektivbüro*. Shaking my head, I put the driver's license back, leaving the business card as I slid the wallet back to him.

"You licensed to carry?" I asked him.

"Certainly not. This is not America, Mr. Dixon."

I leaned back in my seat, a bit more relaxed. "I'll take your word for it. Who hired you?"

That brought a smile to his round face. "Come now, Mr. Dixon. You know better than that."

He was right and I could only agree. This was not the hired thug I had expected. This was not someone who could be pushed around, this was a career detective of one of the oldest bureaus in the country. He knew the score.

"Seems to me we both need information. We could part here, and you could continue to try to follow me around some more, or we could negotiate some sort of trade," I suggested. "What are you looking for from me?"

He studied me for a moment. This man would be easy to underestimate. His age along with that portly round body, skin bags under his eyes, and chin could easily give the impression of someone over the hill. Someone who's no threat to anyone. But those eyes probing me left little doubt - those where trained and alert eyes, missing nothing.

"You have involved yourself in a developing situation around a certain bank. You are fronting for someone. Can you tell me who your client is?"

Now it was my time to smile. I mimicked his body language from a minute ago, smirking and shaking my head at him.

"Oh, please. Come now, Mr. Adler."

"Quite. I hope you take no offense in me trying my luck. Allow me to volunteer some information in the hope that you will reciprocate. From my client's point of view, you represent a wild factor in what should have been a simple situation, Mr. Dixon. A monkey in the wrench, is that the correct American colloquialism?"

"Close enough. I can appreciate that."

"My client is concerned as to your motives and the attention that your actions are drawing to the situation."

I felt my eyes flash with rage for a moment and he saw it. "You better not be insinuating that the murder of my friend was due to my actions."

He held his palms up in a gesture of apology. "A poor choice of words, I do concede. Mea culpa. I merely meant that a sudden influx of violence is a concern." He made a pause for me to nod, accepting his apology.

"My client merely wishes to ascertain the nature of your interest. The task I am charged with is risk assessment, Mr. Dixon. To establish if you are part of the problem or part of the solution," he continued.

I studied his eyes as he spoke. Sharp, piercing eyes. Not a hint of uncertainty.

"I'll buy that. My interest in this situation is monetary, Mr. Adler. I have been contracted to facilitate a transaction, and I have been offered an attractive sum for my services. My part is about making a deal happen for a third party. That's it."

My true interests were far more than monetary. The money mattered - it actually did. But money was not my real motivation for doing any of this. Not that it was any of his business.

"Do you have any thoughts on why you have been offered such an attractive sum, Mr. Dixon?"

I turned and made eye contact with the waitress behind the counter, making a hand signal to get two more coffees.

"Your line of work has similarities to mine, Mr. Adler. We both get paid well to handle aboveboard parts of developing situations. Our respective fields are highly regulated and even respectable. I'm sure you can guess, at times, that there is something larger going on. Something you're not being told. Something you're best off not knowing.

"I stay on the side of the law, Mr. Adler. But like you, I know when not to ask questions. I'm sure a man like you can appreciate that."

We were interrupted for a moment as the two diminutive ristretto cups were placed on our table. The man in front of me didn't take his eyes off mine as he emptied the scalding-hot cup into his mouth.

"So you have no interest in any underlying value? Merely in an... aboveboard transaction fee?"

I nodded as I brought my own cup to my mouth. Far too hot for me to drink, but for some reason I still pretended to take a sip.

"I would prefer it if I never find out. As long as I get paid, of course."

He drew air slowly. There was a pause, a lull in the conversation. A time for us both to study each other, measuring each other up once again.

"As you say, Mr. Dixon, I will buy that. Does this imply that you are open to alternative business arrangements? Better deals, so to speak."

I shrugged back, blowing on the hot coffee before taking a small sip.

"Business is business. If you've got a deal to propose, go ahead."

"That is hardly my place, Mr. Dixon. But I will convey the possibility to my employer."

"Tell him one more thing." I set the cup down and stood to my feet. "If he's responsible for what happened in my office, no amount of payoffs will keep me from destroying him. Thanks for the coffee."

Penn and Teller

She was on the phone when I got back up to the office. I threw my coat over a chair and went up to her desk. Without finishing her private phone call, she pushed over a note to me. There was a local phone number on it along with the scribbled name *Mister C*. She pushed the note over to me without even glancing my way, continuing her phone conversation.

I picked it up and walked past the trading room into my office, shutting the door behind me. I set the note down on the desk in front of me. Reaching for the phone, I caught a glimpse of the dark spot on the floor. I wouldn't have it removed. I wouldn't change the carpet. I wouldn't forget and I wouldn't forgive.

He answered on the first ring. Must have been expecting my call. Even though the reply was simply, "Yes?", there was no mistaking the Russian accent.

"I just spoke with your errand boy. I suggest we drop the intermediaries and meet face-to-face," I started and he didn't miss a beat, didn't hesitate and if there was any surprise he didn't show it.

"I hear you're a man I can do business with, Mr. Dixon. A straight shooter," he said.

"It's not a metaphor I'm particularly keen on at the moment," I said.

"You have been a hard man to reach, Mr. Dixon. I shall very much like to have you over for dinner. There is a car waiting downstairs, unless you have any pressing engagements, of course."

"I'll be there," I replied and set the phone down.

Russians. Russians with means. The last complication this situation needed. I sat there a few minutes staring at the wall, and the wall stared back at me.

She was off the phone when I got back out there, looking at me as if demanding answers. She was entitled to them. But I had none to offer.

"Would you look in on Chris for me? Just keep her company this afternoon?" I asked her. She must have seen the worry in my face. She didn't even ask.

"Of course. Where is she?"

Trusted old dependable Sandra. Always there when she's needed.

"My suite at the Hyatt. My car's in the underground garage too. She's got the key. Listen, I'll explain when I can, but for now—"

"It's fine, Jim. I've got this. Any danger?"

"I'm not sure. Might be. I just need you with her and her out of sight. One more thing… If you haven't heard from me by tomorrow morning, call Guy. Tell him to find me."

She reached for my hand on her desk but I pulled it away.

"Jim. You're scaring me. Where are you going? Are you in danger?"

"I'll call you in the morning. If not sooner. Gotta run. Got a car waiting."

I took my coat under my arm, wishing I had my hat. Sure enough, a black Mercedes was waiting downstairs, parked illegally halfway up the sidewalk with the engine running. That ruled out a Swiss driver. Hardly a surprise. The city of Zurich employs an army of parking attendants and anyone local knows better than to stop like that.

Two men were up front. The driver was a large man, the shape of a snowman with shirt buttons over his belly straining. The round head appeared to be mounted straight onto the torso, and only the cold hard eyes prevented him from giving a comical appearance. The passenger was his mirror opposite, a slim man whose shirt buttons bulged over his chest rather than his belly. Their physiques aside, they shared the same cold, dead eyes.

As I approached, the slim man in the passenger seat nodded to me and I opened the back door, jumping in. I hadn't even closed the door fully before it took off. The driver was apparently not used to how an overpowered AMG engine revs up, the deep roar turning tourist heads along Bahnhofstrasse.

"Hiya, fellas. Where're we heading?" I tried.

"No English," came the unconvincing reply from the Slavic voice of the driver.

"You wanna give me some names? Laurel and Hardy? Chip and Dale? Penn and Teller?"

"No English!" insisted Penn.

I didn't believe that but no sense in arguing. If they're told not to talk, they're told not to talk. As they headed toward the Milchbuck tunnel, I opened my mouth, ready to explain to them about the ongoing roadwork up ahead. About how we'd be stuck in traffic this time of the day. But if they wanted to pretend not to speak English, let them. I leaned back in the comfortable leather seat again, getting ready for a long drive.

Predictably, the traffic came to a crawl, and the equally predictable Russian profanity came from the front seat. Serves them right.

Exiting the city to the northeast, I had my guesses. I was hoping that I would be wrong, but we kept following the autobahn along a familiar path.

"Airport?" I tried. No reaction. "*Aeroport*?" I tried in my best imitation of a Russian accent. I got a look from Teller that suggested that I might want to cut it out.

Penn took the airport exit off the autobahn but didn't follow the usual approach. Not toward the parking garage and not toward the drop-off area. It had been a while, but I knew this path too. A smaller road by the side of the airport, something that most regular travelers would assume to be for maintenance vehicles. Now I knew exactly where I was heading.

The door buzzed open mere seconds after they pressed the button. I glanced up at the camera as we entered the discrete side door of the airport. Something of a miniature of airport security checkpoint was in front of us, complete with a tired-looking border officer who didn't even bother to get out of his seat.

Teller went through the metal-detection frame first. The detector went off like a Christmas tree, red lights blinking along with a loud beep. He kept walking, and the officer didn't even turn his head. I went next and there was no surprise that my phone and keys set off the same alarm. Still, no one cared. After me, Penn carrying a suitcase. The machine beeped for the third time, and the supposed security guard finally spoke up.

"Enjoy your flight, gentlemen," he said.

"Thank you," Teller replied.

I shook my head, "No English, huh? This terminal is nice. I don't know why I don't check in here every time."

My attempt to get a reaction fell flat, and the three of us exited straight onto the tarmac. Another Mercedes was waiting for us there. No longer surprised, just eager to see whose plane we were heading to and what he wanted with me, I jumped in the back. Not bothering with the seat belts, we headed out toward the private hangars.

They say that deep down, everyone is poor. Nowhere else is

that principle better demonstrated than at the private hangars at Zurich's Kloten Airport. Just like the guy driving a Porsche feels poor when he's parked next to a Maserati, the owner of a Gulfstream V is the big boy on the block until someone shows up with a G650.

The planes were lined up near the hangar almost as if the purpose was to facilitate such comparisons. Closest to us was an Embraer Phenom 100, tiny in comparison to the others. Takes five passengers and could take you from Zurich to Istanbul, but no farther. We passed it and the Citation XLS next to it.

I was hoping that we were heading for one of the smaller planes, but this didn't seem to be a day where wishes come true. The Mercedes came to a halt by the steps leading up to a Bombardier Global 5000. Not the largest plane around, but certainly not among the smaller.

The tarmac smelled of jet fuel. It was windy here with only the hangar to break some gusts. Gray skies, heavy dark clouds approaching in the distance.

I stepped out of the car and was approaching the stairs leading up to the plane door when Teller stopped me.

"Phone," he demanded, holding his hand out.

"Forget it," I replied, trying to stare him down. He looked tough for a little guy. His was nose crooked, likely from being broken more than once. A boxer. Some other kind of fighter.

"You give telephone and walk on plane, or I take telephone and throw you in plane."

Penn had moved up behind me, and the situation didn't leave much room for negotiation. Reluctantly I fished the phone out of the inner jacket pocket and handed it over.

"I'm gonna need that back. Hey!" The man behind me was actually frisking me. Grubby Russian hands feeling me up.

"What, you think I've got a weapon? What's wrong with you?" After a quick search, he shoved me to the stairs.

"Push me again and you and me have a problem," I said as I walked up the stairs. The man with my phone stayed on the tarmac. The other followed close behind. As I came to the top of the stairs, I saw the plane's name painted on the fuselage. The *Rubicon*.

How fitting, I thought as I stepped inside.

Kyril Chekhov

The maître de cabine had a beaming white smile on her face as she greeted and welcomed me on board. Six feet, flowing blond hair, built like a model.

"Mr. Dixon, welcome aboard the *Rubicon*. My name is Stephania and I will be in charge of cabin service on board. Anything you need, don't hesitate to ask," she said with the happy, bubbly voice of a twentysomething with only a slight trace of a Slavic accent.

"Parachute, perhaps…" I muttered as I walked past her into the cabin.

The aircraft had the standard layout for this model. At least that's what it looked like. Three sections all with wooden panels that can be closed off for privacy. In the first, four large armchairs in cream leather faced each other. Two on each side of the isle. That's where the fat comedian from the car sat down.

The next partition also sported a cabin attendant. It didn't feel like a coincidence that another tall, slim blonde was greeting me. Perhaps they got a discount deal on blondes.

"Good afternoon, Mr. Dixon. My name is Alexis. This way, please," she said rather superfluously given that there was really no other way to go. "Dinner will be served shortly. I do hope you are hungry."

I nodded a silent greeting and stepped past her, into the middle section of the cabin. The dining area. Another group of four leather armchairs, this time close together, all on the left side of the aircraft with a dining table between them. A white cloth on the table, the setting prepared for two. This section looked more like a VIP room in a Michelin restaurant than what most people would associate with aircrafts.

I continued forward, to the final section. It too looked as I would have expected. The lounge area, a three-seater couch, two armchairs, and a little coffee table in the middle. That's where he was waiting for me. A face I had only seen in the news.

"Mr. Chekhov. Thank you for the invitation," I said, extending my hand to him.

"Call me Kyril. Please, please, have a seat," the gray-haired man with the well-kept beard replied. His voice was heavy and coarse, and even the polite words sounded like an implied threat. His shirt did little to hide the physique of an aging prize boxer, his dark eyes deep set and narrow, his gaze painfully piercing.

He was seated leaning forward, an elbow supporting against his knee, the other hand extending to shake mine. His white shirt sleeves were rolled up over his elbows, and his forearms were covered in faded tattoos. A large scar over his left forearm, long since healed, and hands that betrayed the experience of a man not unaccustomed to hard work.

Kyril Chekhov was a familiar face. In the past decade he had moved from a minor and relatively unknown player in the presumed Ukrainian underworld to a respectable international businessman. Amazing what buying a Premier League team can do to rehabilitate your respectability. Makes me wonder why everyone doesn't do it. Of course, it didn't hurt that he was locked up on racketeering charges when Uncle Sam made a move on Crimea. Being in prison at the time made you an instant freedom fighter. They even gave him a seat in the new Mickey Mouse parliament after the revolution.

He motioned to the closest armchair opposite the coffee table after the vicelike handshake that nearly crushed my hand. I had been too focused on him to notice what was on that coffee table. Well, there was no way back now.

"I am a man who likes to indulge in life's little pleasures, Jim. One never knows when one's pointless little existence will end. Better to enjoy it while it lasts, I say," he growled as he filled the two shot glasses with vodka.

"Without a bit of fun, life makes little sense," I agreed and swiftly downed my shot, slamming it down on the table at the same time as he did. The fact that I didn't cough on the strong vodka seemed to amuse the old Russian bear. He reached for the bowl next to the bottle of vodka. The bowl with the flour-looking powder which I hoped in vain was actually flour.

"Tell me, Jim. A man of your background must be a man of discretion, no? A man who likes to keep his mouth shut," he continued as he shook the bowl to build a little pile of the powder on the mirror next to it.

I shrugged back. "I've got a big mouth. It's not easy to get me to stop. Takes a whole lot of dough to shut me up."

That made him break into a big, wolfish laugh.

"Splendid, splendid. A man of my own taste. What's worth doing is worth doing for money, is that how it goes? Just splendid. I distrust people who claim to be tight-lipped. More often than not they turn out not to be. So much the better with a man who makes his interests clear."

There was a razor blade on the mirror next to the newly created little mountain of powder and he used it to part the mountain in two before proceeding to reshape the two piles into two straight lines making sure to break all the little lumps. He had a white straw in his hand, and he leaned down over the mirror, holding his left nostril while putting the straw to the other, pulling in air hard, and sucking up the left line of the powder.

He sat back looking up at the ceiling, holding his nose for a couple of seconds before pushing the mirror with the remaining line over to me. His face showed clear disapproval when I waved off the plastic straw but shined up in a big toothy grin when I took my wallet out and rolled up a twenty. His red eyes watched me closely while I replicated his action and leaned down over the remaining line, pulling it up into my left nostril, holding the right one with my finger.

I held my nose shut for a moment, closing both nostrils, nodding slowly to him.

"Good quality. Own import?" I asked him, letting go of my nose.

He brushed off the question. "Good, good. Very good. I distrust a man who does not indulge. People who don't trust themselves enough to enjoy. Those who are worried about what they might do after a bit of stimulation. But you, Jim. I think we can get along, you and me. I do think we can get along."

I ran my finger over the leftovers on the mirror where my line had been, scooping it up on my fingertip, rubbing it over my upper gums.

"Are we getting to the point any time soon, Kyril? Or are we doing a few more lines first?"

That made the bear of a man in front of me break out in a loud, almost violent laughter. I sat back to watch and wait.

"A man who is afraid to speak his mind is not much of a man. I am sure you would agree. I do like a straight-up conversation. Yes, to the point. Very good. Very good indeed, Jim."

"You wanna have a straight-up conversation about Bank Niederhauser?"

That made him laugh out loud again. A loud, bellowing laughter that no one from the cabin crew to the bodyguard to the pilots, if there were any in the cockpit could have missed.

"I do. I do indeed. That is, after all the purpose of your little visit. Yes, no beating around the bush with you, is there? To the

A Most Private Bank

point it is. Straight to business without the foreplay, as it were. Yes, I do think we can do business, Jim. Let us talk about the bank indeed. As a straight shooter, do tell me, Jim. Are you here on the behest of young Ms. Walker? Do you speak for her?"

"I speak for no one but myself," I replied, attempting to show no surprise over the question.

"Very good, very good, sir. You are then representing yourself and your own interests? I do respect that. A man not afraid to look out for number one." The grinning bear continued to test my patience as the coke started to slowly make itself known in my brain. I took a deep breath feeling that all-powerful sensation, the buildup of endorphin and adrenaline, the razor-sharp focus, and the lack of any fear of any kind.

"Did she tell you what this is all about? What the angle is, what she is looking for? Why this is worth so much to her? Worth enough for her to do all the things she did?" he asked while shaking out a new white mountain range on the mirror. *Good*, I thought. *At least with the coke I can still focus. Too much of that vodka and God knows what happens.*

"Didn't ask. Don't know, don't care to. My part is to make the deal happen. That's it. I've got no other stake," I lied, repeating the same line I had told others this week.

"Ours is not to reason why, ours is but to do and die?" An amused faced grinned at me.

I shrugged back. "Not sure I'm your man for charging Sevastopol, but I suppose Tennyson had a point. Properly compensated, I'm perfectly happy not to reason why."

I wasn't sure if I should feel offended when this highly successful mobster gave me an impressed grin as if he hadn't expected me to recognize that poem. I tried not to show him that I was equally surprised to realize that he was an educated man, or at least that he made pretenses of being one.

"You really have no idea what storm you are in the middle of. And you really don't care. I can respect that, I really can. Well then, tell me your interests in the outcome of this affair, and I shall tell you mine."

Again he parted the powder into two and made neat lines as if the very motion was second nature to him, something entirely locked in motor memory. Not little bumps. Full lines. The first line had just started to take effect, and this pace was far too fast for my liking, but I wasn't about to kick up a fuss.

"My interest," I said as I picked up the twenty I had left on the table, rolling it back into a proper straw shape, "is to see this deal through. To facilitate the buyout of Bank Niederhauser through the entity I arranged. If that deal goes through... I'm happy. I have zero interest in the supposed hidden value of the bank, nor do I want any ownership stake. I get paid if the buyout goes as planned."

I couldn't tell him the full extent of my interest. It would not have been to my advantage to show curiosity or to tell him about the rest.

After snorting his own line, he pushed the mirror back to me, and my own makeshift twenty-franc straw was at the ready. I listened to him as I pulled the line up into my right nostril, hoping to alleviate the blocked nose issues somewhat by alternating.

"My interests do not necessarily conflict with yours. Though I do need a favor. And you may just be the man to grant it to me."

I nodded to him while holding the nose shut, taking in the powder. "Favors cost money, Kyril."

"There is something in the bank that I require," he said, ignoring my comment. "Something that should not land in the wrong hands. Something that would make me upset... were it to land in the wrong hands. Get the picture, Jim?"

"In Technicolor." I sighed.

A Most Private Bank

"My interest, the hidden value, as you put it, is in information. Papers. Papers with names on them."

Can opening. Worms starting their crawl to freedom.

"What I am in the market for is small, light, easily carried. Likely stored in a safe box inside the bank, a safe box that very few people would have access to."

I already knew. Perhaps I should have already known before. The can was wide open. No way to get those worms back in. No need to play ignorant anymore.

"Beneficial ownership statements. For yourself or others?" I asked outright, my judgment impaired by the cocaine in my membrane.

I wished I could have remained ignorant, that I could have at least pretended it might be something else. Beneficial ownership statements were the secret documents, the papers that identified the true owners of accounts and assets. Information not found on any computer system, information that could destroy so many rich and powerful people if it were ever to be made public. Information worth killing for.

My question was met by another giant bear grin. "Just get me all of it, and let me do the sorting."

"I'm not in the business of corporate theft, Kyril. You got the wrong guy."

"I started out with the wrong guys. The kind of dogs that bite their master's hand for a tiny bit more meat."

"That why you put Petrov down?" I asked. He scoffed off my question.

"I'm a businessman, Jim. What happened at the Dolder strike you as good business?"

I shrugged, reaching for the bottle of vodka, pouring up two fresh glasses for no other reason than to stall for a moment.

"I've heard what you have to say, and I will take it under advisement. If I do find myself in a position to assist, it would cost you. We done here? I've got a busy day."

At first I thought it was the Gulfstream next to us that was taxiing out. That feeling you have when a train on the next platform starts moving and for a few seconds you can't be sure if it's you or them moving. It was us.

"My chef makes an Entrecôte Café de Paris to die for. Truly spectacular. I hate to dine alone and, in particular when such interesting company is at hand."

It was too late to object. We were on the runway and the engines were powering up. Nothing to do but to lean back as the plane took to the skies.

Cruising Altitude

Once the plane was at cruising altitude, we moved to the middle section of the cabin where the table had already been prepared. Four seats, but the table was set for two. The smell coming out of the galley was appealing, that was hard to deny. But the fact that we were airborne on a plane with a reach of six thousand miles was concerning. Enough for a nonstop flight to anywhere from Tokyo to Cape Town to São Paulo.

The two model-like cabin attendants were on standby as we took our seats, placing the white napkins in our laps, moving the vodka and coke from the lounge area to our table. When they showed me the wine menu, I jumped on the opportunity to move from vodka to wine. Quite an impressive wine cellar for an aircraft. I picked a nice Bordeaux, swirled it in the glass, smelled and tasted it before nodding my approval.

The two wine glasses filled in front of us, he lifted his to mine. "To a profitable cooperation." I touched my glass to his and took another sip. The girls were serving us the starters, some sort of French-style seafood salad and he veered back to business.

"Tell me, Jim. Where did you hide away young Ms. Walker? A good job dodging my surveillance, you did. Twice you lost them. And she hasn't been back to that roach-infested hotel since this morning. Say, I would very much like a word with her."

"Not sure I'd call Flemings roach infested," I replied, glancing at how the girls expertly started preparing new lines on the mirror.

"Don't tell me you've developed some sort of attachment, Jim." He grinned. "It would be unbecoming. You and me are alike. Mercenary."

I can't really remember snorting the line, but I must have.

"Can't blame me for protecting my interests, Kyril. I need her, to see this deal through."

"And you believe that without your benevolent protection she would be found floating facedown in the Limmat? I should be offended. You hurt my feelings, you really do," he said with that big white bear grin on his face, holding the nostril that he just pulled the coke into.

"You wanna tell me where we're heading, Kyril?" I asked, looking out the window. Clouds there and nothing else. I could see the sun and I should have been able to figure out if we were heading east or west but couldn't.

"Funny thing, having your own plane, Jim. No manifests. No security checks. No real ones anyhow," he said opening his armrest compartment taking out a nine-millimeter Beretta and casually placing it next to the coke mirror on the table. "No one ever checks what or who goes on the plane. Or what comes off."

The black automatic laid on its side on the table, pointing toward me, he picked up his knife and fork and started cutting the sirloin beef, which had arrived without me noticing. I looked down at the gun and the little red dot near the hammer. He made no attempt to stop me as I reached over and flipped the safety catch on, covering that red dot, and swiveled the gun to have it point to the fuselage rather than my gut.

"Melodrama is no excuse for poor firearms safety," I told him and picked up my own knife and fork, digging into the meat. That set off another thundering laugh from the old thug. Even the girl refilling my glass seemed to think this was particularly funny. Made me wonder where one finds young stewardesses who think drugs and gunplay on aircrafts is amusing.

"Yes, indeed, sir. Well played, well played indeed. A man cowering at the sight of a barrel is not much of a man. No, you may keep your little secret. And your little girl. For now. But scores will be have to be settled. I'm sure a man of your background has no problems with that. No, we shall see this through. You will get me what I need. And then we shall tally up."

The plate of meat in front of me was gone. Did I eat it? When did it disappear? I wasn't hungry anymore. The drugs were messing with my sense of time. I felt strong, focused, determined. But I had no idea how long we had been in the air. We could be over Siberia for all I knew.

"So we understand each other?" he asked me.

Had I been dozing off? Had I been asleep? I felt so focused, so determined, but still I had the feeling that I'd missed something, that I hadn't been paying attention. As if out of motor memory, I pulled another line of powder before replying.

"I got the message. All will get sorted at the cocktail party," I said confidently while another part of my brain wondered what cocktail party I was talking about. "No sweat, Kyril. I'll get it done. I always do."

The flight attendants were topping us up. Stephania was replacing the empty wine bottle, corking up a new bottle of the same vintage, while Alexis made a few more lines on the mirror for us.

"Good man. We'll be landing in an hour. Plenty of time. Which one do you like?" he asked me.

Cocktail Party

When I exited the aircraft, I had no idea where I was. Private plane hangars look the same all over the world. Cocktail party? What cocktail party? I staggered down the ladder, down to the tarmac, with the Russian heavy behind me. It was bright outside. Not sunny, but bright. There was fog around the tarmac and the air was moist. Cold. At least we're not in South America. I checked the Patek on my wrist. Why hadn't I done that before? Seven. A.m. or p.m? Had I reset it during the flight? Was this local time or Zurich time?

A Mercedes was waiting for me. A driver behind the wheels. I came down to the tarmac and turned to look back up. Stephania was smiling at me. "Enjoy your day, Mr. Dixon," she said.

I tried to remember. Had I..? I wasn't sure.

I got in the back of the Merc, and the gorilla got in the passenger seat. The driver reached back, holding out something for me. "Your phone," he said in an Eastern accent.

"No English," I replied for some reason, mimicking his accent, taking the phone. Was this the same thug? It must be. Yes, that's Teller all right.

I looked around me as we drove out of the hangar, approaching a terminal. Passing the main terminal, the sign was clear. *Zürich Flughafen.* The bastard had circled over Switzerland for half a day. Sure, at ten thousand a flight hour, why not take a little joyride.

The same sleepy customs officer attended the private jet arrival and departure area. All three of us beeped loudly as we walked past the metal scanner while the officer kept reading his book. I knew the drill by now. The next Mercedes was still waiting

A Most Private Bank

in the parking spot where we left it earlier.

"Take me to the Hyatt," I told the driver, but no such luck.

"Niet. Cocktail party," he replied.

Goddamn cocktail party.

"Fine. Got any water?"

A bottle of Evian was handed to me, and I leaned back in the seat for some rest. I might need it. My brain went over the conversation on the plane again and again, searching for missing details. The fight between the alcohol and the coke raged in my brain. Stay focused. Stay clear. This is important.

It was starting to come back to me. I watched the road, trying to focus on the task at hand. Everyone will be there. Everyone who matters. This is where it all gets settled, where it all gets tied together.

I saw the car turn up the lake, away from the city, and I wasn't surprised. It had to be a larger place down the lake. He must have told me, but it didn't seem important. What did seem important was that I was starting to come down from the coke. The last thing I needed was the severe hangover that comes afterward. It had been many years and I had no tolerance. Nor did I care to build one. Focus.

The car came to a halt. Where were we? Küsnacht? Meilen? I couldn't tell. A tall gate opened and we pulled in slowly. An array of luxury cars, all neatly parked in front of the main building. The valet was waved off as I got out and my escort rounded the fountain in the middle of the driveway and made their way out again. I was on my own.

Music and chatter came from the nearest building, and a few people in cocktail dresses and evening suites mingled outside over champagne and cigarettes. I made my way inside, lifting a glass of bubbly off a tray that a waiter held out for me. The place was a veritable who's who of Swiss finance. You couldn't swing a cat here without hitting at least seven bankers and six financiers.

Making my way in took time. The finance community isn't all that big, and I had to make my way from table to table, shaking hands, exchanging a few words with the gnomes and their silicone-infused companions. Some fund manager just wouldn't shut up, pitching me his next big idea from the second he saw me. I lied and told him that I'd call him next week. Stuffing his card in my pocket, I found it. I didn't take it out. No need. I knew what it was. It felt like a gram.

Did he put it there? Was this his idea of a joke? Did I ask for it? I can't remember.

The living room was larger than most people's villas, and I bravely negotiated the terrain making it to the other side of the room. The plan was starting to come back to me along with bits and pieces of memories as the airplane vodka started to wear off. I scanned the room. This was a target-rich environment.

I spotted Todd Preston first. Looked like the same suit he had on yesterday in the meeting. Nina was there too. A long blue dress. High heels. Giggling at some fat old financier's jokes. Playing the game.

I waded right in. Ignoring the conversation they were in the middle of. Not caring.

"Todd. Good to see you. Need a word in private," I said, interrupting his anecdote mid-sentence. "Nina," I added with a polite nod to her. Based on the look she gave me, this must be a potentially valuable client they were in the middle of greasing.

"Of course. Excuse me, Mr. Bertschi. Nina, please explain our new custodial services to Mr. Bertschi," he said to his junior. If looks could kill, my troubles would already be over. I took the American banker aside, and we stepped out in the fresh air. I waited for us to be out of earshot from the tipsy people around us.

"It's screw or walk, Preston. In our out, right now."

He looked surprised and it didn't look like the usual bad banking theater.

"But... You got my message, didn't you? I called your office hours ago."

The phone. I still didn't turn it back on. And now I looked like an idiot.

"Been out all day. What's the score? In or out?"

"We're in. In like Flynn."

"Libor plus five?"

"Libor plus five. We're golden. In the kill zone. Locked and loaded. Provided you've got the equity part covered, of course. Forty mil. We match it in debt, dollar for dollar. Secured against your equity. We already drafted the contracts."

"Have them sent to my office in the morning."

"All done. Signed and everything. Just countersign and send back. Hey, why don't we get together next week to discuss next steps, perhaps over a round of golf? We'd love to have on you onboarded on the prime brokerage platform and—"

"I'll get back to you, Preston. Enjoy the evening."

One down. Easy. Greedy bastards. Sucking my kneecaps to get me back in. So much for due diligence. So why am I angry? No. Not now. I can't deal with the dopamine drain, not now. Need to stay focused.

I checked the Grand Complications. Good thing I hadn't switched. It was perfect for a place like this, for a mission like this. There was still time. These high-society mingle group jerks lasted for hours and hours. I searched around for a bathroom, and it must have been obvious. One of the penguins with an hors d'oeuvres tray cleared his throat next to me.

"Sir, around the corner to the right," he said discretely.

"Thanks, buddy," I replied and headed in the direction he indicated.

I nearly took the wrong door, not expecting there to be separate men's and ladies' rooms in a private home. But this was no ordinary private home. The guest bathrooms had multiple stalls, for lack of a better word. Small rooms inside the bathroom, each with a toilet, sink, and various amenities.

There was already a mirror on the sink. I looked closer at it. Yep. That was cocaine residue on it. Welcome to high society. I made a little bump with that gram bag I found in my pocket.

I had asked for it. For this exact reason. I knew I was going to come down at the worst possible time and that I'd need a bump to stay focused.

I pulled the line up my left nostril, thinking back to the plane. Most was clear to me. Not all. The actions required tonight. His promise to back off of Evelyn. Chris. Until everything is done. My own plan. The parts I lied about.

The lies I told a man who murdered his way to a Premier League owner's box.

I looked at my reflection in the mirror, wiping off a bit of visible powder on my nose. This was not what I needed, not today. It'd been years. Many years. Even then I barely touched the stuff.

Stephania. That smile. Oh, God. I had tried. The coke... didn't let me.

I gave myself a disgusted look in the mirror.

"Life all comes down to just a few moments. This is one of 'em," I said aloud and corrected my nonexistent necktie.

I flushed the toilet, as if anyone out there would have cared or paid attention, washed my hands, and stepped out.

The Boathouse

I was on the way to the boathouse, taking the small marble paved footpath from the back of the main house, when I heard my name. I hadn't expected him to be there. But then again, why wouldn't he be part of the same incestuous circle of the rich and dysfunctional. Why indeed.

"Jim. Need a word," he called out as I nearly passed without noticing him.

"Not a good time, Hill," I told the pudgy little spook without stopping.

"It's important. You'll want to hear this."

"Catch me later," I replied without turning my head to look at him.

Last thing I need now is the law. Or whatever it is that he represents.

There was soft lounge music playing from the boathouse. Soft-spoken conversations, occasional polite laughter from mingling financiers and their sycophantic hang-arounds. A hundred feet sailing catamaran in the dock, the centerpiece of the three-wall structure leading out into Lake Zurich.

Of course he was there. Standing by the stern of the catamaran in that navy-blue double-breasted jacket with shiny brass buttons. The right hand casually half tucked into the jacket pocket while the left held a champagne flute as he explained the finer points of yachting to some female junior banker a third his age, standing far too close and hovering over her.

Looks like a peacock in that ridiculous ascot. He actually thinks he's got a shot with that girl. He can be a sleazeball on his own time.

"Dick!" I called out from across the room, turning heads.

"Roll your tongue back in your mouth and get your checkbook out!"

I'm causing a scene. And I don't even care. Goddamned coke.

He was startled. Uncomfortable with the sudden attention. The room hushed up, discretely glancing at the out-of-control American.

"Could we perhaps talk outside?" he said softly before turning to the girl he was chatting up. "I'm so sorry. I promise to finish that story in just a moment."

He motioned for the open door and the path leading to the stables. First now, I noticed the other woman standing to his right. Must be at least fifteen years his senior, in her late seventies with a face that probably paid for a new beach house for some lucky plastic surgeon. That necklace was likely worth as much as the catamaran and the Jaeger-LeCoultre surprisingly tasteful. He was trying to usher me away from her. That made me curious.

"Jim Dixon, how do you do?" I said extending my hand to her.

"Mr. Dixon." She smiled. "I've heard so much about you. Ursula von Burg. Dick has been so excited about working with you. It would be good for him to build something on his own. Do let me know if I can be of any assistance, of course."

"Yes, I'm optimistic about my project with Mr. von Baerenfells as well," I replied while he seemed increasingly apprehensive next to us.

"Von?" she asked, but didn't wait for a reply. "Well, I'm sure you boys have a lot to talk about. Don't let me get in the way."

"Enjoy your evening, Mrs. von Burg."

Somehow the sleazy banker looked smaller as we walked out.

"I've got the info you need, Dick. I know where the stuff is and I've got forty-mil debt financing ready to go. I want your commitment right now. Handshake today, signed contract first thing in the morning. Yes or no, right now."

At least my lie had some element of truth in it. I knew where his secret gold was. I knew that it didn't exist.

His voice was muted. Soft and careful. "You... you found out the number of the boxes? How?"

"I know exactly where it is. Straight from the source. From the guy who told your guy. I can do this with or without you. Are you going to make a decision? Or do you need to go ask your girlfriend for permission?"

A tall man, his head tilted upward he looked down at me with contempt in his eyes. He remained quiet and so did I. A full-minute staring contest.

"Bühler will send you the contract. I'll get the wire done by the end of the week," he finally said between gritted teeth.

"Not good enough. Wire the proceeds first thing tomorrow morning."

I was pushing it. But he was desperate. I could smell it. *Bet it has something to do with that plastic patchwork over there.*

There was another pause, this one lasting shorter, and now his upper lip quivered as if he was holding back a rage. A big man and seemingly in good shape. A man used to playing the big shot, a man used to people backing down and giving him what he wants.

"The money will be on the account before lunch tomorrow. Now, if you excuse me." He strode off, back to the boat house.

I could have laughed out loud then and there. Two down. One to go. Where is he? I'll find him. After a mid-flight refuel.

I looked around for the restrooms. Too far back to the main building. I needed a jolt before the next step, and I made my way down to the water. The calm water washed against the boulders -

no one around but a family of swans. I didn't want to, but I knew I had to. I squatted down by one of the larger rocks and took the gram bag from my pocket and tipped out a bit on the stone. A bit too much. Never mind.

I leaned down to it and pulled it up my nose. The nostrils started getting blocked already. I wondered how much I'd had. I couldn't remember. The powder sloppily spread all over the stone, and I made another pass moving my head over it like a Stuka making a bomb dive. It hit me hard and fast this time. Made me feel strong. Smart. In control. Invincible.

King freaking Kong!

I beat my chest, making some sort of animal grunt. The family of swans gave me a disapproving look. Not that I could blame them.

I wiped the leftover powder off the stone, down into the water. The mother swan gave me another disapproving look.

"Hey, better you than me, lady," I told her and headed off toward the stables.

The Stables

Long, swift strides in the brisk evening air, eyes straight ahead, straight on target, ignoring bankers, asset managers, gold diggers, and the idle rich along the way. No time for pleasantries. It was almost done, almost locked, almost in the bag.

There he was again. Not giving up easily. And this time his handler was with the annoying little pug. I kept my eyes forward, dead set on ignoring them. Donahue stepped into my path. Hill by his side.

"Jim. The situation is escalating. We need to talk. Now."

You didn't need to know a thing about him to spot the American bureaucrat. He was in an off-the-rack black suit, nearly fitting but not quite, with a slim black necktie, as if he was auditioning for a high school production of Men in Black. Nobody dresses like that. Nobody but unimaginative American government men.

"Subpoena me or get the hell out of my way," I said as I speed walked a half circle around them down the stone footpath. My nose was blocked and I could hear it.

He grabbed me by the arm as I was heading past him, pulling me back. It took me by surprise. I didn't think the little bureaucrat had the guts to lay a hand on me. I stopped dead in my tracks and stared into his eyes point-blank. He spoke before I did. His words were calm and measured.

"Your country requires your cooperation. Incidentally, such cooperation may also help keep you out of prison."

"The hell you talking about, Donahue? You think you can throw some ridiculous threats at me like some schoolboy? Hill, get this guy out of my face before I break his."

I didn't like the smug grin on his face. He knew something I didn't, and it amused him.

"Two possibilities. Either you don't know, and that makes you incompetent. Or you do know, and you're just a common crook. Either way, you're exposed, Jim," he replied, keeping his calm while I was losing mine.

"You're out of your mind. You can go to hell, Donahue! That goes for you too, Hill!"

I slapped his hand away, freeing my arm of his grip.

"Touch me again and you'll draw back a bloody stump," I told him and turned to continue the path leading to the stables. It was stupid and I knew it. Drugs and stress doing the talking, brain trying to play catchup.

"Your funeral, Jim. Bet you'll look great in orange," that smug voice behind me replied. It was an absurd threat. But that's what worried me.

I tried to get his voice out of my head, approaching the stables, getting my game face on. The lights were on all around the riding pen and the nearby stables area, and there was the same soft buzz of a few dozen mingling guests. I scanned the crowd as I approached, trying to avoid making eye contact not to lose time getting stuck in polite conversation.

It really wasn't difficult to spot him. At least a head taller than the other men around and towering over the women. Cream-white double-breasted jacket with brass buttons, hair slicked back to cover the bald patch, a crimson pocket square, brown loafers, and blue jeans. Upper-class casual.

He was entertaining a woman just by the round pen, showing off a thoroughbred to her, patting the stallion's head while a handler held on to the reins. I locked on like a cruise missile and

A Most Private Bank

headed straight for them. The last piece of the puzzle.

I was so concentrated on him that it wasn't until I got all the way up to them that I saw whom he was talking to.

The devil was she doing there?

I froze up as I came all the way to them, face-to-face with the old sod. My loss of words did not afflict him.

"Ah, and there you are, Jim. Good man, just in time too. Jolly good. I was just in the middle of relaying last week's Ascot race to Ms. Rosenbaum—"

"Chris, please, Mr. Niederhauser," she said in that sweet bubbly voice that made men's knees week.

"Of course, and call me Nick. Everyone does, my dear," he beamed back at her. "As I was saying, Dancing Cloud here was my star performer last week. He just arrived back from Berkshire. Poor boy, such a long journey. Came in second, he did. By a nose, by God, by a nose! Next time, he'll do even better. Not bad for a four-year-old, eh, old boy?

"I believe you already know Chris? Part of your acquisition team, I understand. You have found a very competent lady here, Jim. That's what good breeding does for you. Just like with Dancing Cloud, a Rosenbaum is sure to excel. I was distraught to hear about your father, Christina. He was a dear friend and a client."

I was breathing hard but not out of breath. I was furious.

"Nick, I'm sorry do to this on your big night," I started while trying to remember if I even knew the reason for this little garden party for a few hundred of his closest friends. "Need to talk shop. Time is of the essence. Is there some place we can talk on the q.t.?"

He gave me a knowing smile and a nod, like a child thinking that no one around can see that you've got a secret.

"Of course, of course. Business before pleasure, that's what I always say."

He looked around, making some hand waving here and there and the hang-arounds cleared off one by one. Made me wonder if this was a common occurrence, to wave away the servants and guests from the racehorse pen to talk secrets. Probably was too. Even the handler started walking off with the thoroughbred trotting beside him. Left were me, the Swiss aristocrat, and her. Not what I had in mind. I glanced at her and back at him.

"Oh, I'm sure we can speak in front of Chris. She is a Rosenbaum, after all."

I shouldn't have given that Bolivian marching powder to the swans. Could use it right about now.

I took a deep breath and tried to focus. She didn't matter, not now. She could wait.

"Listen, Nick. It's decision time. I've got a deal in place, but it needs to be now. I've got eighty lined up, and I want as many percent for it. Deal expires at midnight."

"Turning into a pumpkin, will you?" the old banker mused. "A hundred million valuation seems a little tight. Need to speak to my brothers, you see. And my uncle. Nephews and such. You understand. Perhaps a hundred for eighty would make them act more swiftly, if you follow."

"Yeah, I follow. But eighty's all you gonna get, Nick."

The old man nodded and started walking slowly along the pen, expecting us to follow. I shot her a look. Hating that she was there. She just smiled back.

"If eighty is all there is, then fifty percent would be a more reasonable number."

What the devil is she doing here? Going behind my back?

"Sixty-five. Expiry just moved to five minutes from now. Tick. Tock."

A Most Private Bank

Silence. Two sets of sharp eyes staring at each other. Two men squaring off in an old-fashioned staring competition. Battle lines drawn. Whoever speaks first loses.

Soft lounge music from the nearby stables. Some light chatter from oblivious minglers outside. A goddamned frog croaking on a mossy stone by the shoreline.

All that's missing is rolling tumbleweed. I hope those swans are okay.

He put his hand out to me, those small, sharp translucence-white teeth grinning.

"Deal."

I took his hand. I shook it.

"Have the contract sent to me in the morning," I told him as I turned to take my leave.

"I would have given you seventy-five," he said as I turned my back.

"I would have taken fifty-five," I replied without turning back.

My heart was racing but it wasn't the negotiation. This bozo couldn't negotiate himself out of a barn. If he wasn't born with a nine-figure wealth he would have been fixing streets or sweeping floors.

Perhaps it was the powder. Perhaps it was anger. She was not supposed to be here.

I walked at a brisk pace back toward the front of the house, past the boathouse, past the white garden tent that had been set up on the lawn, past the gloved servants holding out drink trays, ignoring the voice behind me. But it was persistent, and it was gaining on me.

A Drive in the Rain

"Jim, wait up!"

I had pushed my way through the crowded ballroom, navigating the sea of tipsy bankers, c-list celebrities, and clueless heirs, and made it out the wide-open glass doors facing the front lawn. I made it all the way outside before my arm was grabbed. I spun around to face her.

"So much for laying low at the hotel. Got bored with CNN, did you?"

She frowned to me. Then she grinned. Finally she chuckled. Nearly laughed.

"That's why you're upset? You think, what, that I'm here because I'm secretly sleeping with that sleazy banker? Or that I'm in cahoots with him to screw you over?"

"Which sleazy banker? There's quite a few of them in there," I shot back.

"Take your pick! You want to hear what I'm doing here or not?"

Another black-clad man with white gloves and a tin tray and a French accent interrupted.

"Champagne, madame? Sir?"

I waved him off, nearly knocking his ridiculous little tray off his hand to send the neat formation of glasses crashing down.

"Spill it," I said to her.

She sighed as if she was dealing with an idiot. In all fairness, perhaps she was.

"That sleazy banker, the one you found me talking to.

Niederhauser. He called your office three times, looking for you. Your phone was off, and no one knew where you were. He said that he needs to see you today, urgently."

I already knew where this was going, and I felt like an idiot already. I put my hand up to stop her, but she would have none of that.

"Seems like he called half the town trying to get hold of you. Good job turning your phone off in a situation like this. Finally Sandra came to see me at the hotel. Well, you weren't going to show, so someone better get over here, don't you think?"

I looked at her shoes a moment as my breath steadied. I knew what she wanted to hear. No way I would actually apologize.

"You got my car, I suppose?"

She held the key up.

"Give it to me."

She yanked the key back again.

"Not a chance. You'll wrap it around the nearest tree. You high or just drunk?"

She had a point. I could hear how the alcohol had made me slur, and my heart was still doing Hula-Hoops from all the powder.

"Bit of both. Drive me home, then. To the hotel, I mean."

We walked the curving path from the left wing of the main building up to the horseshoe driveway with the fountain in the middle. I hadn't really looked around before, hadn't paid attention. The chemicals starting to reduce their concentration in my brain, I took a look around. What was it with the ultra-wealthy and their morbid lack of taste? I watched the slowly spinning round stone block on top of the fountain, the size of a Toyota. Not that this driveway would be caught dead with a Toyota. The most low-key of the cars I saw double-parked round the horseshoe was a dark blue Maserati. It looked a bit sad next to cars you could hear from across the lake with their engines off. The yellow Lamborghini. The neon-pink Ferrari with Russian plates. The red Porsche convertible with the white racing stripes. This was a place that Tony Montana would approve of.

She handed my key to a valet, and the car came rolling up in front of us. A gloved hand opened the driver-side door for her and she got in. The glove floated around to the other side of the car and it held the door open for me. I took out a twenty to tip the valet and got a disgusted look back as the white glove took the bill between the thumb and the index finger as if I'd just handed him a dead rat by the tail. Europeans.

I got into the passenger seat of my own car. Not a place I prefer to sit. Not a place I ever like to sit. The engine growled as she pulled around the horseshoe on too high rpm in first gear. I wanted to tell her to go easy on the gearbox, but she didn't look like she was in the mood for driving lessons.

"Off the grid all day. Great day to pick to go on a binge with your drinking buddies. Hadn't figured you for a coke fiend, though. And you smell like cheap perfume."

I wondered which part upset her the most. Not that it mattered.

"Well, are you going to explain yourself?" she demanded, like a stern headmistress scolding an insolent child.

I lowered my head like the naughty boy I apparently was and sighed.

"First some goons picked me up and drove me to the airport, and then a Russian gangster pulled a gun on me in his Global 5000 somewhere over the Alps before he plied with me enough coke and vodka to sedate a medium-size bear, and I suppose the smell is from the stewardess who sat in my lap during much of this, but I really can't remember all the details."

A Most Private Bank

I breathed in and waited as she digested that. She was doing sixty-five kilometers on Seestrasse. I cringed, knowing this road all too well. Even at the state I was in I knew exactly where the speed traps were usually placed. At sixty-five kilometers an hour, she was a measly three miles per hour over the limit, and I clinched my teeth, squinted my eyes, bracing for it. The six-feet gray metal tower with a large bulky foot and a window for a face must have been designed by George Orwell. Designed to instill fear and a feeling of being constantly monitored. Three miles or not, a sudden bright flash hit us in the face to notify us that we had violated Swiss law, had been photographed, and would receive a fine in the mail. Goddamned Swiss efficiency.

She eased back on the gas after that.

"Fine, tell me when you sober up, then."

I wanted to explain that what I had just said was true, but this was not the time.

"Are you at least sober enough to hear what I've found out? At least one of us has actually been working."

A single drop of rain hit the windshield just in front of my face. Large enough to leave a round puddle of water on the glass the size of a silver dollar. Then another. I watched and tried in vain to predict where the next one would land. The glass in front of me turned into a canvas with a beautiful artwork of Pollackian water splashes. Then the cruel and destructive wipers moved over the canvas without regard or remorse, wiping the slate clean. I still hadn't spoken.

"You may want to know a little bit about who you're doing business with. The sleazy banker, the other one, Baerenfells. He's as dumb and as greedy as they come. Got a huge chip on his shoulder. Married a twice-divorced society lady two decades his senior.

"Imagine that. He was a twenty-eight-year-old junior when

they met. She was a forty-seven-year-old Botoxed high-society lady just finishing up her second successful multimillion-dollar matrimonial exit. She got him that job at Niederhauser. She got him the promotions, she got him everything.

"Those watches he wears... they're hers. She lets him use them. Got them in her first divorce. The cars too. That ridiculous black Lamborghini. He loves to show off wealth, but the truth is that he doesn't have any. For all the posturing, he makes a measly two hundred at the bank. Another hundred in bonus if he's lucky. He's a nobody. Just a peacock.

"This secret so-called hedge fund he set up, well, that's her money. She lent it to him. Actually made him sign a loan agreement, can you believe that? She's letting him play this hedge fund fantasy, indulging his little boyhood dream. But he's a greedy little boy, isn't he? So now he's risking it all on this bank scam, trying to make some real money for himself for the first time in his life!"

I paid attention to her every word, to her smug, satisfied review of the evening's gossip. She took a sadistic kind of pleasure in this. And for some reason, so did I. I was impressed. The wipers were moving faster. The rain that had started with just a few large splashes had grown into a relentless whipping of cold and harsh waves slamming down on the screen.

"You got all that from some casual chat at a cocktail party?"

"Men like to brag to girls. I just happen to be very good at playing dumb, reading between the lines, and getting the information I need. In fact, I've made a pretty decent career out of it."

"Conclusions?" I asked.

"He's motivated by greed an inferiority complex. He lived a lie in the shadow of this woman for three decades, and he's desperate to get out. Sick of being treated like a little boy, getting an allowance, while playing the big shot to the outside world. He played it safe his whole life and doesn't know how to take calculated risks. Now he's in way over his head and doesn't understand the risks he's taking. He's ventured far across the Rubicon and has no way from here but forward. He can be pushed much further if needed."

I froze up for a moment when she used that word. *Did she know? Had she been on that plane? No. No, it's just an expression.*

I nodded to myself, feeling reluctantly impressed. She's good. A stone-cold killer.

"He has a weakness for young girls as well, but that's hardly unusual for middle-aged bankers. But I'd say his pressure point is money and pride, not sex. He even has the gall to call himself '*von* Baerenfells'. She's from a noble background - he's not. Kept her name when they got married, didn't let him share it. Probably eats him up inside. She's not a dummy, though. Shrewd, focused. Must have made at least fifty mil on her divorces. Picked the young banker as a toy boy and kept him around on a short leash. You don't want to cross her."

"Yeah... Good job," I said, nodding along. That's when she dropped the bomb.

"He's the leak, you know."

As if hit by a lightning strike, I sat upright in the shape-fitted Merino seat. Any residual effect of alcohol or cocaine vanished along with any fog of my mind.

"What makes you say that?" I fired back.

"He's practically advertising it, isn't he? All the leaks so far concern his clients. Clients he would have full insight of. Now, that might be a coincidence, sure. But then add in that he's been on a spending spree. He couldn't wait to tell me about his new Maserati GranCabrio. Four hundred and sixty horsepowers, V8 engine topping out at 288 kilometers an hour. He was so eager to explain all the little details. Got a bonus from the bank, he said. That sugar mama of his was so proud. She speaks to him like a son, you know. Telling him how proud she is and all. Really quite amusing." She grinned.

"Niederhauser was bleeding money even before the leaks. There's no way he just got a six-figure bonus payment," I said, even though I had already seen her conclusion.

"He's talking about buying some vineyard in Tuscany too. Says that he'll probably get another bonus payment soon."

I took a deep breath and took all of this in. It mattered. It fit.

"Right. So he decided to get out from under her shadow. To try to become an actual man, fending for himself for the first time in his life. To become the person he's pretended to be for so long. So he starts by selling information. Probably shopping it around. Starting off with nickel-and-dime stuff, selling embarrassing things to the press," I said, thinking out loud.

"Until he realizes that the big bucks is in selling wholesale, giving raw data dumps to foreign governments," she added, completing my thought. "And getting himself up on the radar of the big boys in the process."

"This… this is all his doing. He's the prime mover. Unwittingly. The greed and pride of this man-child set this in motion and got people killed. And now he believes that there's gold at the end of the rainbow. Does he actually believe in that story?"

"The lost Jewish gold in the vault? That's the amusing part. He's the one who started this information wholesale business, and he still hasn't figured out the value of it. He's old school, seeing more value in gold than information. He's risking prison time violating Swiss banking secrecy laws for a couple of hundred grand, not to mention the risks in waking up governments and dangerous high-net-worth individuals along the way."

"He's a blind child walking through a minefield. But if greed and pride has pushed him this far, we can surely push him a few more steps. You speak to anyone else?" I asked.

"In the three hours I was there before you bothered to show up? You bet. The investment bankers were so eager for my attention. Seems like you have somewhat of a reputation. They assumed that we're an item, you and I."

"Are we?" I asked for reasons that defied logic, but to my relief she barely acknowledged the question with a brief eye roll before continuing.

"That blonde did her best to stare a hole in my head anyway, not that it matters. Her only interest is in climbing the old corporate ladder, and she seems to have a nice promotion and a bonus lined up if she brings your business. Doesn't hurt your ego too much, I hope," she lied.

"Not at all," I lied back.

"The American, Todd something, doesn't like you very much, but he really wants your business. Thinks you're an arrogant bastard."

"I wonder how he could have gotten such an idea."

"Yeah, I wonder. So what happened back then?" she asked, glancing at me as we were stuck at yet another traffic light. By now the wipers worked overtime, swooshing back and forth, slapping away the torrent of rain now pouring down over the windshield.

"Back when? Back in New York? I'm surprised you haven't figured that out already."

"Who said I haven't? You had a hedge fund back then. Few hundred mil, I gather. Before they shut you down for cause."

I sat there watching the bucketloads of rainwater splash on the glass in front of me. I glanced up above me at the glass roof, watching the raindrops come at me like a guillotine's blade, relentlessly pounding down, one after another. I wish I could see the moon up there. Round and bright. A full moon.

The moon. I had a telescope back then. In New York. I got it because you're supposed to have a telescope if you have a balcony facing the park, and I bought it because I wanted to see the mountains of Mars and the acid rain of Venus and the colors of Andromeda.

But those things are just fantasies to anyone not having their own Hubble, and not even a balcony facing the park can house an orbital telescope. Mars is a tiny little pinkish dot, and Venus is just a shiny white dot, and Andromeda is merely imaginary.

But the moon. But the moon was the only thing worth watching with that blasted telescope. A car honked. The light had turned green without her noticing, and she raised a palm up between the front seats to apologize to the impatient driver behind us as she took off.

"For cause. That was he said? For cause," I grumbled. "My fund had three hundred million with Pierce & Pierce. Up from my start of twenty. Not a bad five years. The bank seeded us, housed us and provided certain informational advantages."

"Advantages?" she asked.

The car turned left up the bridge crossing the Limmat river, passing the Swiss National Bank. Any other day, the view from here would be spectacular. The small marina with the view over snow-covered mountains on one side and the Old Town of Zurich with its centuries-old churches, bridges, towers, and buildings on the other.

"You know what's under us right now?" I started, changing the topic. "The world's second-largest gold deposit. The vault down there makes the one in *Goldfinger* look like a piggy bank. Even has a little train system to take you around."

A Most Private Bank

She wouldn't let it go. "What informational advantages?"

"There is... a lot of information in a bank. Information that the bank itself may not be able to take full advantage of," I tried.

"But a fund would?"

"Flow data, for instance." I sighed. "Information on orders and trade patterns of the bank's customers. And at times there may be some upcoming merger or acquisition or news that the bank is privy to."

"Isn't that illegal?"

I took my eyes off the rain and stared at her. *A career criminal, a professional grifter, someone who lies for a living. And she's judging me?*

"Oh, don't be a child, Chris. That's how the business works. Everyone does it. Not like there's a victim here, is it?"

Even in my current state, the irony wasn't lost on me. She had found herself in a world where everyone lies, cheats, and steals for a living. She had adapted to it, learned the game, and excelled at it. Much as I had found myself in a similar situation.

"It was symbiotic," I tried, justifying myself. "Our office was at the bank's building by Times Square. Just down the hall from their trading floor. They'd share useful information with us, and we'd act on it. Sharing the profits. It's a common arrangement."

I stopped talking and it was all quiet in the car for a moment. I was a successful financier, a self-made man. A supposedly independently wealthy former hedge fund manager, a respectable man. And here I was, trying to defend my actions to someone who steals for a living.

"There was an investigation," I continued. "My fund wasn't the only one they fed information. Caught the attention of the SEC. You can imagine how that went."

"No. No, not really. How did that go?" she asked. I'm not sure why I thought she would know. It would be an easy guess for anyone in the business, but she wasn't in the business.

"Everyone working for the SEC hates working for the SEC. Their big dream in life is to get a job with a prestigious outfit like P&P. Situation like this, they'd just ask the bank. Bet you can figure out what the bank had to say."

This she got. This part was predictable. "They pointed the finger at you?"

"They were shocked and outraged over how I had abused their trust. Hell, I never asked for any of that information. The entire thing was their suggestion, their standard setup. And here they were, telling the SEC that I must have stolen documents or eavesdropped on their traders. The kids at the SEC were all over it. The bank became a poor victim, working with the SEC to track down those who traded on their good name.

"There was no evidence, not enough for a criminal case. The bar for an SEC ruling is lower. I got shut down. Massive fines. Civil suits. P&P walked away as the heroes, even planted some news stories about being whistle-blowers, fighting financial crime. It would be laughable if it wasn't so dumb. The real criminals become heroes and the innocent suffer."

"But you did commit a crime, didn't you?"

"I did what everyone does!" I said. "What I had to do. You think anyone becomes financially independent in this world without bending a few rules?"

She was quiet, navigating the dark and wet streets. I had snapped at her for pointing out what I didn't want to be said. She's the criminal, not me.

"They didn't have anything on me. Circumstantial. SEC still yanked my license. Forced a fire-sale liquidation. Had big options bets on and now the whole Street knew I had to off-load. Got squeezed from all sides, P&P joining in to take advantage of the forced liquidation. Total bloodbath. Twenty cents on the dollar. Had to fire my whole staff. Took a big hit myself. A fortune in legal bills."

"Still made some money on the fund, though, didn't you? On the whole?"

"I had made a whole lot more, and they took it away from me! P&P cost me millions, and they get to play the heroes in the press? They get bonuses and I gotta leave the country? Where's the justice in that?"

I stopped talking and my words lingered in the air like a brick that just wouldn't fall. I hadn't planned on telling her this, telling her that much. I never told anyone that much. After all these years, I had started believing the alternative version of events I made up, the story I told everyone. I wasn't even sure why I had admitted this to her.

"But you knew all of this. Didn't you?"

The car had been parked in the underground garage for a few minutes, and we still sat there, talking. The echo of a powerful engine reverberated and echoed as it slowly pulled around and parked opposite us.

"What I don't know is why you still chose to do this deal with P&P," she finally said. So that's what this little Q and A was all about. She was far too used to being the one with all the angles. I hadn't realized how much it must bother her to be part of a play like this without being in control, without even knowing all the details of the play.

"Look, I'm dealing with them because I can. Their main office back home wouldn't take my phone call, but over here I'm a big fish in a small pond. They don't like me, they don't trust me, but they want my money."

She nodded, slowly taking this in. Her pretty little head housed an impressive brain. Something I had better remember.

Something that was all too easy to forget. I watched her mull it over, seeing her furrow her brow. It was the first time I saw her like that, openly showing her thoughts.

"They think you have nine figures. Hundred million. Or more."

She said it as if it was a question. I looked out the passenger-side window, at the Mercedes parked next to us. Hoping she would let it go.

"You don't have a hundred million. If you did, you wouldn't care about any of this."

There was no avoiding it. A subject like that just wouldn't be raised, not here, not in this town. No one would ever ask such a thing. A direct question is dangerous - it leaves only three courses of action. Refuse to answer. Lie. Or tell the truth. The garage was all quiet.

"It... It's all about perception, Chris. Never about reality. Everything from the watches to the car, everything is about projecting humble, understated wealth and power. I'm a powerful man in this town because I project a certain image. A wealthy man, a bully, someone with power, someone you don't push around. Perception becomes reality. The power is real, even if the wealth might not be.

"Nine figures... Good. Hope that rumor spreads. Hell, I don't even have eight. Seven figures, sure, but who doesn't in this town? A few mil doesn't go very far around here."

She wasn't shocked, not like most people would have been. I had turned my face back to her to try to read her reaction, and I had clearly told her more than what she had figured out in the past days. It was hard to tell if that look on her face showed impress or disgust.

"So you pretend to be something you're not, build a false front, and lie until your lies turn into reality? At least I understand why you're so accepting of my own past. That why you demanded my hundred and fifty thousand?" There was a certain edge to her voice, coming out clearly in that question. I had blackmailed the money off her, and she hadn't liked it. Probably was all she had too.

"Yeah," I admitted. No sense in going back to lying now. "Needed it too. Not like I don't have anything, but most is tied up. Got a divorce settlement coming up, legal bills, fighting over the house…"

She was still upset about that money, and now she was hoping I'd hand it back, now that we got close, now that we were partners. Now that we had slept together. But I really did need that money, and I had no intention of handing it back for sentimental reasons.

We had left the garage and were heading up the elevator toward the room. She had been quiet awhile, hoping the uncomfortable silence would make me feel guilty about the money. She'd have no such luck, not today.

"We pull this off, and that money won't matter to either of us, Chris," I said as we exited the elevator. "Stakes are high - no mistakes."

"I'm not the one who got high and partied all day, Jim. I paid well for your services, and you better stay sharp tomorrow. Time is running out."

"You're right. Tomorrow it's all business, tomorrow we settle this. I can do this, trust me, Chris."

She gave me a smile at last, whether real or part of the act. I kissed her forehead and headed into the suite.

The room was neatly kept and the bed turned down, with a little piece of chocolate shaped as a ladybug wrapped in red-and-black foil on each pillow. I fell asleep on top of the cover with most of my clothes still on, unable to keep my eyes open, unable to think of anything but rest after this day.

Thursday

A Beautiful Morning

I hadn't moved all night. I woke up in the late afternoon when sunlight from the balcony window reached my face. The Complications lay there next to me on the bed stand. It showed quarter to twelve. It must have been decades since I'd slept that late. It had been a good day yesterday. On balance. Laying there on the soft king-size bed with a squashed chocolate ladybug under my chin, I had the first time in days to stop and think, to contemplate the situation. My mind now clear, clear from the chemicals and clear from the stress.

I was on my side, facing the window, facing the rising sun that nearly blinded me. Welcoming the light after yesterday's darkness and torrential rain. I was summing up the last day, making sure no details of it had escaped me. Running through the events in my mind, what was real, what was imagined, what was said, what was implied, what was true, and what was a lie.

What was clear was that she had given me a vital missing piece of the puzzle. The unwitting prime mover. It fit now, it all did, and I was more certain than ever of what had to be done. It wouldn't be difficult now. All the pieces were lined up, all the players on the field, all knowing their position and their role. Even if they couldn't know the endgame. Not my endgame.

The chocolate ladybug under my chin was sticking to my face and I picked it up and gently placed it on the nightstand. I had my pinstripe pants and a white shirt on, in all likelihood wrinkled beyond rescue. At least I had managed to kick off the Oxfords before crashing on the bed.

My arm reached behind me. It didn't feel anything. Stretching my body, I turned first on my back and then a full one-eighty to face the other side of the bed. It was empty. The covers piled up, showing signs of having been used, having been slept in. An envelope on the pillow. Hotel stationary. Red writing on it. My name. Cute.

Dear Jim,

Didn't want to wake you. Thought you could use some sleep. Will come to your office by lunch. Today's the big day, let's get it done!

Chris

She signed with Chris. And a little hand-drawn red heart. Funny. I had no idea what business she had to take care of, but it really didn't matter. Not at this point. The girl wanted a controlling stake in a private bank. We had it all lined up. I had it all lined up. By the end of the day, the bank and its secrets would be ours for the taking.

It had been an unlikely week. Nobody could put together this kind of deal in just a few days. Nobody. The pieces had just fallen into place. The mission was to gain control of the bank, and I had achieved it without spending a dime. Without putting up any collateral, without any risk.

I parted the curtains more for the sun to fill the room and let the warm beams caress my face for a moment. It was a good day, and it could only get better. There was an orange Nespresso machine in the kitchenette, and after a flick of a switch a little yellow light started blinking as the machine heated up and prepared for its coffee-making duties. Not even the thought of industrial Nespresso coffee could bring me down. I stretched and yawned and smiled. Actually smiled.

The light on the Nespresso machine had just turned from blinking to solid when a cloud covered the sun and the room suddenly got both darker and colder. There was a knock on the door.

She had a key card. She wouldn't have to knock. Not many other people knew I was there. Not many others should know

A Most Private Bank

anyhow. A knock on that particular door, a knock not followed by the words "housekeeping," could not be good news.

Perhaps it was the sudden shift in mood effectuated by the dark rain cloud that covered the sun. Perhaps it was premonition. Perhaps it was childishness. But I whispered quietly to myself.

"It's the wind, and nothing more."

The first raindrops hit the balcony while I tried staring the intrusion away. It would be early for the maid to call, but not impossibly early. It had been a moment since the first knock and even if she forgot to call out "housekeeping," this is when she would swipe the key card. Instead there was another knock.

"Somewhat louder than before," I muttered as I went to open the door, hesitating no longer.

She stormed into the room before I could greet her.

"This is a really bad time to make yourself unavailable, Jim. You just woke up? You don't know yet, do you?"

"Morning to you too, Sandra. Calm it a bit, will you? Got a hell of a hangover. Didn't have my coffee yet. What gives?"

"Get your coffee, Jim. Gonna need it. Niederhauser got himself pinched on US soil."

The words floated around in my head as if trying to grab onto a ledge, trying to stick but without finding something to hold on to. The word *pinched* was knocking around the inside of my skull while the coffee machine slowly squeezed out an espresso in the tiny white cup. Lifting the cup to my nose, smelling the strong robusta, the words *US soil* knocked *pinched* away and took its place by my forehead.

"That's just not possible. He's in Switzerland. Met him last night. Supposed to finalize a deal today."

"The wife's vernissage. Heard you were there and made a fool of yourself. Small town. He got a better offer. Thought he did. Got caught in a fed sting," she said, waiting for my coffee to kick in so she could lay it all out. I took my espresso like a shot of vodka, turning it upside down and swallowing it all in one go. That woke me up.

"I'm good. Go."

"Niederhauser's desperate to cash out. Word is there's a toxic asset that could sink them. He tries to appear as if he's only taking in a partner, keeping majority stake, but he's really interested in a payday before the whole thing collapses."

"With you so far." I nodded, hitting the button for another espresso.

Most people saw her as just a secretary. That was just fine with her and just as fine with me. I didn't just keep her around for her loyalty. You can get loyalty from a cocker spaniel. She's a sharp cookie. Tuned in.

"He had you and an American venture capital firm lined up. They gave him a better offer, and he took the jet last night to New York to sign with them. Only problem is, the VC was a front, a shell company run by the FBI. A sting vehicle."

I stood frozen for a moment. How could this man, this senior banker, be so incredibly stupid? People born with more money than they could ever spend tend to be arrogant by nature, but not necessarily stupid. Complacent, sure. Lack of work ethics, often. But gullible enough to be taken on such a ride?

"They did a proper job on him. The VC had years of operations, passed reasonable due diligence. The feds are getting pretty wised up about the business. Could have fooled most people," she added as if reading my thoughts. "It's gonna make this morning's newspapers, will be front-page stuff in the Post. *New York Post*, that is. *WaPo* wouldn't bother. Quite a feather in the hat for the feds, especially after the scene he caused when they arrested him."

A Most Private Bank

The rain was increasing in intensity. On a sunny day, this room had a view of Lake Zurich stretching out from the bridges over the Limmat river, expanding out in the distance toward snow-covered Alps. Most days this would be a breathtaking view in the most literal sense of the word. But this was not most days. This was the day when a bold and brilliant plan laid down to die.

I nodded for her to go on while I looked for some fresh clothes in the wardrobe. There was a bird on the balcony. The cold and wet little pigeon looked as miserable and pathetic as a soaked cat unable to find cover from the rain.

"What they book him on?"

"The usual. Aiding and abetting tax evasion. Facilitation of tax fraud. Money laundering," she explained, none of which was terribly surprising to me.

"They probably have him cold on the tax stuff. Doubtful on money laundry," I said with her confirming my line of thought with a slow nod. "But it's bad enough. If the bank took undeclared money from US persons, if they solicited clients in the US, he's done for. And so is the bank. That's how they brought down Wegelin. It was the oldest private bank in the world, you know. From the 1740s, used to be another bank of choice for Napoleon's family. Then they went and got all greedy and started helping Americans hide dirty money.

"Generally speaking, it's not a great business plan to piss of the only country in the world that claims global jurisdiction and is willing to use economic blackmail to impose control over allied countries' legal systems. Didn't take long for Wegelin to go belly up."

"If you told me what your shot is, I could give you better info, Jim."

"Not a question of trust, Sandra. Not even a need-to-know situation. It's a want-to-know situation and you really don't want to know."

"He's gonna talk. Cutting a deal with the feds."

I had moved to the bathroom for a shave while talking, leaving the door open. I stopped the blade mid-motion as it was passing up over my neck, resisting the urge to pull it sideways just to slit open a wound.

"You know what he's giving them?" I asked after a brief pause before finishing up the shave.

"Enough to get them salivating. Lot of excited people in the J. Edgar building. Big scoop for them. US attorney's office is involved. Already working on a deal. That's where it's leaking from. Feds run a tight ship."

I gave her a look of incredulity. She's good but not that good.

"How would you possibly know that?"

"You have your sources and I have mine, Jim!" she said in that same tone I use when I don't want anyone to ask follow-up questions. But this was just too important. I had to know.

"Cut it, Sandra. This is important."

"Calm down, Jim. It's reliable. Got a friend at the Post. Someone I trust. They're not uncertain. This happened."

Some might have compared that feeling in my chest with a small hole in a balloon, slowly seeping out air until it's all empty. But the *Hindenburg* seemed more apt. I was halfway through buttoning up my shirt when it hit me. I sat back down, into that black armchair near the window. The rain was heavier now. And I was slow. Unfocused. Depressed. The price to pay for the yeyo yesterday.

"Game over. It's... just over," I said to no one in particular.

"Yeah, it is game over. If you're planning on sitting there and feeling sorry for yourself! So what's it gonna be? Should I go back to the office and take the sign down? You want me to leave you here so you can cry your troubles away?"

Sometimes you need a strong drink. Sometimes you need a line. And sometimes all you need is a middle-aged woman to call you a wimp.

"Get back to the office. Get me Guy. Ask him to come to the office as soon as he can. No phones. And try to set up a meet with those bastards at the consulate."

She was giving me a scolding look as she picked up her handbag to leave. "Don't take too long or I'll be back for you!"

The Dossier

The person staring back from the reflection in the elevator mirror wasn't me. It resembled me. But this person was pale as the corpse I had seen just a few days ago. God, it seemed like weeks ago. Months. But it was just three days. Those eyes were wide open, dilated pupils, red and watering up. I wiped them with the back of my hand, and the person on the other side of that glass did the same. Lips cracking up, a drop of blood on them. Wiping that sweaty forehead with a pocket square, crumpling it up and pushing it back down. I could have killed someone for a glass of water.

Pull it together, Jim!

Sandra looked unimpressed when I entered. It couldn't have been more than twenty minutes at the most, but she looked at me as if it had taken me days to get here. I threw my coat over a desk by the entrance and realized that I'd forgotten to put the watch back on this morning. There is something about not wearing a watch, even about not wearing the right watch for the occasion, that makes a man feel vulnerable.

"We got the contracts?" I asked, rubbing my naked wrist.

A brief, if somewhat judgmental, smile lifted the corner of her lips. "Two manila envelopes on your desk, marked private and confidential. Also, two matching phone messages, both urgent."

"The first one must be from Piece & Pierce. Preston? And then what, Baerenfells?"

"Close," she replied, handing me the phone notes. "Preston, yes. And then that talkative Swiss fellow, Bühler. Just won't shut up, will he? Told me all about the party last night, about the deal, about how worried he is now that Mr. Niederhauser got

A Most Private Bank

arrested."

"Useful idiot. He can wait," I said, heading past the trading desks into my own office.

"Guy's on the way too," she called after me.

Sure enough, there were two unopened envelopes on my desk. The two envelopes looked comically identical. Comical, given the identical situation the senders were in. And would be in. Flipping them over, one bore the crest of an American investment bank and one did not. The crest of a crimson shield, ordained with an intricate pattern of tiny crosses, angels, and lions, a royal crown above and two lions flanking it, holding the shield from either side. The kind of crest a dodgy American investment bank would have designed to make it appear as if they have actual heritage.

I was just removing the metal clip to open that one when the phone rang. I knew that number. I never forget a number.

"Todd, how the hell are ya?" I tried, but he would have none of that.

His words whipping out like machine-gun fire, hurling at me at a thousand rounds a minute. "Gotta call the whole thing off, Jim, new developments, you understand, can't take the risk, you know, gotta wait and let the whole thing blow over, let's touch base in a couple of months, when things calm down, better to wind down now and revisit once we all have our ducks in a row, you underst—"

"Not a chance in hell," I interrupted, pulling out the contract from the manila envelope. I pushed the cover letter aside, flipped to the last page, and moved my eyes rapidly over it, making sure. Yeah, it was there all right. He was screwed.

"I got a contract in front of me, Preston. Looks alarmingly much like your signature at the bottom. And guess what, I just countersigned it."

"Now listen, Jim. Let's all be reasonable. Niederhauser's valuation will take a hit on this news and—"

"Don't want to hear it. Pacta sunt servanda. Honor the deal, or I'll sue both you and P&P into oblivion. Release the funds in time, or I'll destroy you in court."

The receiver slammed down in the middle of a feeble reply. I sat motionless for minutes, staring at the desk phone, minutes turning into hours. Or so it felt. Financing wasn't the problem. Not anymore. Pierce & Pierce had no way out and neither had the garage-band hedge fund. No, the contracts were signed all right and that was that. The money will be there. But what of the seller?

There was a chance. A slim one. The last thing I wanted to do. This was going to be a long day. First things first.

The floor safe in the back corner of my office was of the same brand as Niederhauser's, even if it was smaller and less showy. I spun the dial of the old Franz Jäger safe until the heavy door clicked open. Reaching in, I took out the box with watches, the ones that were left. It was a mahogany box with clear glass cover, making each of the twelve slots visible from the outside.

The slots were divided by a gray silk-covered grid, a watch pillow in each slot, a watch around the pillow. Apart from those stolen a few days earlier. I needed something comfortable, something solid, something to help me through this.

My father's old Submariner would be just the thing. The same Rolex model that Sean Connery wore on a too-slim NATO strap in *Dr. No*. This watch had taken plenty of abuse for over half a century, and it was just as reliable as the day it was made.

The other envelope contained just what it should. A binding commitment for forty million for the purpose of acquiring an equity stake in a certain private bank. Even a confirmation of the wire that had already been done to the escrow account.

I had the money. Now all I needed was the bank. And for that

I needed the old banker. The bell interrupted my thoughts. He sure got here quickly. Then again, when was he ever late. Men in his line of work were always on time. Most of these corporate intelligence people boast colorful military backgrounds and flash their pedigree on their websites. Words like *agency*, *SEAL*, *GRU* and *Mossad*, all as ubiquitous as *MBA* or *CFA*. It rarely meant much in the real world. Far too many people have had some peripheral role in such organizations only to use them for bragging rights later on. But he never needed a website. I never asked what he did before, and I never needed to. Just like I never asked where or how he got his information. All I knew was that I could trust him. His competency and his discretion. The rest didn't seem important.

A brown leather messenger bag under his arm when entered my corner office, he took a seat in front of my desk with no need for polite pleasantries.

"You've got more than one problem, buddy. Which one first?"

"The situation in the States," I replied, suspecting what the second problem may be about.

"Sandra's source is solid. Niederhauser is jammed up tight and leaning toward making a deal. If they start a full federal case on tax dodging, that'll take years to unravel and the first thing they'll do is to get the Swiss to secure physical evidence. Assume a total lockdown on the bank by end of play tomorrow, sanctions against the other owners, and a loss of bank license in a matter of days. I can only assume such developments would be detrimental to what you're up to."

There had been no reason to doubt Sandra, and none of this came as a surprise. The clock was ticking and options limiting.

"T minus thirty-six hours. To complete the transaction or derail the investigation."

True to form, he pretended not to hear that last part. "They'll move fast on this and will likely secure digital storage and hard copy files before the weekend. Plenty of chatter around DC on this one. Seems like a bigger deal than it should be, but I can't tell you why."

"Can't or won't?" I asked him.

"Can't. Don't know. Trying to find out, Jim."

"Right. Can't blame me for being a little paranoid this week. The second issue?"

He flipped open the leather flap on the messenger bag and pulled out a dossier, on the outside looking exactly like the one he had handed me a few days ago. Except that it was thicker. That's never a good sign.

"Impressive CV for her age," he said and slid the dossier across the table for me. He was right too. This was more than I had expected. The name she had given me was real enough, and so was the background she had told me. Key parts were left out, of course.

He leaned back in that leather chair, patiently waiting for me to get to the punch line. This was put together in a hurry. All raw data from different sources and no executive summary up front. Must have been a rush job.

Evelyn Walker had started out as a small-time con artist in Manchester. Running the whole cute-little-girl-in-trouble gag. Teamed up with some low-level Albanian for a while before graduating to the big league. Interpol didn't seem to know how she fell in with the Russians. She had been a seemingly respectable front for them. Dealing with banks, mergers and acquisitions. Money laundering. She understood the world of high finance. But that alone didn't explain the Interpol red notice on her. A rare distinction not bestowed on just about anyone. Only 7,430 people currently had a red notice, 842 of them women. She was one of them.

An overwhelming number of red notices are terrorism-related. It's not easy to earn this illustrious distinction with petty crimes like money laundry. He was getting impatient, even if he was trying not to show it. He was glancing at his black Breitling Avenger. I flipped to the red notice. Terrorism financing. I closed my eyes hard and whispered a profanity to myself.

"She middled a deal a few years ago. Off-books small arms to Russian separatists in Ukraine. Not a biggie compared to what both the Russians and the US government did, but these particular guys were on a list. So now she's on a list. These kinds of things don't need much evidence. Guilty until proven innocent."

"Photo must be from grade school. Blond. That's all they've got?"

"She's been careful. They have that description there, but that could be just about anyone. What they do have is fingerprints. Never been arrested, must have lifted the print some other way."

"They looking for her?"

"Looking, sure. They're looking for all seven thousand of them. But not specifically in this part of the world."

I flipped a few more pages, taking this in. That put a whole different light on things. When it comes to the big T word, there's guilt by association. Simply being seen in the same room could put a very unwanted spotlight on you. No more fun and games. These were not the sorts of things you skirt.

"Keep it on the q.t., will you? Need to figure this out first. How to deal with it."

"Sure thing, Jim. That's the only copy. Nobody knows I've been digging in this. My offer on the hardware still stands."

Lost in thought, I kept looking at the dossier for a moment

before realizing that he was waiting for an answer.

"No. Thanks, but no. A gun won't do much good. Getting caught with an illegal gat around here would sour things real fast."

He flipped the bag closed and stood to his feet in one motion.

"Get yourself a double espresso, Jim. You look like they just fished you out of the Limmat. You know where to find me. Good luck."

"I'm gonna need it too," I muttered quietly to myself while the door closed behind him.

He had a point. I studied the face in the bathroom mirror. It still didn't look quite alive, even after plenty of cold water splashed onto it. It wasn't just cosmetic either. I was tired. Slow. Depressed. Everything had looked so good yesterday, and now it was falling apart in front of my eyes.

My entire face under the facet, tap open. Trying to focus. I knew what this was. This wasn't me. This wasn't who I am, who I was.

A hangover could get bad enough at times, but this was worse. Coke gets you euphoric. High on dopamine. You feel invincible, like you could take on the world. But the day after, you pay the price. You get the opposite feeling. The lack of dopamine in the system makes you feel depressed, sad, and worthless and helpless. You saw this in others all the time in this town. In any town with enough money slogging around. No. Any city, period, now that powder was cheaper than a drink in the pub.

Awareness helps. You have to know what you're fighting to stand a chance. This was not me being depressed. This was not me making a rational assessment of the situation, determining that there was no winning outcome. No, this was a chemical reaction in my brain, and one that I could defeat.

Closing the faucet, I stared at my reflection a moment. The coke was dumb. Did I have a choice? Probably not. But no more. This was the time to put the game face on. Make-or-break day.

I went through it again in my head. What needed to be done. What was clear and what was not. What conclusions to draw. But mostly what needed to get done. That hadn't changed. I hadn't forgotten.

With steel in my eyes, imagined or not, and an almost certainly imagined new resolve, I started setting things in motion. Line 'em up and knock 'em down. Time to get back out there.

"Sandra, need you to set up a meeting with Donahue at the consulate. No, just call his people and tell him that I'm on the way, whether he's got time or not. He's gonna want to hear what I've got to say. Then check the accounts. Should have gotten one-fifty K in today. From one of Chris's entities. Another half a mil from Baerenfells," I said as I headed past her desk by the front door.

"Saw the payment already this morning. All fine."

"After Donahue, call Bühler, tell him everything's on, financing in place, deal secured," I said as I grabbed my coat.

"Is it?" she asked while I headed out the door.

"Damned if I know," I muttered as the door closed behind me.

The walk from the office to the consulate would take at least fifteen minutes. You could do it in half with the tram, but I needed the time. I needed a way to get them on my side without compromising my endgame. Fifteen minutes in the fresh air should do it.

Down Bahnhofstrasse was an easy stroll. Bit of light drizzle. Once I hit the lake, I regretted not taking the hat. The wind picked up and the dark clouds got darker and meaner. The drizzle turned into rain, which turned increasingly heavy. By Bürkliplatz the skies opened up on me. Good. I needed the shock to the system.

Cold, hard rain whipping my face. I stopped a moment by the life-size bronze sculpture of Ganymede pleading to Zeus, in the shape of an eagle, not to take him away to Mount Olympus. At least that's what I had been told the statue of the naked boy and the bird to be. It was just by the water, where the small riverboats were moored, next to the yacht club. The river Limmat on one side and the medieval Schanzengraben moat on the other. The bodies of water, together with the river Sihl, enclosing the old city and faithfully serving Zurich as the outer defense against neighboring city-states for centuries before the unification.

Plenty of blood had been spilled here. Town against town, village against village, for centuries. Every Swiss town worth a damned had its own defensive walls, cliffside fortresses and hand-dug moats. All untouched by both German and Allied bombs, all just as spectacular as they stood hundreds of years ago.

This was not the time to reminisce on ancient history. I kept moving, kept picking up the pace, kept going over the plan in my head. It had looked so easy. But that was before. Way before. When they were out of their league. But that was then. Now I was the one out of my league.

An angry tram rang out its scolding bell as it nearly hit me. Bellevue was a mess. It was always a mess. Trams, people, bikes, cars. A busy inner-city junction, poorly planned and accident prone. I'd been told that one-third of Zurich citizens get hit by a tram at some point in their lives. I'd also been told that one-third of all statistics are made up on the spot. The tram driver appeared to be screaming at me as I jumped to safety, as if I was the one to inconvenience him.

Not much farther now. They better be there. Better take the meeting. Or I'm done for.

Mike Donahue

It took a moment for the door to buzz open. No one there to receive me this time. No lance corporal with a broom up his butt, no salutes. I stepped in and saw only a few poor saps sitting in the waiting area, probably there to apply for US visas. Perhaps expats looking to renew their American driver's licenses. Three counters, only one open. Seven people waiting around. This was a dentist waiting room. A post office. The DMV. Anything but what I was here for. And I had myself to blame.

A marine PFC made for a symbolic guard by the door to the inner chambers, short-sleeve khaki shirt, blue pants with the red stripe at the sides, white cap. Not as much as a sidearm on his person.

The world was falling apart around me and they decide to play childish games. They want to see if I sit down and wait like a good citizen or if I'll make a scene. Bet they're watching right now. Sitting down is a losing move. They'd have me wait for hours just to make a point.

The marine kept staring out into nothing.

"Private, I need you to locate Mike Donahue or Steven Hill and inform them that Jim Dixon is here on an urgent matter," I said in my best Lee Ermey impersonation.

"Sir, you'll have to have to take a seat and wait for your turn," the man replied with a hint of uncertainty in his voice. This kid was barely old enough to shave and probably had no idea what I was talking about.

"You wanna pay attention to what I'm telling you, marine. You have a choice, right now. Either throw me out of here or go get 'em. Now."

He was most certainly new at this. He was on guard duty and shouldn't let some civilian get in his face like this. He hesitated. He turned his head and looked at me. By any normal guard protocols, he should have me thrown out. Before he made up his mind, the door to the inner sanctum clicked open from the other side and a familiar grin poked out.

"Jim, stop giving the kid a hard time, will ya? Just running a bit late, busy day. Come on in. Coffee?" Donahue had probably been observing the whole thing through that one-way mirror in the door. I had flipped him off last night. Now I needed him. And he knew it.

"Black, thanks. Got a proposition for you."

"Seems to me the balance of power shifted a little overnight, Jim. Not sure we have much use for your propositions now."

Smug bastard. He was toying with me, and he was enjoying it. I had been a bastard to him for the past few days and now it was his turn. But he did have use for me. He didn't take this meeting for my charming personality. I had to just lay down and take it for now. He had a right to land a few blows before we were even. If I got what I wanted he could land as many as he liked.

The room was as Spartan as the one I saw here a few days ago. No shelves, no decoration, no pictures on the walls. A glass table and designer plastic chairs. No place to hide anything, no place to plant a bug. Donahue was wearing the same bland, ill-fitting black suit. Cheap off-the-rack kit, with the obligatory thin black tie. I wondered if they're issued this stuff in Langley or wherever he crawled out of. No one would actually go buy such an outfit.

The only thing that made him stand out from other government paper pushers was the bimetal Datejust. At thirty-one millimeter, quite a small watch for a man. A classic entry-level Rolex, perhaps the most recognizable. This particular one combined a steel case with a fluted yellow-gold bezel and sported a jubilee bracelet in the same two-tone configuration. For an honest G-man, even one climbing the corporate latter, it probably took years to save up to it.

He was proud of it and he saw me noticing it, and he looked over at my own wrist. He was comparing, measuring us up, and, judging from the nearly unnoticeable way his left lips curled, he thought he was coming out on top. You could hardly fault a government employee for assuming the shinier toy to be of higher value.

"I have to say, I'm surprised to see you back here, Jim. You weren't overly receptive on your previous visit," he started off.

"You asked for information I can't give. You tried to threaten me. If we avoid those things going forward, we may actually find some common ground here, Donahue."

When he was done laughing, he mocked me. "Well, well. Steve told me you had a bit of an ego issue, Jim. Seems like I stepped all over it. Yet here you are, about to ask for a favor."

This time he held the cards, and he knew it. Like a Montgomery Burns parody, he leaned back in his chair, fingertips against fingertips, and waited for my play. Like a cat lifting its paw from the mouse's tail just to see which direction he'll try to run. But he still had use for me. If he didn't, we wouldn't be having this meeting.

"You got it the wrong way around, Donahue. I'm here to offer you a solution to your problem."

That didn't throw him off. Not for a second. He was there to negotiate. He expected a little banter. A little sparring to feel each other out.

"I got a problem?"

"Yeah, you got a problem all right. Those klutzes at DOJ are compromising your operation. They nailed the old man in the

States, and they'll tighten the thumbscrews until he cuts a deal. Then you need to go through proper channels. Bilateral agreements, procedures, local cops, local regulators, weeks and months of territorial pissing between the US and Switzerland until your side eventually wins."

"Our side, isn't it?" he interjected. But he didn't protest the pipes I was laying.

"Sure. And you'll shut down the bank and get a few convictions. But that's not your endgame here."

I had his attention. I still wasn't sure if I was going down the right street. I had to wing it. I had to take my shot. He leaned forward like a vulture towering over me, like a predator studying his prey. He was enjoying this game. So was I.

"Enlighten me, Jim. What is my endgame?" he asked without giving away if I was onto something or if he was just letting me dig a deeper hole for myself. It was time to try it. Time to see if my little theories held water.

"You're looking for beneficial ownership documentation for politically exposed persons, and you want them before anyone else gets hold of them. The last thing you need is to lose control of the narrative."

I tried to sound irritated. As if all of this was obvious. As if we were simply wasting time. His face still didn't give away what I needed to know and neither did his voice. This was a man well accustomed to interrogations. And I suppose that was what this really was.

"Am I now?" he asked, trying to drag more information out of me. Like a sucker, I kept talking. Kept digging it deeper.

"The mole approached you like they approached everyone else. Trying to sell juicy details of the rich and unscrupulous. But you didn't care about a few millionaires hiding some money from the IRS. So they tried to up the ante, baiting you with some

A Most Private Bank

politicians. But then they got all scared and went dark on you. Now you have no idea who the mole is, but you buy their story of the paper-only records for key clients. You just can't risk sending a team of ninjas in to blow that safe open, not in the middle of Zurich. A flap would be quite embarrassing."

I was so far out on a limb I couldn't even see the tree anymore. It was all or nothing and this was my only shot. If I was too far out, if my guess wasn't close enough, that's it. And still, the bastard didn't show any indication.

"That's quite a story," was all he said while barely parting his lips.

"You probably had your doubts about the whole thing. But then all of a sudden all kinds of external parties started showing interest for this otherwise quite mundane little bank. And now you're thinking that the only thing worse than not getting those documents is to have someone else get them."

"You know who's been selling information about Niederhauser?"

Did he change subject because I was getting close, or because I was too far away? *He keeps playing this like an interrogation. Dragging information out of me, hoping to catch me in a lie. Had I lied? Perhaps. Bluffed, certainly.*

"I'm the guy who can solve all your problems, Donahue. I'm the only one who can get you those documents. I can even give you the identity of the mole. After I close this deal. After you help me close this deal. Make it happen and I'll make it rain."

"It sounds like you're building up to some sort of proposition, Jim," he said. That blank face was impressing me as much as it was annoying me. It's not easy to keep a blank face in these situations. I wouldn't play poker with this man.

"I need you to stall the DOJ investigation for a few days. I need access to Nicholas Niederhauser. He needs to sign some papers and give me some information."

"I'm not sure what you think we do here," he said. "Obstruction of justice wasn't listed in my job description."

"And here I thought that was the main purpose of the CIA," I shot back.

This was the first time he lost his poker face. This wasn't a bluff, this was a genuine reaction. He couldn't hold back his laughter.

"That what you think I am? You've seen too many bad movies, Jim. Or perhaps you listened to those childish stories Steve likes to tell. I told you I'm State Department, and I meant it. I've got a reasonable clearance level but I'm not a spook. And as much as Steve likes people to think he is, the same goes for him. What, you think I carry a pistol under the jacket and have a, what did you call it, a team of ninjas on standby to raid banks in the dead of night?"

He wiped his eyes and shook his head, finding my CIA guess amusing. Made me feel like a complete idiot.

"Look, Jim. I'm not in a position to confirm or deny any of your wild speculations. But I can listen to your proposition, and I can take it to the powers that be. Tell me why we need you."

"You're not as dumb as I had you pegged. You know exactly why you need me - that's the only reason I'm in this room. If the deal goes through, I'd be the custodian of the bank. At least initially. I alone would have full access to every part of the bank. If there are papers or items you would prefer not being found by nosy Swiss cops or other parties, I can get them before anyone else does. Of course, it would help to know exactly what you're looking for."

"You still think we're bank robbers, huh? Your proposition is that the US government spring a criminal from jail so you can complete a business transaction with him and make a buck? In

A Most Private Bank

return, you'll steal something that you believe we want, violating laws, bank secrecy, and your fiduciary duties?"

He wanted me to compromise myself. To say it out loud in plain text for whoever was listening or whoever would read the transcript. A room this clean is supposed to look safe from bugs, but of course they were recording this. I would be crazy to give them anything to use against me. But I was way past the point of no return. In for a penny, in for a pound.

"Yeah. That's the gist of it. Make sure Niederhauser can sign off on the deal, and I'll swipe your stuff for you. I'll even throw in the mole. I'm sure you wanna know who's been shopping bank data. Caused quite a mess for you, didn't it?"

He sat back in his chair, tapping his thumb on the table. That was a good sign. He was considering what I was offering. I had to be close. Close enough, anyhow. The room was quiet for nearly a full minute, bar the soft tapping of a thumb against the glass table.

"Gonna need your client, Jim," he said when the silence finally broke.

It was my turn to be silent. That was the one thing I wanted to avoid. He wanted her. I took a few deep breaths. This couldn't be done without Niederhauser, and I had to make a deal. But I couldn't give her up.

"Look, Donahue. Getting you those documents is a major crime in this country. I'm way out on a limb here. My client should be of no particular importance to you, not compared to those documents. I'm sorry, Mike, I can't betray my client."

He stared me down, and I felt my pulse rising. He had the upper hand, and he was all too aware of it.

"Sure about that, Jim?"

"Yeah," I said. "Time is ticking here, Mike. This deal needs to be done by tomorrow or won't get done. The natives are slow, but not that slow. They'll move in by the weekend to secure the premises."

With that he stood up and shook my hand. "I'll take it to my people. We'll be in touch."

"Don't take too long," I replied on my way out the door.

The Armory

Lunchtime. She was there, all right. She was there in spades. A skintight white Gucci dress with a thick black square pattern, ending exactly by the knees. The kind of dress that makes any red-blooded man instinctively check for visible underwear lines. There were none. The slim tall legs were bookended with the dress on one side and white Louboutin stilettos on the other. Sitting on the visitor's chair, one knee over the other. A tiny green Chanel bag hanging off the armrest.

I had seen her before. With and without dress. But she still took my breath away.

"All set for lunch?" she chirped as if she was going on a date. I wanted to ask where she'd been all morning. I wanted to confront her about the red notice. But she caught me off guard and my mind was already elsewhere.

"Of course. Shall we?" I replied, offering my arm. "I'll take you to a real local Swiss place this time. Not that the Swiss are famous for their cuisine."

I didn't tell her the real reason why I wanted to go to this particular restaurant. A single large hall where everyone can clearly see everyone else. It had two exits leading to their own sides of the cobblestone maze that makes up the Old Town and inside the acoustics of an old cathedral, should you put a kitchen and fifty dinner guests in there. A surveillance nightmare. And I was feeling more than a little paranoid.

The joint wasn't far. The house itself was a fixture in the Old Town landscape, just off the main Bahnhofstrasse, and, like most of its surroundings, it had stood there for centuries. The windows were deep-set Palladian style, arched and with intricately carved wooden ornaments. Even the doors matched that same design, and it looked just the same now as it had a hundred years ago.

She noticed the lettering on the facade, above the arched doorway. Large yellow text in old German Gothic style. *Fraktur*, they call it. The old calligraphic typeface preferred in this part of the world since the sixteenth century. Of course, these days it was less common, owing to the little detail that it was also preferred by a short Austrian fellow with a funny mustache and his merry band.

I really should have been taking things more seriously, but I couldn't help enjoying her reaction. If the *Fraktur* outside got her concerned, the interior had her properly worried. With the old Bavarian-style decor, complete with eggshell-white walls, brown wooden beams and round brick pillars, the restaurant could easily be mistaken for an old German *Bierhalle*. But what really got her was the weapons.

Her hand tightened against mine and she moved closer to me as we were shown to our table.

"This is the *Zeughauskeller*. The Armory," I explained. "It's not a gimmick, it really was an armory for quite some time."

I pointed to the text on the menus in front of us. "Fourteen eighty-seven. That's how old this place is. It was the main Zurich armory for centuries. That's why the walls are full of swords, crossbows, and old rifles. Quaint, isn't it?"

"And the Nazi antiaircraft cannon?" she whispered and nodded toward the cast-iron wheeled piece on an oak pedestal.

"Don't be silly. That's just a German light artillery piece, and I doubt it has any strong political convictions either way."

We got a good table. Only an impenetrable stone wall behind me and a clear line of sight of both exits. Perhaps the paranoia was getting the better of me. But can you really be called paranoid if they're actually out to get you?

A Most Private Bank

"When did you plan on telling me about the red notice?"

I threw it out there when she least expected it. We were having a laugh, feeling relaxed. But I had to know. That pearly white smile was gone. She was busted and she knew it.

"Would you have helped me if you knew?"

Her reply was soft, low and quiet, her big puppy eyes imploring me.

"No."

"Listen, Jim... I'm in a bad spot. I, I had no other way. I never meant to play you. No. No, that's not true. But that was before. Before I knew you. Before we... knew each other."

"I can walk right out of here and forget this whole week ever happened. I'm not committed," I lied. "You are. Any more deception. Any secret. Any omission. And I walk."

She was scared. You can fake fear but I knew her enough by now to tell the difference. Fool me once.

"I understand. No more secrets. I need this, Jim. I need you. If you walk... I'm dead before the end of the week."

"Tell me about the charges."

She closed her eyes a moment. This was hard for her, this was deep. She leaned forward, speaking softly. Not quite whispering.

"Four years ago I was asked to turn half a billion rubles in cash into pristine sterling. That's about five million pounds. Not a big deal."

I nodded silently, with her so far.

"I had a solid contact. Had done the same for me many times. Getting the cash into the Russian banking system is easy. The tough part is—"

"You ran the old mirror trade?" I interrupted. This part was predictable.

"Gazprom and Sberbank mostly. Buy the shares in Russia, sell them in London. Have the bank map it internally. And just like that... you have clean Western money. Only cost 15% plus... slippage. The bankers who came up with it make good money."

"That hole got plugged years ago. Must have been fun while it lasted. Should net you a couple of years at the most, not exactly red notice stuff. Can't say I approve, but I've done business with people who did worse."

"Nobody would have found out either. It's not like the UK police or regulators care. Their entire economy is based on laundered Russian money, and they're not about to kill the golden goose."

"So what happened?"

"What you have to understand is that these methods... these ways of cleaning money, they depend on implicit approval. On both sides. The Russians aren't dumb, but they're greedy. At least they're smart enough to get paid. The Brits... they're in on it but not in the same way. I mean, the politicians know they need Russian oligarchs, and they don't want to know where the money came from. Enforcement is simply not, well, prioritized."

I didn't speak. She hadn't answered me. None of this was news to me. Anyone in the business, clean or dirty, knows that the two best places in the world to launder money is London and Delaware.

"This time, they came at us hard. The Brits. Made it their business to hit everyone involved."

"Because the money was proceeds from illegal arm sales?" I should have remained quiet and let her speak but I couldn't stop myself.

"Everyone's got a finger in the supposedly illegal arms business, Jim. The Russians, the Americans, the Brits, the French. They deal in secret with gray arms dealers who do the dirty work

A Most Private Bank

for them. No one cared in the past."

"But this time they did."

She nodded slowly. "This time… The Americans saw a chance to put a carrier group at Crimea. It would have been poetic justice for them, after nearly getting Soviet nukes on Cuba."

"Right. So you became collateral damage. When elephants fight, grass suffers."

"I'm not saying I'm innocent. But terrorist financing? It's not like I raised money for bin Laden!"

"Yeah. A little excessive, perhaps. If my side gets you, you're looking at twenty years. At least you're too pale to be hooded and flown to Gitmo."

"Don't even joke about that!"

"Sorry. But you seem like someone who's comfortable on the run. You probably have a few quality passports. A few identities. Enough cash to stay afloat and the skills to get more."

"I can stay away from the law. If it's in my interest."

"But you're more concerned with Chekhov? Is that where you were this morning?"

To my disappointment, she didn't seem surprised. She simply nodded, confirming my suspicions.

"It was his money. His money I lost. But they never got to him. Because they never got to me."

"I'm surprised you're still alive."

"I'm alive because I'm good at what I do. It's not like he didn't try."

The pieces were falling in place as she spoke. How could I have been that blind? I thought I was a mile ahead of everyone. In my arrogance, I saw myself as the smartest guy in the room. The one who knows who the sucker at the table is. This slipup made me wonder.

"So that's what this is all about," I muttered quietly to myself.

"What's in that safe implicates us both, implicates everyone involved. Names, signatures, the lot. The companies we used and everyone behind them. I'm only alive because those documents are in the wind."

The waiter interrupted with perfect timing. I needed some space to consider this. I ordered for her without asking. This place didn't have an English-language menu and even if it had, she wouldn't know what any of these dishes were. I got her the cordon bleu with röstli and beef tartare for myself. Pinot noir to share.

"You went to see him this morning. Alone. Brave girl."

"I convinced him that I'm the only one who can get him his files."

"He seems to be under the impression that I can get it," I objected after tasting and approving the pinot noir.

"You're needed, yes. But hardly trusted. I'm not either, but me he can threaten. Well, he can threaten you too, but I can be disappeared without headlines. You can't."

"And you said, what, that you've played me, that you've made me fall madly in love with you, and that I'll give you the papers? No questions asked?"

"Close. I said that I can steal the documents without you noticing. And give them to him."

"You won't give him anything."

"No. If I give him the documents, I'm dead. Perhaps I am, perhaps not. If he's got those papers, he has a choice. To trust me or not."

"Sounds like you've got a plan."

"We keep the files. We have a trusted law firm keep them, sealed. With instructions to post them to authorities and media if anything happens to us. We disappear together, Jim. New lives. We'll live in Brazil or Israel or... We'll start fresh. You and me. No more secrets."

I couldn't help being impressed. Here she is, this fragile young girl. This one-hundred-pound cute little thing. Going toe to toe with a Russian oligarch. And winning. She had thought this through, and she knew what she was doing. Her proposition made sense, and for a moment my mind drifted off to a warm beach in the Caribbean, the two of us sharing a drink at sunset by our very own private stretch of sand by our mansion.

I moved my left hand to hers, resting it on top of her hand, lifting my crystal glass to hers.

"No more secrets," I whispered.

She seemed suspicious when her cordon bleu arrived but after she saw my tartare, she had no complaints. Raw minced meat with an equally raw egg cracked on top of it isn't for everyone, even with a fancy French name.

"It's not done yet," I reminded her. "We have a problem."

"You're good at solving problems. That's why I picked you."

"Sure. That and the fact that I'm the only one in this town who could actually land a deal like this. Still, we've got quite some distance left.

"Until this is all done, one way or another, you should stay in character as Chris. There's no one but Chris, not now. Not yet."

"Yeah. Got it," she said, overdoing the American accent on purpose.

"And stay with me, or where I tell you to be. I can't protect you if I have no idea where you are. I assume you already know about the New York situation?"

She nodded. Not surprising. Chekhov would be well-informed and the subject likely came up.

"How's the cordon bleu?" I asked, seeing her careful examination of what was on her plate.

"It's... different. But not bad. What is it?"

"That's veal, wrapped around ham and cheese. Breaded and panfried. Well, Swiss food takes some getting used to, I suppose. Try the rösti. It's a Swiss potato pancake - you'll like it. You got checked out of Fleming's?"

She washed down the mix of veal, ham, and cheese with a gulp of red wine and tried the fried potato pancake. That seemed more palpable to her.

"You told me not to go back there," she pointed out.

"Good. I'll have Sandra check you out and get your stuff. You should be ready to travel. Either way, no matter what the outcome, you would be in danger. Even if some deal can be made with Chekhov, your presence has raised questions. The powers that be are asking about you."

"And did you... tell them about me?" She was looking into my eyes. Those big blue eyes, those eyes that must have melted many hearts. They must have separated many men from their money. But this was no act. She was concerned. For herself. And perhaps for me.

"They don't know much. And I haven't volunteered information. They know I have a client. Someone who initiated all of this. They know I wouldn't suddenly wake up one day and decide to take over a bank on my own."

"Did you—"

"No. I've said what I need to say to get what I want. But I haven't named you or compromised you."

"When will it be over?" Her voice was soft. Quiet even. There was no doubt in my mind that this was a woman who could be as tough as any man, when that's what was required. She'd a rough life and she'd come up the hard way. She was also under a tremendous amount of stress. This must have been building up in her for a long time.

One wrong step to the left and she'd be looking at life in a federal prison. One wrong step to the right and she'd be found duct-taped in some river. No safe harbor, no place to let your guard down. And now she was forced to. Now it was out of her control. All up to me.

I put my hand back on hers. I wanted to tell her that all will be fine. That I could solve this, that I could fix any problem. But that would be a lie. Perhaps it would work out. Perhaps it would all fall in place. Perhaps.

"Tomorrow. Tomorrow we'll know. It won't be over tomorrow. But we will know. And until then, we're safe. It's in everyone's interest that tomorrow is seen through. Even if everyone has a different interest in how the day turns out."

"How will it turn out?" she whispered. The stress of the week was palpable, and her original British accent was shining through.

"If the last pieces of the puzzle fall in place… the day will turn out as I want it to," I said, squeezing her hand.

"No matter how it turns out… thank you. And… I'm sorry for dragging you into this."

Nina Meier

We ended up having a second bottle of pinot noir, and our lunch lasted over two hours. It had been quite a week for us both, and this was a welcome break. By the time we left, the place was almost completely cleared out. Both because it was way past Swiss lunchtime and because the weather was picking up again. A storm was brewing, and the trees along Bahnhofstrasse were bracing for the assault.

I walked her back to the Hyatt. She held my arm with both hands the entire walk back and we made it there just in time before the rain. The concierge spotted us and held the side door open for us as we approached. All I wanted was to rest. One uneventful evening, a brief rest before the big day.

But of course. There she was. The other one.

Not that many people knew I had been living at the Hyatt for the past four months. Nobody's business. But she knew. Nina Meier knew. And there she was. Waiting for me in the lobby with all the cheerfulness of a Pamplona bull.

"Hey, Chris... Why don't you go up ahead?" I tried. But it was too late.

Nina had turned one of the large armchairs so that it faced the entrance. From the looks of her, she had probably waited there for some time. Now she stormed toward us like a freight train.

"You've been impossible to reach all day! We're at battle stations on the trading floor and you go AWOL? We've got to sort this right now!"

She was pissed. She should be. Her job was on the line. She put me back with P&P, she vouched for this deal. Now the bank was on the line for $40 million.

Hardly an enormous sum for the bank, but enough to derail her career. But I hadn't put her in this situation. Her own greed and ambition had. She was the one who signed off on anti-money-laundering and know-your-customer documents without having done any actual due diligence.

"Hey, Nina," I started. After a couple of bottles of nice red and a surprisingly pleasant time at lunch, I was in no mood for some childish scene. Two nights ago she had slept in my room upstairs. Here I was with another girl around my arm, and she's yelling about a business transaction. "I've already spoken to Preston. The deal is on, just some details left."

"What's she? Goldman? JPM? Hooker? I don't care, get rid of her!"

So she had noticed. But she didn't see a romantic rival. She worried about another investment banker taking her place.

"Chris, honey, why don't you wait upstairs? You've got your key card, right?" That was childish of me, but she deserved it. For all the times she'd been up there, Nina never had her own key card. And she never would.

She waited with her arms crossed, waiting for Chris to make her way to the elevators. I wasn't about to tell her that the person she just insulted was the one her bank was about to wire $40 million to. She never even asked who was the beneficial owner of the shell company they were lending money to. Bankers rarely ask questions they may not want answers to. Not if there's enough profit potential for them.

I looked at my wrist. The old Submariner always made me smile. Something of the pinnacle of stealth wealth, a piece that would evoke diametrically opposite reactions from different people. Sold as a tool watch and used as such for decades, considered expensive back when it retailed for a few hundred bucks. Now a vintage piece, visibly weathered by experience and greatly underestimated by the uninitiated. More than twice as old as the furious investment banker in front of me, and it told me that I really didn't have time for a pointless argument in a hotel lobby.

"Look, Nina, is there something I can help you with?"

"You can explain yourself, for starters! We're just doing this deal to get you back in. Seemed low risk anyhow, but now. Now with the CEO arrested. We have no idea what the exposure might be. What's the rush anyhow, can't we just wait a few weeks and see what's going on?"

"No. The deal was very clear. I will proceed this week and P&P is committed. The money will be there by tomorrow morning, or my lawyers will go to the mattresses."

"You could at least explain what's going on. What's the rush? You have a lot of people really worried back in the office."

"I'm afraid it's a little above your pay grade. You've played your part and if all goes well I'm sure you'll get a nice bonus. Was there anything else?"

"Enjoy your hooker," she said in a well-honed icy tone and walked toward the big revolving doors. At least she didn't make a scene.

Chris was on the living room couch when I got up to the suite. Her high heels kicked off and her tight Gucci dress replaced with a robe, her dark hair flowing over her left shoulder down over her chest.

"Your ex?" she asked, sounding more teasing than upset. She blew her smoke away from me - she knew I didn't care much for cigarettes.

"An investment banker. She thought she was playing me and now she's in tears when it turns out I was playing her. She's a big girl, she understands the game."

"She gonna come out ahead in the end?"

"Wouldn't expect so."

"Good," she said, putting out her cigarette in the ashtray. "Didn't like her much."

"You gonna be okay here this afternoon? I need to take care of some things out and I'd feel much easier knowing you're safe back here."

She was half reclining on the couch in that robe, nodding slowly to me. "I'll behave. I need the rest anyhow - I left really early this morning. No promises about that minibar though."

"Minibar's useless. Call room service instead. Don't open the door for anyone but room service."

I kissed her forehead. Hard to imagine what she'd been through. Not just this week but in her life. How does someone go from a regular Manchester teenager to learning how to navigate the Russian underworld? Dealing with the worst of the worst, gaining their respect, becoming one of them, laundering their money. And still remain such a sweet girl.

The words lingered in my head a moment. Sweet girl. Was that all she was, how I saw her? A sweet, fragile girl in need of rescue? No, not anymore. That was how I saw her before. Before I knew, before I saw what she really was. I had swum in the shark-infested waters of high finance far too long not to recognize one of my own.

Her lies were different from mine, her acts, her personas, the characters she put on. All well-honed, practiced, and polished. No, sweet girl or not, she was skilled in lying, manipulating, and getting what she wanted. Just like me. Sharks aren't usually pack hunters, but you don't see them eating each other on the Discovery Channel either.

She was still lying to me, I knew that. I didn't mind - I didn't need total honesty. I had my secrets and she had hers.

She was asleep by the time I got back. It had been a long afternoon and an even longer evening. It hadn't been easy to get it all done. Nothing this week had been easy. Perhaps it wouldn't matter anyhow. Perhaps the entire day was wasted. The entire week. If not for that greedy old banker, it could all have been over. And now. Now I needed to put my faith in the hands of the only people I despised more than bankers. Government bureaucrats.

I had lost my temper at Sandra back in the office. Wasn't her fault. She was just concerned. I was a total wreck all day. The dopamine drain had me looking like a ghost, playing tricks with my mood, pushing me from exhaustion to rage to despair. It had taken all my remaining energy to keep it together during that lunch. That was important. She had to feel safe.

The wine we had over lunch didn't help. It had reminded my body of yesterday and it was crying out for more. For more than alcohol. Damned Russian.

I had been screaming, on the phone and at people. I was barking orders like an insane leader during his last stand in some bunker with no one around having the guts to stand up to me. No one but Sandra. My rock of sanity in a sea of madness. I fired her on the spot.

It wasn't the first time I fired her, and she replied with the words I deserved. It had been quite some years, but she knew this routine and she knew very well that she wasn't actually fired.

There I was, back home. Home. In my semipermanent suite at the Hyatt. The jacket thrown over an armchair, the shirt halfway opened up, staring at myself in the mirror. Reminding myself of why. There had been ample opportunity to simply walk away.

The money didn't matter. No, that's not true, money always matters. But the money wasn't the reason. It had nothing to do with it. The money served a purpose, but none of this, none of this insane week would be worth it if this was about money.

I stood there in the bathroom for what felt like hours, just looking into my own eyes. I was staring down the abyss and the abyss was staring back. This time, I liked what I saw.

Friday

The Price

"Are we on or what?"

"Morning to you too," replied the man who had just called me.

"If it was a flat-out no you wouldn't bother calling. What're your terms?"

"Have it your way. Any document pertaining to politically exposed US persons belongs to us. Physical paper data on numbered account holders. Any leak and all bets are off. Open season."

"No need for threats. I got no dog in that fight. What else?"

I got up from the bed and walked over to the window, glancing out through the small sliver of light coming in. I didn't want to pull the curtains yet - I preferred if she slept through this particular call.

"Copies of the other client files. Do what you like with the originals. And the identity of the leak."

"Don't push it, Donahue. I'm in deep enough with lifting your files - no way I get caught photocopying the lot just so you get a slight head start. But you'll get your leaker. I got no reason to protect that bastard."

"Figured as much. But there's one more thing. Nonnegotiable," he continued.

I was holding the old-fashioned hotel phone in one hand, receiver in the other. Standing by the window, stretching the cord, trying to be as far from the bed as it would let me. The receiver pressed hard against my ear, I looked back at her while Mike Donahue laid out his final demand.

She slept on her tummy, the blanket halfway down, her face away from me. She had been asleep when I came back last night and hadn't woken since. Not as far as I had noticed anyhow. It was her deception that had led me down this path. Her lies had put me in a position where I needed to break the law. A situation that could result in my own bones being broken. Or worse. But looking at her sleeping there, I couldn't bring myself to fault her, not for that.

I knew she was lying. I knew from the day she showed up in my office. Perhaps I didn't know why. Even about what. Certainly I didn't understand the severity of the situation. But I knew something was wrong. This is finance. People here lie for a living. Trust is a scarce commodity in my world and I'd been around been long enough to know. No, I couldn't blame her for her lies.

He didn't know about her, didn't know who she was. All he knew was that whoever had put me up to all of this was a prize worth catching. There was only one way I could get Mike Donahue to agree to do what I needed done. Only one way forward.

"After the deal's done. I'll get you that piece of information," I told him. I turned away, turned my back to her and the bed, as if that would ease my conscience of what I'd just agreed to. There may still be time to play it my way. "All I care about is my deal and my fee," I lied.

"We can live with that. Look, Jim, we can't do a thing about the local authorities. But we'll stay clear. You'll get no interference from us. We'll be watching, though."

"Leave the natives to me. How do we proceed?"

She was awake. I could see it in her breathing. No longer slow, deep breaths.

"Mr. Niederhauser wants to talk directly to you. Got a secure channel prepared. When can you be here?"

A Most Private Bank

My wrist was empty and I didn't see any clock on the wall. The sun was low, had just risen.

"Half an hour. Less if I get off the phone now."

"Then don't waste time talking to me."

The phone went dead and I put the receiver back down. He had called me at the Hyatt. I hadn't told him about the hotel. Perhaps he wanted to show that he was not completely without resources.

"Good news?" she asked, opening her eyes. She had probably been awake, listening the entire time. Probably out of habit. At least she could only hear my side of the conversation.

"Good news. The Americans are in. I need to get to the consulate and make a secure call, and you don't want to show your face there."

"What are they asking for? Why are they making the deal?"

She was trying to sound curious, but she was worried all right. She had plenty to be worried about.

"They want all files on politically exposed US persons. All off-digital files on numbered accounts. Exclusive access."

"Why? Won't that be handed to them by the Swiss anyhow? Now that there's a criminal investigation building up?"

I was getting dressed as we spoke. No time to shower and shave. Not the start of the day I'd prefer, but time was of the essence today. Today it would all be settled. One way or another, it would all be over soon.

"Could be that they just want a head start on high-profile prosecutions, but the cynical side of me doubts it."

"Oh? What else then?" she asked, sitting up in the bed with the blanket over her chest.

"I'd guess there's some embarrassment they'd rather keep in-house," I replied as I was buttoning up my shirt. "They're just asking for PEP files, politically exposed persons. If they cared about crimes, they'd go after the lot. No, they're looking to avoid a scandal."

"Like what, corrupt senators or something?"

"Mayors, governors, congressmen, senators... presidents. Don't know, don't care. Don't want to be anywhere near anything like that. Nothing to gain, plenty of risk."

She was sitting up in the bed, wearing a far-too-large white t-shirt. Mine. She looked into my eyes in silence, searching for answers in what I had not told her.

"Is that... all they want?" she finally asked. She wanted to trust me, like I wanted to trust her. She still wasn't sure. Even though I was.

"They wanted copies of other documents. And they wanted to know who my client is."

Her eyes were those of a deer, looking at the sudden movement of a bush, weary of hiding predators.

"Did you agree?"

I put the jacket on and folded my coat over my arm, walking up to the door.

"I said no to the documents. But I agreed to tell them who my client is. Hell, they'll find out sooner or later anyhow. These days, bank secrecy only goes so deep, and Christina Rosenbaum would have a tough time hiding the ownership of a bank. Look, I don't think you want to show your face at the consulate, so stick around here until I call you, okay? We'll hit the bank together and get what's needed."

I saw her nod slowly and she even gave me a smile. She was still worried, and after all I now knew, I couldn't blame her one bit. Stuck between a rock and a hard place, going at it alone for so long and now she'd got to trust someone she'd only just met a few days ago.

It'd been a weird week for us both.

Escape From New York

This time there were no childish games. No formal welcome and no stonewalling. Donahue was waiting for me and ushered me in quickly with only a brief handshake to slow us down. This time it was business, and this time we were on the same side. Presumably.

"All set up for you, Jim. Got a secure line, nobody listening in," he said as we walked into a small conference room.

"No one but your guys, I suppose," I added. "That's okay, I don't expect privacy. Not asking him on a date."

I threw the coat over a chair, unbuttoned my jacket, and took a seat. The room was smaller than the one I saw yesterday with just a round plastic table with a phone on it, a chair on either side. No windows in any direction. It gave the impression of absolute privacy even though there was no doubt in my mind that this call would be anything but private.

"Pick up the handset and press line seven when you're all set. He's standing by."

I was curious what kind of a deal the old banker had struck. He was a product of old money, self-confident to the point of arrogance, born into a family where etiquette and arcane social rules were hammered into your backbone before you could walk. A world impossible to enter for those not born into it, a society that politely allowed us mortals to occasionally interact with them as long as we never aspired to become like them.

Even for those of us who had been visiting their world for long enough to almost qualify as friends, it was still a minefield of impossible rules. By the time you were seated at the dinner table you would already have committed at least seven infractions

A Most Private Bank

of their unspoken code. Perhaps you looked people in the eye in the wrong order, perhaps you touched the wrong cutlery at the wrong time, or held your elbows at the wrong angle, or perhaps you simply just smiled when you were not supposed to.

The people produced by such an environment are often assumed to be lazy by those who have made their money the hard way. We see them as dumb and fat. Cake eaters. Despite their inevitably impressive list of academic credentials from the top schools of the world, more often than not this assumption holds true.

But I had known Nicholas Niederhauser for the better part of a decade, and he was anything but dumb and lazy. He could compete in arrogance with the best of them, but he was not stupid. The feds may have gotten the better of him with that sting job, and that could have happened to any of us. It was arrogance that got his nose stuck in that particular honeypot, arrogance and greed.

"Morning, Jim!" a voice called out to my ear. It was a poor connection with a loud whirring background noise.

"Nick, I hear you got yourself in a bit of a jam," I replied, projecting my voice to overcome the noisy line.

"I hear you had a hand in getting me out of it. I can only assume that you have some nervous gentlemen around you right now and that you are all very eager to get to the point."

"Getting to the point would be good, Nick. You know what I need?"

"Everybody knows what you need," laughed the old man on the other side. "The purchase documents are signed and notarized. Electronic copies sent, originals in the mail. Effective as of transfer of funds."

I looked at my wrist. The Sub showed a little before eight. The government man across the table nodded to me, confirming it.

"Impressive, given the hour over there."

"We've been at it all night. You don't think they'd let me take off without securing the papers, do you?"

"You're airborne? Where are you?"

"Oh, that would the coast of Newfoundland that's growing smaller in the distance. Should be back in Zurich in around… six hours. But surely you didn't arrange for this little phone call to inquire about my travel arrangements, Jim."

"Gonna need the details, old buddy. Where to find it and how to access it."

A hearty laughter came from the crackling line after the usual delay of satellite phone transmissions. "That was part of my deal, of course. To provide the new administrator of the bank with information on how to access certain files. Well, rest assured, Jim, that information will reach you before noon today."

"That's not what we agreed!" yelled the man in the cheap black suit in front of me. "You'll give us the details we need, and you'll do it right now!"

"Ah, that must be Herr Donahue. I expected you to be on the line. Our agreement stipulates that said information shall be communicated to our common friend this morning, meaning before lunchtime. It did not in any way indicate that I would tell you over an open phone line."

"Listen, you son of a b—"

"We've departed US airspace and unless you intend to scramble Raptors to bring us back, I suggest you quiet up and listen. I have sold a controlling stake of my family bank to Mr. Dixon's enterprise, and I shall make sure that Mr. Dixon receives all the information he requires. That is the extent of my arrangement. Handing client information to a third party would be a serious crime, and I cannot be expected to violate Swiss bank secrecy laws. If you believe that you have a claim on such information, do feel free to take it up with the new majority owner of the bank."

"I'll have you arrested and deported the second you land," Donahue tried.

"I'm sure you would do your best. But I suspect that you and Mr. Dixon will already have concluded this affair by then. Now, if you excuse me, I had a long night and I intend to get some sleep."

The line went silent. The reaction on my face and the face of the man in front of me could not be more different. I was smiling for the first time in days. He was not.

"Well, not much we can do about it, is there? Can't blame him for playing it safe. Look, if he says I'll get the info in a matter of hours, I'd take that seriously. Besides, once I've completed the transaction I can access anything in there. I might just find what we need all by myself."

If looks could kill, I'd be at the bottom of the lake by now. He hadn't counted on the old banker having a backbone.

"I don't need to explain to you what happens if you try to screw us over, do I?"

"Boy, am I glad you don't have those ninjas." I stood up and grabbed my coat. "We have a deal, and I intend to honor it. If you messed up your negotiations with Niederhauser, that's on you. Now you have to excuse me, I've got work to do."

Transfers

Having to actually search the bank for the files would be a problem. Highly confidential files were kept apart for a reason. Nothing digital, nothing that could be searched or leaked. The best way to keep a secret is to avoid anyone realizing that a secret exists in the first place.

Hollywood films are full of scenes where secret agents access anonymous numbered Swiss bank accounts by reciting a series of digits or having their eyeballs scanned. It makes for a tense scene in a movie, but that's not how these accounts work. Even in the old, Wild West days of Swiss banking, private banks didn't just open an account with no owner, an account anyone could access with some secret password. The idea of having huge amounts of money, potentially tens or even hundreds of millions, secured by the kind of combination an idiot would have on his luggage is simply preposterous.

An account will always have beneficial ownership registered. Granted that in the old days Swiss banks were exceedingly flexible in how much they verified documents they were given, but someone or something was to be the owner of the assets. The way to hide ownership was not relying on anonymous numbered accounts. It was based on offshore shell companies and fiduciary holdings, with side letters confirming actual, ultimate beneficial ownership.

You simply open an account for ACME Holdings Panama or Johnny Smith from Arkansas and, to the outside world, that's the owner as far as everyone but the bank is concerned. As long as there's a contract somewhere stating that ACME or Mr. Smith are just fiduciary owners, getting paid a small fee for pretending to be the owners, the bank has their backs covered. Those documents name the actual, secret owner. The beneficial owner. When done right, such papers were kept off the grid, accessible only to a few key personnel.

This is what we were looking for. The secret stash.

Nick Niederhauser probably knew exactly what we were after. What the government was after. Perhaps even what the Russian was after. It would be his business to know. If he wanted to avoid the risk of the US government getting its grubby mitts on those files then he probably had good reasons. All I could do was to go about my business and trust that he really did have a plan.

I was thinking all of this through on my way to the office. I walked up the riverbank by the Old Town. This stretch was what you'd see on Swiss postcards. Stone building after stone building, not one of them younger than a few hundred years. Each one in a different matte color. Gray, beige, eggshell, even pinkish. The bottom part of each building housed a restaurant or shop, with colorful flags flying from the ornate balconies. On a nice day, this place would be crowded.

But I didn't take this detour for the scenery. I still had a nagging feeling of paranoia, and I was heading for the Mühlesteg bridge. Just in the short walk from the lake to the train station, there were a total of six bridges over the Limmat. But only one of them was a narrow pedestrian bridge with clear sight in all directions. The kind weighted down by thousands of padlocks placed on the side grid by confused teenagers. This extra precaution was worth a minor detour.

I didn't see anyone. Not even when I stopped at that little platform in the middle of the bridge to pretend to admire the view. All I saw was a family of white swans passing below me and I imagined them looking up at me, judging me, and I turned away. Once I was satisfied that I wasn't tailed, I picked up the pace and headed straight to the office. It didn't really make sense. Anyone could have guessed I was heading to the office and taken a different route there.

I passed the coffee shop at the corner and headed up the stairs. There was a nagging feeling at the back of my head that I had missed something. Something important. I continued up the stairs, opened the door to Dixon Capital, and entered.

She was already there. Of course she was. My rock, my one constant.

"Need you to check the accounts of—"

"Eighty million on the Orphelia account, Jim. Forty from P&P, forty from Global Opportunities Fund," she interrupted.

"And the con—"

"Signed and notarized, both fax and electronic. Cover letter says originals on the way by FedEx. LGT are notified about imminent urgent transfer and standing by."

I had barged in like I was raiding the place all set to start barking orders on what needed to get done and fast. Now I was stopped dead in my tracks. She had anticipated what had to get done this morning and she was way ahead of me. I'm not sure why I was surprised.

"Looks like someone's got all her ducks in a row," I said and threw my coat over an empty chair. "Not sure what I would do without you, Sandra."

"You just remember that at bonus time, boss."

"I'll see what I can do… I'll see what I can do…" I repeated on my way to my inner office. Two men were already in there. Neither looked like a threat.

"Hey Jim. Almost done here, just installing the final camera." Guy shook my hand and nodded towards the man on the ladder. He was mounting a camera in the corner of the room. Small, discrete, and painted in the same eggshell white as the walls, it would blend in well.

"Listen, you asked me to keep a tab on anything of interest."

"Looks good, Guy. Barely even noticed the cameras myself. Yeah, what'd you hear?"

"Request for search warrant filed this morning at the Zurich district court. For Bank Niederhauser. Being processed today."

"A search warrant for a private bank must be quite a big deal. They can't have done many of those before."

"Yeah, highly unusual. You know how the Swiss cherish their bank secrecy. Civil proceedings are one thing, but they're asking for a proper raid."

"You know who filed it?"

"An Inspector Schmidt, major crimes unit. Signed off by the Zurich chief himself. They wouldn't try this unless they have something. My contacts in the force are quite excited about this one. It's not every day they get the chance to take a shot at big game."

Time was already short, and it just got shorter. It was nearly ten already.

"Any idea of when the judge makes a call on it?"

"There's a meeting at 2:00 p.m. If the cops got it down solid, and the judge has a pair, they'll get it. But it's Friday already, and if the judge isn't sold on the urgency, he'll push it to next week and play it safe. If they do get it approved, the cops will go in fast and hard. Before some lawyer can stop them."

"Got it. Thanks, Guy. I hate to do this to you, but I've got a helluva day and I need the office."

"Sure thing. Let me just show you where the panic buttons are and we'll be out of your hair."

Six panic buttons around my office. Cleverly placed, both for convenience and inconspicuous access. By the edge of my desk, on the wall by the safe, by the desk phone. Someone could study these little devices for quite some time without realizing what they were. The common feature of all of them was the two parallel openings, separated by a thin metal sheet. You would need to use two fingers, pushing both buttons at the same time. No way you do that by accident.

A signal from these little puppies would trigger an immediate armed response, and with the local station just a block away, you'd only need to stall an intruder a few minutes. If I had bothered installing this earlier, Raph would still be here.

The floor had been cleaned, but the pool of blood had left its permanent mark. The only way to get rid of that would be to replace the carpet. But I had no such plans. Not anymore. That dark circle next to my safe was a reminder. A reminder of my mistakes. My arrogance. A reminder to see this through.

First things first. It was game day. Today it would all be settled. Perhaps. This day could also be my last. I picked up the desk phone and dialed the number. Rehearsing it all in my head, reminding myself of what needed to be done today. She answered on the second ring.

"Hello?"

Good girl. No name, no accent, just a brief word. Playing it safe.

"Chris, it's me. All systems are go, and we're ready to get this done."

"Great, what do you need me to do?" she replied, sounding American now that I'd called her Chris.

"First call LGT and release the funds. All eighty's in the Orphelia account, contract is signed, and the deal is in effect upon receipt. Transfer needs to be immediate - they have the account and all details. They just need your say-so. It's your company, after all."

A Most Private Bank

"I'll call right away. And then... we have the bank?"

"Then we have the bank. But we're not out of the woods yet. After Dumas confirms the transfer, come meet me by the bank. I'll wait for you outside. Just need to make some calls. I'll see you there!"

I shook off any sense of doubt and told myself that there was only one way. Forward. A shark keeps moving forward or he dies. Next call.

"Bühler, Jim Dixon. We're on. Should be all set in an hour or less. Tell Dick that I'll be there soon. He'll get what he paid for."

I listened to the excited young man's questions and comments. This was quite an adventure to him. This kid had probably never even been inside a private bank. As Swiss as he was, he probably believed in the American movie versions of how private bank vaults worked. Still, he wasn't a bad kid. Just got mixed up with the wrong banker.

"Hey, Bühler," I interrupted him. "The weather is clearing up out there. This might not be a bad day to call in sick. I'd go for a hike in the mountains if I were you."

I clicked off. Didn't waste time waiting for his questions. There were far more important considerations.

The Information Vending Machine

I grabbed my coat, folded it over my arm, and put my hat on in one movement, heading out the door and down the stairs. Time was of the essence. Somewhere some smug cops were waiting around, ready to go raid their first private bank as soon as they got their authorization. At the bottom of the stairs, I kicked open the front door of the building with my foot while swinging the coat around me, passing the coffee shop while pushing my left arm through the sleeve of the coat, nodding a quick greeting to the private eye having his espresso, walking up the narrow and slanting cobblestone path between the stone buildings, picking up the speed in the direction of the bank.

Private eye?

I was already halfway to the bank when the thought that had been rattling around my brain finally took root. Private eye.

I stopped a moment by a display window. A Japanese lady holding a yellow flag on a stick passed me, a flock of her countrymen following like a row of ducks, all with a little earpieces telling them what they were pointing their heavy SLR cameras at. The thought was firming up in my mind. Private eye. Yes, that made sense, didn't it?

Standing there, looking into the display window, it was starting to crystallize in my mind. I only snapped out of it when I realized that the window belonged to Victoria's Secret and that I had been absentmindedly staring at the crotch of a mannequin for a few minutes.

I turned on my heal and headed straight back down the hilly cobblestone footpath where I had come from. Turning the corner, toward the coffee shop, there he was. He and his walrus mustache.

He was at the same table as he had been a couple of days ago. The best table to pick if he wanted me to spot him. Carelessly sipping a tiny little espresso, smiling to me as if I was right on time for some prearranged meeting.

"Mr. Adler. You got something for me?" I asked him as I approached.

"Please, do sit down, Mr. Dixon. Have a coffee. Americans are always in such a… rush."

"Either you got something for me or you don't," I replied without sitting down. "If you pardon my French, I've got a helluva day and time is running out fast."

"Patience is a virtue, my dear. I can assure you that sitting down and having a coffee will be well worth your time."

He moved his hand, gesturing to the chair in front of me. He moved slowly and he talked slowly. He was an easy man to underestimate. Easy to write off as yet another slow, lazy European. But the eyes spoke a different language. Sharp. Deadly.

I pulled the chair out and sat down.

"Espresso. Make it a double."

The slow-moving man lifted a light brown leather binder up to his lap. He pulled the elastic strap to the side and opened up the binder. Taking his sweet old time, he studied the documents for a moment, testing my patience. It took restraint to keep my mouth shut and sip my espresso.

"It would appear, Mr. Dixon, as if you now belong to the very select group of private bank owners," he finally said. Slowly.

"I'm afraid you're misinformed," I cut him off. "I am merely the administrator of a holding company. I have no stake in any bank."

"Ah, but of course. If you say so, sir. But semantics aside, Mr. Dixon, it is you who now holds the authority over the bank. And everything in it."

"And what exactly is in it, Mr. Adler?" I asked, getting tired of this little game.

"Come now, Mr. Dixon. Knowledge of such matters is neither something which I should have, nor is it something I desire to possess. What I do know is that whatever is in the bank is, shall we say, unhealthy. Knowledge can be a dangerous thing, Mr. Dixon. But possession… can be fatal."

"I'm aware of the risks, thank you very much. Look, time is ticking. You got something for me or not?"

The Swiss way was never direct. To simply cut to the chase just wasn't in their DNA. The old sleuth grunted back. He had been enjoying this game. Until the loud, rude American cut him short.

"I have been authorized to provide you with these documents, Mr. Dixon. They are attested originals signed by Mr. Niederhauser and the other owners, authorizing unfettered access and full cooperation on the part of the bank."

"That would certainly save me some time arguing ownership questions with bank security. But how could you possibly have signed originals? Nick's still on a flight over the Atlantic."

"Mr. Niederhauser likes to plan for all eventualities, Mr. Dixon. It was all prepared before his travels. And left in my care."

"How very Swiss of him. Any particular reason you didn't tell me the other day that you work for Niederhauser?"

The old private eye smiled again. As much as he annoyed, me I couldn't help but respect him. Here was a man who did what he loved doing and didn't care who didn't like it.

"Of course there was a reason, Mr. Dixon. As I am sure you

understand, I am in the information collection business. Not the information disbursal business. My directives from my client were somewhat different a few days ago."

"And what are your directives from your client now, if I may be so bold?" I tried.

"My new directives are to make myself helpful to you and your endeavor, Mr. Dixon, in any way I am able and at my own discretion."

I sat back on my chair for a moment to think about what this meant. Yes, an easy man to underestimate. He says what he's supposed to say, no more no less. A man of his profession and experience, in this town, can be trusted. Trusted not to break the rules, not to take risks.

"Unless you advise otherwise, I intend to open a large, floor-standing green safe box. You wouldn't happen to have any advice on how I should accomplish this?" I tried.

"Of course. Do you have a pen handy, Mr. Dixon?" he replied without batting an eye. He had expected this question.

"Don't need one."

"Eight, five, three, seven, nine, ten, eight," he said slowly. "Would you like me to repeat?"

"Eight, five, three, seven, nine, ten, eight," I repeated. "Got it. Anything in particular I should be prepared for in terms of the contents?"

"I understand that Mr. Niederhauser is very fond of color coding. I hear it's a common habit among dyslectics. Makes it easier not to mix important things."

I listened intently. He was right. This little game was worth sitting down for. Not as dumb as he looked. Both Niederhauser and Adler. He was playing it safe, talking in generalizations. Avoiding liability.

"Makes sense. I had no idea he's dyslectic."

"He likes green for financially, or shall we say fiscally, complicated situations," he started. I saw no reason to interrupt. "The color blue signifies political issues to him. And as it turns out, he tends to use red when there is a more… physical risk involved. I do hope this is clear to you, Mr. Dixon."

"Crystal. Am I correct in assuming that this is the only reason for the sudden interest in the bank? Nothing special downstairs, for instance?"

"I am unaware of any further items of note," he replied curtly.

The man was an information vending machine. Told to volunteer nothing but to answer direct questions. At least that's what it seemed like. I paused a moment.

"Is there anything else I should be asking you?"

"Really, Mr. Dixon?" he proclaimed, as if such a question was violating the unspoken rules of this game.

"Right. Well, as fun as this is, I really do have to get going," I said as I stood to my feet. I watched his face, looked into his eyes for an answer to that final question. He folded up his little leather binder, and there was nothing in his eyes that told me that I should worry.

"Happy hunting, Mr. Dixon."

Breach

The cold wind ran through the narrow footpaths like rats in a maze. The smell of the lake was inescapable in any part of the Old Town's myriad of wind tunnels. The troop of Japanese tourists hadn't gotten far, but now their identical white umbrellas were all folded up. The theme of *The Godfather* came from an open window by the Croatian-run pizzeria. The lunch crowds of bankers filled the tables rapidly. The fog was thicker by the square, the cathedral tower fading out halfway by the large gold clock on the facade, with the year 1732 written just between the clock and the ornate window below. Squinting, I looked up at the time.

The window was open. Halfway open. A rifle scope! No. A camera lens. Sneaky bastards. No sense in hiding my face, they already got it. Hers too. The cathedral was just across the square from the bank. Not easy getting in or out unseen. If all went well it wouldn't matter. And if things went bad, it would matter even less.

She could have used one of those white umbrellas. Her long black hair all wet from waiting out in the rain for me. At least she had the sense to wear that green Gucci coat. Must have been here for twenty minutes, maybe more. Surprised she didn't seem upset about it. She smiled when she saw me and even tried to kiss me. I pulled away.

"Is everything all right, Jim?" She sounded concerned.

"Fine."

"Did something happen?" she asked.

"I... I'm just stressed."

I led her inside the outer doors of the bank, to the marble

landing. The two security guards in dark suits took little notice of us. A couch and a coffee tabled on one side, a receptionist behind ballistic glass on the other, and security doors leading to the stairway and elevators in the middle. Safe from prying long lenses, I turned to her and kissed her.

"It's not over yet," I whispered. "There's a thousand ways this could end badly. And if it does... if it ends badly... I just want you to know that I, that I care. That I tried."

"That wasn't so hard to say, was it?" she asked.

"You have no idea how hard that was to say."

"If things do go south, I want you to know that I wouldn't regret at thing. I came to you because nobody else could have gotten this far, this fast. Nobody. And... I really care... too."

We both smiled to each other for a moment. There was an unspoken and very real sense of mutual respect. No, something deeper. Admiration. More. But I didn't dare to think that word. Not now.

"You ready?" I whispered, having been lost in her eyes.

"I was born ready!" she replied, and I had no reason to doubt it.

I turned on my heel and walked up to the receptionist counter. The lady behind it seemed somewhat familiar even if I couldn't figure out why. I spoke English, making sure Chris could understand. Chris. That's how I thought of her. That's how messed up my brain had gotten this week.

"Jim Dixon. I represent Orphelia Holdings, the new majority owner of the bank, and—"

"But of course, Herr Dixon, you are expected," she interrupted. I had been all geared up for a fight, to have to play the loud American who just wouldn't accept no for an answer. To make a scene and demand the in-house lawyers come review the papers I had in my hand. But she had been forewarned. By whom?

"Herr Niederhauser has requested that you be extended every courtesy, Herr Dixon."

"The entire staff is informed of this?" I asked her.

"Just key personnel. Upper management, security and myself. I am Frau Schubert, Herr Niederhauser's personal assistant. I do not normally man the front desk, but I thought it may be helpful on a day like this."

"Of course," I said, feeling like an idiot. "We met briefly the other day. I apologize, I had a stressful day. I appreciate the assistance, Frau Schubert. That's all I can ask for. We will be up by Nick's... well, the CEO office in a moment. Please meet us there. I'm sure one of these ladies can take over the front desk."

The old fox had called ahead. Once more he was a step ahead of me, once more he had surprised me by not being as dumb as he looked. He had gotten his money, and that was perhaps his most important goal, but that didn't mean he was happy handing the keys over to the authorities.

"Chris," I said, sticking strictly to her cover identity, "stay close to me and act as if all of this is normal."

She played the part to a T. She looked arrogant, entitled, and impatient. The look of someone used to being waited upon, someone who hardly gets excited about the takeover of an insignificant little bank.

I walked up to the security doors where the older of the two guards was standing. He was in a dark suit and black necktie. A skin-colored plastic wire curled from his ear back into his shirt.

"Need you to follow us around, opening locked doors and overcoming unexpected obstacles," I told him without bothering to check his name tag.

"Yes sir," he replied and swiped his card to open the security doors. I nodded a silent thank-you and walked in with her following closely behind. She didn't say anything, but I could see what was on her mind. She glanced at me and nodded discreetly toward the security guard.

I grinned back at her. "These aren't just security guards, Chris. They are private bank security guards. Swiss private bank security. This guy has probably seen more personal details than an army doc and heard more secrets than a catholic priest. Isn't that so?" I directed that last question toward the man following us.

"I wouldn't know about that, sir," he replied.

"See, Chris? The main qualification for their job isn't to be tough guys. It's to be able to pretend they've never seen some Disney starlet do coke off a meeting table while discussing her hidden millions in the Bahamas."

Her laughter made me feel more relaxed. She was cute when she laughed.

"A bank like this isn't exactly like your local HSBC branch. When you bank with Niederhauser, you get personal service. And that means personal," I explained as we walked up the marble stairs with the security guard right behind us. "They do whatever it takes to make the ultra-wealthy happy. Twenty-four-hour concierge service. Sometimes some sheik and fifty of his closest friends just touched down in the middle of the night and now they want the LV at Bahnhofstrasse to open up at 3:00 a.m. for a private shopping spree. Sometimes a rock star needs twenty grams delivered to his hotel in less than half an hour. A movie star needs a couple of call girls, or boys for that matter. Some tech entrepreneur needs help in disposing of the body of the hobo he ran over in a rented Lambo. Am I right?" I knew he was listening behind us, and I kept talking to set her at ease.

"Never had to dispose of a body, sir, not yet," he replied with

A Most Private Bank

a face straining not to smile.

"Well, the day is still young. Would you open this for me, please?"

The guard pulled his card through the slot and fingered the keypad. He held the door open for us and stood aside as we walked in. He didn't have to be asked to wait outside.

They insist on calling it a trading floor even if it bears no resemblance to an actual trading floor. This was a part of the bank that no client, no matter how important, would ever see. A client would be met downstairs and ushered into the luxurious meeting rooms, the lounge, library, or the dining hall. Some may even get to see old man Niederhauser's office. But certainly not the trading floor.

Anyone seeing a picture of the room could have easily mistaken it for an insurance sales operation. Back office at a car dealership, perhaps. Beige divider screens parted the Ikea desks, two twenty-four-inch Dell monitors on each with the ubiquitous Bloomberg keyboard next to their most important professional tool - the telephone.

The people manning these phones weren't traders. They were relationship managers. They were responsible for their allocated set of clients, in whatever form those clients may require. If a client asks them to jump their job, is to ask, "How high?" The two-thousand-dollar-a-month Bloomberg terminals they had in front of them were not for trading. They were in case a client asked the price of IBM. If a client wanted to place a trade, they would put them on hold and call UBS or Credit Suisse to let a real trader execute it.

The relationship managers were all semi-casual, in white shirts with rolled-up sleeves. Full set of suits and shirts hanging in the wardrobe, in case a client showed up unexpectedly. The ones not on the phone were glancing nervously toward us as we walked past. By our outfits, we probably looked like clients.

We were heading for the back row. His unmistakable gray slick-back hair was sticking up over the divider screen. He was on the phone and hadn't seen us yet. I could hear his voice, speaking French, reassuring some wealthy schmuck that some options losses were a temporary setback, the cost of doing business, and that steady players stick to the path. Something along those lines.

I called out to get his attention.

"Hey, Dick!"

He looked up, surprised to see us but unable to hide his excitement.

"Pardon, monsieur, puis-je vous rappeler? Bon. Mais oui, bien sur. Bon journée, monsieur, au revoir," he finished up his conversation. "Jim! How did you get in here? Well, never mind that, how are things looking? Where do we stand?"

I accepted his outstretched hand. A firm grip and a cocksure look in the eyes. A well-trained salesman.

"We're golden. We hold the bank and have full access. Total control."

"We? Who exactly has control?" he asked.

"We, Orphelia Holdings. Of which a local startup hedge fund appears to be the controlling partner. I suspect anyone who holds sway with them could do just about anything they want around here."

He looked around over what apparently passed as a trading floor around here and lowered his voice.

"Don't play games with me, Jim, not now. Can you get me into the vault or not?"

I couldn't resist a playful grin on my face. I had no intention to stop playing games, not now.

"I'm not sure if you've met Ms. Rosenbaum. She is the CEO of Orphelia and the one who has the authority to make such decisions."

"Yes, yes, we met the other day. Well, can I get into the vault?"

She looked at me and I just smiled and shrugged back.

"Well... I don't see why not," she finally said. "As I understand, you do represent a majority owner of this bank now."

I held back my smile. This was simply too much.

"Chris, why don't you accompany Dick to the vault? The security staff will let him in on your say-so. Come meet me up on third at the CEO office right away afterward. It's the big corner office, you can't miss it."

She gave me a suspicious look. She had been suspicious of people all her life and she had had good reason for it. More often than not, her suspicions had been accurate.

"Look, time is of the essence, and we have lots to get done. You want to switch the tasks?"

"No... No, it's fine. Mr. von Baerenfells, if you show me to the vault, I'll make sure it opens for you."

"Open sesame!" He grinned. "Let me just get my gear and call my associate."

When I saw him pull out a large, black-and-red plastic case from under his desk, I turned and started walking out. I had already seen the sticker on it. A Black & Decker pneumatic drill. Whatever this lunatic intended to do with it, I hoped to be out of the building before he did it.

Dumb and Dumber

They left through the door at the back of the room. The three of them made for quite a sight. The exceedingly polite gorilla in the black suit. A diminutive socialite in a form-fitting green Gucci outfit with long, flowing black hair on his left flank. The right flank sporting a silver-haired banker in rimless glasses, gray pinstriped three-piece suit, carrying a plastic case for an industrial drill.

A chilling notion sent a shiver through my body as it made its way through my spine up to my brain. This week had taken its toll. It had worn me down, and there had been little time to question my initial assumptions. What if this old banker was not as dimwitted as he appeared to be? Could he really be that daft? Could anyone? What if he was actually on to something with the vault? What if he was the one playing me? Then again, there was that other notion. The much worse one. What if she had the upper hand? What if she was the one playing him? And me.

I was in the web, that much was for certain. But was I the spider, or the fly? And if I wasn't the spider, then who was? The Rubicon was crossed long ago and whatever lay ahead, there was no turning back. Not now, not ever.

The trading room sported a pungent assortment of odors, the most overwhelming of which was the stench of stale cigarettes. The *No Smoking* sign on the wall had round burn marks on it, as if someone had used it as an ashtray. The remaining relationship managers in the room continued their phone calls with hushed voices, glancing suspiciously at the intruder in the room. I had neither the time nor interest in whatever schemes they were cooking up for their clients.

A Most Private Bank

My strides back toward the door from which I came in were long and increasing in speed the farther I got. Once outside the door, I took off.

The marble stairway was carpeted down the middle. Royal crimson with ornate gold decoration by the sides. A white alabaster railing followed the curvature of the stairs all the way. Oil portraits of old Niederhauser patriarchal figures, former heads of the family, hung on the wall. Dark paintings in Renaissance style, showing powerful men at a slight upward angle. This entire place, all that the customers were supposed to ever see, had an emphasis on history, tradition, and heritage. At the top of the stairway, the Niederhauser family crest, positioned in a manner impossible to miss. The unmistakable smell of old money.

I suppose that when the office looks like the west wing of the Versailles Palace, it's easier to overlook that this was primarily an outfit based on hiding illicit money.

This staircase had seen its fair share of tax-dodging businessmen, kleptomaniac oligarchs, and corrupt politicians. Safe to assume, they hadn't seen many of them sprinting. Not until now.

At the top of the stairs, the crimson carpet flowed seamlessly from the stairs out over the white marble floor all the way up to an oak door. Outside the oak door, a neat desk. A telephone on one side, a discrete monitor on the other and an immaculate elderly lady behind it. One who had been expecting me, if not the fact that I would be out of breath after sprinting up the stairs rather than taking the elevator.

If my mode of arrival surprised her, she didn't show it.

"Bit of a rush, Frau Schubert," I said on the way up to the oak door. "I don't want to be disturbed."

No time for polite conversation. I hurried past her into the room I had seen last only days ago. That time the room was Nicholas Niederhauser's office. An office designed to make a visitor feel small, to make him feel as if he was in the presence of power. Elegant tapestries on the walls. An antique globe in wood, at least three feet tall, a painting of the bank's founder sitting in an armchair next to his German shepherd. The desk was larger than a conference table. It too antique, in ornate mahogany. Not as much as a computer on it. Nothing on the table would have looked out of place fifty years ago. Not the phone, not the mail out-box, not the leather-encased notebook or the Mountblanc fountain pen.

The room had a soft smell of sandalwood and cigars. A wooden cigar box placed on the drinks table by the side of the room, next to the decanters of whiskey and cognac. Time had not managed to make a dent in this room in the past century.

Neither whiskey nor cigars were my interest, not today. Time was running out fast. There it was, the 1944 Franz Jäger. The gold standard of traditional safe boxes. A huge green box, paint-chipped and faded over the years. A piece of furniture, a throwback to a different time. So antique, so cartoonish in its appearance, it was impossible to imagine that whatever it contained could be so dangerous.

I hadn't been in there for more than a few minutes, perhaps less, when the intercom buzzed. As stressed as I was, I couldn't help but marvel at the old-fashioned intercom. At least the office showed remarkable consistency. The intercom was of 1960s style, with a button to press when speaking.

"Mr. Dixon?" her voice called out.

I pressed the red button on the intercom, hoping it was the right one, and snapped back at her. "Thought I said I don't want to be interrupted!"

"There are two men in the lobby demanding to see you.

A Most Private Bank

Causing a bit of a scene. Security asking for instructions."

"Police officers?" I asked, trying to focus my mind without stopping what I was doing. A personal assistant to the chief of a bank like this knows her job. Had she been ordered not to interrupt, but interrupts anyway, she had a reason. Likely following protocols instilled in her over decades of service.

"They appear to have frightened the staff," she said. "The scene is escalating. We could lock down the entrance and call for police assistance."

"No! No, that won't be needed. Last thing we need. Tell them to stand down. Deescalate."

I dropped what I was holding and hurried out of the office. The elevator announced its arrival with a discrete ding. I stepped behind Mrs. Schubert's desk to see what she was motioning at. Chris was back with the security guard I left her with. The monitor on the desk showed two confrontational figures in the lobby. She had come back quickly, must have rushed to the vault and back. Penn and Teller in the lobby. Beads of sweat on my forehead.

"You okay, Jim? You look like you've seen a ghost," she said.

"There's a situation in the lobby. Associates of your old friend."

The gorilla next to her was wearing the same earpiece as the other guards I had seen around. He knew all about the situation - I could see it in his eyes. But he hadn't told her. Good man. Niederhauser ran a tight ship.

"Mrs. Schubert, please inform the lobby that these are my invited guests. Ask to have them escorted to the elevators and sent up here. No need for security. We'll be fine."

Chris walked around to my side of the desk to see for herself. My eyes on hers. She let out a soft gasp. Barely detectable if you weren't looking for it. Like a short, sharp inhalation.

"You know them?" I asked her.

She nodded slowly and I felt her fingers touching mine. Mrs. Schubert was clever enough to sense danger but experienced enough not to ask questions.

"This wasn't part of the plan. They are here. And we need to deal with it," I tried to reassure Chris. "We're in a bank. In the middle of the city. We'll be fine."

I felt her fingernails digging into my hand. She was afraid of them. She had reason to be. There was little time to do or say anything else. The elevator opened once more, and this time it contained two Eastern Europeans. One slim, one fat, zero smiles.

I moved out from behind Mrs. Schubert's desk and opened the oak door. "Gentlemen, step into my office."

They didn't need an invitation. Mrs. Schubert rose to her feet as the pair marched right in. The security guard who had escorted Chris back was nowhere to be seen. Perhaps dismissing him had been premature.

"Would you like some coffee? Tea?" Mrs. Schubert asked the two figures as they sat down in the visitors' chairs in front of the antique desk.

"Thank you, Ma'am, we're fine. But thank you for asking," the smaller and younger of the two replied in surprisingly good English. I hadn't realized until now that I had barely heard him speak before. Second-generation gangster.

I walked around the old wooden globe all the way behind the desk. Only one chair behind that desk. Three in front of it. I saw her eyes, her eyes pleading for assistance. She wouldn't be any safer behind the desk. It would offer nothing but psychological defense. I took a seat and so did she. Next to Teller. The three of them seated in front of my desk. My desk. As if this was somehow my bank now.

"That'd be all for now, Mrs. Schubert. Please hold my calls. We don't want to be disturbed."

They waited until the door was shut. Teller sat with one foot over the other leg's knee. He brushed some nonexistent dust off the side of his knee. Penn was leaning back in his leather chair, his knees and feet wide apart.

"Right, then," started Teller. A trace of an Eastern accent, but this thug sounded like he finished high school. Probably abroad. "We let you finish your end. Now it's our turn. You have something we want."

She was quiet but her ears were perking up. Sharp eyes, moving from Penn to me and back to Teller.

"And what exactly do you think I have?"

"Everything. You have everything, don't you?" the little bugger replied.

"Gonna have to be a little more specific there, Teller."

A little smirk on his face. The confident smirk of a spider, sizing up the fly stuck in his web.

"Give us the documents. And we'll be on our way."

"I just got here five minutes ago. How would I know where your documents are?"

He had a friendly smile. The kind of friendly smile that would make a man feel almost flattered to be murdered by him.

He opened up his jacket. His hand went inside and came back out with a Makarov pistol. The hand and the gun casually rested on Chris's thigh next to him as if it was an armrest.

"I understand you have grown somewhat affectionate toward Ms. Walker. That's good. She might need someone to care for her."

The pistol in his hand rested there, on her thigh. Aimed just a tiny bit downward. I couldn't see the safety catch, but his finger was on the trigger. Guess he went to the same firearms safety class as his boss. At least the Makarov had a safety catch, unlike its notorious TT-33 predecessor.

She was absolutely still, like a gazelle hoping the lion wouldn't see her if she didn't move. I saw her chest move, breathing slowly. Her eyes on that pistol aimed at her knee. If discharged, it would blow her knee clean off. She'd never walk again. I could have used a line right about now. Dismissing violent threats is a whole lot easier when you're high.

"We should be busy searching for the files. Whatever you think you're doing here isn't helping," I tried.

"By all means. Get busy finding."

The gun didn't move an inch. Neither did Chris. I grinned at him with stiff lips. Second-generation gangsters. Punks with attitudes.

"Chekhov knows you're busting in here like this? Jeopardizing the entire mission?"

"My *krysha* wants to make sure that you do what you say. Our methods are our own," the confident little man said. Penn had a tired, almost disinterested look on his face. The visitor's chair he was seated in looked far too small for him.

"Your boss wouldn't be too happy if you mess things up."

"No, no, no. Not boss. *Krysha*," he corrected me.

I glanced over at Chris and she spoke. She had to clear her throat halfway through her words. Her mouth sounded dry.

"Roof," she said. "*Krysha* means roof."

This appeared to amuse the two armed comedians. Even the fat man let out a little chuckle hearing this.

"So you haven't forgotten your time with Mother Russia after all?" Teller said. "Yes, yes, she's correct. A *krysha* is your roof. Your... protection. Everyone has a *krysha*. My *krysha* has a *krysha* and his *krysha* has one. All the way up."

"All the way to the Kremlin, I'm sure," I said. "And how would all of those people feel if you two geniuses manage to sink this entire project? Barging in here like the Red Army nearly bringing the police down on us."

"You met Mr. Adler on the way here. What did he give you? The location of the documents? Keys? Combination to that safe, perhaps?"

"Tell your *krysha* that he will have his papers tomorrow morning. At 9:00 a.m. And that I'll only give it to him personally," I said.

"Search him," Teller said to Penn. The fat man moved as one would expect from a person of his size. Slowly but with purpose. He was in no rush as he got up, cracked his enormous knuckles and moved toward me.

I rose to my feet, my hands at the ready. "Like hell he will!"

Teller's thumb moved and I heard the safety catch flip. The mountain approaching me showed no concern with my defensive stance nor could I see a reason why he should.

His big grubby hands rose up, and in the face of overwhelming odds I lowered mine. Penn seemed like an old-school Russian thug. The kind who came up the hard way. Easier to understand a man like that.

Teller was different. Second generation. Western educated. A privileged kid who did this for fun. The kind of kid who'd pull wings off insects and burn them with a magnifying glass. The kind who'd think that shooting off someone's knee would be amusing.

"All right, all right!" I said, putting my hands on the desk. "Search if you like. I got nothing on me, not a thing. Get it done so we can finally start searching for the papers!"

I stood leaning over the desk, meaty Russian hands going through my pockets. The sharp smell of cheap cologne and vodka made me grimace. My eyes locked on hers. A bead of sweat running slowly down her forehead.

That's when the intercom buzzed.

The Raid

"Mr. Dixon, we have a situation," the intercom announced.

My palms on the desk, hands going through my pockets, lining up my belongings on the desk. Not the first time he'd frisked someone.

"I need to answer that," I said with gritted teeth to the man holding a gun to her knee.

"Mr. Dixon, are you there?" the voice asked. "I'm afraid it's rather urgent."

I moved my hand slowly toward the intercom, my eyes not on her but on him. On the little wing puller.

"Careful now. Real careful," he urged.

I nodded to him that I understood. I didn't take my eyes off him, pressed the button, and spoke. "I thought I said I didn't want to be disturbed."

She rightly ignored my comment. "It's the police, Mr. Dixon. They appear to have a search warrant for the premises. In-house legal team are down there now, but they won't be able to stall very long. Not if the warrant is valid."

"Thank you, Mrs. Schubert. Thank you for letting me know."

My finger came off the intercom and only the two thugs and Chris could hear me. "Well, gentlemen. Congratulations, your little initiative has lost valuable time and attracted the law. The firearms alone will get you jail time if they catch you with them. But I'd worry more about your *krysha* if I were you."

"You're bluffing," he said with a hint of uncertainty.

"I bet this office will be their first stop. What do you think,

Teller?"

"I think that if you're bluffing, if you try something, it won't end with a busted knee. For either of you."

"You wanna stay here and get pinched? You plan a shootout with Zurich's finest? Or would you like to know where the back door is?"

Teller finally rose to his feet, gun in his hand, motioning to Chris to get up. "The girl comes with us. If the police get the documents—"

"Yes, yes, you'll kill her and probably me too. Save the threats for when there's time."

He wasn't used to being spoken to like that. The younger of the two was clearly in charge. The big guy was muscle. Teller held the Makarov pointed at the floor, staring at me for a moment. He wanted to shoot me. Wanted to teach me a lesson. Lucky for me, there was no time for games, and even this punk knew it.

He grabbed Chris by the shoulder and pulled her to her feet. She was scared. Her eyes pleaded with me for help.

"Jim?"

"Take her with you," I said to them. "Hurt her and there will be a fun little story in the *Washington Post* over the weekend. And I bet your *krysha* will want to blame some people for it."

I walked over to the door and opened it. Mrs. Schubert was watching her monitor when we came outside.

"My friends here need to leave discretely. Would you arrange for someone to help them exit through the garage? Rather urgent, I'm afraid," I told her.

"There's a better way. A side door leading to the alley, often used by more recognizable clients wishing to avoid drawing attention," she replied. Cloak and dagger was everyday routine. A top-tier tennis player didn't want to be seen coming through

A Most Private Bank

the front entrance any more than a rock star.

"That'd be fine, thank you," I replied.

She got up and walked to the elevators. "This way, gentlemen."

The pass card touched against the sensor and her finger pressed a button. "I will have someone meet you and take you to the exit. I wish you a pleasant afternoon," she said as if these men were wealthy clients like anyone else. Teller played the role well. Exceedingly polite as the three of them made their way into the elevator. At least they were moving. Getting out of here. They would be hard to explain away.

No sooner had the first elevator left with the three of them, the second elevator opened. There I was, standing by the elevators as some sort of welcoming committee. Two plainclothes policemen, one of which I had met before.

"Inspector Schmidt. Anything I can do for you?" I asked as if I had come to the elevators to meet him.

"Hadn't expected to see you today, Mr. Dixon. You care to tell me what you're doing here?"

It was an interesting question. My impression of him from our brief interaction in my office had been positive. He was a man of my liking. Competent, smart, and with no affinity for pointless small talk. If he asked, he didn't know. They hadn't caught up to the ownership change yet.

"I represent the new owners of the bank, Inspector," I told him. This part he could find out himself and there was no sense hiding it. "Bank changed majority owner this morning."

His narrow eyes pierced me, studying me, evaluating every word every intonation that came out of me. A suspicious man, one who had reason to suspect people of lying or obfuscating the truth.

"You bought this bank? This week of all weeks, you bought this bank?"

"No. I facilitated the purchase of this bank on behalf of a third party. And right now, I'm the acting administrator of the bank. I have no financial interest, or legal liabilities, for that matter."

"But you are then effectively the manager? You are in charge of the bank at this moment?" he probed.

"I suppose I am," I had to concede.

"Very well. In that case. We have a search warrant for the premises, and we expect full cooperation. We are granted access to any part of the bank, any locked area, and any documents," he said in a monotone voice as if he was reading me my rights.

I took the paper he handed me, and I took my time studying it. "Well, I just got here. Not sure how helpful I'd be."

The junior of the two plainclothes officers stepped up to Mrs. Schubert's desk and started rummaging around. She didn't like it one bit. I looked at her and she looked at me.

"I'm sure you're not looking for whatever letters might be on her desk. Tell me what you're searching for, and I'll see if I can help."

"As I'm sure you saw on the warrant, we are here for everything, Mr. Dixon."

"No. I did read the warrant. You can't lay a hand on any client assets. Only bank property."

"We might just take it all and sort it downtown," he suggested as his partner kept going over pointless papers on the assistant's desk.

"Sure you will. You take client assets, you open yourself to all kinds of lawsuits."

"There were two men entering the building half an hour ago.

A Most Private Bank

I wonder if they were perhaps visiting you, Mr. Dixon," he said, changing tack.

I could only shrug back at him. "There are lots of people coming and going in a bank."

"I'm sure there are. These particular individuals happen to be known members of the Ukrainian organized crime world."

"They were looking for change on a twenty. What's it got to do with me?"

Those keen, sharp eyes homed in on me. Most cops his age were tired old administrators who stopped caring a long time ago. He was a different breed. "Is there a reason for you to be hostile, Mr. Dixon?"

It made me pause. It made me consider what I was really trying to achieve here. And what I was trying to prevent. I drew in a breath hard, held it, and slowly exhaled.

"No. No there's not. Would you like to come into my… to the office? I have a good idea what you may be after. And I believe that I could be of some assistance."

He smiled and motioned toward the door, as if to let me go first. I did. He followed close after and so did his partner. They had no interest in that desk he was searching. That was just to get on my nerves.

I took a seat, once again, behind the deliberately intimidating old desk. Three chairs neatly placed in front of it. The two plainclothes policemen sat down in the same chairs that had been occupied only minutes earlier by quite a different type of individuals. I tried my best not to smile at the absurdity.

"So what are we looking for, Mr. Dixon?" said Inspector Schmidt.

"You're looking for off-the-books beneficial ownership statements. Physical papers with information not entered into any computer."

If I was correct, he sure didn't show it. Another poker player.

"And why do you believe we are looking for that?"

"I'm sure you've already got a team of propeller heads backing up all the servers right now. But you don't expect to find what you need there. No, you look like you've been around long enough to understand how this game is played." I paused to give him a chance to save some time and get to the point. He wasn't in the habit of making it easy for those he interrogated.

"Would you care to enlighten me, Mr. Dixon?" came the trained reply of someone used to dragging information out of unwilling participants. At least this back-and-forth gave me some time to consider my best move and my best chances.

"We have a rather unique legal system, in terms of fiduciary ownership, don't we?" I didn't pause for a reply to the rhetorical question. "If you wanted to keep your ownership of something a secret, it's really not that difficult. Not here, not in Switzerland. You simply register the asset on a fiduciary party. A bank account, a company, a yacht, whatever the asset may be, as owned by someone else. In all the official documents, that is."

"And you're saying that this would be perfectly legal, then, Mr. Dixon?"

His one-liner questions designed to trip me up were slowly getting on my nerves. My tone of voice sharper, I snapped back at him.

"Yes. As long as you have an official fiduciary agreement. As long as that agreement is held by the bank or financial institution. Signed, notarized, and all of that. But there's nothing in the law that says that this paper has to be in some database. It's perfectly fine to keep a document like that in, say, a secret safe box only accessible to a few key individuals."

A Most Private Bank

"Are you aware of any such documents, Mr. Dixon?"

That did it. He was getting on my nerves and he was doing it on purpose. He was talking to me as if I was some blue-collar criminal.

"Listen, Inspector. You can sit there and play your little games and treat me as a suspect, hoping I'll get scared out of my pants. But then I'll get up and walk out of here. And if you try to stop me, I lawyer up and all kinds of hellfire will rain down on you from above. Maybe you win, maybe you lose, but you'll burn days and weeks. Time you ain't got.

"How many private banks are raided in a year? In a decade? You're here because of political pressure. You need to show results and you need to show them fast. If you roll a donut on this outing, it's your job. So how d'you wanna play this?"

I had lost my cool. Lost my temper. Broken my own rules. Pretending to lose your temper is one thing, but actually losing is quite another altogether. Shouting rarely solved any practical issues, and bullying your way to a solution often backfires.

The left side of his mouth pulled farther left. Slowly his mouth grew lopsided before the right side decided to partake. Once the lopsided smirk had grown into a full-sized symmetric grin, he replied.

"They told me you'd be testy."

"Who's they?" I shot back, now more upset with myself for having lost my temper than with him.

"Yes. I'm looking for fiduciary agreements. The physical papers. As you have probably guessed, the reason for a surprise raid is to prevent anyone from, well, accidentally setting them on fire. We are not naive to which kind of individuals may be named on such papers and what length they may go to.

"We had planned on going in this afternoon. But seeing two,

shall we say, somewhat suspicious individuals entering the bank, we had to act swifter. And yes, I would appreciate your cooperating in obtaining these documents. Is that honest and direct enough for you, Mr. Dixon?"

Those goons. The stupidity of barging in and creating a scene. This entire mess could have been avoided - the situation could have been resolved hours before Johnny Law bothered to show up. But here I was and here he was. And there was nothing to be done about it.

"Fair enough. Fair enough, Inspector. You need to secure those papers, and you need to do it fast. There's a lot of money involved. By tomorrow someone may have managed to get an injunction, stopping the search. But you're not really taking any risk telling me this.

"Either I turn out to be helpful and all's fine. Or I start to lawyer up now and stonewall you, in which case you're back to plan A and bring in the welder crew."

"And which will it be?" He was good under pressure. Powerful forces in this town, not to mention around the world, would be alarmed by this raid. Even those with no stake in this bank. Dangerous precedents and all of that. Within hours the pressure on him would be overbearing.

"I'm told that those kinds of documents reside in the somewhat antique-looking box in the corner. In this very room." I motioned toward what most would dismiss as simply quirky decoration, no more valuable than the huge wooden globe next to it. "I've been given the code eight, five, three, seven, nine, ten, eight. You're the one with the warrant."

He rose from his leather chair, the same chair that had been warmed by the very thugs who had now put us in this mess. I heard his scoff at the faded green safe box with its chipped rounded corners.

A Most Private Bank

"Franz Jäger. You don't see many of these anymore," he said as he started spinning that round black dial. An audible click for each time the dial spun to the left or to the right. A throwback to a different era. A time of simplicity, of straightforward banking. Not cleaner, not less unethical, not by any means. But nevertheless a nobler time.

I kept quiet to let him concentrate until the mechanical ticking was followed by a louder, metallic snap as the door opened. His junior partner had turned his chair toward the safe box and was leaning forward, hands on his knees, staring intensely at the box. They both had plenty riding on what was inside.

"If it's all the same to you, I'd rather not know what's in there," I told the inspector who was now looking into the safe box like a child who just took the wrapping paper off his brand-new bicycle.

There was a knock on the door before it opened.

"The police have requested for all nonessential personnel to vacate the building, Mr. Dixon. Would you be needing me for anything?"

It was Mrs. Schubert, and I didn't mind her interruption. I hadn't minded her interruptions the previous times either. More often than not, the personal assistants were the most sympathetic people in banks. Bankers caught in illegal acts invariably used the Nuremberg defense, and they almost always got away with it. Among few people in a bank, even a highly corrupt bank, who could actually claim ignorance with plausibility would be the assistants. Loyal and discreet, never involved in any questionable dealings, never a party to shady agreements, but always there to take care of the things people took for granted.

"No, that's fine. You've been most valuable, Mrs. Schubert. Please take the day off. Just finish up your usual end-of-day routine, please."

She went about her routine while the junior officer stood up to watch as his boss started lining up folders of papers on the floor. They seemed to have found enough to warrant excitement. Mrs. Schubert emptied the wastebasket, collected the outgoing mail, closed the windows and locked the file cabinet.

"Oh, and please leave the keys for the file cabinet, Mrs. Schubert," I said as she was about to take her leave. "I wouldn't want the police to break it open."

She put them on the table, and that's the last I saw of her. I sat there a while watching the two men line up the documents on the floor, photographing their findings.

"I've got places to be. Can I go now?" I sighed.

The Krysha

The steep cobblestone path at the side alley was wet. The cracks between the stones filled with water that had not yet had time to drain. It must have rained hard while I was in the bank. At least the rain had cleared the air. The fog was gone and there was a refreshing smell in the air, of the river, of the trees of the Old Town restaurants.

The fresh air aided my thought process. I needed that. My plan had looked so good this morning. Until Dumb and Dumber raised hell in the lobby. All wasn't lost. But the risks had gone up.

I needed an aspirin. I needed a walk in the mountains. A piña colada at the beach, with a little umbrella in it. What I didn't need was for the first girl I cared about in years to be taken hostage by a psychotic Russian thug.

The documents were the key. That set of documents could get you killed seven ways to Sunday. They could also give you leverage, give you power to negotiate nearly any deal.

If the State Department didn't get their documents, they'd find a way to burn me. I wouldn't be able to set foot on US soil again. But that was hardly a concern, not in the current situation. If the papers on Chekhov got out, if he thought for a second that I was to blame for that...

I had walked up and down the narrow alleys of the Old Town, and I had long since lost track of time. I had been thrown off the path somewhat and my seemingly solid plan had been derailed. I had lost my leverage. Part of it.

It was getting darker but I didn't see any rain clouds. I must have been walking for longer than I thought. Perhaps I had been deliberately wasting time, hoping for a magical solution. It was time to face the music. Time to go back to the office.

By the time I reached the office the big hand of the Submariner had passed the five, heading toward the six and the dusk was already settling over the city.

Sandra was at her desk as she always was. I saw the concern in her eyes before she spoke. Concern, and that accusing look she would give me when I had been misbehaving.

"You keep making yourself impossible to reach. You can't keep doing that."

I was in no hurry taking my coat off, hanging it up. Still deep in thought, and I took my time before shrugging and replying.

"Took a walk for a while. Had to clear my mind. You, you look pale. Anything the matter?"

She nodded with her blond head toward my inner office. Toward what had been a crime scene just days earlier. Her voice lowered and she leaned forward in her chair, closer to me.

"Chris has been waiting for you for some time. She… and her friends. That's how she introduced them."

I blinked. More than once. The word *friends* went through my head like a seed trying to find soil to stick to. Friends.

"Friends?" I whispered back, without fully understanding why I was whispering.

"Friends," she repeated. "A slim chatty man, probably thirtysomething. A big, violent-looking man perhaps forty-five to fifty. Both in bad black suits. And… a man with a big black beard, friendly smile, and… dead eyes."

"Oh," I said. "Those friends. Suppose I better go see them, then."

"Should I call the police?" she whispered.

"No. No, that wouldn't do any good. Why don't you take off.

This is something that I need to… handle."

She didn't like that one bit. The way I sent her out of harm's way as if she was a fragile dame in need of protection. But she didn't want to stay either, and there was really nothing she could do to help. Not now.

"Enjoy the weekend. I'll see on you Monday," I said, trying to sound reassuring. We both knew that Monday may never come.

She didn't say goodbye. She just looked at me for a moment before turning and walking out.

So they were here. All of them. That meant Chekhov was concerned, that there was plenty on the line for him. What names were on those documents in that safe? The private files, the fiduciary confirmations in Nick Niederhauser's safe. Marked in red. Perhaps Chekhov's name was on them. Perhaps someone bigger. His roof or his roof's roof. I was glad not to know.

The time for procrastination was over. It was time to face the music.

I cracked my neck first, then my fingers. The door to my office was open and I walked toward it with wide, determined strides.

"Gentlemen. I apologize for having kept you waiting," I said as I entered my office. The big thug, Penn, had perched himself in a chair by the left wall, slumped down as if by fatigue or boredom. He gave me a disinterested look as I entered, nothing more. In the three-seater couch by the coffee table half laid a younger thug with a sadistic grin on his face.

In front of my office, on the usual visitor's chair, sat a frightened-looking girl with her back as straight as a floorboard. She spun around and saw me. Her eyes were red, but she appeared unharmed.

Behind the desk, in my chair, sat the proud owner of a Premier League team, swiveled back with his sneakers on my table, flashing a big white, psychotic grin.

The Waiting Game

"You're in my seat."

"I was beginning to think you wouldn't show," he said in a jovial manner as if I was late for a date.

"I said, you're in my chair."

"Have a seat, Jim," he replied without moving an inch. "We have some important business to finish, you and I."

I stood my ground.

"You got my chair and you got your feet on my desk and I don't like it one bit. You want to talk shop, we can talk shop, but you're a visitor in my office and by God, you'll behave like one. Get your own chair."

It wasn't bravery talking. It was the stress of a long week starting to eat its way into my brain. Whatever this man had in mind, his plans wouldn't change over me demanding my chair back.

He broke out in one of his roaring fits of laughter. Something between a hyena and the sound of a grizzly about to take your head off.

"You want your desk back?" He laughed, lifting his designer sneakers off the table. "You are a character, I do say. Quite a character indeed. Yes, it is your desk, and I am a visitor. A man's office is his castle, after all."

Chekhov motioned to my now-empty swivel chair and even gave a somewhat sarcastic bow as if it was a valuable gift from him to me.

I sat down. My forearms on the table, my fingers interlaced, I waited for him to move around, pull up a visitor's chair next to

Chris, and take a seat. Then I spoke.

"What can I do for you, Kyril?"

He put his left foot over his right leg, his left hand on his knee. His white shirt sleeves were rolled up to his biceps, and it was impossible not to notice what he was wearing on that hairy, tattooed right arm.

The untrained eye may easily mistake it for a plastic gimmick watch, something you might get in a vending machine. A tonneau-shaped black carbon case on a bright orange rubber strap. A huge watch at fifty times forty-three millimeters, the face was utterly illegible. With no actual dial, the hands were seen at the backdrop of the watch movement, with the cogwheels, oscillators, and tourbillon in plain view from the front. A bright orange crown with matching highlights inside the actual movement and with custom screws to hold it in place, requiring custom tools.

It would be impossible to explain to regular folks why a Richard Mille like this is worth more than the house they live in.

"My associates tell me that you allowed the police to recover the documents. I thought my wishes in that regard were expressed quite clearly. I am disappointed, Jim."

I forced myself not to let my eyes stray from his. Not to show thoughts, emotions, fear, or hope.

"Your associates are mistaken, Kyril."

"Is that so? They tell me that they arrived just after you did. That they were in that office with you until the police arrived. That they watched you exit the bank carrying nothing at all. Please do enlighten me, Jim. In what way are they mistaken?"

"There's nothing wrong with their powers of observation, Kyril. Merely with their abilities to draw conclusions. Neither of them appear terribly clever."

The slim man reclining in my couch jumped to his feet in one swift move, his mouth opening to issue retort or threat. A raised hand from his *krysha* made him close his mouth and sit back down.

"Very good, Kyril. Does he roll over on command too?"

"Watch yourself," Teller hissed under his breath. But he stayed put on the couch. Chekhov seemed somewhat amused over my slight toward his ward. Then again, Chekhov seemed rather easily amused.

"You were saying," he said and motioned for me to continue.

"I was saying that these two klutzes here nearly lost us everything. Charging in like the Red Army invading Bratislava. You should put a leash on your puppies, Kyril."

He wanted to murder me, and he wanted to do it slowly. He wanted to show me, to teach me. I saw it in his eyes. I was humiliating him in front of Chekhov, and I did it on purpose. He deserved what he got.

"Suppose you stop stalling and tell me where those documents are," Chekhov said. This time without a smile, this time in a slow, deliberate tone. Playtime was over, at least for the moment.

"Suppose we make a deal first," I replied.

"Suppose I let my associates finish what they started," he said and nodded to her. "Left knee, was it?"

"I want your word that neither I nor Chris, well Evelyn, will be harmed. After tomorrow I don't want to see your thugs ever again. And I want your watch for my trouble," I countered.

He paused and studied his opponent. Many years earlier I had been trekking the Serengeti. Days on end, walking among the nature. Well-equipped but unarmed. The first thing they teach you is not to run. In Africa, they had told me, only food runs.

"What do you have to bargain with?" came his reply moments later after he looked at his Richard Mille.

"If you agree to my terms, I will have the documents you're looking for by 9:00 a.m. tomorrow morning."

"Tomorrow morning, is it?" he said, back to the usual amused smile.

"And if I don't, you could always have Tom and Jerry here plug us full of holes and dump us in the river."

"They would be rather fond of that idea, I'm sure." He grinned. "But I am somewhat reluctant to simply let the two of you walk out of here, as you can understand. We'll find you, I'm sure, but imagine the time and trouble to have to chase you two down in rural Kansas or wherever you might decide to slip away to."

"I don't expect to part company until the documents are in your hand. What do you say to my terms? Do I have your word?"

"You would simply take my word for it?" he asked.

"I trust your word, your handshake, and your own self-interest, Kyril. Threats of violence are cheap, but the consequences of carrying them out can be costly. You're a businessman, and you'd much rather have a clean solution. A bullet hole in a knee is hard to explain. Missing persons and bodies reemerging from the lake draw attention."

"Listen to this man and learn something," he told the furious man on the couch. "Young people these days. Too quick to violence. It's not a matter of principles, I'm sure you understand. It's just terribly bad business. Violence should remain a last resort. Who was it who said it? War is merely a continuation of politics with other means. Kissinger?"

"Believe it was Clausewitz. The deal is about as good as you're gonna get. We get safety, and I get a little souvenir to remember you by. You get the documents. Everybody lives."

He thought about it for a moment, at least he looked as if he did. His eyes moved from me to her to his Richard Mille. She had been reduced to a bargaining chip, a damsel in distress to be rescued by her knight in shining armor. Not a role she was particularly used to or keen on.

Then he bared his pearly white fangs and extended a grubby hand in my direction. "The documents tomorrow morning, for your safety and peace of mind. But you're crazy if you think I'll give you my favorite watch. Do you have any idea how hard this was to come by?"

I reached forward and shook what felt like a brick. It was impossible not to notice the wave of relief washing over her. She looked at me and I looked at her. Had I asked for protection just for myself, she wouldn't have been around by sunrise, and she knew it.

"Done. The documents will come to us. Right here. At 9:00 am. Since you don't seem to have a very trusting disposition, I suppose we all stick around here until then."

The man with his feet in my leather couch stood up again, his voice raised, his posture that of a man itching for a fight. "He's bluffing. Stalling for time, that's all. Probably has the cops arriving in the morning!"

"I'd put a leash on that doggie, Kyril. A leash. And a gag."

Chekhov raised his hand once more without looking back at the boy, and once more he sat back down in anger. The now crimson face glared at me, blood vessels pumping by the side of his forehead, murder in his eyes.

"Better make ourselves comfortable. It's going to be a long night," Chekhov said. "Got any coffee around here?"

"Kitchen's out that door, straight ahead and to the left.

Bathroom's right next to it. I can get you a cup, Kyril."

"No, no," he said waving me off. "I'm quite capable of making my own, thank you."

Chekhov got up from his chair and headed in the direction I had indicated, leaving the door open. Teller appeared to have accepted the situation, at least for now, and was reclining on the couch again. His older and considerably larger colleague sat slumped back in his chair with his usual utterly disinterested expression.

As soon as Chekhov was out of the room, Chris pulled her chair up closer to my desk, leaned forward on her forearms, and whispered to me.

"You can't trust him, Jim. He'll kill us both," she said.

"We'll be fine," I reassured her, moving my hand to hers. "He's a businessman. I can deal with him. And right now, I'm the only one who can solve his problems."

"He might let you go. I'm not so sure about me," she said. She was no stranger to physical threats. She had been around men like these for most of her life and she had come out on top. There was concern in her voice, a soft whisper of worry, but she was not one to panic. It was difficult to be certain whether she was more concerned with the danger or with being relegated to a spectator, having to rely on me to navigate the situation for her.

"All cards are not played yet," I whispered. "Tomorrow morning, the three of them will walk out of this office and leave us here, unharmed."

She relented and didn't press the matter further. There was plenty going on behind those pretty eyes. They had likely been instrumental to her illustrious career. A pair of pretty eyes and a matching smile can get someone far, in particular if a sharp mind is well hidden behind them. She looked into my eyes and her long black eyelashes seemed to smile at me.

"Whatever happens, Jim," she whispered, "I'll always be grateful. I have no regrets and wouldn't change a thing." She paused a moment, hesitating a second before adding that last part. The part that will always haunt me. "I love you, Jim."

I saw him walking toward us from the corridor outside. He was holding two cups of coffee in his hands. She let go of my hand and moved her chair back a little, seemingly embarrassed over having had Kyril Chekhov see her holding my hand.

"I took the liberty, Jim," he said as he handed me a cup of steaming-hot coffee, keeping the other for himself. "You strike me as someone who takes his coffee black."

He hadn't even acknowledged anyone else's presence, not even looked at the girl in the chair next to him. Two coffee cups, two men.

"You can tell a lot about a man from his taste in coffee," he started. A moment's pause for him to lift the cup to his nose, twirling it like a wine glass while taking in the aroma. "De'Longhi PrimaDonna. I have one myself at my dacha by the Black Sea. I cannot claim to be familiar with these beans, but let me try."

He took a sip of the coffee, tasting it as a connoisseur tries a glass of fine wine. Swirling it around his mouth a moment before letting it move down his digestive system.

"Full body, somewhat fruity… Rustic, a tint of bright acidity. Arabica, of course. Ethiopian?"

"Close enough. Tanzanian. A small plantation on the slopes of Kilimanjaro."

"Of course. Good region. One of the best. Some swear by kopi luwak and wouldn't drink anything but it. I don't know about you, Jim, but I prefer coffee beans lacking the illustrious experience of passing through a monkey's backside."

"It's quite overrated," I agreed and tried my own cup.

"Scarcity does that. The more you can't have something, the more you want it."

With his rolled-up sleeves, thick black hair covered only part of the many tattoos. My own preconceived notions told me that they were Russian prison tattoos, but my only basis for such an assumption was bad movies.

On some level, I couldn't help respecting him, even liking him. A little theatrics aside, he hadn't been incorrect toward me. We were both from very different walks of life and very similar at the same time. Here was a man who had played the cards he was dealt, and played them well.

"Now please enlighten me, Jim. What will happen at nine o'clock tomorrow morning?"

"At nine we tally up. You get what you're looking for. We shake hands and part ways," I said.

"Just like that?"

"Just like that," I replied.

"I'm beginning to think that there is a reason why you are not telling me why we need to wait for nine and what will happen then. Forgive me, Jim, but I am by nature not a terribly trusting person. You understand, I'm sure."

"What's life without a few surprises, Kyril? I could tell you all about it. I could also serve you some Nespresso capsule coffee, if you prefer predictability to excitement."

The roaring bear laughter had Teller briefly jump, but he quickly settled back down again. Must have been half asleep, taken by surprise by the sudden noise.

"Quite a character, as I said, quite a character. Yes, let's play it your way. We'll wait for morning. Can I at least offer you a line?"

He reached for the left pocket of his pants and his hand came back up with a gram.

"I'll have a hard time sleeping after that coffee anyhow, and I'll be damned if I'm gonna stay awake all night."

"Suit yourself," he said and started building a white line on my desk. He didn't offer Chris or the goons. She looked as if she wanted to blend into the wall, and the way she was ignored, she nearly did.

The Deal

I waited for him to pull the line up his left nostril, tilting his head back a moment, taking it all in. A situation like this made it tempting. That gram bag was right there on my desk. If things were to go badly, if Teller would eventually get his way, a bit of powder would go a long way to making it easier. But this was not the time to restart bad habits.

Recreational use, a few times a year wasn't a problem. That's what I had told myself back then. The danger is when it spills over into the day. Just like drinking to sooth anger, frustration or pain is a bad idea, so is doing coke to ease your nerves, to focus on work, or simply to pass the time.

"What did the police ask you? At the bank," he said.

I leaned back in my chair, my hands on the armrests. "Nothing about you. But this guy is clever and he won't stop digging. Not until he's got his cases wrapped up."

Whether from what I said or from the Bolivian marching powder making its way through his cerebral cortex down toward the cerebellum, his eyes got sharp and his ears perked up.

"His cases," he repeated, letting me continue.

Swiveling my chair to the left, I pulled out a drawer. It was right next to my safe box, and it made me see that discoloration on the floor again, where the pool of blood had left its unmistakable trace.

I pulled the drawer out slowly, to show him that there was nothing threatening inside. Lifted out a bottle of Macallan 18 and set it down on the table. Without asking him, I reached for two glasses, short with wide bottom and narrower top, one for me and

A Most Private Bank

one for him.

Just as he had done, I too ignored her now. In the corner of my eye I saw her looking. Nerves running high, she was probably itching for a drink. But I wouldn't offer one. I simply poured up two glasses of the eighteen-year-old single malt.

"This is not Russia, Kyril. People have died and the authorities will not rest until they have those responsible. Cheers."

He lifted his glass to mine and we both took a moment to savor the scotch.

"Most unfortunate events," he said and I saw his eyes move toward the dark stain on the floor.

"Yes. And bad business. I hope you forgive me for saying that the police might have accepted an unresolved killing of a minor crime figure at some hotel. He lived a dangerous life and associated with dangerous individuals. But they will not let the murder of a civilian stand. An educated young Swiss man with no criminal record, a securities trader from a good family with means and connections."

He hadn't turned his glass upside down in one go as I had expected. He was rolling it around in his hand thoughtfully.

"Bad business. I hope you don't believe that I was responsible for your friend's demise, Jim."

"If I believed that, we wouldn't be having this conversation. No, you're a businessman. That's why I don't worry about you having Mr. Happy over there plug me full of holes. He doesn't look clever enough to get it, but it would be terribly bad business. No telling how far such an investigation may go.

"I have, however, been a little concerned for my new companion. Me, I cannot simply disappear. But she's traveling under an assumed name, with false documents. There's no one who would miss her if she's gone, no one to file a report. She could simply go up in smoke."

She was staring holes in me, her chest heaving, glancing at the door, at the thugs, back at me. Her fight-or-flight instincts kicking in, and she must have been using every ounce of her self-control to simply sit still and keep her mouth shut.

Chekhov, on the other hand, was amused. He was enjoying this conversation. He was listening intently with the facial expression of a man enjoying the setup of a joke, eagerly anticipating the punch line.

"I have to admit that similar thoughts have crossed my mind, Jim. Indeed they have. So then? If you believe yourself to be so sacrosanct, if you think you are above physical danger, then enlighten me, I pray, are you really doing this for young Evelyn? You care about her so much that you want to save her from the Big Bad Gangster?"

"That is part of it." I shrugged. "Scores have to be settled and debts have to be paid. But if it's all the same to you, Kyril, I prefer to avoid further bloodshed."

"Bloodshed is necessary at times. But costly. Often more costly than one may think. You have a proposition?"

I refilled our glasses. She was on pins and needles. She wanted to be part of this conversation, she wanted to regain control, she wanted to be an equal. What she did was keep her mouth shut and her ears open.

"Like I said, Kyril. The law won't stop until they have their murderer. I know the inspector in charge. It's a matter of time before he figures the connection to the bank, to the papers, to you and beyond. And don't even think of trying anything with this guy - that'll get you nowhere."

"Your proposition being?" he asked without attempting to hide his growing impatience.

"They're looking for a murderer. They won't stop until they have one," I said as a matter of fact.

"And you have someone in mind, have you?"

"I was thinking that your charming young companion over there would make an excellent fall guy," I said and motioned over at the younger of the two goons. "He fits the bill. A hot-tempered thug, not too bright. And I'm sure he'd understand the consequences of not playing his part, if told to."

Teller jumped to his feet. He hadn't been sleeping after all. His hands went straight into his jacket and the Makarov was still there. In an instant that barrel was trained on my face, the arm held out straight.

"Who do you think you're talking to? I'll kill you! I'll f—"

"Sit. Down." Kyril spoke slowly and deliberately. "The grownups are talking." Without turning around, he lifted his hand up, palm down, and slowly moved the open hand down.

Teller's hand was shaking, his knuckles white and his face red. He looked at his partner for help, but his older and fatter companion did not move from his chair. Still slumped back, still arms crossed, still the same disinterested expression.

"This boy and his temper are starting to get tedious," I said without looking up at the man with the pistol.

Chekhov was the kind of man whose face often shifted from one extreme to another. Seconds ago he had looked almost jolly, someone you'd like to have over for a barbecue in the garden. In an instance his features had shifted to something that could give Charles Manson nightmares.

"Out. Leave us. Now," he said with gritted teeth.

"Kyril—" the young man with the pistol started.

"Out!"

The man I had been calling Teller looked like a ghost. I saw his hand tremble as he secured the Makarov in the shoulder holster. He didn't say a word. Penn had already gotten up and opened the door.

If it would have been possible to sink through the floor, that's what she would have done. She was making herself as small as she could, hoping to melt into the background.

"You too, sweet cakes. Scram," he said to her.

She looked at me. Her big blue eyes silently begging me, her lips parted without emitting a sound. Whatever happened next, she wanted to be part of it. Wanted to know, to be included. But the decision was made, and Chekhov was in no mood to be argued with.

I looked into her eyes. For a moment, I was lost in them. She was really something. My head moved slowly from side to side. There was nothing I could do. Even if I wanted to.

When she stood up, I saw her eyes change, I saw anger in them. She certainly hadn't minded the goons being dismissed, but she was a principal, she was integral to all of this, and she had a lot at stake. Being sent off to sit outside like some low-level assistant wasn't something she was used to.

The two of us, me and my new oligarch friend, sat quietly until she had picked up that tiny green leather Chanel purse, left my inner office, and closed the door behind her. Through the glass panels, I saw how both Penn and Teller had made themselves comfortable in the leather swivel chairs by the trading desks. Chris picked the chair farthest from the two of them.

"I apologize for my nephew," Chekhov said to me. "Young people these days. All tempers, no patience, no proper respect."

"Can't say I like him very much. Didn't know he's your nephew," I said.

"I got many nephews. You are correct, of course. Not bright. But he is family." Chekhov seemed embarrassed by the outburst.

"Suppose we settle the final parts of our deal and finish this bottle," I said.

That brought his face back to what it had been before the interruption. For a moment, the big white smile and the thick beard made me think of Santa Claus.

SATURDAY

The Delivery

When the phone woke me up, my face was resting on my arms, slumped over the desk. I ignored it at first. It had been a long night. A grunt seemed to urge me to make the noise stop. I sat back up in the chair and rubbed my eyes. Two scotch bottles on the desk, two empty glasses and one half-asleep Russian.

"Yeah, Dixon Capital," I muttered to the phone. "Jim Dixon speaking."

I grimaced and leaned back in my chair to avoid the foul smell of his yawn.

"One, seven, three, four. Half an hour. Confirmed."

After I set the phone back down, he raised his eyebrows in a silent question.

"In half an hour our business will be concluded, Kyril."

He stretched out his arms, buttons straining and nearly popping off his shirt.

"You're sure this is the way you want to play it, Jim?"

I looked out through the glass panels. I could see the three of them clearly. Penn's huge frame was lying back in Raphael's old office chair, his feet on the table, his mouth wide open, and his massive chest moving slowly.

Teller was laying on his side, arm under his head on the carpet. I saw his eyes open - the phone had probably woken him and he was gazing over at us.

She was curled up sideways in an office chair, her knees on the seat. I couldn't see her face - perhaps she was awake perhaps not.

"This is the way it has to be." I took no pleasure in saying it. I felt no joy over what should have been a victory. Over what we had agreed to.

Chekhov nodded slowly and he too glanced out the glass panel.

"If that's the way it has to be," he said.

"There's no perfect solution here. But this one is the least bad. My turn to get that coffee - I'll just be a moment."

Teller glared at me when I left the inner office. He was angry but he was also scared, and I liked that. Chris, I still thought of her as Chris, wasn't asleep. She saw me and she got up. Her high heels kicked off, she walked up to me barefoot and followed me to the kitchen.

"Please tell me what's happening, Jim," she said. I wished she had stuck to the American accent.

"Everything is back on track. In an hour all of this will be over."

I placed two cups in the machine and hit the button. It was a loud coffee maker. The fresh beans were ground up first, before the noise shifted to the pressurized water pushing the coffee through, slowly filling the cups. It was impossible to speak while the cups were being filled, and we simply looked at each other.

When the noise finally stopped, I picked the two cups up. "Hang in there, Chris. I'll explain it all soon."

She didn't like it, but she had little choice but to accept my reassurances. She returned to her chair, and I returned to the inner office and shut the door. We had our coffees in silence, my Russian counterpart and I. A sense of mutual respect and understanding had grown from a night of bonding over eighteen-year-old single malt.

The office remained dead calm until the doorbell rang. The three out there were taken by surprise, but neither I nor Chekhov were caught off guard. "After you," he said, getting up and opening the door for me.

I marched straight out past the lobby to the entrance. Outside the door, a blond man in a gray-and-yellow uniform with a sidearm, carrying a large steel case. I opened the door and let him in.

"Morning, Mr. Dixon," he said and set the case down on the floor in front of us. "Today's code, please."

He looked away as I squatted down to enter the four digits I had been provided with earlier. The case was large enough for quite a few gold bars, should that be what you wanted moved. This time the case was nearly empty. Just a thick manila folder with messy black handwriting on it, as if a child had scribbled on it. Or someone under pressure had jotted down an address with a Montblanc fountain pen.

Apart from this address and my name, the text SECUREPOST and NINE AM SHARP were drawn in large writing, underlined and in all capital letters at the upper left side of the envelope. A rubber stamp on the back identified the sender as Bank Niederhauser.

You could have cut the air with a butter knife. Even the armed deliveryman could sense it. He must have seen his fair share of situations in that job and he looked into my eyes for an indication.

"All fine, thank you," I told him, and he returned down the stairs.

With the deliveryman gone, I turned to face Chekhov, holding out the still sealed brown envelope. "I believe this belongs to you, Kyril."

I waited for him to open it. He moved over to the counter, where Sandra would usually sit, and he flipped through the pages.

"You read this?" he asked me.

"Uh-uh. Don't want to know anything about it."

"No curiosity over what all this has been about?" he asked.

"Curiosity can be a dangerous thing. I assume there are some names on those documents. Names I might even recognize. Perhaps yours, perhaps other names. And I suspect that it can be quite detrimental to one's health to have seen such names on such papers."

He pushed the pile of papers back into the envelope. Whatever he had seen, he was content. He looked like a man who had run a marathon and finally hit the finish line. Perhaps he had been as much at risk as anyone if those names would have been exposed.

"You kept your word, and I will keep mine," he said. "I have similar situations developing. Different banks, different places. I could use a man like you. I could make it worth your while."

"Much appreciated, Kyril, but this is the end of the line for me."

His white shirt sleeves rolled up to his biceps, his hairy tattooed forearms on display, he made a menacing figure the way he approached me. He looked into my eyes for a moment. Hard, sharp eyes, eyes that had probably seen more than I could imagine, stared into mine.

Then he snapped open the deployant, took the Richard Mille, off and held it up to me.

"I have a condition. This is a collector's item. Only one hundred ever made, this one has number zero zero two. It would be disappointing if you were to ever sell it, Jim."

"It would be the pride of my collection, Kyril," I said and held out my right hand.

An enormous meaty hand shook mine and a pristine carbon

watch was placed in my left. Whatever was in those files meant a lot to him. Perhaps his life.

"It has been a genuine pleasure, Jim. I hope we can do business again."

I held his hand, a firm and lasting handshake.

Repercussions

She had clutched that green Chanel of hers hard when they walked past her. She was still barefoot and considerably shorter and smaller. They towered over her but hadn't even stopped, hadn't even spoken to her as they exited.

I confess to having felt some degree of satisfaction over how Teller looked nervous. He too had been sent out of the room and couldn't be sure of his safety.

The door had shut behind them and their footsteps down the stairs had faded. I heard her breathing. It was as if she had held her breath since last night and just now drew in air once more.

"That... that's it? Just like that?" she asked.

"Nearly," I said. "There's one last part. Let's sit down, I'm exhausted."

I went back to the inner office, to the chair where I had been sleeping, and I heard her soft bare feet on the carpet following me. *Just one last part*, I thought to myself, careful not to step on the discoloration on the carpet. *Just one last part*.

"I thought you made a deal with Kyril," she said. "About him. That awful little sadist. Thought you were throwing him to the cops?"

"He's a bad apple. He's also Kyril's nephew, and I doubt he'd throw his own family to the wolves."

"You said that, that this won't be over until they get their man."

I took a deep breath and nodded to her. "I did say that. And I made a deal with Kyril. The only deal that'll keep everybody alive."

"Tell me. Don't do this to me - don't keep me in suspense, Jim. Tell me what's going on?" The nerves were getting to her at the tail end of a very long week. I couldn't blame her, not for that.

"The cops will get their murderer. But not that angry little fellow with the gun. He's all bark and no bite. Probably never killed anyone."

She was shivering. Holding that Chanel purse so hard her fingers were turning white.

"Who then?" she demanded.

"They will get the person who actually pulled the trigger."

She didn't speak. Her eyes razor sharp, her body tensing up.

"Mikhailov was your partner, was he?"

"My... krysha," she said softly.

"Why'd you do him?"

"He was going to sell me out, Jim. He was giving me up to Kyril. I'm telling you, Jim... I had no choice. It was him or me!"

"I might not have cared all that much about that," I said. "But you shot Raphael." Nothing escaped my gaze at this point. Not a slight tremor in her hand, not a tiny vibration in her eyelash. Certainly not the shift in the color of her face.

"I... Jim..." She was lost for words, she was scrambling for an explanation. Whatever she had expected, this was not it.

"Raph was a greedy bastard, but he was my colleague and my friend. You shot him. You shot him in the back. You shot him in my office. In *my* office!"

A week's worth of pent-up rage was slowly surfacing. The wheels under my chair were touching the edges of the dark, crimson stain on my carpet. And there she was. The prime mover. The one who had set this all in motion.

"It was Alexander. It was Mikhailov who did that. I had no

part of that. You have to believe me, Jim."

"Uh-uh. I saw the body, I saw the scene. He was shot in the back. From down low, upward angle through his torso. Raph wouldn't have let your late *krysha* in the office, and he certainly wouldn't turn his back to him."

Her mind was racing. She looked at me, she looked toward the door, she looked back at me. I kept my right palm on the desk and my left hand on the desk apron running along the sides.

"What do you intend to do?" she asked me. She looked at me in a different way. A look I hadn't seen from her before. She looked at me as if I was a threat. Her usual big innocent eyes narrowed, her voice harsh and firm.

"It's all been agreed to, Evelyn," I said. "You take whatever sentence they give you and you keep your mouth shut. Deny everything if you will. Not a word about anyone else. You'll be protected inside, and you'll come out alive."

"Alive!" she yelled. "Alive!"

"You'll do fifteen years at the most. You're still young, and you'll have plenty of life left. And if you're not too upset about how things went, come and see me when you get out. I'll miss you."

"You bastard! I trusted you!" She reached into that Chanel bag. The hand came back up with a Colt Cobra, a thirty-eight snub-nose revolver in black matte finish.

My left index and middle fingers gently pushed two buttons, separated by a slim metal sheet.

"Kyril would have killed you," I said. "That the gun that killed Raph?"

She held the revolver so hard her hand was shaking. From this angle I couldn't see if her finger was on the trigger or not. A tear was building in the corner of her left eye, only to slowly run down her face, dragging a black line of mascara with it.

"You wouldn't have helped me. You wouldn't have cared. Getting those papers was my only chance to survive. I, I was going to use them. To buy my way out. Forever. I was going to have a normal life. Just, just disappear to some quiet place."

"You can still do that, Evelyn," I said. "Fifteen years will pass. Then you'll be free. Free from the gangsters, free from the law."

"I should just shoot you now and run!"

"How far would you get? If the law won't get you, Kyril will."

I looked at the chronometer on my wrist. She saw me look and I wanted her to see.

"I'd say you have less than five minutes to make up your mind, Evelyn."

She hesitated. She wasn't sure if I was bluffing. Her thoughts were interrupted by a banging on the front door, followed by a loud noise and a German voice.

"*Polizei*! We're coming in!"

She let out a gasp and turned the revolver around, under her chin. More tears ran down her face, her makeup smeared down her red cheeks.

"Damn you to hell, Jim."

"Evelyn. Chris. Please don't," I said quietly. I heard the noise of the police clearing room after room. Impressive response time.

They got to our room. Black uniforms, body armor, and helmets. Full tactical gear, the only visible insignia a round patch with the white outlines of a tiger.

Loud voices. Commands shouted both in German and English.

"*Waffe runter*! Drop the gun!" They were closing in behind her, Heckler & Koch MP5 submachine guns trained on her center mass.

"I… I hate you, Jim."

She let the revolver fall, hitting the carpet with a loud thud.

Settling with the Law

She wouldn't take her eyes off me. Not when they slammed her face to the floor, not when they cuffed her, and not when they dragged her out.

I kept my hands in front of me, palms toward the masked men. They showed little interest in me. I kept the hands up anyway. They stayed up until the ninjas stood aside and a familiar face in civilian clothing entered.

"That's quite an impressive response time, Inspector," I told him and slowly lowered my hands back down to the desk.

"Not at all. We've had this office under surveillance for days," Inspector Schmidt replied and sat himself down in the very seat recently occupied by a member of the Russian underworld. The fatigue was wearing me down, and I rubbed the base of my nose with two fingers.

"Well, if you bugged me, I'd be really impressed. Had the place swept recently."

"No bugs, Mr. Dixon. Just a physical presence. Couldn't be sure which team you were playing for."

I reached for the bottle of scotch that had enough left in it for a drink, but changed my mind. "And now you are?"

"Nearly. You want to tell me what just happened here?"

I took a deep breath and tried to collect my thoughts.

"I was approached some days ago with a proposition. I was to assist a wealthy socialite, the daughter of a man I had known for decades, with a takeover. She was looking to buy herself a bank. The very bank where we met yesterday."

He motioned for me to go on.

"Her intention was to set up an offshore SPV, that's a special-purpose vehicle, a shell company, to take over the bank. Half the money in debt, half in equity. My role was to secure the loan and raise the equity from external parties."

"And you would be paid for this, I presume?" he asked.

"Naturally."

"Would you know why this lady would be looking to buy this particular bank?" he asked. He had a way of making each question seem innocent. It sounded more like personal curiosity than an interrogation.

"In my profession, Inspector, there are questions you ask and there are questions you'd rather not."

"I see. And purchase the bank you did, as it would appear."

"That we did, Inspector."

"Which brings us to what just happened," he suggested.

"I had reasons to doubt her identity. Naturally, I had obtained the required due diligence documents. Copies of passport, proof of residence, and such. I had a bad feeling, shall we say, and made some inquiries. When I confronted her this morning, she pulled that revolver on me. Luckily I had panic buttons installed just a few days ago."

He leaned closer, his elbows on the desk, his chin leaning on his hands.

"And the gentlemen who have been spending the night here in your office along with you and… your client?"

"You know I can't talk to you about my clients, Inspector. I'm bound by banking secrecy, unless of course I suspect a serious crime. And as I said, in my profession there are questions you don't want to ask. I'm sure your profession is similar in that regard."

"We didn't find all that we were looking for in that safe," he said.

"I'd imagine you found enough," I replied.

"Enough for what, Mr. Dixon?"

"Would you like me to speculate? To make a hypothetical reasoning?"

"By all means, Mr. Dixon."

"Well. I suppose it takes quite a bit for the Swiss police to get a search warrant for a private bank. It's probably been tried and denied many times. Simple things like garden-variety corruption and tax evasion wouldn't be enough. No, I suspect it would take some serious political pressure to get such a warrant signed off. Perhaps something that could be used for international bargaining or to further someone's political career."

"You think that is what we do at the Swiss police? Run political errands?"

"Not at all. You're looking for the regular criminals. Political exposure wouldn't exactly be beneficial to you. You'd get all the blame and none of the credit. Makes me think that a good haul for you would be to find evidence of large-scale white-collar crimes. Rather than ending up in the middle of some political situation that would quickly spin out of control."

He thought about what I had said for a moment. We studied each other, like I and Kyril had done last night. Sizing each other up.

"Suppose we found enough," he finally said. "And if there was ever anything else, I suppose it would be quite difficult to obtain."

"Suppose so," I replied.

"I'm going to need you to come down for a statement. But that can wait till next week," he said as he rose from the chair.

"Not a problem, Inspector," I said and shook his hand.

"Say, you wouldn't know anything about the banker we found in the vaults? Drilling up dozens of client deposit boxes."

I furrowed my brow and gave him a puzzled look.

"That sounds like a really dumb thing to be doing."

A New Week

Aftermath

It seemed strangely fitting that I was lying in the couch with her sitting in the swivel chair next to it. Made me feel like back home, back where everyone for some reason needed a shrink to cry to.

It was over. It was finally over. That goddamned week was finally over.

I knew I had to take whatever time it required - I had to tell her, explain it all to her. Perhaps explain myself. I owed her that. I had kept her in the dark all week. It wasn't a matter of trust. It was never a matter of trust, not with her. The less she knew the safer she was. Until all the cards were played.

It was Monday morning, and I hadn't left my room at the Hyatt all day yesterday. The stress, the alcohol, the blow. The stakes had been too high, too high to relax all week. Once it was over, I crashed for a day and a half. Even now I wasn't back to normal.

I had been lying on that couch for the past hour, explaining the week. I was a mess, I was a wreck, I was rambling.

"They had it coming, Sandra," I said once again. "I never screwed anyone over in my life who didn't have it coming."

I wasn't sure which one of us I was trying to convince. My mouth had been running for some time and she let me run it. Perhaps I had made sense, perhaps not. I was running out of steam and she saw it.

"So you get it?" I asked her.

"You haven't made sense since you got here. You haven't made sense all week."

She had a point, and I tried to collect my thoughts, tried to focus.

"Baerenfells is arrested. Not sure if they'll get him on the bank secrecy violations, but drilling safe boxes should land a conviction. Probably suspended, but he'll never work again. Blew up forty mil of his girlfriend's money too."

"Because you don't like him?" she asked.

"I was planning on giving him an out. Until Chris figured out he was the leak. Betrayed his bank, betrayed his country and got some friends of mine in hot water. Serves him right, the greedy bastard!"

"Nina, what did she ever do to you?"

"Don't be so naive, Sandra. Nina was sleeping with me to get my business. You think I was the only one? The first one? She played the game and she got played. Oh, she'll bounce back. They'll fire her today. Perhaps Preston too. What, you think it's unfair? After what they did to me?"

"You never intended to go back to them, did you?"

"It took quite a bit of self-control to even go into that cursed building. Can you imagine the greed? These people despise me as much as I despise them. They saw money, and like some bull charging a red flag, they waved all due diligence, skimped on all the checks and balances, and rubber-stamped an insane deal for me. Wish I could hear those guys try to explain away a forty-mil loss to their bosses. That and being associated with a toxic bank, a messy upcoming bankruptcy, and having lent money to a woman on a terrorist watch list."

"Terrorist?" she asked. I must have missed that part in my rambling.

"LGT is a different story," I continued. "They did nothing wrong, nothing out of the ordinary. They sold a clean shell company to someone who presented false documents, good fakes too. No, they're clean as a whistle. Gave them a heads-up too - they already filed a report against her."

"What terrorist watch list?" she asked again.

"Chekhov will be fine too. No sense going up against someone like that, not healthy. Besides, he never did anything against me. Theatrics and threats, but he didn't really do anything to piss me off."

"What list?" She was getting impatient with my rambling.

"Niederhauser cashed out just in time. Good for him. The name will suffer a while, but he'll be fine. Just can't set foot in the States, but I don't think he'd want to. I could, though. They owe me a favor now, you know."

"Who does? What?"

"The home team. My team. The US government. They got a surprise delivery this morning. The papers they'd been looking for. Got them off my back, got them to owe me. Got a chip to call in some rainy day. Might even be able to go back home."

"The list, Jim!"

"She's on a list, all right," I said. "Chris. Evelyn. Got on it by bad luck, nothing more. I don't care about the list. I care that she murdered my friend."

"You... you still spent a week with her? Sharing a bed with her?"

"Uh-huh. Had to keep her close. Keep an eye on her. At first. Then I grew to respect her. Hell, I grew to like her. A lot. She's just a cornered animal desperately doing whatever it takes to get out. Hell if I know what I would have done in her place. Few different steps in life and it might have been me with a red notice and murderous gangsters in pursuit."

"You would kill? Kill an innocent man?" she asked.

I thought about it. I tried to look deep within for an answer.

"I believe anyone's capable of nearly anything. It's easy to judge. But none of us would ever know, not until we faced what she's faced. Hell, I don't think I would kill anyone. But we all have a breaking point."

"What... what happens now? It's really over?"

"Press will have a feeding frenzy. My name's not on any papers. Should be a minor mention of me, nothing big. For her... for Evelyn, it's not over. God, I still struggle with that name. I had to compartmentalize it, like a submarine. I had to separate them. Evelyn is a murderer. Chris... Chris is something else to me. I had to keep her in character, keep her Chris. That was the only way I could deal with it. That's the way I want to remember her.

"She'll be okay. In time. She'll do a decade and a half in Swiss prison. Perhaps a few more years back home in England. I hope she'll be okay. No matter how much I try, I just can't hold a grudge, not against her."

She was looking at me. She was judging me - I could see it in her eyes. Judging me for my actions, for not telling her, for what I had done to people this week. Who knows what she was judging me for? She had the right.

"You have no regrets? You think you had the right to do this? To cause so much pain to so many people?"

I kept my mouth shut a moment and thought it through. Who got what and who deserved what. What I had done and why I had done it.

"Bühler. I guess I just blew up his career in the process. Someone like Nina is fair game, accepted collateral damage. She knew the game she got into. Bühler's a good kid who got mixed up with the wrong banker. Remind me to give him a call. If he took my advice not to show up at the vault, I'll give him a job."

She was shaking her head at me, judging me.

"You're some piece of work, you know that? Made a bit of money on all of this too, didn't you?"

"I'll have to give up the cash Chris wired me. Evelyn. Goddamned Evelyn. I don't hate her, I hate that name. No, her money's dirty, and if I keep it, I'm dirty. But I made a little on the side this week. Half a mil from Baerenfells's little fund should cover my expenses."

"Is that what you used to buy that piece of plastic on your wrist?" she asked.

I looked at the Richard Mille. By any reasonable definition, it truly was a ridiculous thing. Loud, showy, colorful, and impossible to tell time from. Not my style, not by a long shot. Still, it would forever be the centerpiece of my collection.

"This... is just a trophy. But I wouldn't worry about that bonus of yours, Sandra. Year's almost up and it looks like there's a bit of a bonus pool to go around."

She gave me one of those looks. Money hadn't been on her mind. It never left mine.

Her mouth opened and she was probably about to explain a few things to me. The bell saved me as it had so many times. The front door to the office.

Sandra looked at her wrist, at the Franck Muller Casablanca I had given her for her birthday last year. "That'd be your nine o'clock. Mrs. Fischer, out of Vienna."

I took her word for it, still struggling to read the time on that huge orange thing on my wrist.

"Park her in the meeting room, will you? I'll be there in a moment. And do me a favor and interrupt us in ten."

By the look on her face I knew that this conversation wasn't over - far from it. She got up and walked toward the sound of the bell.

"Not a chance. You're on your own on this one," she lied.

Printed in Great Britain
by Amazon